Patricia Favier was born in New Zealand of French and English parents but has lived in many countries, including France, Canada and Britain. She began writing fiction and drama in her teens and, after completing a degree in history, went on to become a journalist and a local politician. She co-founded a book publishing company and was for many years an editor. She is also the author of numerous non-fiction titles, as well as a book for young children. She now lives in Auckland, New Zealand, where she enjoys writing, gardening and music.

A TEMPTATION TOO GREAT

Final book in The French Legacy Trilogy.

Fate has dealt a cruel blow to Jean-Michel de Chambois, once a French viscount but now an American citizen, drawing him into a secret life on the fringes of piracy. Revenge may be sweet, but he discovers there are greater forces at work when Sophie Lafleur, fleeing her own demons, embroils him in a far more dangerous game. Both Jean-Michel and Sophie discover that vows only whet the appetite for forbidden desires — and that those vows could cost them their hearts as well as their lives.

Books by Patricia Favier
Published by The House of Ulverscroft:

THE FRENCH LEGACY TRILOGY:
A MASQUERADE TOO FAR
A PRICE TOO HIGH

PATRICIA FAVIER

A TEMPTATION TOO GREAT

Book Three of The French Trilogy

Complete and Unabridged

ULVERSCROFT
Leicester

First published in Great Britain in 1999 by
Robert Hale Limited
London

First Large Print Edition
published 2001
by arrangement with
Robert Hale Limited
London

Jacket Illustration by Barbara Walton

British Library CIP Data

Favier, Patricia
A temptation too great.—(The French
legacy trilogy; bk. 3)—Large print ed.—
Ulverscroft large print series: romance
1. France—Exiles—Fiction
2. Boston (Mass.)—History—18th century
—Fiction 3. Love stories
4. Large type books
I. Title
823.9'14 [F]

ISBN 0–7089–4346–2

Published by
F. A. Thorpe (Publishing)
Anstey, Leicestershire
Set by Words & Graphics Ltd.
Anstey, Leicestershire
Printed and bound in Great Britain by
T. J. International Ltd., Padstow, Cornwall

For Joyce and Bernie

1

Windward Islands, 1794

Jean-Michel de Chambois was no longer a dreaming man. Bitter, sometimes; cynical, often. Some called him a waster, a layabed, the black sheep of his noble French family, and he did not demur. Perhaps they were right. Sometimes.

Yet as he grasped the rail of his sleek Baltimore Clipper and watched the vessel slice through the crystal waters of the Caribbean, he knew there was something far more dangerous in his heart than the idle pursuits of the new American rich. Inside, he knew who he was.

He turned his attention to the horizon, lifting one hand to shade his eyes against the late sun. They would make anchor by dusk. If they were lucky, they would come upon their prey soon after. If not . . . Well, he could wait. He'd grown some talent for that over the years.

He turned at the sound of footsteps. It was his *capitaine de vaisseau*, a blackamoor originally from the Île de France, whose

1

skill at the helm had rendered him both an indispensable ally and friend.

'Almost there, *monsieur*,' the man murmured, his black eyes touched with unusual reserve. Jean-Michel frowned.

'There is a problem?'

'No, sir. Everything is ready.'

'Except you, *mon ami*.' He turned back to the rail. 'You dislike this mission.'

The captain stood tall, clasping his big hands behind his back and staring out at the passing ocean. 'I dislike waste, sir.'

Jean-Michel allowed himself a small smile. '*Bien sûr*. So you think I should keep the wretched ship and make us all rich at Jack Morgan's expense.'

His companion was silent. Jean-Michel felt a twinge of frustration. 'I know 'tis hard for you to grasp, Captain, but I have no *lettre de marque*. I cannot sail the *Deliverance* into port as though I were a licensed privateer.'

'Better that than be labelled a pirate,' came the soft reply.

His eyes widened. 'Clearly you have lost the stomach for this, my friend. Perhaps you should find less dangerous work.' He turned away sharply, ashamed at the flash of pain in Zamore's eyes. 'Forgive me. I forget myself.'

They stood side by side for a while,

watching the tropical sun slide towards the sea, firing the sky with flames of red and orange. Dusk would follow quickly, and the tide would be turning already in the islands, bringing the *Deliverance* to them like a sacrificial lamb. Although she was a sloop, highly suitable for carrying cargo, she was cumbersome next to Jean-Michel's rakish little porpoise of a boat. The *Némésis* was small, but she was fast and easy to handle, and her false bulwarks hid some very unpleasant surprises.

The *Deliverance* would be easy game.

'I shall not ask you again,' Jean-Michel said at last, though he knew he would miss having Zamore at his side.

He felt the man glance at him. 'The crew are not happy, either, *monsieur*. They have families to feed.'

'I pay them, dammit! And handsomely.'

'They see others, sir . . . '

'Ah.' Jean-Michel bit his lip. So that was the real issue. Now that England and France were at war, privateers — even the lowliest cabin boys — could make vast profits in only a few voyages. Enough to set themselves up for life.

'That is not what I do, Zamore. You know that and so do they.' He sighed. 'I shall make you an offer you may convey to the crew:

You may sail the *Némésis* where you will, after I have Morgan . Get yourself a *lettre de marque* and — '

'That is impossible — '

Jean-Michel waved an impatient hand. 'I will have the lawyers draw up papers giving the *Némésis* to you — with the proviso that I can use her when I wish. Will that satisfy you?'

'It is very generous.'

'Hah! Well, that's a change, by all accounts.'

'But I cannot accept.'

'*Tiens!*' Jean-Michel was beginning to wonder whether he knew Zamore at all. 'How much more would you have of me? My boots and coat? Perhaps I have a horse you would like?'

He saw a flush creep over the captain's dark skin, but was too incensed to care. He turned away, striding across the deck towards the helm. He felt the grip on his arm and swung around. 'Well, Captain? Have you decided upon your pound of flesh?'

'I merely meant, sir, that I have no wish to be a privateer. The *Némésis* should be used for protection, not piracy.'

Jean-Michel raked a hand through his hair. 'Damn me for a fool, Zamore.'

'And I, sir.'

4

They glanced at each other. Somewhat ruefully, Jean-Michel grinned. 'Come, let us placate the crew and make ready before we all end up in the hangman's noose.'

★ ★ ★

Sophie Lafleur pressed her palms against the lid of the reeking puncheon and edged it gently upwards. For a moment the wood stuck against the sides of the barrel, then it let go with a little pop. Sweet fresh air rushed in, salty with the tang of the sea.

She drew a deep breath, feeling it clear some of the dizziness caused by the rum-soaked wood, and peered out into the early morning light.

'Prepare the magazine, Master Gunner, and make a good show of it,' called a rich voice across the deck. Sophie's heart pounded, for the words were in French, and cultured French at that. These were not the voices of the rough English crew of the *Deliverance*. She squinted into the bright light, but could see little of the speaker beyond his worn brown coat and a pair of black top boots that bore not the slightest shine. A battered hat covered his hair but she could not see his face, for he was turned away from her.

She saw him gesture. 'Hurry about it, *messieurs*. There's a foul wind coming from the south. We must make landfall before she hits or the *Némésis* will be doomed as well.'

Sophie shivered, despite the sticky heat she had endured for so many hours already. The *Némésis*? God was not smiling on her this day.

She pressed her lips together to suppress the tears that threatened. They would not help her now. Be brave, Sophie, she whispered silently.

When she'd arrived at the harbour in the dark of night and had seen the *Deliverance* loading its final cargo, it had seemed like an omen too strong to deny. Terror had driven her, given her a courage she hadn't known she possessed. She had taken her chance and it had worked. But then, barely an hour before dawn . . . chaos. A vessel — no doubt the aptly named *Némésis* — had accosted the ship, surprising its crew, who had resisted but little. Nausea, hunger and discomfort had faded into insignificance before the snap of muskets and the single, deafening cannon shot that had felled the *Deliverance*'s mast with deadly accuracy. Peeking from her hiding place, she had witnessed the huge sails tumbling to the decks upon the English sailors. She had heard their cries, understood their meaning, even if she spoke barely a word of their tongue. It was soon over.

And now, the captain of those same brigands was ordering the ship's magazine prepared — for what? Sophie knew as little about ships as she did about the world beyond Guadeloupe, but she knew that a ship's magazine was where gunpowder was stored.

She saw a blackamore approach the man she supposed to be the captain of these brigands. In his hands he carried a sheaf of papers.

'Well done, Zamore. Do you have them all?'

'*Oui, monsieur.* There are invoices, some marked as paid, others as promissory notes. And the bills of lading, sir, all signed for.'

'So what is he carrying today? Have you verified the cargo?'

So that was it, Sophie thought. Privateers gloating over their spoils. They were no better than common thieves, taking law-abiding trade vessels on the high seas with the blessing of their governments. Despite her revulsion for the practice, she felt less outrage than she might in this case, since she had every reason to despise the English herself.

She listened to what she could hear of the conversation between the two men, not much interested in the inventory of cargo. She knew much of it was first-class Caribbean rum, worth a small fortune in the north. She sniffed, knowing she would forever associate the smell of the liquor with this terrifying ordeal, for her clothes reeked of it.

'*Monsieur*,' she heard the man tell his captain, 'there is one more thing.'

The captain turned slightly and Sophie observed that he wore the bushiest set of black whiskers she had ever seen. It covered most of his face, except his eyes, which she could not see anyway since they were deeply shaded by his hat.

'And what is that?' The voice somehow did not suit the face. It was vibrant and touched with a good humour that seemed out of place.

'Morgan is not aboard, sir. The *Deliverance* is under the command of Captain Daniel Blackthorn.'

'I know. Morgan is in New York trying to buy back one of his other ships at auction. He's not having a good time of it lately, is he?'

'You knew, sir?'

'I make that my business. Now, let us send this tub to her final resting place and be off before that storm swallows us all.'

Sophie let the lid of the puncheon slip back into place and pressed her fingers to her mouth. The magazine! Surely she could not have heard aright? Surely they did not mean to blow up the vessel? It made no sense. If they had taken the ship, it was surely to obtain its cargo. Pirates would simply take what they wanted; privateers would sail the vessel into port and legally claim a share of its bounty. But to take a ship and then callously sink her? What possible motive could there be for such an action?

She knew there was bounty to be had, for the very puncheon in which she was hiding had once contained a hundred gallons of first-rate Caribbean rum — until she had knocked out the plug and allowed it to run harmlessly into the sea below the wharf. There had been as many as eighty further barrels of equal size awaiting loading, and much else besides. A cargo certainly worth plundering.

Her eyes wide in the gloom, she listened, praying that she had been mistaken. Yet the sounds of men hurrying about the decks and the companionways left little doubt, for no one came near the cargo on deck. And then she heard another sound, a sound that filled her with even greater dread. Footsteps and the unmistakable sounds of irons. Men in chains.

Gingerly, she eased up the lid of the puncheon once more. A stream of men — sailors from the *Deliverance*, she could only assume — were being led away. Their gaolers led them calmly across the deck, chivvying them down a ladder and into boats that would take them to land. She heard the sailors' pleas, heard the mixture of English and French they received in reply, telling them not to be babies, that they were no more than a few hours' good rowing from land.

The ship grew quiet as the last of the prisoners left, followed by their captors. The vessel rose and fell on the gentle morning tide with no sound beyond the quiet creaking of the boards. The *Deliverance* was abandoned. They would not sail her into port.

Sophie now knew with certainty the deadly intent of these pirates. There could be no mistaking it. Whatever their reasons, they would sink the sloop — and her with it. She swallowed against the tang of fear in her mouth.

She took a deep breath, for her whole body was trembling. She had escaped certain death once; she must do it again. If these pirates could spare the lives of the sailors aboard the *Deliverance*, then perchance they would spare hers, for even if she survived the blast, she could not swim a stroke.

She pushed aside the heavy lid of the barrel, and stiff from her self-imposed captivity, climbed out painfully only to see the last man about to depart the ship, leaving her behind!

★ ★ ★

Jean-Michel looked about him at the deck of the *Deliverance*. A pity to send her down, he thought, scratching idly at his heavy black beard. But Jack Morgan was an evil man who richly deserved to lose his most valued ship, cargo and all. It would scarcely ruin the blackguard. Prick his conscience, maybe. Show him that even if *he* didn't care what cargo he carried, he'd not be allowed to prosper from it.

He turned as Zamore approached with the gunner and one of his men. They were the last souls aboard, apart from himself.

'All clear, *monsieur*,' the captain said.

Jean-Michel looked enquiringly at the gunner, a wiry man named Gazel.

'Ready to go up like a cannonball from hell, sir,' he said grinning.

11

'Then let us depart, gentlemen. We don't want to accompany her on *that* voyage. There are too many sharks in this water for my taste!' He tucked the papers he was holding securely into his coat pocket and grinned.

They crossed quickly to the rails where a rope ladder led down to the waiting skiff. Gazel and Zamore went first, but just as Jean-Michel leaned over to grasp the top of the ladder, his eye was caught by a flash of yellow flying across the deck like a suicidal parrot. He turned sharply. Too late. The creature launched itself at his legs, enveloping him in a wild tackle that brought him crashing to the newly tarred planking.

The world went momentarily black as his head smashed into the boards, then changed to stars, which in turn dissolved into a blanket of suffocating yellow. He closed his eyes, only to have his senses assaulted by the pervasive smell of apples and herbs . . . and something he could not immediately identify. The *mélange* of scents reminded him of a time long ago. It brought happiness and then a pain so sharp and savage that he gritted his teeth.

He groped wildly against the yellow creature that lay atop him, registering shock as his hands came into unmistakable contact with a pair of firm, perfectly rounded buttocks.

'What the devil — ?' He spat out a mouthful of silken hair. So that was what smelled of apples and sunshine.

'Oh, please, *monsieur*, I beg you. Please, do not leave me here!'

Jean-Michel shoved himself to his feet, dragging his attacker by the elbows. The woman came willingly; indeed, she had little option, for she was feather-light in his hands and stood no higher than his shoulder. Her wide blue eyes stared up at him in terror and supplication, and her yellow dress, plain and yet elegantly simple, reeked of alcohol. He held her at arm's length, for he had never been fond of the smell of rum.

'Who the hell are you and what are you doing on my ship?'

The creature looked about her fearfully, licking her lips with a soft pink tongue that stirred unwelcome feelings in Jean-Michel.

'*Je vous en prie, monsieur*. Please, do not make me go with those sailors. I throw myself upon your mercy!'

He stared at the woman. She was French, which seemed odd on an English vessel, even if it had docked in Guadeloupe. And she was not ill-looking. In fact, cleaned up she might be halfway presentable. But how on earth had they missed her when they'd searched the 'tween decks? Zamore and his men were very thorough.

'Sir!'

He looked down at the waiting skiff. 'Sir,' Zamore called, 'we must away — now! The powder is ready and anything could set it off.'

Jean-Michel looked at the woman he still held, astonished that she had managed to divert him from his course so effortlessly. He shoved her down the ladder towards his captain. 'Take this . . . this . . . creature aboard the *Némésis*. There is something not right here, and I mean to find out what. But not now.'

Sophie scrambled down the ladder willingly, for she had no desire to be blown skywards with the *Deliverance*. She felt the black man take her arm in a grip of steel and push her brusquely on to a bench in the bow. He did not look at her, but his firmly clenched jaw showed just what he thought she had been doing aboard the ship. She must not care what anyone thought. She would be free soon enough and they would never see her again.

The bearded captain climbed quickly aboard and pushed the vessel away from the side as the gunner and another sailor

14

took the oars. She wondered that the Negro was not pressed to the task.

She stared about her, spying a Baltimore Clipper half a league away, its slanted masts showing only a French flag while it lay at anchor. As the dinghy crossed the sea towards it, Sophie found her eyes drawn across the heads of the sailors to the man she assumed to be their captain. His unmistakable air of authority was so much at odds with his tatty clothes and the preposterous black beard that covered most of his face. Who was he, and why was he destroying a beautiful ship without apparently rescuing any of its valuable cargo?

The brigand turned, his grey eyes connecting with hers over the heads of the men. Sophie looked away, but not before a most unsettling feeling had enveloped her.

She had no time to contemplate these sensations, however, for at that moment the Negro lifted a musket to his shoulder. Sophie drew a sharp breath, wondering if he was about to make a bid for his freedom and kill them all on the spot, but instead, he aimed calmly at the *Deliverance*, firing a single shot into a pile of torn sails on the deck. The sails burst into a small flame that glowed orange across the water, and then sizzled like a snake down towards the companionway. A small puff of smoke rose from the spot, but that was all.

Sophie frowned.

No one on the skiff moved.

Suddenly, there was an ear-splitting roar, echoed almost instantaneously by others as the powder magazine exploded in a gigantic ball of acrid smoke and flame. Sophie ducked, covering her ears with her hands against the noise. Pieces of flaming timber floated down from the sky like dying firebirds and hissed into the ocean all about the stricken vessel.

Then, in the eerie silence that followed, the *Deliverance* trembled, shuddered and slid quietly beneath the waves, the flag atop its one remaining mast waving farewell as it sank forever into its watery grave.

2

'You are a madman!' Sophie cried as the skiff rocked in the wake of the dying ship. 'How could you wantonly destroy such a beautiful ship — and all for nought?'

The captain turned his gaze upon her as the men took up their oars once more. 'That is scarcely your affair, *mamselle*. I might better ask how you came to be upon the vessel. At the behest of Jack Morgan's men? Did they offer you rum in exchange for your undoubtedly sweet favours?'

His gaze roamed over her, slowly and with a thoroughness that left her in no doubt that he saw everything in her attire that was implied by his words. She flushed hotly, tugging the drawstring front of her gown higher. She was uncomfortably aware of how she must seem, for her white fichu had been lost when she clambered from the puncheon, and her breasts threatened to spill from the scanty neckline at any moment. She had tossed her straw hat into the sea long ago, for it was unwieldy in her hiding place. As for her dress, it was torn and filthy, the stripes in the muslin faded by the grime that covered her from head to toe. What she would give for a bath!

'I have never heard of anyone by the name of Jack Morgan,' she replied, avoiding his eyes. Her voice was soft, but she was determined not to be cowed by these villains. 'And as to my reasons for being aboard the *Deliverance*, I have not the least inclination to explain myself to a lawless pirate. Your despicable behaviour earns you no such right.'

His dark brows rose slightly and Sophie was appalled to see a touch of amusement in his eyes. She turned away, blinking back tears of humiliation. So what if he thought she were a common harlot? He was at least that far down the ladder to hell himself. The thought crossed her mind that she no longer had the right to cast stones, even at pirates, for she was as damned as any person on earth.

She turned as the sound of his laughter reached her ears.

'Such lofty talk, *mamselle*, and from such a precarious position, too. But if you will not tell me the real purpose in your skulking aboard the ship, then what other conclusion can one draw? Especially,' he added, 'when you are dressed in such a . . . ' He shrugged slightly, as if words failed him, yet the amusement in his voice was clear.

Sophie glanced down at her ruined gown. She tugged again on the drawstring, to no avail. Her cheeks flushed with shame, but she met his grey eyes with as much coolness as she could muster. 'I repeat, sir, my business is private. You need not concern yourself with it. I ask only that you set me down so that I may find another ship — one that is owned by honest citizens. As to this morning's . . . activities, I shall say nothing. You have my word upon it.'

'Indeed? A woman of easy virtue but impeccable honour. As delightful a mix as I have ever encountered, I'm sure.' She squirmed as his mocking eyes slid down her neck and roamed over her half-exposed bosom. Then his gaze turned cold, chilling her to the marrow. 'But I shall not set you down.'

'*Monsieur?*' Sophie felt real alarm at his quiet assertion. The skiff was drawing close to the *Némésis* now and she heard a voice hail them from the vessel. She must not get on that ship. She glanced about wildly at the ocean, seeing a small island not far distant. With luck it was not the one to which the sailors from the *Deliverance* had fled. She would have to take her chances on that.

'Please, Captain, I assure you my lips shall

be sealed forever. Whatever your reasons for your actions, they shall remain known only to you. If you would set me down upon that island over there, I shall be gone and you need never hear of me again.'

But he appeared not to be listening. Instead, he gazed at the sleek clipper that lay awaiting them at anchor, rocking with the steadily increasing swell. This close, Sophie could see how aptly the *Némésis* was named. Her masts were mounted at an alarming angle and she was painted entirely black, giving her a rakish air that fitted her black-whiskered captain perfectly. Sophie thought she had never seen so evil a ship.

'*Monsieur*? Please, you have nothing to fear.'

He turned back, reaching a hand to steady his hat as a sudden wind buffeted the little rowboat.

'Indeed I do not, *mamselle*.'

Hope quickened her heart. 'Then you will take me — ?'

'I will take you nowhere, until I know precisely who you are, and what your business was aboard Jack Morgan's ship. After that . . . '

'What possible difference could that make?'

'To me, a great deal.'

She stared at him, desperation emboldening

her. He was a pirate, cast to the fringes of society by his very occupation. Surely, he did not represent a serious threat to her. And once she was gone, he would likely never think of her again.

'Very well,' she said softly. 'My name is Sophie Lafleur and I am travelling north. To — ' Should she admit that much, she wondered? Yet if she did not . . . 'to Acadia,' she added quickly. 'Now, may I go?'

'Acadia? In Canada?' He grabbed the side of the boat to steady himself as they bumped against the rope ladder that hung from the side of the *Némésis*. She watched him jump to his feet as nimbly as though he were on land. 'You have quite a journey ahead of you, Sophie Lafleur.'

She glanced at that tiny green island that seemed to beckon. 'Then will you ask your men to take me — ?'

He leapt to the ladder and mounted effortlessly, climbing almost to the top before he cast his answer back over his shoulder.

'Zamore, take Mademoiselle Lafleur aboard and lock her up. We have a storm to ride.'

Before Sophie could so much as open her mouth to plead her case, the villain had disappeared and she found herself being helped — none too gently — up the ladder and across the deck of the small ship. She stumbled as she was unceremoniously pushed down a narrow companionway and into a dark and narrow passage, lit only by what meagre sunlight could penetrate this far. The Negro fitted a key into a lock and pushed her inside.

'Wait!' she cried, when she realized he was closing the door upon her, but the door shut firmly, the key turned and Sophie was alone.

She gasped in despair, spreading her arms and letting them fall to her sides. How could this have happened, and what did they intend to do with her once they arrived at their destination — wherever that might be? She had heard stories of women who fell into the clutches of pirates. They were not nice stories, nor did they have happy endings. That they might make enquiries concerning her did not enter her head. These pirates were as unlikely to return to Guadeloupe as she was.

She turned, gazing at her little prison and steadying herself automatically against the rise and fall of the vessel. The cabin was tiny, but well apportioned, with a cot built into one of the panelled walls and a desk into another. Aside from a few rolled maps and a quill in an empty inkstand, there was nothing in the room, as though it was seldom used. She spied a door beyond the desk and pushed it open to find a tiny quarter-gallery with toilet and commode.

Water! At least she could use this time of imprisonment usefully. She peered out of the tiny open window from whence a small breeze carried hot sticky air into the already humid room — too small to climb out, she decided, even supposing she could swim. The sky was darkening as purple clouds began blotting up the sunlight, and the sea was rising and falling as though a monster hidden beneath the waves stirred in restless sleep.

At least the storm would keep her captors busy. She closed the door to the quarter-gallery and stripped off her filthy yellow gown. The muslin was torn in two places, but she could do nothing about that in her present situation. The stench of rum was another matter.

She poured water from a large pitcher into the matching bowl. There was a bar of expensive sandalwood soap on a dish and she quickly washed herself. Her hair smelled like an inn, too, so she washed that as well, squeezing the water from the blond curls as best she could. At least in this heat she had no fear of catching a chill.

She picked up the gown and began rinsing it one section at a time in the small basin. At

23

last it was done. She tipped the dirty water into the toilet, watching it tumble into the churning sea, then refilled the bowl, rinsing first her own hair and then the dress.

This activity had taken some time and as she looked around for a hook upon which to hang the gown to dry, she realised the ship was under sail, moving at a rapid clip over the heaving sea. She steadied herself as she reached up to hang the dress over a lamp hook in the ceiling. There, it could swing freely, attracting as much of the sultry breeze as possible from the little window.

Sophie sighed. At least she was a little cleaner than she had been since her precipitous departure from Mon Bijou. She flicked out the folds of soft muslin so they could dry quickly, and returned to the cabin.

She licked her dry lips, wishing she had reserved some of the water in the pitcher to drink. It was many hours since she'd had refreshment of any kind. She looked about her. A small cupboard built into the wall above the desk contained only what she took to be nautical instruments; another, books. In a desk drawer she found a half-empty bottle of cognac, but set it back in its holder, for she had no desire to add drunkenness to her woes.

This is ridiculous, she thought, suddenly furious with the world. None of this was her fault! For a moment an image of her mother flashed into her mind, searing her heart.

'Oh, Mama,' she whispered. 'How could this happen to me, after all we had dreamed and planned?' She squeezed her eyes shut, forcing the memory aside. Her mother was gone. She was alone, and she could never go back. Not ever.

Rage replaced self-pity and she stormed across to the door. But at that moment a particularly vicious wave sent the clipper crashing into a trough, throwing her off-balance. She crashed into the wall, jarring her shoulder, but the pain only made her more determined, more frustrated that she should have allowed herself to be taken captive by this strange crew. She beat upon the door with her fists, yelling for someone — anyone — to let her out.

She paused to listen, but could hear no sound beyond the creaking of the ship, the crash of breaking waves and the rising howl of the wind. Again she hammered against the timbers. Again, she stopped to listen. Still no response. The storm was clearly upon them now, and maintaining her balance was ever more difficult.

Sophie gave up. Her knuckles were red

and raw from beating them against the heavy door, her shoulder hurt and she was bone weary. She let the next roll of the ship carry her to the bed, then fell upon the coverlet and closed her eyes.

'God forgive me,' she murmured. She knew she owed Him a great deal more than that poor supplication, but she was *so* tired. Perhaps in the morning . . .

★ ★ ★

Jean-Michel tugged at his sodden jacket as he gave up the wheel to the helmsman. He crossed the spray-slick deck, careful where he trod in the darkness, for dawn was still a few hours away. God, he had never felt so tired. The storm had been a bad one, and the *Némésis* had almost succumbed, showing every weakness in her light construction. How many times in the past twelve hours had he wished she might magically transform into a nice ponderous brigantine that would plough through the sea like a water buffalo in mud.

But it was not to be. The words of his brother-in-law, the Duc de Beligny had rung in his ears over and over as they'd ridden the storm: 'No Baltimore Clipper can stand up to a big sea! It's a suicide boat.'

Well, she *had* stood up to a big sea; the foulest Jean-Michel ever wanted to experience. Perhaps he was getting old. He should get rid of the ship before she became his coffin. But while he'd heard that from his family a few times, he couldn't part with her. She was a scorpion of a vessel; fast and furious when he needed her to be, with a sting in her tail that allowed her to bring down any ship twice her size. She could race and tack and come about like lightning in a decent wind. And she was painted black from hull to rigging, rendering her nearly invisible at anchor.

No, he was not finished with the *Némésis* yet. Not by far.

He reached the companionway, shaking his head as he remembered how stunned the crew of the *Deliverance* had been when his crew uncovered the false bulwarks on the *Némésis* and exposed the 6-pounders hidden there. And when the master gunner uncloaked the massive 12-pound cannon mounted on the upper deck, primed and ready to fire . . .

The sailors aboard the *Deliverance* had laughed. Joked that the recoil would smash the *Némésis* into firewood and save them the trouble.

He grinned with satisfaction as he fished

in his breeches pocket for the key to his cabin. The sound of that shot splitting the main-mast of the *Deliverance* was the sweetest thing he'd heard all year. And it wiped the gloating smiles off every last man aboard that ship.

He was glad of the privacy of his cabin, though it was not a place in which he spent much time. He tossed his jacket on the desk and ripped at the beard on his face, surprised to find the irritating thing still there — normally he removed it as soon as the chance arose. The storm had preoccupied him tonight.

With a grunt of pain as the glue pulled his skin, the whole contraption tore from his face, moustache and all. He threw it on the desk, then froze as he heard an unmistakable sound.

He turned softly. His eyes, while accustomed to the dark night above decks, could not penetrate the deep blackness here. But his ears were no less acute.

Breathing.

There was someone in his cabin.

He listened for a moment, reaching out silently with one hand to feel for the oil lamp that hung above his desk. In utter silence he slid it off its hook, lowered it to the desk and searched for a tinder-box in the drawer. The strike of the flint sounded loud in the virtual silence.

He squinted in the sudden brightness, cursing softly, then shading his eyes from the glare, held the lamp high.

An expletive that would have made his hardy sister blush fell from his lips. How could Zamore have put that woman in here? There were plenty of other places aboard the little vessel. A closet would have been generous.

He crossed to the bed, steadying himself on the wooden sides of the cot, and stared down. In sleep she seemed much younger than he remembered. And much more innocent. Sophie Lafleur. Even her name was sweet. Her hair splayed out around her head like a halo, glowing like spun gold in the lamplight. He reached out a finger and touched it. It was damp, soft as silk and —

He felt a strange tightening in his body and drew back his hand sharply.

She was a trollop, he reminded himself. Nothing more. Stowed away on the *Deliverance* to sell her favours while the vessel was at sea. A nice way to make a living, if you enjoyed sweaty sailors and the taste of rum — which clearly she did, since she'd reeked of the stuff.

Telling himself he was merely curious,

he leaned closer, studying her face, which seemed perfectly composed in sleep. She did not snore, nor sleep with her mouth ajar like some women he'd known. And she no longer smelled of liquor.

He frowned. Her face was innocent, now that it was clean. Too innocent for the likes of those tavern rats they had thrown off the *Deliverance*. Her features were fine and her skin satiny in the soft light. Her mouth was full, the lips parted ever so slightly in sleep. Her face was turned slightly into the pillow, displaying a length of milk-white neck adorned with a wisp of golden hair that curled behind her ear. And just below her ear was a tiny pink birthmark in a curious shape that reminded him of a butterfly. He leaned forward, feeling the strongest urge to press his lips to that —

'Oh!'

He leapt back as her eyes sprang open. Blue eyes, like the forget-me-nots his mother had always favoured in her garden in France. He frowned, irritated at the intrusive memory. He had no interest in this woman, except in ensuring she kept her mouth shut.

'Y-you — ' she stammered, sitting up with a rush and tugging the thin coverlet over her. He noted that she wore only her shift and wondered what had become of the canary yellow dress. But then, women in her line of work didn't need a great deal of clothing.

'You've shaved!'

She was staring at him in amazement. At his face, his hair, his mouth — Damn, but that was unnerving. Then her eyes fell upon the desk where the beard lay atop his coat. He cursed himself silently for a fool.

She let a small gasp fall from her lips. 'Who are you?' she asked. 'And why are you in my room?'

'I thought to ask you the same question, *mamselle*.' He turned away, returning the lamp to its hook and ripping off his sodden shirt. There was no point pretending. 'So you know my secret. Congratulations. But while you have the advantage, I have the upper hand, *n'est-ce pas?*'

He glanced at her, seeing the blankness of her look. 'You are my prisoner, if I want you. I have no reason to give you up, after all.' He saw her blush and caught a flash of pure venom in her eyes that surprised him. Then she glanced down, almost demurely. Oh, she was good. Very good.

He laughed softly. 'Very well, if that is your best offer.'

He crossed to the bed, pulled her small body against him and ploughed a hand into her silky hair so he might tug back her head,

31

claiming her mouth with his own. At least, that was how he had intended it to be. Yet the touch of her lips sent a frisson of flame through him, burning with pain and memory. He gentled the kiss, recognizing something, though he knew not·what, then eased apart her soft lips with his tongue and gently probed the sweet recesses of her mouth. The small sound that issued from her throat was almost his undoing. A wash of tenderness unlike any he could remember flowed over him, filling him with a bolt of desire that stole the breath from his very lungs.

He pulled back sharply, breathing hard. She stared up at him like a frightened rabbit, her lips still wet and parted from his kiss.

Then, to his absolute amazement, she raised her hand and slapped him fiercely across the jaw.

The force of the blow and the surprise of it knocked Jean-Michel backwards. He raised a hand to his face, rubbing the tender spot in amazement and staring at the blue eyes that gazed back in shock. There was something in those eyes, a determined quality, that he had not expected to see. And something else. Something of the defensive yet helpless animal a moment before slaughter.

'I apologize,' he said, surprising himself. 'That was unconscionable.'

'You don't look sorry.' Her voice shook.

He raised his brows a fraction. 'Are *you* sorry you hit me?'

'No.'

'Then we are even. I enjoyed kissing you.' Too much, he thought, surprised that it had been so. No woman had moved him even the tiniest bit since — He stopped that painful train of thought instantly. He had vowed never to torture himself with remembrance of what had been. Action was his only comfort these days.

He stared at her. She was a timid little thing. Edgy. She cast furtive glances around the room, at the door — which he wondered if he should have locked behind him — at the lamp, the desk — anything but him.

And she was pretty. He frowned. Too pretty to be aboard a shipful of men. His first impression of her made no sense to him now. She seemed scared of her own shadow. She must have been beyond desperation to sell herself to a pack of Caribbean sailors.

'Who are you, Sophie Lafleur?'

'I am nobody,' she whispered, her eyes meeting his.

'Hah! You slap altogether too firmly for a ghost,' he answered, rubbing his chin. 'But I see I was mistaken.' He turned away, bending over the wooden trunk that stood against the wall — the only clue that the room was inhabited at all. He withdrew a soft velvet frock coat and tossed it to her.

Sophie caught the garment, her eyes wide. 'Where did you get this?' she demanded, looking from the expensive jacket to the bedraggled pirate.

'My tailor in Boston made it.' His voice held a touch of surprise, as though the question were somehow out of order. 'Not his best, but adequate for day-to-day wear, I think. Don't you approve?'

'That is not what I meant. It is very fine. I merely wondered . . . ' Her voice trailed off and she bit her lip. This man was more of a mystery than she had first thought.

'You wondered which poor soul I had stolen the thing from,' he said grimly. 'Well, you may put your mind at rest — I paid a good penny for the coat. Now kindly oblige me by putting it on, woman! You may not have scruples, but I do.'

Sophie flushed red, clutching the fine cloth to her.

He wandered off into the quarter-gallery, having withdrawn other items from the locker, but he did not close the door. She could clearly hear him moving about as she slid her arms into the frock coat and closed it over her shift. The sleeves were vastly too long

34

and the shoulders broad enough for two, but it was warm and smelled of cedar from the chest. Madame had always liked her things packed in cedar.

Madame Guillaume. Fleetingly, Sophie wondered how the woman fared, even though she knew the mere mention of the name Sophie Lafleur would cause an outpouring of vitriol. The thought made her sad and more lonely than she could have thought possible.

She started as the man's head appeared in the doorway.

'That looks better,' he said, eyeing her attire.

Sophie stared at him in dismay. He too, looked better. Better than any man she had ever beheld. She swallowed.

'Would you please put on some clothes?' she squeaked.

He looked down at his bare chest. '*Je m'excuse.*'

She breathed a little easier when he disappeared once more. This time she made sure she concentrated on what he was saying, rather than on the way his skin had glowed bronze in the lamplight, or on the breadth of his muscled shoulders.

'You definitely have the advantage, Sophie,' he called as his trousers swished onto the floor. She heard him kick the breeches into the corner and licked her lips. She hadn't said her prayers, that was the problem. Perhaps if she said a novena? But she had no rosary beads.

'In what manner, sir?'

His head appeared again. He was buttoning a shirt over his chest, covering the light scattering of reddish hair that grew there. She suddenly noticed that without the hat he had worn earlier in the day, his hair was a deep Titian red, neatly cut and glowing like coals in a brazier as he moved near the light. And he was a lot younger than she had at first believed.

Hail Mary, Mother of God . . .

He ducked back into the gallery. 'You have seen the real me, Sophie Lafleur. And you have seen my ship and what she can do.'

Sophie had indeed seen altogether too much of the man for her tastes.

'You have nothing to fear, sir. I gave you my word I would speak of this to no one.'

Holy Mary . . .

'I dislike surrendering the advantage,' he replied, finally returning to the cabin. Sophie gasped at the transformation, for she had seldom seen such expensive or fashionable raiment. At Mon Bijou she had met plenty of rich plantation owners, ship owners and

36

local gentry, but this . . . this was something quite different.

'You are a gentleman,' she finally said in awed tones. 'A gentleman pirate!'

He waved a hand. 'I am scarcely a pirate, Sophie, difficult as that may be for your ears to accept.'

'But the ship — you sank a perfectly good vessel with the entirety of its cargo — '

'Precisely. What pirate — or privateer, for that matter — would do such a thing?'

She frowned. 'Indeed, sir, I have no experience of either, so I could not possibly say.'

He perched on the bed beside her.

Sophie's heart pounded. She edged nearer to the wall.

'Pray, do not call me sir all the time. My name is Jean-Michel de Chambois. I was once a viscount, but that was before the Revolution and before I became an American. Now I am a man of the New World.'

Sophie paled. Her situation appeared to be worsening by the minute.

'*Oui, Monsieur le Vicomte.*'

'Jean-Michel.'

'Jean-Michel, sir.'

He sighed. 'I expect you will get used to it. In the meantime, you may tell me what you are running away from.'

She gasped. 'Why do you say that? What could you possibly know of me?'

His eyes took on a speculative gleam. 'So, I am right. A simple guess, my dear.' He stood up and began to pace the few steps across the room and back, without being the least put off his stride by the constant rising and falling of the ship, though that, too, was easing now. The storm was past its worst.

'When you attacked me on the deck of the *Deliverance* — '

'I did no such thing! I was merely running and lost my footing. I feared you would be gone and leave me to be blown into the heavens along with the ship.'

'Well, it worked,' he said mildly. 'However, as I was recounting, having at that point smelled the rum upon your person,' — he wrinkled his nose — 'I dislike the stuff intensely, myself, I could only assume that you were a lady who, er . . . '

She tilted her chin. 'You were mistaken, sir, if you thought me aboard the vessel for the comfort of the sailors. They were, after all, English!'

He looked at her for a long moment, until Sophie felt herself grow quite warm, but she held her head high.

'Not that their being English was the

38

reason I was not there . . . for that purpose,' she added. 'But *that* . . . well, it would have been altogether too much.'

'You dislike the English, I gather.'

'I have reason.'

'We are more or less at war,' he said matter-of-factly.

'We?'

'The French and the English. Not the Americans. And the Spanish.' He waved a hand. 'It is all too confusing.'

'Not to me,' Sophie replied, pressing her lips together. To her, it was a great deal more than war.

'I can see how mistaken I was concerning your reasons for being aboard the *Deliverance*,' he said at last. 'And while that relieves me of one anxiety, it presents another more confounding problem: what am I to do with you?'

'You have no need to do anything. Set me down when next you make landfall, and forget you ever saw me.'

He shook his head. 'Impossible.'

'You cannot keep me prisoner!'

He gave her a meaningful look, got up, went to the quarter-gallery and returned with her still-wet gown. 'So you have a few dozen gold coins secreted in the folds of this, do you?'

'Of course not.'

'Then you are hiding them beneath your shift, perhaps?'

She pressed her lips together, fingering the place where her mother's wedding ring hung on a long, gold chain beneath her shift. To a man such as he, it would be barely worth a second glance; to Sophie it was priceless. 'You may be assured I do not. If you are hoping to rid me of secret wealth, you will be sadly disappointed.'

'On the contrary,' he muttered as he threw the gown over the foot locker, 'I would be surprised to find you have a penny to your name.'

He sat on the bed, reaching out and taking her hand in his. Sophie wanted to snatch it away, yet his touch sent a curiously hypnotic warmth through her veins. She stared stupidly at his thumb as it brushed to and fro across the back of her hand.

'Why won't you just tell me what it is you are running from and why, and then perhaps I can help you? I am not an ogre, although having seen me in action today no doubt you find that rather a leap of faith.'

His touch was causing strange little tremors to flit through her. Sophie wanted to pull her hand away, but the sensation was so very pleasurable. Why couldn't she remember the words to that prayer?

'But something tells me you are a lady,' he continued, 'and since I know I am a gentleman, I could not possibly abandon you in some strange port, alone and penniless.'

Sophie regarded him with dismay. This would not be as easy as she had first thought. Anger, she could deal with. Lust . . . well, she knew she could defend herself against that. But chivalry?

'There is no need.' She was about to say she was not a lady but a lady's maid, when the words of her mother came back. *Before the British came, your grandfather was a seigneur with a hundred families in his service.*

Instead, she pulled her hand from his grasp. 'Since you say you are a man of honour, I will ask you to take me at my word. It is a matter of life and death that I return to Acadia with all haste. If it will satisfy your conscience, I will gladly accept a small loan, which I will repay the instant I am reunited with my family there. With interest, of course, at whatever rate your bankers deem suitable.'

'My bankers!' He ran a hand through his dark red hair, making it even wilder than before. 'I don't give a . . . a . . . toss about my bankers. Why in the name of Hades do

41

you want to go to Canada?'

'It's my home.'

He frowned. 'Then what are you doing stowing away on ships in the Caribbean?'

'Trying to get there.'

'From where?'

'Guadeloupe.' She twisted her hands in the velvet coat, annoyed to have given away even that morsel of information. Much more could hang her.

'So you have been living in Guadeloupe, while your family is — where, exactly?'

'My mother is dead, my father, too. I have, I believe, an uncle in Acadia.'

'You *believe*? You mean, you aren't sure? When did you leave Canada?'

She looked down at her fingers. 'I — I have never been there.'

He cocked his head on the side. 'Ah. I believe I am coming to comprehend. Your family was exiled by the English?'

She nodded miserably. 'I was born in Georgia and moved to Guadeloupe at the age of four. But it was always my mother's dream that we should return to our rightful home.'

She peeked up at him through her lashes, only to find him gazing thoughtfully at her. Before she could look away he had hooked a finger under her chin.

'Sophie Lafleur, forgive me if I don't understand all this. Clearly, you are a gentlewoman, yet you are without either a companion or any means of support, trying to travel two thousand miles as a stowaway. That is a very dangerous game, and one which I simply cannot allow.'

'Please, you must! I like to be on my own.'

'And I like to sleep at night.'

Her heart plummeted as he got up and went to the door. He paused with his hand on the latch and looked back at her.

'We have many days before we make port, *mamselle*. We shall speak no more of this now, but you may rest assured that you will no longer be travelling by stealth while there is breath left in my body!'

And with that, he left her in his cabin, closing the door behind him.

She lay back upon the cot exhausted, knowing that stealth and speed were the two things she most desperately needed at this moment. Yet despite everything, she was almost glad to have this voyage ahead of her, filled with days when neither would be an issue. Those days might be all the better for the company of such an intriguing and unusual man, she thought, then chided herself sharply. Not for her, such fancies of the heart. Not ever.

But despite her sternest attempts to keep her thoughts on other matters, she found herself thinking so much about *Monsieur le Vicomte* that she was still awake when dawn broke suddenly across the tropical sky.

She slept then, until the sun hung high overhead at the zenith of the day. Someone had brought a tray with fruit, sweet rolls and a delectable juice of squeezed pineapple. She sat up in bed and ate ravenously, the first food she had consumed since her flight from Mon Bijou.

Her thoughts returned to the plantation, the only real home she could remember, the place where she had grown up, played with the many young slave children until that was forbidden on her eighth birthday. Despite all that had happened, she had many happy memories of the place. And her mother was buried there, in the tiny graveyard surrounded by a picturesque white picket fence. Madame had allowed it. Sophie's mother was a lady born and bred, so she had said, and she would not have her buried alongside the slaves.

Monsieur Louis, her son, had not approved. But then, nothing was ever to his satisfaction.

Sophie grimaced, setting down the succulent

banana she was about to peel. She had lost her appetite suddenly.

She clambered from the bed, pushing aside the food tray, and hurried to the window. The sea was calm and blue, with scarcely a cloud in the sky, and the *Némésis* was skipping over the surface like a happy dolphin.

A quick investigation showed her yellow gown to be quite dry, if in dire need of smoothing. But Sophie could do nothing about that. She dressed quickly, performed her ablutions and was about to leave the cabin when she looked down. Her breasts were once again half-exposed by the low neckline of her bodice.

Her eyes fell upon the trunk at the foot of the bed. Hoping Monsieur de Chambois would not mind, she lifted the lid and began delicately poking through the contents. There was not much. Shoes, gold buckles . . . *Gold*? She shook her head and continued her search. Stockings. Breeches made of heavy cotton — clearly not the type of garb she had witnessed him wearing last night. She blushed, recalling that she had also seen him in very little last evening!

Then she spied something she could use. Two white stock cravats, of ample length for her purpose. She pulled one from the trunk and shook it out, then wrapped it about her neck, crossing it over at the bosom and tucking it, fichu-style into her neckline.

It was not overly long, but it would do. She contemplated asking her involuntary host whether he might lend her a pin with which to secure the silk, but thought better of it. She had no desire to draw his attention to the possibility of her tumbling suddenly from her clothes!

She tidied the foot locker, satisfied she had done all in her power to make herself presentable. Pleased to find that the cabin door was no longer locked, she left the cabin and went above.

The day was perfect, warm and clear, the sea an unrepentant blue. The tangy scent of the ocean teased her nostrils and made her think of her destination — the ocean margins of Lower Canada. She knew from stories her mother had told that the weather there would be quite different from anything she had known. The notion excited her, filling her with hope.

She gripped the railing, staring about her at the small neat deck. A couple of sailors sent her curious glances, but then turned to mutter amongst themselves as though they had already been told of her existence.

'*Bonjour*, Mademoiselle Lafleur,' said a voice at her elbow.

She turned, her heart beating a sudden tattoo.

'*Monsieur le Vicomte.*'

'Jean-Michel,' he corrected.

'Sophie,' she replied archly. Two could play at that game.

'Very well. A truce. May I offer you refreshment?'

She shook her head, smiling shyly in response to the twinkle in his eyes. How she had ever thought him an ill-looking pirate, she could no longer imagine. He was very tall and well built for a nobleman — not that she had met many of those in her twenty years. Without that awful beard, his face was youthful and yet experienced. There were lines about his eyes that made it hard to guess his age, but she would put it at no more than thirty-five.

'Someone left fruit and pastries in my room, thank you,' she said, allowing him to take her arm and lead her towards the stern where he seated her upon a wooden bench.

He propped a foot up beside her and leaned on his knee, tilting his head down so he might speak without being overheard. 'You will be comfortable and quite safe while

47

you are aboard the *Némésis*, my dear. The crew is small and discreet and the captain a man of scrupulous honour.'

'I thought you were the captain?'

'No, indeed. I bought this tub in an auction for three hundred and ninety pounds — a considerable bargain — but I leave her in the capable hands of Zamore.'

'The Negro?' Sophie was stunned.

He shrugged. 'No doubt after life in Guadeloupe, you find it hard to believe. There are those of us in America who dislike slavery and take no part in its misery.'

'Then I, too, shall like America,' she said forcefully.

'Aha,' he said, pushing away from the bench and turning to survey the ocean. 'So the mystery deepens. A gentlewoman who's spent her entire life in Guadeloupe, surrounded no doubt by black slaves, yet who disapproves of the convention. Tell me again, my dear Sophie, where exactly have you been living?'

She trembled. She must have more care around this man. 'I did not say, sir, so I can scarcely tell you once more.'

'So tell me for the first time,' he replied, unabashed.

'I cannot.'

He turned the full force of his stare upon

her then. She glanced quickly away.

'*Will* not, don't you mean?'

'It is of no consequence, *monsieur*,' she responded quietly. 'All that matters is that your ship is taking me north, faster, I suspect, than I had dreamed possible, and for that I am grateful.'

'Save your thanks,' he responded dryly. 'For I do not go as far north as Halifax.'

'I shall find someone who will. Oh, look!' she said suddenly jumping up. 'Are we near land?'

She hurried to the railing and pointed to a large bed of kelp through which the vessel was sailing.

He joined her, and she was relieved that the distraction seemed to have worked, for the moment. She had no desire to enter into an interrogation concerning her history each time they met.

'We are entering the Sargasso Sea. I like this route. It is faster and one is less likely to encounter other ships.'

Sophie turned to him, her eyes wide. 'But I have heard tell there are monsters in these waters and that the ships can become embroiled in the seaweed beds.'

He laughed. 'And some people believe in dragons.' He shook his head. 'I have never seen anything here to alarm me. The soundings we have done show only the deepest water, despite the kelp and the creatures that inhabit it as though it were close to land. I do not pretend to understand, but since I believe the shortest journey is a straight line, I cross the Sargasso and trust in God.'

Sophie turned back to the waves, wondering that anyone could have so straightforward a view of life. All she had heard of this part of the ocean was that it hid unmentionable dangers. Yet if Jean-Michel de Chambois said it was safe, then she would trust him.

The idea gave her pause for thought. For some reason she did trust him. Had circumstances not dictated otherwise, she might even have considered such a man for a husband. But that could never be.

She had made her choice when she set out on this perilous journey, and she had made a deal with the Almighty: if God would forgive her, she would give Him her life. And that meant poverty, chastity and obedience.

No matter how many temptations He put in her way.

3

By the third week in April, the *Némésis* was north of the Sargasso Sea, in the colder waters of the Atlantic. Sophie stood at the rail, wrapped in a heavy woollen coat, and stared at the endless ocean speeding past. She had grown to like the strange vessel with its backward-leaning masts and small, efficient crew. She had seen how much they admired the vessel's owner, and how skilled a captain Zamore was. He had surprised her by sending his valet, a boy of fourteen called Pierre, to her, so that she might have a servant for the remainder of the voyage. Her protests that Pierre's services were unnecessary went unheeded; Captain Zamore wasted few words on argument, she discovered. He merely stated his business and had done with talk.

So Pierre became her cabin boy, bringing her breakfast so that she might lie abed in the mornings, and even occasionally amusing her with tunes played upon a battered hurdy-gurdy, his only treasure. She enjoyed the way bashfulness gave way to pleasure as he wound the handle, manipulating the ivory keys with a skill beyond his years.

Otherwise, there was little to fill her days. Jean-Michel (for she had finally succumbed to calling the viscount by his first name) had presented her with two sets of men's clothing. It was all they had on this ship full of men, he had told her ruefully. The breeches were small enough to have come from Pierre, but he was so painfully shy in her presence that she never dared enquire. She had retired to Jean-Michel's cabin, now given over entirely to her use, and adjusted them to fit her comfortably with needle and coarse thread from the sailmaker's workshop. She was grateful for any alternative to her yellow gown.

Seeing her in her 'new' clothes of loose shirt and sailor's culottes seemed to amuse Jean-Michel. He mentioned something about his sister having gone to sea dressed as a man, but would not be drawn further on the subject except to say that she could ask her when they met.

Sophie did not wish to meet the viscountess, or whatever she was called now. She wanted only to find another vessel taking her to Acadia and never set eyes upon Jean-Michel de Chambois again.

Or so she told herself. Over and over.

It was nearly dark. The sun was sliding

into the ocean, trailing golden scarves behind it. Not a trace of red, Sophie was glad to see, for the storm they had experienced at the start of the voyage had not been at all to her liking.

Still no land in sight. Perhaps tomorrow.

She turned towards the companionway and headed for her cabin. As time had passed, she had become less afraid and more at peace with herself — with the future, at least, for she could not change her past. She had made up her mind what she must do, and she was determined that nothing should stand in her way.

Her only fear was that she would be found before she could return to safety in Canada. Jean-Michel had not brought up the subject since their first days at sea, and she hoped this meant he had accepted her choice.

If he didn't, she would still go.

She was surprised, when she entered the cabin, to find him at the desk, pen in hand. He looked up as she came in.

'*Pardon*, Sophie. I had need of my papers. I must write to Jack Morgan before we make landfall.'

Her step quickened as she entered the room and closed the door behind her. She tossed the coat on the bed and crossed to the desk.

'You are writing to the man whose ship you sank?'

'*Bien sûr*. 'Tis the only polite thing to do.'

She stared at him. 'Have you gone mad? He will send you to the gallows!'

He glanced up, sending her a grin that sent her pulse flying. 'I shall not sign it, my dear. I am not that kind of fool.' He turned back to his work, dipping his quill in the ink and dabbing off the excess. 'But I would dearly love to see his face when he gets this. I doubt he even knows the *Deliverance* is missing, yet. This may break the news in quite dramatic a fashion, do you not think so?'

'Indeed I do,' Sophie responded, perching upon the edge of the desk to watch him complete his task. She did not know what to make of this enigmatic man. That he should pursue such a fool-hardy occupation — whatever it was he did — was one thing, but to spell out his actions to his victims . . . She paused.

'Have you done this before?' she asked suddenly.

He sprinkled some powder on the sheet and tapped it lightly with one finger. 'Written a letter? I can, you know. Even we aristocrats from the *ancien régime* had some skills.'

' 'Tis not what I meant,' she scolded him.

He blew the powder off the letter and looked up at her. 'You meant have I stolen any other ships and blown them into the abyss?' He stared at her for a moment, as though assessing the risk of trusting her with his answer.

'I won't tell anyone.'

'Ah, but will you tell me *your* secret, sweet Sophie?'

'Mine?' She felt the heat rise into her cheeks.

He grinned, reaching up with one finger to touch her nose admonishingly. 'You see, you are as itching to know my evil past as I am to know yours.'

She jumped up from the desk as though burned. 'I am a private person,' she replied, picking up the woollen coat and hanging it on a peg. 'I do not go about exposing myself to strangers.'

'Really? 'Tis not the thought that crossed my mind when I first saw you in that yellow gown.'

'Oh!' She turned away, fuming. 'My fichu was lost in my hurry to escape the vessel you were so wantonly destroying,' she answered, cross that she had let him needle her. 'And for what good purpose? None, except for the pleasure it gave you to do it.'

She jumped as she felt his hands grasp her shoulders. He turned her around forcibly, tipping up her chin so she was forced to look him in the eye. A frisson of awareness skittered up her spine, making her knees tremble beneath her coarse matelot breeches.

'I gained no pleasure from sinking the *Deliverance*. I did it to teach Jack Morgan a lesson he will never forget. I risked no man — or woman's — life, and I gained no profit from the act. Indeed, it cost me a great deal to set up the mission. But I will do it again, in a moment, if I see the need.'

Sophie's voice cracked as she tried to speak. 'B-but why?'

He released her abruptly, pointing at the letter that lay discarded on the desk. 'See for yourself.'

She crossed to the desk and picked up the note. Holding it by the light of the candle, she read:

Mr Morgan
  You may find the Deliverance *a short distance north of the Leeward Islands at approx. 19°20' lat. 64°15' long. In view of the proximity of the Puerto Rico trench I relinquished the pleasure of performing a sounding, but I suspect what is left of the*

ship and her cargo may be found in less than two thousand fathoms of water.

I have taken the liberty of forwarding all documentation concerning the cargo to your creditors, so that they may be assured you had received all the goods into your crew's care.

Captain Blackthorn, for his part, can no doubt attest that all cargo went down with the vessel.

It was signed: 'Your conscience'.

Sophie stared at the missive, shaking her head. 'I believe I almost feel sorry for the man. What, pray, has he done to deserve this?'

Jean-Michel stared at her for a moment and she feared he would not answer. Then he leaned his back against the cabin door.

'Morgan is a privateer, licensed out of Halifax. He and dozens of others are getting rich on the backs of half the honest shipowners of New England. The British Parliament set them to it late last year, since France and Britain are at war. Its ships may seize all vessels — of any nation, mind you — carrying goods to or from France or her colonies.'

'But what has that to do with American shipowners?' Sophie was sceptical.

'The burden of proof lies with the owner. The British need merely state that they believe the cargo was intended for France or French foreign soil. It's hard for the owner of a fishing schooner in Maine to prove that his catch will not be consumed by a French mouth.'

'That's preposterous.'

He shrugged. 'Some privateers go one better. They sell the sailors from the vessels they capture into service in the British Navy — they're very short of men these days.'

Sophie stared at him. 'And the Americans allow this?'

He pushed himself off the wall. 'When I left Boston in March, they were preparing for war.'

★ ★ ★

Sophie had a great deal to think about after Jean-Michel had gone. That he was telling the truth she did not doubt. But she also believed her own inner voice that told her there was something more personal in the Vicomte de Chambois' crusade against Jack Morgan. Something a great deal more personal.

Three days later, as she dressed in her yellow gown for dinner, tucking the makeshift fichu securely into the neckline, she wondered whether she would ever discover the truth about Jean-Michel. There was a bitterness inside him that surfaced sharply whenever the subject of the *Deliverance* or Jack Morgan came up.

She ran a hairbrush — another item borrowed from Jean-Michel, she thought — through her hair, tidying it as best she could. No doubt she looked a fright, as her mother would say, but there was no one to see her except the crew of the *Némésis* and its captain, the taciturn Zamore. And Jean-Michel.

She stared at the ebony brush, inlaid with silver, wondering whether he would let her take it with her as a keepsake.

Silly! She tossed it upon the desk. She had no time for such sentimentality. Was she not determined to give her life to God? What use had a holy nun for such fripperies?

She turned as Pierre entered the room to escort her to dinner.

The *grande chambre* was empty that evening, and Sophie wondered if she was to dine alone, when the door opened and Jean-Michel entered.

'*Bonsoir, mademoiselle*,' he said as he sat and flicked a serviette over his knee. 'Monsieur Zamore will not be joining us this evening. We are sailing close to the Nantucket Shoals tonight and he prefers to be at the helm.'

'We have reached land?' Sophie could not keep the excitement from her voice, though her delight was instantly replaced with more sombre considerations: the thought of returning to civilization filled her with dread. She had become accustomed to the false security of life aboard the *Némésis*.

'Soon. We'll round the Crab Banks in the morning and you'll see Cape Cod.' At her blank look, he explained, 'Then we'll have a straight run across Massachusetts Bay and into Konohasset.'

'I thought our destination was Boston.'

'It is. But in Konohasset there's a small and very discreet shipyard where the *Némésis* will be repainted in glorious blue and white. Then she'll hoist the American flag and be ready for business once more.'

Sophie picked up her glass of claret and took a sip, considering his words. 'And what business is she in when she is blue and white?'

'Mail.'

Sophie choked. She set down the wine and reached for her napkin, unable to stop the laugh that bubbled in her throat.

'May I help?' He was out of his seat in a

moment and rubbing her back.

Sophie froze. He stepped away and resumed his seat, glancing only furtively at her before picking up his spoon and paying attention to his soup as though he hadn't eaten in weeks.

'I'm sorry,' she said contritely. 'I was not prepared.'

'There is no shame in running a mail boat.'

'No, indeed. But it makes quite a contrast to piracy.' She stifled another giggle by stuffing a small piece of bread in her mouth.

Jean-Michel looked at her blue eyes twinkling with merriment across the table. She didn't smile often enough; laughed even less. He liked it.

He felt something twist deep inside him and recognized it as loneliness. He would miss her.

He stared down at his soup. No, he would not. For two reasons: one, he had no room for special relationships in his life, and two, he would not let her go.

He looked up, realizing she had spoken. '*Pardon?*'

'I merely said I did not mean to offend you.'

He waved it away. 'You are right to laugh. I did not purchase the ship so she could make a pittance out of carrying the mail. I bought her because she was fast and quick and had already been spectacularly successful as a privateer.'

Sophie bent her head over her soup. 'You are a man who likes to plan well ahead.'

That observation pleased him. It was not one his father would have shared. 'Perhaps I am.'

'So,' she went on, sending him a furtive glance. 'What plan have you in mind for me in . . . Kohasset, was it?'

'Konohasset. Actually, it should be Quonahasset, according to the Indians.' He passed her a covered silver dish. They did not bother with servants aboard the *Némésis*. Pierre brought the dishes up and cleared away, and they usually helped themselves.

'I have another vessel waiting, a sloop named the *Lady L* — for my sister, whose name is Léonie. The boat belongs to her husband, the Duc de Béligny.'

He saw Sophie's eyes widen. 'Don't worry. They're as Republican as I am these days.'

She seemed unconvinced. She helped herself to a leg of chicken and then passed him the server. 'How can a duke be a Republican?'

'Good question. Things are not what they were, are they? Let's just say that France

62

needed a shake-up, and that the Revolution in America was a healthy thing, at least in the end. Maybe France can grow through this recent madness and find a better path. If not, there will soon be no one left with his head still attached to his shoulders.'

She shuddered and he was instantly repentant. 'Forgive me, I did not mean to spoil your dinner. Let us talk of Boston and the *Lady L.*' He refilled their glasses as he talked. 'We shall transfer immediately — and under cover of darkness, which is how we shall arrive in Konohasset — to the sloop and sail for Boston Harbour. Once there, I shall take you to my sister's house, where there will be plenty of very respectable females to ensure that no further stain can impeach your character. Will that suffice?'

'I am not going to your sister's house,' she responded quietly, without meeting his eyes.

He tossed his napkin on the table. 'We have discussed this.'

'I cannot,' she said imploringly. 'Please understand. I must leave immediately for Canada.'

'That is not possible.'

'You cannot keep me prisoner! What would your sister, the duchess, have to say of that?' She pushed back from the table and got to her feet, eyes ablaze.

Jean-Michel seemed unperturbed. 'You are not going anywhere until I can ensure your safety.'

Sophie made a disgruntled noise in her throat, and turned to the bench that ran under the windows. She sat down mutinously. 'I will not go.'

He smiled a little to himself, then got up and crossed to stand in front of her. He deliberately stood too close, just to goad her, she was certain. 'My, my, Mademoiselle Lafleur. We are scarcely behaving in an adult fashion about this, are we?'

Her head shot up and she glared at him. 'It is you who are behaving like a child, *monsieur*, bullying and threatening me and saying it is all for my own good.' She stood up abruptly, bringing her nose to within a breath of his chin.

It was a mistake, but she recognized it too late. He tilted his head down the merest fraction and their foreheads touched. Sophie could feel the wooden bench pressing against the backs of her legs — she could not move unless she were to admit defeat and sit down once more. And she would not give him the satisfaction.

For a moment neither moved. Then slowly she tilted up her face so she could meet his eyes. She read something there, something that made her tremble and yet warmed her deep inside. Barely an inch separated them, and she could feel his breath, soft on her cheek. She closed her eyes, anticipating the touch of his lips. Ever since that first night when he had kissed her thinking her a loose woman, she had longed to experience the feel of his mouth upon hers again. Just once. Just one sweet memory to carry her through a lifetime of loneliness.

He made no move. She opened her eyes again and his mouth curved in a teasing smile. 'I do believe you want me to kiss you.'

Fury slammed into Sophie. She brought up her hands and shoved at his chest, but it was like hitting a brick wall. 'I was not the one who stood so . . . so . . . indecently close. How dare you take advantage of me!' She pummelled him again, but he merely grabbed her fists and held them against his chest. 'Let me go! You are nothing but a.. but a . . . '

And then he kissed her.

Sophie gasped as his mouth slowly enveloped hers, drowning her furious words and turning them into soft whimpers of pure pleasure. He released her hands and she spread her fingers unconsciously across his chest, feeling the heat of his muscles beneath his silk shirt.

His hands slid into her hair, tangling in the curls and stroking the back of her neck.

In response to the urging of his tongue, she opened her mouth, letting him explore, giving herself over to the exotic sensation. Somewhere deep inside, an ache began to build, a hunger unlike any she had ever experienced. His hands roamed over her back, stroked her shoulders, slid up the curve of her neck. She gasped as the backs of his knuckles encountered the mound of her breast beneath the silk fichu.

She pulled away, eyes wide with fright.

'I've been wanting to do that for a very long time,' he murmured.

'But you didn't,' she replied in a breathless whisper.

'Zamore was always watching.'

'Or Pierre was playing his hurdy-gurdy.'

'Or there were sailors about.'

They laughed quietly. Sophie marvelled that she could find humour at such a moment.

'Come,' Jean-Michel said, taking her hand and leading her back to the table. 'The cook will cry if we do not sample his offerings.'

They sat once more. Sophie watched him as he ate, for she had little appetite. She was thinking of the Devil and how hard he was working to keep her in his grasp.

'You look so forlorn, Sophie,' her companion observed. 'Does kissing a man usually make you gloomy?'

'I — I have never . . . that is, I don't usually — '

'You have never been kissed before?' He seemed astonished. 'Then you have led a truly sheltered life. Has nobody even told you how beautiful you are?'

'Never!' She stared at him. 'And nor must you. It is not true, anyway, and telling lies is a sin.'

He frowned. 'I am not very much on religion, I'm afraid, but it was no lie.'

She stared down at her plate, wishing childishly that she could run and hide, or climb the old apple tree as she had done when life was too much for her as a child.

'Tell me, Sophie Lafleur, what are you going to do if — sorry, *when* — you return to Acadia and find your uncle? Will you marry some French civil servant and mother dozens of children?'

'I shall never marry,' she replied shyly.

He sounded genuinely surprised. 'Never? But why? What will you do?'

'I . . . I have made a vow.'

Jean-Michel had a feeling he wasn't going to like her answer to his next question. 'What kind of vow?'

'To the church. I am going to join the missionaries.'

He stared at her, at her flawless face with its cornflower-blue eyes and its halo of golden hair, and tried to imagine her as a *réligieuse* working with unwashed Indian children in a wattle-and-daub hut in the middle of a Canadian winter. He shook his head to clear the vision.

'Forgive me, Sophie, but I cannot picture that.'

'Why not? Do you not think me capable of devoting myself entirely to the care of others?'

'Utterly. But I doubt you would survive your first winter. Sophie, you are a child of the tropics. You have never known a day of frost, let alone the bitterness of a northern winter. Or the hunger. To say nothing of the disease.'

'I must suffer those things, and if I do not survive, then it will be God's will.'

Jean-Michel frowned. 'Is this a recent vocation, or does it have something to do with the reason you were fleeing Guadeloupe?'

She jumped up sharply from the table, her face stained red. 'I will bid you good night, sir. I am very tired.'

And still without looking at him, she fled the room.

But she had answered his question, in her own way.

* * *

Sophie saw little of the tiny fishing village of Konohasset, for not a single light glowed from any dwelling as the *Némésis* glided into the harbour. Not even the moon shone to mellow the darkness. In eerie silence, they were towed to the dock by a waiting skiff, without any lights to guide them. Jean-Michel, with Sophie and young Pierre close behind, quickly transferred to a small sloop. Captain Zamore and his crew remained behind with the *Némésis*. As soon as her refit was complete she would sail to New York.

Meanwhile, the crew of the *Lady L* set about putting to sea with scarcely a word uttered between them. Sophie followed her cabin boy, in complete silence and without even a candle to guide their way, to her new quarters.

He left her then, returning to other duties, and Sophie felt her way cautiously to the window to see what she could in the blanket of darkness. Already they were on the move, for she spied a faint glimmer of sky above tall trees that edged the narrow waterway. The sea was calm, with a gentle breeze just strong enough to fill the sails. Water slapped faintly against the wooden hull and the canvas snapped as it caught the breeze.

She stood there until they cleared the point and headed north once more, picking up the now familiar swell of the ocean. But despite her fatigue, Sophie was too agitated to sleep. There was so much to think about, so much to plan. She had tried to organize her thoughts while at sea, but the strange voyage aboard the *Némésis* had lulled her into a misleading security. It had felt so safe, so far from prying eyes. So endless.

Now reality had returned. In a matter of hours, they would return to the real world.

She turned to survey her cabin, trying to distract her thoughts from what might await her in America. The *Lady L* was certainly a vast improvement over the Spartan *Némésis*. Everything was cheerfully decorated in gold and white with touches of blue. With its cheery curtains and elegant cheval mirror mounted on the wall, she realized this was a woman's quarters. The duchess, no doubt. She may have been to sea disguised as a man, but clearly she now liked to sail in more feminine comfort!

Sophie was almost disappointed she would not get to meet her.

She tugged off the woollen coat that had

become her constant attire on the chilly North Atlantic and rubbed her arms through her shirtsleeves. The first thing she would need to obtain in Boston was suitable clothing for the final portion of her journey. Despite his implacability, she still hoped to persuade Jean-Michel to advance her a small loan for this purpose. If he refused, well . . .

She turned as a knock sounded on her door.

'*Entrez!*'

It was the *vicomte*. He ducked his head to enter the room, then stood awkwardly, looking about him.

Sophie eyed him carefully, purposefully refusing to take note of the way her heartbeat raced whenever he was this close. In a few hours, he would be but a sweet memory.

'Was there something you wanted, *monsieur*?'

He closed the door.

'I . . . just wanted to see that you were settled.' Then looking about him, added sheepishly, ' 'Tis not like the *Némésis* is it? This was my sister's doing. Her folly, François calls it.'

'François?'

'The duke. François de la Tour. You'll like him.'

'No doubt. But I shall not have the pleasure. I shall be leaving your' — she sought for the appropriate word — 'protection, once we reach Boston.'

He turned his full attention on her then. 'Sophie, that is utterly foolhardy. You have no money — '

'Then be my friend and offer me a loan as I asked you. Have no fear — your money will be returned as soon as I reach Canada.'

She saw his jaw set in a firm line, felt the chill of his grey eyes, and had no need to hear his answer. She turned away, pulling down the white coverlet on the bed, deathly tired now the excitement was over. 'Very well, if you feel you cannot do me that honour, then I shall manage on my own.'

'You'll do no such thing!'

She jumped as his hand gripped her arm. 'Sophie, look at me!'

She turned, reluctantly. 'I am very fatigued, sir. Perhaps we may discuss this in the morning.'

'We will settle it now.'

She sighed.

He released her arm and she sank onto the bed, wishing with all her heart that she could just lie back and close her eyes and never have to have this conversation at all, for she was certain it could only lead to further unpleasantness.

He pulled an elegant *fauteuil* across the

room and sat heavily on the velvet seat, unmindful of his working clothes.

'I have given this much thought, Sophie, and my offer is this: let me find you a safe passage on a vessel going to Québec. The town is not large, but it is still French, which Halifax is not. From there you should be able to find news of your family, even these nuns you are so anxious to join.'

'That is most generous, but . . . ' To do that she would have to remain in Boston. Panic made her hands tremble.

'But,' he went on, 'until I can do that, I want you to stay at my sister's house as a guest.' She opened her mouth to object, but shut it when he held up a hand. 'I shall introduce you as a friend of a business acquaintance in Charleston and tell them the truth — that you are staying with us until I have booked you a passage north.'

'Us?' Sophie frowned, momentarily distracted.

'I live at my sister's house while I am in Boston. The place is big enough for ten families.'

More strangers to face. 'How many families does it house?'

'Only my sister's, though I very much fear it will soon be accommodating my beloved parents, who have taken it into their heads that the English are boring and that a visit to America would bring light relief.'

Sophie experienced a sinking feeling. 'And your father is . . . ?'

'Another duke. Or was.' He stood up, jabbing a hand through his hair. 'Dammit, Sophie, why does it matter? They're just people. You have no need to be over-awed by — '

'You do not understand, *monsieur*. I cannot. Your gesture is most generous, but it is out of the question that I break my journey in such a fashion.' She spread her hands, as if begging for his understanding. 'I must continue to Canada, by one means or another.'

He frowned, beginning to sense some of her own panic. Her eyes held a desperation he was totally at a loss to comprehend.

'Sophie, why do you act as though the very Devil were snapping at your heels?'

'Because he is.' She looked away instantly, her cheeks pink. Jean-Michel felt his unease deepen.

'Perhaps you are right. We are both tired. Let us speak of it tomorrow.'

She nodded, staring down at the braided rug beside the bed, but did not meet his eyes.

'I bid you goodnight.'

He paused, waiting for some response, but she made none.

He closed the door softly.

★ ★ ★

The next day brought little relief. Sophie was ready soon after dawn, standing at the starboard rail to catch her first glimpse of the harbour.

Jean-Michel was there already. He tried to talk to her about how she would be safe at his brother-in-law's house, but she seemed terrified of the very notion. He had never thought of his family as intimidating before, and made every effort to view the proposal from her point of view.

It was impossible. His own pragmatism was too strong. Were he in her place, surely he would be grateful for the offer?

They approached the point and spied a pilot vessel making towards them in the pale light. Jean-Michel accepted the pilot's offer of guidance through the channel, leaving himself free to enjoy the beautiful scenery at Sophie's side. She exclaimed at the green fields and trees heavy with blossom as the vessel passed up the narrow roadstead. Finally the sun broke through, reflecting its spring warmth across waters as smooth as glass. The beauty seemed to calm her, for he felt her relaxing at his side.

'It would be just for a few days?' she said suddenly.

His expression lightened as he realized the import of her words. 'Not long, I promise. You will be quite safe.'

Sophie spread her arms, though they trembled with the enormity of the risk she was taking. Why she was even contemplating such an action, she scarcely knew, for speed was of the utmost importance.

'Perhaps I have taken leave of my senses,' she said quietly. 'But this land is so beautiful, so serene — how could I come to harm in such a place?'

'I am glad,' he replied. 'La Tour House is set well apart from the town, and is well hidden from the street. You need not fear discovery there.'

'Very well.'

He beamed.

'But please,' Sophie added, alarmed at her own foolishness, 'I wish to see nobody, nor go about any more than I must. I shall need . . . ' She coughed. 'I shall need a few things. Some clothes, for instance.' She looked down at her sailor's attire. 'I cannot imagine what your family will think if they see me like this.'

'They have seen worse, I assure you,' he said without hesitation. 'Take this.' He withdrew a small purse from his pocket and passed it to her. It clinked in her hand. 'I will give you more when we've landed. Pray do not concern yourself about money. It is of no importance whatsoever.'

She frowned at the thought of accepting his gift, knowing she should accept it — after all, had she not begged him to make her a small loan? — but hating herself for falling into such a predicament. 'Perhaps its importance is relative to the quantity one possesses,' she said as she tucked the purse into the pocket of her shirt and turned once more to observe the scenery. 'But I do thank you. I shall pray for you.'

He turned his head towards her, a bitter laugh on his lips. 'Don't waste your prayers on me, sweet Sophie. I am entirely beyond redemption.'

4

Sophie was dismayed by the beauty of Boston on this crisp spring morning. She rode along in the carriage with Jean-Michel, feeling dreadfully out of place in her tatty yellow gown. The *vicomte* had donned a fine suit of dark grey, with a matching topcoat and beaver. She, on the other hand, had neither cloak nor hat. Indeed, she had been obliged to fashion her companion's spare stock into a bandeau for her hair as a token effort at performing her coiffure.

She pulled the curtain closed, pressing herself as far back into the upholstered seat as she could.

She was miserable, her black mood only worsened by the glorious morning. She wished she had not made such a rash promise. She had tried to change his mind, had begged him to let her remain in a hostelry near the Market Square, where she might stand some chance of finding the only two things she needed — suitable clothes and a passage to Canada.

But her entreaties had met with uncompromising silence.

She risked a glance at her companion. Jean-Michel sat relaxed upon the seat, his beaver hat clasped lightly in his hands and a careless whistle on his lips.

He turned to her suddenly. 'I know. I can't hold a tune. It's just such a glorious morning, don't you think?'

She looked away, her face burning that she had been caught observing him. What he must think of her she dreaded to imagine.

'Is it always so cold?'

'Cold? Forgive me, I had not thought . . . ' Instantly he shucked off his coat and wrapped it about her shoulders. 'Here. It is only a light frost and the sun is already turning warm.'

The coat was warm from his body and smelled of cedar and Jean-Michel. Her cheeks burned with embarrassment, but she was too cold to be anything but grateful. She snuggled into it, glad as much for the way it hid her hideous yellow dress as for the warmth it provided.

'I thought that was snow,' she grumbled.

To her discomfort, he laughed. 'On April 21st? No, my dear Sophie, 'tis but a touch of frozen dew. When the snows come, they bury the town in feet of the stuff. Ah, but then you have never seen either, have you?'

She shrank further into the coat. How stupid must he think her?

'Forgive me, *ma petite*. I forget that everything will be new and a little strange.'

Sophie blinked at the endearment. He was in good spirits.

'No doubt you are looking forward to seeing your family,' she said, purely for the sake of a rejoinder. She had no wish to allow the conversation to turn to her appalling lack of knowledge of the conditions she might encounter further north.

His face grew shuttered suddenly. The horses turned on to a rutted road that led between much finer houses surrounded by large leafy gardens. Apple blossoms had begun to open on the trees, and the morning air was redolent with their perfume.

'I do not spend much time there,' was all he said.

Sophie lifted one corner of the curtain and peered out at the town and the fine houses that graced the roadway. They were not as grand as Mon Bijou, but they still made her feel uncomfortable. This was a pretty town. She would rather it were ugly, for she had no wish to like it here. She wanted to be gone as quickly as possible, and without regrets.

She cast a quick sideways glance at Jean-Michel, admiring the bold lines of his face. The cut of his jaw, the way his lips seemed both sculpted in stone and yet warm and inviting. At the moment, he was humming a little ditty to himself, the corners of his lips curved upward in a way that made her breath catch in her throat. She looked away quickly. That way lay temptation.

'How long will it take to find a passage to Canada?'

'I cannot say. But I shall make enquiries as soon as we have settled in.'

'I have no wish to settle, sir,' she replied more curtly than she had intended. She must, at all costs, keep her sight on the final stage of her journey. Nothing else mattered.

He pretended not to hear. 'Look. We call that Beacon Hill.' He pointed to a green mound that rose beyond the trees. It was topped by a tall wooden structure that she lost sight of behind a large three-storeyed mansion.

'John Hancock's house,' Jean-Michel explained. At Sophie's blank look, he explained. 'He was the governor — and self-appointed king — till he died last year.'

She nodded, thinking it a curious description in such a new republic, though she forbore saying so. 'There is a beacon on the post up there?' she asked, as it once again came into view.

'No longer. They use lights in the Old North Church to send warnings these days, if they need to. But the children love to scramble up the hill.' He glanced quickly at her, a smile dancing on his lips. 'Perhaps I will take you there and show you the view sometime.'

Sophie frowned. Why could he not accept that this arrangement was for only the most fleeting period? She was leaving this town in a few days, with or without his help.

'Children?' she enquired, to change the subject once again.

'A houseful of them. I trust you have no objection to babies?'

'I believe they are best restricted to married women,' she replied haughtily.

He laughed. 'I heartily agree, my dear! My sister, however, has been married these ten years and has developed quite a passion for children. There's Christiane, the eldest, named for our mutual best friend when we were young. She's eight. Then *les enfants terribles*, the twins — named for me, I regret to say — Jean and Michel. They are seven and utterly incorrigible. Then comes — '

'How many are there?' Sophie asked, thinking that this house was going to be anything but the quiet refuge she had hoped.

He laughed as the carriage slowed and turned onto a long driveway lined with trees.

'Six in the house, and one on the way. I am to be an uncle again soon.'

'You like children.'

He nodded. 'They are uncomplicated little souls. They say what they mean and unless they are endeavouring to inveigle some sweetmeats from an uncooperative adult, generally lack artifice. But then, of course, there are the twins. Of them I am less certain. You will have to give me your opinion.'

Sophie frowned. She had no intention of remaining here long enough to pass judgement.

'I think not,' she said quietly lifting aside the curtain to peer out. They rounded a bend and came within sight of an enormous mansion, three-storeyed like John Hancock's, but very much grander. 'Oh, dear,' she murmured. It was built entirely of red brick with a slate-grey roof interrupted at intervals by a row of dormer windows, and each of its many white-painted windows bore a pair of black shutters. With stately symmetry, the house opened from its central core into two matching wings. Even its chimneys were neatly arranged in corresponding pairs, and the front portico, reached by an impressive flight of stairs, was made welcoming with a pair of huge urns brimming with scarlet geraniums that must surely have been grown indoors to affect such abundance in these cool climes.

The vehicle was slowing as it approached a set of wide stone steps at the top of the carriage sweep. 'You don't like it?'

'No! That is . . . 'tis very grand.' She shivered suddenly. 'But so large a house . . . so many people . . . '

His eyes softened. 'There's nothing to be afraid of, Sophie. You will be safe here.'

Safe? She did not feel in the least safe. Not while he looked at her like that. She glanced down, remembering how she was dressed and immediately began shrugging out of his coat with shaky hands.

'Please, sir, you must take this. Whatever will they say . . . ?'

She gasped as his arm suddenly encircled her shoulders in a hug. 'I don't care a fig for what they say about me, *petite*. As for you, they will think you a beautiful young woman with far too many secrets.' He touched his finger to her nose as though she were a naughty child and Sophie blushed.

Then the carriage door swung open and Jean-Michel released her. Sophie felt bereft. She watched him jump lightly from the carriage and hold out his hands to her. Her heart pounded as she stepped down, but whether from the viscount's warm hands

84

on her chilled ones or from the fear of this house and its strangers, she could not say.

A young black man grinned broadly at them, displaying a row of vividly white teeth. '*Monsieur! Vous êtes revenu!*'

'As you see, Maurice. Pray, where is my sister? No doubt still abed at this hour?'

'No, indeed, sir. I believe she is in the garden.'

He bowed to Sophie. Even to her, a total stranger, his manner was easy and familiar, something that would not have been tolerated at Mon Bijou.

'Come,' Jean-Michel said, tossing his coat to Maurice. 'Let us find Léonie and surprise her. She will be delighted to meet you.'

'But . . . ' Sophie looked down at her gown, feeling unbearably grimy and travel-worn. The last thing on this earth that she could imagine wanting to do at this moment was to make the acquaintance of a duchess!

He seemed to comprehend her distress, but he took her hand and tucked it into the crook of his elbow. 'My sister is not the least intimidating, Sophie. Come along.'

She had no choice. She tried to think of a prayer to calm her nerves as they passed around the side of the huge house and through a white picket gate that opened onto a wide lawn.

Sophie stopped, staring at the scene before her with disbelieving eyes.

Jean-Michel laughed, calling out cheerfully, 'Raise your guard when you've parried, Michel, or she'll run you through!'

There was a squeal of delight, and two small boys tossed their rapiers to the ground and rushed across the dewy grass to greet their uncle. They threw themselves at him without a care for his fine clothes, nearly knocking him to the ground in their enthusiasm.

'*Doucement! Doucement!*' he laughed, grabbing a child in each arm and swinging them about. 'You are as wild as ever, I see, *mes jumelles.*'

Sophie smiled a little sadly at the joyous scene. She had never known such affection, such ease. Her life with her mother, after her father disappeared, had been devoted entirely to work and to the dream of one day returning to Acadia. There had been little time for frivolity.

She looked away, startled by the sight of a tall figure coming across the lawn, sheathing her rapier smoothly, her long legs striding in a pair of highly polished top boots. That this was Jean-Michel's sister, Sophie had not the least doubt, for she had vivid red hair that tumbled over her shoulders and down her back, and bemused grey eyes that bore

86

an uncanny resemblance to the viscount's. But Sophie was quite unprepared for the sight of a heavily pregnant woman dressed in men's breeches! Her loose tunic did little to disguise her condition, especially with the addition of a sword belt slung beneath her enormous bulge.

'I couldn't sleep,' the woman explained in a lyrical voice as she drew near. 'And 'twas such a splendid morning!' She waved a hand at the children. 'Michel, Jean, pray leave your uncle alone. You will ruin his clothes.' Suddenly she became aware of Sophie, standing a little behind the boisterous group, and her eyes widened.

'*Mais qui est-ce?* Jean-Mich, what have you been up to this time?'

Sophie cringed at the suddenly haughty tone in the duchess's voice. She swallowed nervously, as the woman's eyes travelled over her attire, noting the mended rips and the makeshift fichu, no doubt, and then inspected her face and her pathetic attempt at tidying her hair with a borrowed stock. The duchess's eyes were wide and grey, so alike her brother's and yet bearing a sharpness that made Sophie want to run and hide.

'You don't usually bring your strays home, *mon frère*,' she said at last.

Sophie blushed to her roots, but the woman's words did not cow her. On the contrary, she drew herself up and returned her stare with equal boldness. Sophie's clothes may have suffered since she left Guadeloupe, but at least they were *women*'s clothes!

She felt Jean-Michel touch her arm. 'Léonie, may I present Mademoiselle Sophie Lafleur. Sophie, my sister, Léonie, Duchesse de Beligny.'

Sophie curtsied deeply, refusing to allow the woman any small triumph at her lack of manners. She was aware of the two small boys watching, their heads cocked to one side in unconscious symmetry.

'*Enchanté*,' the duchess said, though Sophie doubted she meant it. 'Come, you must be hungry. I was about to breakfast on the terrace.'

She turned to the house, striding away in her boots and breeches. The boys scampered off to fetch their swords and then ran ahead of her into the house, their voices tinkling in the crisp air.

'She's really quite a lamb once she gets to know you,' Jean-Michel whispered in Sophie's ear as they followed along in the duchess's wake.

More like a wolf, Sophie thought uncharitably. 'It is of no importance,' she said stiffly.

'I shall be leaving very soon, and in the meantime, I expect to see little of anyone. I shall keep to my room.'

She sent him a meaningful glance, which he returned gravely, though she wondered whether he was secretly laughing.

'We shall see,' was all he said. 'For now, perhaps you would like some breakfast.'

Sophie avoided his eyes. 'I would rather rest. Perhaps . . . '

'Of course. Forgive me.' He ushered her into the house, where they found Maurice. The young Negro cast her a curious glance.

'Mademoiselle Lafleur is my guest, Maurice. Perhaps you will find her a room.'

The servant's dark face was bland as he observed them. '*Certainement, monsieur.* But *mademoiselle* has no luggage.'

Sophie froze. She heard the coolness in Jean-Michel's tone as he replied.

'I do not believe I engaged you in conversation, Maurice. Mademoiselle Lafleur wishes to rest. You will show her to the gold room.'

'*Oui, Monsieur le Vicomte. Excusez-moi.*' he replied, his skin burning deep red. '*Mamselle*, if you would follow me?'

Sophie almost felt sorry for the boy. She nodded to Jean-Michel, whose face was set in a mask of anger, and followed the servant down the hall. They came to the front of the house and mounted a wide curving stairway that led to the two upper floors in a grand sweep of polished oak. Their steps were muted by royal blue carpeting that covered the centre of the stairs and as they passed down a long hallway, Sophie could hear children's voices raised in excited chatter. They sounded so happy, so full of life. She sighed, catching herself before she could contemplate what the future might have been, if only — she would allow no 'if onlys'. The past could not be changed. The best one could do was to shape one's own future.

And her future, she knew, could never include such blessings.

Maurice stood aside and motioned for her to enter the room.

'Do you wish for some refreshment, *mamselle*?'

She hesitated. 'Some tea, perhaps? Thank you, Maurice.'

He nodded, avoiding her eyes entirely, and closed the door behind him. She wondered what he was thinking. What the duchess thought. She shivered. She could not imagine ever liking that woman.

The room was not large, but tastefully decorated and furnished. The bed, so wide after the humble cot aboard ship, looked very inviting. She had been up since before dawn, and had slept little the night before, so absorbed was she by the thought of arriving in Boston.

She inspected the view from the window, finding that she was at the back of the house, facing the wide lawn where the duchess had been teaching her young sons to fence. Sophie had never seen a woman hold a sword before, and the sight had been unsettling. As if the countryside and the very atmosphere here were not strange enough, now she had to become accustomed to women who wore pants and fought with weapons.

A knock sounded on the door and a slender young Negress entered, bearing a silver tray. She smiled shyly and set her burden upon the table beside a *chaise-longue*.

Then she curtsied. 'My name is Danielle, *mamselle*. I have brought your tea.'

'Thank you, Danielle.'

Sophie lifted the china pot and poured some of the golden beverage into an elegant wafer-thin Sèvres cup. She added a lump of sugar and picked up a tiny silver spoon. Suddenly she was aware that the girl was staring.

'Did you want something else, Danielle?'

'I am here to help you, *mamselle. Monsieur le Vicomte* sent me.'

Help me or watch me? Sophie wondered wryly. To the girl she said, 'Most of all, I should like a bath, Danielle.'

'*Certainement*! I shall see to it at once.' She indicated a small door leading off the bedroom. 'There is a bathroom in all the main bedrooms here, *mamselle*. That is very modern, *n'est-ce pas?*'

Sophie didn't know quite what to say. 'Indeed, that is very . . . modern.' She made no move to inspect the facility. It would not do to let the girl know that she herself had never set eyes on a bathroom, let alone used one.

Luckily, Danielle skipped away on her errand and Sophie was free to satisfy her curiosity.

She pushed open the door to reveal a small anteroom, containing an elegant marble-topped table upon which stood a porcelain bowl and jug. The front of the table held a rail upon which towels were hung. On the other side of the room sat a wooden commode with a decorated lid, and against the near wall stood a large blue-painted tub, decorated with flowers that matched the *chaise-percée*.

As she was contemplating the notion of a

room entirely devoted to bathing and bodily functions, there came another knock. She hurried back expecting Danielle with hot water, only to find *Madame la Duchesse* standing there, now dressed in a white sprigged-muslin gown with her vibrant red hair subdued by a simple bandeau.

She looked almost girlishly young, but her expression was not entirely pleasant.

'I wish to speak with you. Alone,' she said, without preamble, and sailed into the room.

Sophie closed the door, wiped her hands against the sides of her gown and followed. 'Y-Your Grace, I really have no wish to impose upon your household. It was entirely at your brother's insistence that I came here. I have begged him repeatedly to let me find more . . . appropriate accommodation in the town, but . . . '

'How is it that you have no belongings?' the duchess asked, sitting herself somewhat awkwardly on the *chaise-longue*, in deference to her motherly girth.

'I — ' Sophie flushed under the directness of the woman's gaze. She did not wish to offend the lady, yet neither did she have any desire to bare her soul. 'They were lost.'

'Rather careless, would you not say?' Her

grey eyes narrowed. 'And you have been aboard my boat with my brother, all the way from Charleston? Without chaperone? Why is that?'

This was worse than Sophie could have imagined. She cleared her throat. 'We boarded the *Lady L* in Konohasset. Before that, we sailed aboard the *Némésis*.'

'*Vraiment!*'

There was a moment of complete silence, during which the duchess stared at Sophie and Sophie stared at the carpet. Finally, the older woman spoke, her voice containing more humour than previously.

'There is something you should know about my brother, *mamselle*. He is perfectly incompetent at lies. They shine from his face like a beacon of denial. And if I am not mistaken, you, too, lack proficiency at that skill. Come here!'

Sophie crossed the floor, sitting primly on the *chaise* where the duchess indicated. She avoided her eyes, enduring the close examination she was receiving only with great determination.

'Mademoiselle Lafleur, are you in trouble?'

Sophie turned, startled by the suddenly gentle tone in the woman's voice. She stared at her, wide-eyed, then blushed when the duchess merely smiled a gentle smile and

94

patted her swollen stomach, her eyebrows raised in question.

'Oh! Oh, no, Your Grace. No. Nothing like that!' Sophie was appalled that she could even think such a thing.

Her adamant response appeared to give Léonie pause. She frowned, seeming almost disappointed. Sophie wondered if perhaps she was a woman given to delving into other people's secrets, and felt a tremor of anxiety.

'*Bien*. I had thought perhaps ... ' She shook her head. 'Then pour me some tea and tell me what brings you here with Jean-Mich.'

Sophie occupied herself with the refreshments, though her hands trembled, her mind whirling as she sought for something to say.

The duchess accepted the tea. 'Well?'

Sophie clasped her hands together. 'I-I fear I cannot satisfy your curiosity, Your Grace.'

Léonie paused, cup halfway to her lips. Their eyes met, one curious and not a little irritated, the other wide and anxious.

'You are not the only one who has ever had a secret, *mademoiselle*. Come, have your tea and we shall speak no more of it this morning.'

Sophie picked up her cup and took a sip, setting the cup back in the saucer with a slightly shaky hand. 'You are most kind, *Madame la Duchesse*.'

'Since you are at present under my roof, would you do me the honour of answering one question?'

Sophie nodded. 'If I can.'

'What were you, before my brother met you?'

Sophie met the challenge in her eyes. 'I was a lady's companion, *madame*. My mother also was forced into that occupation, though her father was a *seigneur*.'

'In Canada?'

'Acadia.'

'Ah.' There was a touch of understanding. 'Your family were forced out with the exiles.'

'In 1762.'

The duchess seemed thoughtful. 'I see.'

'Which is why . . . ' Sophie began, looking about her at the sumptuous room she had been forced to occupy.

'You are uncomfortable, here, in this room?'

'Oh, no! One could never be uncomfortable here. It is . . . it is very beautiful,' she finished lamely, unable to express her true feelings without seeming ungrateful, and that she had no desire to do.

'Thank you. My husband built this house, you know. But the décor, that is my domain. It is not like we had in France you understand. There, we had a château near Bordeaux . . . ' Her eyes clouded with wistfulness. Then she brightened. 'Ah, but that was then, before the Revolution. Now we are Americans, or learning to be so — and must have more modest tastes.' She turned her gaze on Sophie once more. 'And you — why have you come to Boston?'

'Only to find a ship that can take me home. To Acadia,' she added.

'That should not be hard. What will you do when you get there? Marry an Englishman?'

Sophie was appalled. 'Indeed, no! I have sworn myself to God.'

The duchess paused, her mouth dropping open. 'What on earth do you want with Him, child?'

'It is not what I want, *madame*, it is what He wants of me.'

Léonie gave her a sceptical look. 'I see.' Then she shook her head. 'No, I do not see.' She set her cup down hard on the silver tray. 'There was a time when I experienced the cloister. My 'vocation' lasted no more than three days, mercifully, but it convinced me that I could never live that way.'

Sophie bowed her head. 'But I must,' she whispered. 'No matter the cost.'

★ ★ ★

Soon after, Danielle and another servant appeared with the water for her bath and the duchess took her leave.

Sophie dismissed the girls and enjoyed a few moments' pleasure in the scented water, washing away the grime from her pale skin with a bar of lavender soap. She washed her hair twice till her scalp tingled and she felt thoroughly clean again. Then she dried quickly, wrapping a luxurious white towel around her. She contemplated her yellow striped muslin, knowing she must don the garment again, but delaying the moment.

Instead, she wandered back into the bedroom, only to discover a selection of gowns laid out upon the bed. She gasped. These were fine gowns, finer than any she had ever owned.

Sophie's lips tilted into a wry smile. No doubt the Duchess de Béligny did not wish a guest in her house to be dressed in anything less than fashion.

She riffled through the collection, sighing over an exquisite creation in blue silk that would complement her eyes like no other, but finally choosing a demure gown of grey dimity. It was a little long, which made her suspect these clothes had once belonged to Léonie herself, but she tightened the drawstring neck as much as she could and cinched the waist tightly with a blue sash. Satisfied that she could walk in the garment without tripping, she selected a fichu and for the first time in weeks was able to cover herself in a suitably modest fashion.

She wished her hostess had thought to include a cloak of some sort amongst her offerings, for Sophie was unaccustomed to the crispness of the weather here, despite the warm sunshine that now streamed in from the tall windows.

A cloak would have been of great convenience to her, for while she had bathed, Sophie had made a decision.

She would leave this house immediately, without advice to a soul. Jean-Michel would be angry, she knew, while his sister would no doubt think it proved Sophie's weakness of character.

She jumped as Danielle entered the room.

'Oh, *mamselle*. I had thought you would still be in the bath.' She looked approvingly at the grey dimity. 'You look much better, *mamselle*. Perhaps I might dress your hair?'

Much as she wanted to be on her way, Sophie thought it wise to accept. She settled herself at the *poudreuse* and allowed the young black girl to tackle her hair. It was a mess from the vigorous towelling it had received, but Danielle worked quick magic and soon it was tumbling down her back in a soft mass of gold, adorned by a grey bandeau that matched the gown she had chosen.

'Oh, *mamselle*,' Danielle said, as she considered Sophie's reflection in the glass. 'You have the loveliest hair. It is not as curly as *madame*'s, of course, but so fine and silky.'

Sophie smiled. 'Thank you, Danielle. You have quite the knack with a brush.'

The girl seemed inordinately pleased with such praise. Sophie got up from the dressing-table.

'Please, Danielle, will you convey my thanks to the duchess for her thoughtful gifts and tell her that I should like to rest for a while as I am quite fatigued from my journey?'

'*Bien sûr, mamselle.* Shall I say you will be down for dinner later? I can bring you something from the kitchen if you do not wish to join *Monsieur le Vicomte* and *madame* till then.'

Sophie was sorely tempted, for she had not eaten since dawn, but she could not delay any longer. 'Thank you, no.'

The girl tidied the gowns off the bed, at Sophie's insistence merely laying them upon the *chaise-longue* for the moment. She knew she would have no use for any of them, but she hardly wished to make that clear at present.

When Danielle had gone, Sophie quickly retrieved the small bag of coins Jean-Michel had given her from the pocket of her old gown, and let herself out of the room. Rather than use the main staircase, she slipped down the deserted hallway until she found the back stairs. With her shoes sounding loud on the bare wooden steps, she tiptoed down, past closed doors to the outer door. She opened it a mere crack, peering along a short colonnaded walkway towards what she took to be the kitchen and servants' quarters adjoining. With no one in sight, she slipped outside and into the shrubbery that grew beyond the covered walk, where she might be screened from the view of anyone in either the house or servants' hall.

Soon she came to a white pebbled path. She paused while a blackamoor leading a cart and horse passed by, then slipped across and into a copse of trees that grew largely wild beyond. She hurried through the wood in the direction of what she hoped was the lane leading to the road.

The trees grew thickly for a while, the undergrowth snatching at her skirt as she hurried along. She made no effort at stealth, for she was surely far from anyone in this wilderness of a place. Then she saw the lane, a few paces to her right. Beyond was a rough meadow planted haphazardly with apple trees in blossom. Cows grazed on the lush spring grass, their soft lowing carrying to her on the still morning air.

She slowed her pace, slapping at a troublesome mosquito who thought to make a meal of her neck. Her breath was coming in short gasps, for she had run a good distance. Clearly she had become lazy aboard the *Némésis*, with only the small deck for her daily exercise. This walk would do her good.

The trees thinned a little as she followed a route keeping the rutted lane at her right. She stopped as she spied the beacon post high on its hill, using it to orient herself. Satisfied, she continued. She would find the road that adjoined the lane to the house and cross into the large common opposite. If she cut across the park, she could save herself much walking, as well as avoiding any chance encounters with passers-by.

She had tried, on the ride to the house that morning, to maintain a sense of direction, that she might find her way back if she had need. She was glad now, for she knew she could not stay a moment longer. Who knew what might happen if one of the servants were questioned? And why should they not speak of the strange young woman with no luggage who had suddenly appeared in Boston? They had no reason to lie on her behalf.

She stopped, cocking her head for any sounds of pursuit. Aside from the soft sounds of the herd, only the unfamiliar calls of birds in the trees broke the silence.

She continued, hurrying now, for she wanted to be gone from this place as soon as possible. She would not feel safe until she was on another ship, heading north.

★ ★ ★

François de la Tour reined in his horse.

'What the — ?' He peered into the thick maple grove that bordered the lane on his property, shading one hand against the sun.

There. A flash of colour. He spurred the horse into a walk once more. Someone was lurking about in those trees, and their behaviour looked mighty unnatural.

None of the servants had any reason to be there, he thought. But who knows, perhaps the cook had sent them in search of wild mushro —

'Hey!' he called, as the figure began a headlong rush away from the lane. Damn. So it wasn't a servant. He turned the stallion and plunged into the underbrush.

★ ★ ★

Sophie saw the horseman stop and stare straight at her as she stood, frozen with fear. Then he moved on and she thought she was safe. Perhaps he hadn't seen her.

She edged away tentatively, keeping her eyes on the man. Her heart was beating erratically and her breath coming in painful little gasps. So soon, was all she could think. They've found me so soon.

She stumbled on a rotting tree stump, falling heavily onto the soft forest floor. The smell of humus and damp earth assailed her senses. She heard his shout and panic took her. She jumped to her feet, gathering her skirts in her hands and began to run.

Deeper into the woods she ran, heading she knew not where, as long as it took her away from that man on horseback. Even the house seemed like a sanctuary from what awaited her if he —

She screamed. Strong hands grabbed her by the upper arm, yanking her sharply about.

She hit out instinctively, fighting for all

she was worth. She tore at the gloved hand that still held her arm, not caring that its owner was yelling at her. The horse pranced about dangerously, side-swiping her with his flank and knocking her backwards into the bushes.

Winded though she was, she scrambled to her feet and ran. She heard him slide from his mount and give chase on foot.

She was lighter, younger. But he was tall and had a strength she could never possess. Oh, Jean-Michel, she sobbed in terror as she ran, if only I had listened to you!

Then he was upon her, bringing her to the ground in a hard tackle that knocked the last of the breath from her bursting lungs.

She lay face down with the man atop her, gasping ineffectually for air and knowing that she had tried her best. But it was not to be.

His hands stilled, then suddenly he grabbed her gown and plunged his hand into the voluminous pocket, withdrawing the purse of gold coins Jean-Michel had given her. Her eyes widened but lack of air made speech impossible as he opened the purse and tipped the contents onto his gloved palm.

'So, you are just a common thief.'

Sophie wanted to shout 'No!' but the air would not come to her lungs. She shook her head, but he appeared neither to notice nor care as he returned the coins to the purse and tucked it into the pocket of his topcoat.

He helped her up with hands that were not ungentle, considering what he must now think of her, then waited as she recovered from her winding.

Finally, she could breathe again. She straightened slowly and looked up at her pursuer. He was handsome enough, with eyes of midnight blue and hair as black as the devil. The scowl he wore suited his mission.

'So you have finally caught me,' she said, still taking deep breaths to fill her oxygen-starved lungs. 'But I will die before I let you take me back.'

His eyebrows rose.

She ignored him, brushing out her skirts and flicking dead leaves from her hair. 'God will be my judge, not man.'

'We'll see about that,' he said grimly. He took her arm again, pushing her before him through the woods to where his horse wandered, cropping at the short grasses. He bent to retrieve his black beaver, which had fallen to the ground during the fracas. She noticed that he wore breeches of expensive cloth tucked into a pair of elegant top boots. His coat, too, with its high collar and gold

106

buttons, was expensive.

A successful bounty hunter. She should feel flattered.

Without so much as an excuse-me, he lifted her bodily onto the saddle of the great beast and swung up behind. Sophie looked gingerly down. To one not used to horses, the ground seemed a long way below. She clung to the animal's mane and prayed that she would not fall.

To her surprise, her captor headed up the lane towards the house. Hope sprang, sweet and pure in her breast. Jean-Michel was there. For the first time since they had met, she yearned to see his face.

'Why are you taking me to La Tour House?'

'Where else?' was the only reply.

'I am a guest there,' she said, emboldened by sudden hope. 'They will not just let you steal me away like this, from under their noses.'

'A guest?' His voice held a touch in incredulity. 'Guests do not skulk about in the shrubbery.'

'I was not skulking.'

'Oh? What would you call it?'

She glanced over her shoulder at him. 'I was running away.'

He looked no less sceptical. 'From what?

107

A surfeit of hospitality?'

'From you, of course.' His stupidity was maddening.

He called to the horse, halting it at the steps, and dismounted. As he held out his hands to lift her down, two figures came walking, arm in arm, through the picket gate on the west side of the house.

'Jean-Michel!' Sophie cried, never more glad to see anyone in her life.

'François!' said the duchess at almost the same instant.

Sophie ran to them, unashamedly grabbing Jean-Michel's arm as he disentangled himself from his sister. He looked astonished to see her, even more so to see her riding companion.

'Who the devil *is* that young woman, my dear?' came the voice of her captor. She turned, astonished to see the duchess reach up and kiss him quickly on the lips.

A horrible thought came over Sophie. 'Jean-Michel, who is that man?'

'That's my brother-in-law,' he replied. 'François, what the devil were you doing with Sophie up on that damn horse?'

The duke crossed to them in long strides. Sophie gave a gasp of dismay as the full import of her mistake flashed through her mind.

'You know this woman? She claimed she was a guest here, but I didn't believe her. What guest would go running off through the woods without even an escort?'

Sophie cringed as she felt the full force of Jean-Michel's scrutiny. 'What guest, indeed,' he said ominously.

' 'Tis not what it seems!' she said, looking up at him. Her eyes began to ache and she thought she might cry. She willed the tears away, for she had already made herself look a fool.

'Not only that,' the duke continued, 'but I found this upon her person. No doubt she stole it from the house.'

Jean-Michel stiffened. 'Sophie is not a thief. I gave that to her myself.'

François, to give him his due, looked thunderstruck. His face a dull red, he turned to Sophie and presented the purse to her stiffly. 'I beg your pardon. Under the circumstances — '

'There were no circumstances,' she said crisply as she took the purse. 'You merely mistook me for somebody else.'

'What were you doing in the woods?' This from the duchess, who stood at her husband's elbow, observing the scene with confusion. 'Danielle told me you were sleeping. You have quite ruined that gown.'

Sophie looked down. 'Oh dear.' It was true, the gown was badly torn in several places, covered in mud and stained by grass. 'Forgive me, Your Grace. I was — ' She searched for a plausible explanation. 'I was merely out for a walk. For some fresh air.'

This caused the duchess's brows to rise, but she made no reply.

Sophie felt Jean-Michel's hand on her elbow, pushing her towards the path that led around the side of the house. 'Perhaps you had best change,' he suggested levelly. But she knew him well enough to sense the anger hidden beneath the words. She glanced up at his face as she took her leave, then wished she had not, for the anger banked behind his grey eyes caused her knees to tremble.

5

'Dammit, Sophie, why did you run from me?' Jean-Michel demanded as soon as they had rounded the corner of the house.

'Let me go! Please, *monsieur*. I shall bring you only trouble!'

'Not unless you tell me why. And' — he admonished, turning her sharply to face him — 'only if you tell me *all* the truth.'

Sophie's temper flared. 'Why should I do any such thing? What possible interest could you have in me? I am a . . . a nobody!'

'Not to me, Sophie,' he said grimly. 'I doubt I have ever been caused so much trouble by a nobody. Come with me.'

And so saying he took her by the hand and led her across the lawn, up a slight incline that defined the northern edge of the property to a bench set beneath a spreading elm. He pushed her down on the seat but did not sit himself. He propped one foot on the bench and leaned an elbow upon it, his eyes thunderous. 'Now, I am listening.'

Sophie averted her gaze, staring blindly at the grass beneath her feet. How to begin? How could she tell him the truth, and then suffer his rejection? He would hate her, and rightly so. And then he would throw her onto the streets, or even — No, he would not betray her, surely, even though he was angry with her for trying to slip away.

She looked up. 'If I tell you about myself, will you promise to let me go?'

'I'll give no such undertaking.'

She gasped with frustration. 'By what right do you imprison me? You do not own me, sir!'

A burst of fury lit his eyes, melting almost instantly into a bleakness so remote it burned a chill deep into her heart.

He pushed himself away from the bench and paced in front of her, rubbing a hand across the back of his neck, his tone much gentled. 'Forgive me. You are entirely correct, of course. No man can own another.'

'Then . . . ? Then do you promise?'

He gave his head a slight shake. 'We are all driven by our secret demons, and I never make promises I cannot keep. I cannot let you go out into the world with no one as your protector. Dear God, you barely speak a word of English! What kind of man would I be to do such a thing?'

She turned away, staring at the sloping lawn through a sheen of tears. 'Then my secrets must remain my own, and you must beg God's forgiveness for holding me prisoner when it so contravenes your own morality.'

Jean-Michel looked at her in astonishment. 'You lecture me, *mademoiselle*? You, who dared to smuggle yourself aboard a stranger's ship? Methinks you have a plank in your eye!'

'Indeed!' she answered hotly, turning on him. 'But I at least am not a pirate who steals other people's vessels and holds women against their will!'

With that, she jumped up and stormed away across the lawn.

She had not gone three paces when he caught her, snatching her arm and swinging her around to face him. 'All right, Sophie, so I am a blackguard. But I am not so much of one that I would allow a defenceless woman to throw herself on the mercy of the streets of Boston. There is *something* of the gentleman in me, you know.'

She sniffed, abashed by her ill-will when he had done so much for her already. 'Indeed I do, sir. But I merely wish to find my way home. And if you will not assist me, then I shall undertake the journey by some other means.'

'*Nom de Dieu!*' He slapped his hands against his sides in frustration. 'Acadia, Acadia, Acadia! Dear girl, you were not even born when your family left that godforsaken place.'

She tilted her chin. 'It is still my home, as France is yours.'

He frowned. 'France? What makes you think I yearn for France?'

'I . . . I don't know. You are . . . a French nobleman? You grew up there?' He shook his head with each notion. 'Well, you were born there — oh, Jean-Michel, there must be something — '

'Wrong, Sophie. America is my home now. France is my past, a country changed beyond recognition, as yours most surely is. The land that you dream of is only that — a dream. You cannot expect it to be as your mother described it. So many years have gone by, the people gone, names changed by the British migrants brought in to replace them — '

'You've been there!'

'What?'

She stared up at him. 'You speak of Acadia as though you have seen the land. When was this?' She gripped his arm fiercely. 'Please, tell me what you know. Apart from my mother, I have not spoken to a living soul who has seen my homeland.'

Jean-Michel sighed, taking her hand and leading her down the hillside towards a small lake. Ducks and a few geese floated on the glassy surface and nearby a mother goose with a set of yellow goslings grazed on the lush grass.

Jean-Michel sat down unceremoniously at the water's edge, pulling her down beside him. It scarcely mattered. The gown was ruined anyway.

He lay back, plucking a stem of grass and sucking on it while observing her through eyes that squinted against the sun. 'For one so young, my dear Sophie, you are vexatiously sharp of mind. Yes, I have been to Canada. Not when the coastal settlements were part of France, but since then. Halifax mainly. I will tell you what little I know, though I doubt it will cheer you much. But if I share this, will you tell me what you are so afraid of that you cannot rest for a day until you reach the place?'

'If I do, will you let me leave?'

'At least you acknowledge there is something.'

She squirmed. 'Perhaps.'

'Is it a man?'

'No!' Then she frowned. 'Well, not in the way you mean.'

'So it is a man, but not a lover.'

'Certainly not.' She flushed.

'Of course not. You told me no one had ever called you beautiful — nor even kissed

115

you. Such a waste.' He reached out his grass stalk and stroked it down her nose, the playful action in direct contrast to the intent look in her eyes.

Sophie shivered. Her pulse skittered as she remembered the kisses they had shared and the way they had made her feel. Once, she had glimpsed this same intensity in his eyes and had wondered what it meant. It had excited her then in a way she had never imagined, and it still did. She looked quickly away. She could not afford to remember. No doubt he looked at many women in such a way. Women who would suit him far more than she, who had no interest in matters of the heart.

'I cannot tell you my story, for then you would hate me and you might not help me. It is better that I simply leave now, before . . . '

'Before what?'

She sighed. 'Must you insist on such directness?' When he stared at her without response, she continued, 'There may be people . . . looking for me. I simply don't wish them to find me.'

He frowned. 'These people — would they harm you?'

There was a moment's silence.

'I believe they would.'

He stared at her for a moment, clearly troubled by that revelation. She wondered what he would say if she had told him that her capture would mean certain death.

'Very well,' he said quietly. 'Then answer me this: would they have good reason to do you harm?'

She glanced up, meeting his eyes. She wanted to shout 'No!' She wanted to throw herself into his arms and tell him everything, to know that he would understand, that he would make it all right. But she could not. No one could forgive what she had done. There was not a soul to rely upon in all the world, bar herself.

'I see,' he said finally, when she failed to reply. He turned his attention back to the goslings, watching as they took their first tentative steps into the water, their little squeaky voices filling the air.

For a while they were silent, watching the birds experience their first swim. Sophie wished she could take the risk he was asking of her as easily, and that it might have such welcome results. But she knew better.

'You will remain here,' he said at last, in a voice that invited no argument, 'in this house, in this town, until I am satisfied that it is safe for you to leave.' He turned to look at her. 'I must ask for your solemn word on this, for if I do not receive it, I shall personally lock you in your room.'

Sophie saw the glint in his eye, the set line of his jaw. She knew he meant every word of his threat, and saw that she had no choice, though the thought of remaining here a moment longer made her tremble with fear.

'I am not safe here. Already the servants know my name, and they must be speculating on my sudden appearance, to say nothing of my encounter with the duke.' She shuddered.

'You can and will be safe. Did I not give you my word? We shall tell the family that you are recently bereaved and on your way to rejoin your uncle in Nova Scotia. Will that satisfy you?'

At least that much would be the truth. She nodded.

'Then we have a bargain. You will be free to behave as a guest in mourning as long as you hold to your promise.'

This is my punishment from God, she thought as they returned in silence to the house. And His revenge was just beginning.

★ ★ ★

Léonie de la Tour stood at the window of her private sitting-room gazing out upon the wide green lawn behind the house. Perhaps it was wrong of her to spy upon her twin in such a manner, yet something drew her irresistibly to the sight of her brother and his strange new companion sitting in the long grass beside the duck pond.

She was a funny little creature. Quite pretty, with a beguiling freshness. But pugnacious. There was fire in her eye and secrets in her heart, that much was clear. Léonie did not believe for a moment her sorry tale of leaving Charleston for Canada. With no belongings and no companion? *Quelle sottise*!

She tapped her finger thoughtfully against her chin as she saw, even at this distance, that they were arguing. Jean-Mich would win. He always did. Except with his twin sister. But the young woman, Sophie, was clearly frightened. Why, François had related the circumstances of his capture of the girl at the bottom of the lane, and how she had declared she would rather die than return to the house with him! Yet the child knew him not in the least, for they had never met. What could Sophie possibly fear from her beloved husband?

No. Something was amiss here. As she watched her brother and Sophie returning to the house across the lawn, side by side

119

and yet as isolated from each other as two people could be, she wondered if Jean-Michel himself knew what little Miss Lafleur was hiding.

If he did, she would find out, if he did not, then she would discover it for him.

She smiled as she turned back to pick up the baby's bonnet she was attempting to knit. A plan was forming in her mind. One that would suit her current physical requirements — to say nothing of her curiosity — admirably well.

★ ★ ★

After dinner that evening, a meal from which Sophie had excused herself by reason of a headache, Jean-Michel accompanied his brother-in-law into the library.

This was his favourite room in the house. Warm and quiet, it exuded a peacefulness he found refreshing. He accepted the crystal goblet of cognac François passed him and settled himself in a leather armchair beside the fire.

He liked the room and the brandy a great deal more than the expression in the older man's eyes.

'So?' François prompted, as he dropped into a matching chair opposite. 'Are you going to explain the presence of that curious young woman who is hiding in my house?'

Jean-Michel studied the golden liquid in his glass, wondering how much to offer. He and François had always been close, ever since the older man had rescued him on the dockside at Capetown when he was searching for his twin sister. Had he not, goodness knows how many years he might have been away from France searching for her. Time he had been able to spend with Marie. Their happiest years . . .

He shut away the memory. He had learned one could not change the past, one could only atone for it.

'What's to say?' he said, with as much bravado as he could muster. 'I know little of the girl except she is suffering a bereavement and is on her way to Lower Canada when I can find safe passage.'

His brother-in-law's dark eyes were enigmatic. 'I would have thought that an easy task. You go there yourself often enough.'

Jean-Michel blanched. 'Don't let that slip, I beg you.'

'Indeed? And why, pray, should that be a secret?'

'No reason. Except . . . ' He was digging his own grave, but he had made a promise. 'Except I have promised her I will try to

121

find the family she is hoping to join there. I should feel more comfortable knowing she has somewhere to go.'

'Such concern for a virtual stranger.'

Jean-Michel glanced up, then wished he hadn't. 'It is not what you think, François. Damn me if the girl hasn't vowed to enter the church!' He ignored the soft laugh that notion produced. 'I have said I will help her, and I shall.'

'Ah.'

He glared at his sister's husband. 'It scarcely helped that you accused her of being a thief!'

'You can hardly blame me for that. She was running away as though the very Devil were at her heels.' He laughed softly. 'Young women never used to have such a reaction to me. Perhaps I am just getting old.'

'Probably,' Jean-Michel replied heartlessly. Though at forty-four, the duke still cut an extraordinarily handsome figure. Jean-Mich hoped he would look half as good in another dozen or so years.

'I have news you may be interested to hear,' François said, as he got up to replenish their glasses. Jean-Michel was glad he was leaving the subject of Sophie Lafleur's odd behaviour, at least for the moment.

'On what subject?'

'Two, as it happens. Though perhaps during your stay in Charleston — that was where you encountered the lovely Mademoiselle Lafleur, was it not?' Jean-Michel nodded stiffly. 'Then you may have been apprised that war with Britain has been averted, at least for the moment. Washington has sent John Jay to England to smooth things over.'

'That is good news.'

'It will be, if he can get them to agree to uphold their agreements in the Northwest territory and honour America's boundaries. But there is news of more interest, also. We are to have a navy.'

Jean-Michel raised his eyebrows. '*Vraiment?*'

The duke smiled a little wryly. 'The mark of emerging nationhood, I suppose. They are to build six ships and employ over two thousand men. Do you think that will scare the British away?'

'Hardly. But it may offer some coastal protection.'

François's blue eyes darkened. 'Speaking of which, Jean-Michel, there was a man at the docks today enquiring about Baltimore Clippers.'

Jean-Michel glanced up sharply. He read the meaning in his brother-in-law's eyes clearly enough. 'Anyone we know?'

'I think not, but one can never be sure.'

They were silent for a moment. François de la Tour was the only person who knew the real business Jean-Michel was engaged in. He even helped him sometimes. And if someone were making enquiries it could endanger them both.

'Perhaps he only means to purchase such a vessel,' he said without too much conviction, for it was impossible to shake off the sense of unease François's news had imparted.

'And the *Némésis*?'

'Back on her postal run. Zamore was unhappy with our last mission. He thinks we should be doing escort duty.'

'Then better relations with the British should set his mind at rest. There should be less call for protection for a while.'

Jean-Michel thought about Jack Morgan, and wondered whether that would be true.

'I trust you achieved your objective?' This from the duke.

'Perfectly.'

'*Bien.*'

Jean-Mich watched François as he settled back in his chair and stretched his legs towards the fire. There was a troubled look on his face.

'Did something else happen while I was in the Caribbean?'

The older man seemed lost in thought for a moment, then he glanced up, a wry smile on his lips. 'Let's just say that Mr Morgan has dealt me a rather unwelcome blow.'

'Such as?'

'He took the *Gravenhurst* off the coast of Albany. She's awaiting the pleasure of the Court of Vice Admiralty in Halifax.'

Jean-Michel swore. The *Gravenhurst* had once been known as the *Hirondelle*, its name changed to disguise its owner's French origins. But even flying the American flag had offered too little protection from the hungry maws of Jack Morgan.

'So she'll go to auction. You'll not defend her?'

François snorted. 'Would it make any difference? One word from my lips and they would recognize I was French in an instant. They would scarcely feel the need to hear the evidence that she was carrying lumber for New York.' He shrugged. 'No, I'll not give him the pleasure. I only hope the cargo he lost was worth as much.'

Jean-Michel thought of the premium quality rum he had blown into the Caribbean sky and smiled grimly. 'More. Much more. And it won't be the last, I promise you.'

'Are you so determined to ruin the man?'

Jean-Michel looked at him in surprise.

'Somebody has to stop him. Not just Morgan, of course. There are enough others as bad or worse. But there's something about the audacity of the man that galls me.' He swirled the cognac in his goblet, holding it up to the fire so the light sparkled through it. 'I met a man who sailed as a prisoner on one of his tubs recently. A Micmac Indian, sold into slavery in Georgia. He'd tried to kill himself and had almost succeeded. His owner sold him to me for a pittance, since he was too damaged to work the fields.'

He saw the flash of anger in François's eyes, though his voice was deceptively soft when he spoke. 'And pray where is he now?'

'Back with his tribe. Not that he's much good to them as a hunter anymore, but they were pathetically glad to see him. I think he will at least be able to tell them how the white slavers operate, and perhaps they can be more vigilant. They have lost too many.'

They were silent then, each lost in their own thoughts, their own risk-taking and the price they would pay if they, like the natives, were ever caught.

Jean-Michel was suddenly aware of his brother-in-law's scrutiny. He glanced up, feeling instantly ill at ease. François had seen too much, done too much, and seemed sometimes to have a sixth sense that unnerved those around him. Right now, the look in his eyes made Jean-Michel want to squirm in his seat like a child.

'*Quoi?*' he said, rather more abruptly than he had intended.

The duke shrugged. 'You don't trust me tonight, Jean-Mich,' he said softly, dropping his eyes to stare into the amber liquid in his glass. He swirled the brandy slowly, causing little tears of liquor to slide down the crystal. Then he looked up. 'You are too like your sister, even in adulthood. Like you, she should never play poker.'

Jean-Michel laughed, reddening under the older man's assessment which, as ever, was a little too close to the bone. 'I do trust you, François. More than any man alive. Not another soul beyond my closest crew, who could scarcely be kept in the dark, knows of my activities. How much more can one man trust another?'

'Mademoiselle Lafleur is not from Charleston, is she?'

Jean-Michel's heart pounded unevenly for a second at the sound of her name, though he put that down to the suddenness of François's statement, for a question it clearly was not.

He shrugged.

In the silence that followed, the fire crackled and spat, a log shifting restlessly on the embers.

'I don't exactly know where she's from,' he said at last. There, let his brother-in-law make of that what he could.

'*Vraiment*? Yet she is with you. Did she perhaps fall from the sky upon your boat?'

Jean-Michel sent him a dirty look. 'Sometimes you can be altogether too much like my father, François! How does my sister cope?' He held up a hand with a faint laugh. 'No, pray do not answer that. I have no need to hear of your exploits in the bedchamber. Since you are so insistent, she was aboard the *Deliverance*. A stowaway, as it turned out. She threw herself upon my mercy when she realized we were going to blow the ship.'

He could see he had captured the full force of François's interest. 'Why would an educated well-bred young woman like that need to stow away?'

'So far I have not the slightest notion,' he replied with a shrug, resigning himself to telling François everything he knew. Which was not, he realized, very much. Quickly, he shared his knowledge, telling him all that had happened since he had met the intriguing and frustrating Sophie. Except the kisses. Those he would not share.

'So you see,' he finished, 'why I am loath to let her continue her journey. I must see that she will be safe, and to do that . . . '

'You must find out from whom she is running.'

'Precisely. I must return to Guadeloupe as soon as I can.'

François shook his head. 'You must not consider such a course of action. With Morgan out for blood it's a risk not worth taking, and your parents are soon to arrive. You should be here.'

Jean-Michel rolled his eyes.

François ignored the gesture. 'I shall send an agent I can trust. There's a schooner from Carmichael's fleet leaving tomorrow for Saint-Domingue flying the British flag. It should be safe enough. I shall send Jolliet.'

Jean-Michel tossed back the last of his cognac, knowing he was right. It was the best course. Jolliet could be trusted, and then Jean-Michel would be here when his parents arrived in America, though he would have preferred an excuse to be absent, for he was not overly fond of his father's company.

More importantly, he thought later as he lay in the dark, thinking about the young woman who slept a few paces across the hall, he would be on hand to see that Sophie remained right here in Boston where he could keep an eye on her.

⋆ ⋆ ⋆

Tuesday dawned unseasonably warm, so Danielle informed Sophie as she arranged her hair with a white silk bandeau, letting the soft curls frame her face naturally. Sophie surveyed the result in the dressing mirror and was impressed with the girl's skill.

'I believe a walk would do me good,' she said, smiling her thanks as Danielle set the silver brush upon the *poudreuse*. 'After the restrictions of life aboard ship, 'twould be a delight to walk upon green grass again.'

Danielle's guarded expression instantly caused Sophie to wonder whether the servants had heard of her failed flight from the property and had been warned to keep an eye upon her.

'Never fear, Danielle. I shall keep to the paths. No doubt it would be hard to lose one's way in a garden.'

The maid's expression softened. 'The garden is very large, *mamselle*, but if you take the East Walk you will reach the duck pond.'

Sophie turned away, busying suddenly clumsy fingers with straightening her sash as she recalled with painful clarity the scene beside the pond last evening.

'I shall keep that in mind.'

But when she ventured out upon the terrace, she found Léonie sitting awkwardly upon a wrought-iron chair, dressed in a loose Creole gown and a straw hat with emerald feathers.

'Ah, *voilà*! I was about to send Maurice to fetch you. Such a beautiful day, is it not?'

Sophie nodded, perplexed that the duchess should be awaiting her. Before she could say a word, Léonie had thrust a green satin parasol into her hands.

'Here, child, for heaven's sake, you do not even have a hat! I shall have my milliner sent to you this very afternoon. Do you not know your skin is as brown as a matelot?' She laughed suddenly, sounding more like a mischievous child than a duchess. 'Ah, but I know from experience, the tan will fade quickly enough if you apply plenty of rosewater and keep your face hidden from the sun.'

She took Sophie's arm and propelled her down the steps and along a white pebbled path that ran both ways along the back of the house, still chattering about the parasol and apologizing that the colour was an abomination in company with Sophie's blue muslin. However, the sun simply must be kept at bay if she were to regain her looks.

'But *madame*,' Sophie protested weakly, 'you surely have need of it yourself?' It was not lost on Sophie that the parasol exactly matched the emerald gown Léonie wore.

'Fiddlesticks! I have a hat. You do not even own one at this time, I'll wager.'

'Well, I — '

'Exactly.' Léonie would brook no argument this morning. She had lain awake for too many hours last night, consumed with curiosity about this strange little creature her brother had brought home from his latest voyage. François wasn't the least bit of help — all he would say was 'leave the child be; she's grieving now'. So Léonie had been left to speculate on her own, lying on her side in the bed with pillows propped all about her as though she were some building in danger of collapse. And whenever she thought she was finally drifting off to sleep, her unborn baby would commence some gymnastic torture of its own invention, throwing its arms and legs about as though fighting to be free of its prison. Soon couldn't be too soon, she thought, absently rubbing her protruding stomach beneath her gown.

She tucked her hand beneath Sophie's elbow, giving the girl an encouraging smile.

'Come, let us walk and talk. I shall show you the vineyard and the wood, even the pond, though I fancy you have already visited there with my brother.'

She suppressed a smile as she saw a faint flush of colour enter the girl's cheeks.

'Forgive me, Sophie. I have too little to do and too much to think upon these days. Once my babe is born — and I pray God it shall be soon, for I cannot abide the last days of any confinement — then I shall have plenty to occupy me. I detest waiting, as do you, no doubt.'

'I . . . it is sometimes difficult,' she murmured. 'I am most anxious to return to Acadia.'

'There! I knew you would understand. *Sans doute* we shall both achieve our heart's desire in due course. Meanwhile — ' She lost her train of thought, as she so often did during the later stages of gravidity, but it made no matter. She brightened as they reached a long pole fence. '*Voilà*! Is this not extraordinary?'

Sophie frowned, staring at the small field and its crop of woody vines, as yet devoid of leaf. She wondered that such dull plants would cause anyone a measure of excitement. 'What are they?'

'Grapes from our very own vineyards in

Bordeaux. My husband would not abandon our estates without a selection of the best from the fields. Would you believe he chose every one of these himself and had the plants dug so we might bring them with us?' She smiled wistfully, and Sophie could see the real affection she held for her husband. 'Of course, the soil, the climate — nothing is as it was. But we grow them anyway, and make wine when the time comes, and try to pretend it is the same.'

Sophie was certain she glimpsed a sheen of moisture in the duchess's eyes, but the woman turned away quickly and they continued along the path, which began to slope down at that point.

'Do you miss France?' Sophie asked, as they crossed the lawn to enter the edge of a wood where young trees were already showing new leaves.

'Very much, but only sometimes. This is my home, now. After four years, I am becoming as American as sour-dough bread. I am even developing some proficiency in English, though Jean-Mich tells me my accent is atrocious.'

'I do not speak English, beyond a few simple phrases. Mama thought we should retain our heritage better if we did not bother with it.'

'Your mother was right, though it would be wise to learn. Here, especially, English is an advantage one cannot be without. My children are entirely bilingual, you know.'

Sophie contemplated telling the duchess that she would scarcely be in Boston long enough to learn another tongue, but she was forestalled by a sudden weight on her arm.

'*Madame*? Are you ill?'

The duchess was leaning heavily upon her, her breathing uneven. Sophie looked about her wildly, but they were deep in the little wood now, and could not even be seen from the house. She pulled her over to a simple log bench set against the bole of a huge oak tree.

'Rest yourself, *madame*, while I fetch assistance.'

But Léonie was already feeling better and waved the suggestion away. 'Indeed, you shall do not such thing. These spasms are common in the final days. 'Tis good news.'

'It is?' Sophie found that impossible to imagine.

Léonie smiled up at her. 'It is the baby's way of saying he or she is ready to arrive. The sooner it does, the quicker I can be done with living the life of a whale.' She eased herself up from the seat and took Sophie's arm once more. 'Never fear, my dear, you will find out

135

for yourself one day.'

'Are you certain we should not turn back, *madame?*' Sophie asked, preferring to ignore that last comment.

'There is not the slightest need,' replied her companion, shaking her head so that the feathers in her hat bobbed about her face. 'Look, there's the lake. And the children are here!'

She seemed delighted to find the twins and an older child playing at the water's edge. As they left the woods and joined the path that ran around the far side of the pond, they saw that the boys were preparing to push out from a little jetty in a punt. A dark-haired girl, who clearly favoured her father in looks, was untying the small boat.

'Pray be careful, Christiane!' her mother called, increasing her pace. 'Do not lean out so!'

The girl completed her task and stood up, turning her attention from her brothers to the strange woman who approached at her mother's side.

'Dearest,' Léonie said as they drew near, 'say hello to Mademoiselle Lafleur who is staying with us while she recovers from her journey from Charleston. Sophie, my eldest, Christiane.'

The child, whom Sophie took to be about

eight years of age, bobbed a curtsy, looking up at Sophie with curious grey eyes that reminded her of Jean-Michel.

'Where is Nanny?' Léonie asked, looking about her. Sophie noticed an edge of displeasure in her voice.

'She has taken the girls inside, *Maman*. Rose-Marie needed to pee.'

Léonie gave her child a quelling glance, which Sophie could see was entirely lost upon the girl, who grinned mischievously at her mother, displaying a pair of enchanting dimples.

'Christiane, such talk is entirely unladylike. Kindly apologize to our guest.'

The child blushed. *'Je m'excuse, mamselle.'*

Sophie smiled in response, but the child scarcely noticed. She tugged on her mother's arm.

'Maman, please may I go to the stables? Nanny won't let me, but I *so* want to see Mathilde. Georges was going to shoe her today, and he promised me I might watch if I do not get in the way. Oh may I, *Maman* — please, please?'

Léonie laughed, stroking her daughter's soft cheek. 'Very well, child, but you are not to ride unless you have a groom with you — even in the paddock. *Tu comprends?'*

'Oui, Maman!' She shot away across the

137

grass, abandoning the path for the shorter route straight across the wide lawns and up to the house, her skirts hoisted in eager fists at her sides.

'She adores that pony,' Léonie said, as they settled upon a broad bench beside the lake. 'And Nanny likes to punish her for every little thing by preventing her from spending time with Mathilde.'

'Is she very strict with the children?'

Léonie shrugged. 'She has forgotten, I think, what it is like to be a child. The need to explore, to venture out, to scrape one's knees.' She turned to Sophie. 'Were you allowed to scrape your knees and laugh out loud when you were little, Sophie?'

Sophie thought of Pascal, her constant playmate and love of her young life. 'There was not much laughter in my home, *madame*. My only surviving brother died when I was but four years of age.'

She saw a flash of sympathy in the duchess's eyes. 'Forgive me, I had no wish to remind you of such sadness.'

'Do not trouble yourself, *madame*. It was a long time ago.'

'And your mother had no further children?'

'She — ' How to explain that her father had disappeared forever after Pascal's death, leaving the two of them to fend for themselves? 'Papa was lost at sea soon after. My mother never remarried.'

The duchess sighed, turning away to watch her twin sons lowering their fishing lines into the glassy waters of the pond. Their young voices danced on the crisp spring air, full of excitement, full of hope.

'And now, Jean-Mich tells me you have lost your mother as well.'

Sophie nodded, concentrating on the children's antics in an effort not to think about her mother. Not to recall the pain of having been prevented from being with her while she slowly sickened and died.

She jumped as Léonie squeezed her fingers. 'It is good that you have someone new to care for you, then, *n'est-ce pas?*'

Sophie frowned. '*Madame?*'

'Oh, come, child. Surely it is as obvious to you as to the rest of us.'

'I do not believe I take your meaning, Your Grace.'

The duchess's eyes widened. 'Why, I speak of my brother, *mamselle*. You cannot deny that he has developed considerable regard for you. Why, one might even say he is patently besotted, as only a man can be!'

6

Sophie opened her mouth in a gasp, but Léonie never noticed, for she had turned, her attention caught by someone approaching down the path that edged the lake.

She struggled up from the bench, dragging Sophie with her.

'Why, Mrs Otis. How exceedingly good of you to call,' Léonie said in English.

Sophie's head was reeling with the duchess's blithe comments upon the subject of Jean-Michel's feelings, but she, too, stood to receive the bustling lady who was approaching, her person clothed not only in an elaborate velvet pelisse lined with fur, but a monstrosity of a hat bearing feathers, bows and mountains of indeterminate flowers. She sailed towards them like a frigate under colours.

'*Bonjour*, my dear *Madame la Duchesse*. Oh, la, but my French is becoming so *délicieuse*, do you not think so? *Mais* who is this, *cette chantiante* young woman?'

Sophie tried to follow this peculiar *mélange* of language, only grasping its nature from the wry grimace that flitted across the face of her companion. The duchess, however, seemed to comprehend the intent effortlessly.

She reverted to French — for Sophie's sake? — quite seamlessly.

'May I present Mademoiselle Lafleur, recently arrived from Charleston *en route* for Acadia. Sophie, this is Mrs William Otis.'

The woman's brow was furrowed as she concentrated on the words, then lifted as she heard her name.

'Oh, my dear. Pray to God and I am being Muriel. I am fishing women have need of their own names, don't you?'

Sophie stood, speechless. Léonie burst into a laughter so genuine that Mrs Call-me-Muriel Otis could not in the least be offended. She, too, dissolved into gay laughter, leaving only Sophie wondering if all Americans were quite so stricken with madness.

Finally, appearing to notice her young companion's perplexity, Léonie explained. 'Madame Otis is trying to learn French. We meet quite often for this purpose, sometimes speaking English for my benefit, or French for hers. It amuses us, even if we do not *always* succeed in our endeavours.'

Sophie murmured what she hoped were appropriately sympathetic noises, and fell into step with the older women as they headed along the East Walk, back to the house. They skirted the lake this time, avoiding the longer trek through the woods, and leaving the two small boys seemingly content with their fishing.

It seemed French was to be the order of the day. Since the path afforded little comfort to a group of three, Sophie hung back, allowing the effusive Mrs Otis to claim the undivided attention of her friend. However, through the fog of muddled tenses and confused nouns, she discerned a genuine purpose behind the lady's visit. When she heard the word 'pirate', she found herself listening intently.

'*C'est vrai!*' the woman expounded. 'All the world speaks of it. This crazed pirate steals ships and blows them up to hell — '

'Heaven,' Léonie corrected.

'Ah, *oui. Ciel.* Anyway, he takes nothing. *Rien. Vous comprenez? Quelle sottise!*'

This last was rendered with such passion and pride that Sophie clearly understood she had mastered the expression from the duchess's own lips. She smiled quietly, though the news the woman brought disturbed her greatly. If all of Boston was abuzz with news of a pirate who destroyed vessels for no obvious reason . . . She glanced at Léonie, wondering if she was familiar with her brother's activities, whether she might

142

make the link, give away some slight clue to the probing eyes of the undoubtedly sharp-minded Mrs Otis.

But Léonie's frown showed nothing if not genuine bafflement.

'This makes no sense, my dear. Why should any man risk the noose in such worthless pursuit?' She waved a hand dismissively. 'Bah, 'tis nought but delicious gossip. Sometimes, I think Boston needs another tea party to keep idle minds busy.'

'Oh!' Mrs Otis clearly understood more French than she could manage to say. Her horror of the very idea was picturesque. Sophie smothered a smile.

They had reached the terrace, and she was now able to rejoin the pair, receiving the full force of Mrs Otis's considerable personality. They settled upon the chairs surrounding an elegant table set with a fine linen cloth and a bowl of primroses, and within an instant, a maid had appeared bearing a tray of coffee and pastries.

Mrs Otis accepted coffee but coyly rejected the pastries, declaiming in peculiar grammatical fashion upon the importance of maintaining one's figure. Then, realizing her indelicacy, she actually patted her hostess's protruding abdomen. Sophie's jaw dropped at such unprecedented familiarity.

'Oh, my dear Duchess, you must excuse me. I had not fished to implore that you will not eat as I do. You are eating for two, of course. Who can say?' she said, winking at Sophie, 'but there might not be more twins on the journey?'

Sophie choked on her coffee as she caught Léonie's eye, brimming with girlish laughter. It was too much. Why could she not have taught the woman the simple difference between 'to fish' and 'to think'? She giggled into her napkin as she wiped her eyes. Perhaps it was part of the fun. Without her dreadful French, conversation with Mrs Otis would in all likelihood be a chore not to be endured.

Mrs Otis, having made a full — if barely comprehensible — explanation for her refusal of pastries, then proceeded to methodically dispose of two brioches and several slices of dried apple tart. In her excitement with the news of the day, she quite forgot that she was attempting to practise her French with *Madame la Duchesse*, and proceeded to speak in English, which left Sophie entirely dependent upon her hostess's goodwill in translating for her.

Sophie watched the duchess, enjoying a relaxed chance to observe Jean-Michel's twin sister with some ease, since she herself could not enter into the conversation. She found herself admiring the keen intelligence in those fascinating grey eyes, the expressive hands, the casual acceptance of her swollen abdomen, which most women would have kept hidden from all eyes beyond those of their own maid. Yet for Léonie it was as though her confinement were a source of pride, a chapter of joy and anticipation in her life. She was an unusual person, to be sure.

As was her brother. Sophie squelched her suddenly wandering thoughts. She had been doing so well this morning in her efforts not to think of Jean-Michel. She *had* thought of him, of course. Too often. By the lake, where they had sat together on the grass, she had recalled the teasing caress of the grass stalk he had stroked down her nose and the strange intensity of his gaze. For a moment, she believed he had intended to kiss her. Her cheeks flamed with the realization that she had wanted that, very much. Even recalling it now caused her skin to tingle, as though a ghost had kissed her. She shut the foolish notion away, determined not to wallow in such temptation.

But, as she sat sipping her coffee on the terrace with the sun doing unmentionable things to her complexion, and staring at his beautiful sister, Sophie found herself drawn to the woman, as though she herself held the secret of Jean-Michel's attraction. Ridiculous. How could a sister — even a twin — shed light on so intriguing a man?

Yet there was something about her. The way the light played in her grey eyes, or her auburn hair caught the sunlight as she tilted back her head to laugh. No. It was more than that. Somewhere within Léonie de la Tour was a spark of rebellion, a spark of unconventionality that lay at the very heart of her mysterious brother.

She jumped as Léonie spoke suddenly in French, causing her near-empty cup to rattle on its saucer.

'Mrs Otis tells me that some Englishman named Morgan is offering a reward for news of his ship that was sunk after leaving Guadeloupe. He seems to think they should be hanged for mixing his premium quality rum with seawater!'

'M-Morgan?' Sophie squeaked, covering her outburst with a little cough.

'You know this man, Sophie?' Léonie asked with a frown.

'Oh, no, indeed, Your Grace!'

Léonie gave her a thoughtful look, but turned back to Mrs Otis with whom she continued to share gossip about such unlikely events. Sophie caught some of the conversation, since French and English were employed in roughly equal doses, and did her best to join in their laughter, though her heart was thumping so fast she could scarcely breathe. Morgan? The very name swamped her in dread. She must pass this news to Jean-Michel, as soon as she were able. If anyone were to know that she herself had come from the island, both she and Jean-Michel would be undone.

But no one knew. Not a single soul, bar Jean-Michel himself.

Or did they?

She stared out across the spring-green lawn, her eyes capturing not the sight of a fat robin plucking worms from the damp grass, but the dark night of panic during which she had bashed the plug from a puncheon and waited in terror while the rich black rum had flowed out, sloshing through the boards of the jetty and into the ocean below. Though she had hurried it in her mind, her body had been forced to tolerate the interminable wait while the barrel slowly emptied itself into the bay. No sooner had it done so, and she was set to prise off the lid and clamber inside, than she had perceived a sound, faint, but distinct, from the shadows of the wharf.

She had turned, her eyes long since

accustomed to the gloom. Eyes had stared back at her. Young eyes. A boy, perhaps. Black as the night which hid him, his curiosity palpable. She had stared, unmoving, until the tiny shadow had detached itself from the wall and slunk away.

How far away, she knew not.

Now, she wondered whether it had been far enough.

★ ★ ★

Though the night was quiet, Sophie could not sleep. Her thoughts were entirely consumed by the disturbing news brought by Mrs Otis, and while she told herself repeatedly that it was nought but idle gossip, fear nagged at her mind. Jean-Michel had failed to appear for dinner that evening, and François informed her that he had gone to spend the night on his ship now docked in Boston. Someone had been seen prowling about the decks of the *Némésis*, apparently, and he wanted to check that nothing was amiss.

Had it not been for Mrs Otis's news earlier in the day, Sophie would doubtless have thought no more about the matter, but as midnight came and went, she became increasingly concerned. What if the supposed prowler had been more than some idle vagabond looking for a few valuables to gain money for drink? What if he were searching for one particular Baltimore Clipper in the hope of finding some evidence to expose that 'crazed pirate' who destroyed ships complete with their cargo?

Perhaps the rumour of a prowler was merely a trick, a ploy to entice him to his vessel. Alarmed by her own worst imaginings, enhanced as they were by the darkness of the night, she shivered, pulling the blankets closer. There would be no mercy if Jean-Michel's secret were exposed, to say nothing of the disgrace it would bring to his family. Why, they might be forced to leave Boston in disgrace, just as they had finally made a new home for themselves!

Oh, why did he do it? she wondered as she stared into the dark. Were there not other ways to punish the likes of Jack Morgan? And how in all of heaven had *she* managed to become embroiled in all of this!

She turned restlessly, punching the pillow and forcing herself to think no more of it. It was none of her concern. She lay down and closed her eyes, determined to put it from her mind. It would seem better in the morning, God willing.

Just then a lone owl hooted from beyond the window, making her jump.

With a cry of frustration, she sat up. It was quite useless — she would never sleep until she had at least warned Jean-Michel. Then if the reckless man continue to scoff at the danger, she could at least be satisfied she had done her duty.

She jumped out of bed and lit a candle. For a moment she contemplated summoning Danielle to take a message to the docks, but abandoned the idea just as quickly. To do that would only be to fuel suspicion and rumour, for then the servants would gossip that *Monsieur le Vicomte* was in some kind of danger from a bounty hunter. No, this was something she must do herself.

She searched the drawer at the bottom of the armoire for the clothes she had been given on the voyage from Guadeloupe. Holding them up in the faint light, she wondered what had possessed her to keep the pantaloons and shirt, for wearing men's apparel was definitely not to her taste. However, she shed her nightgown quickly and dressed in the rough garments, twisting her blonde hair into a knot atop her head and fastening it roughly with an ivory comb. She found the battered hat she had worn aboard the *Némésis* to ward off the bright Atlantic sun, and jammed it onto her head, then tugged on the heavy woollen coat that had once belonged to Pierre, the cabin boy, and still smelled strongly of mothballs. It was not the best of disguises, but it would do.

She doused the candle and let herself out of her room, tiptoeing down the stairs in order to avoid waking the household.

The darkness of the night confused her at first, but her eyes adjusted quickly enough. She would dearly have liked to borrow a horse from the stables, but she had never learned to ride. So she set out quickly down the lane, keeping to the grassy verge to muffle her footsteps.

As she came out into Beacon Street, she knew only that she must travel east and, hurrying along, soon found herself within the built-up part of the town. The first pale shards of dawn were lightening the sky now, making it easier for her to gain some sense of direction.

She had only the vaguest idea of the route, but it was less difficult than she had anticipated, as from time to time she would gain glimpses of tall masts in the distance as she rounded a corner or descended a hill.

She soon found herself outside an imposing structure where men and women were unloading produce onto market stalls, even at this early hour and, as she wound her way past pens of squawking chickens and snuffling

151

pigs, she soon came upon the harbourfront. Here stood the offices of importers and purveyors of all manner of goods, and tall buildings belonging to shipping companies whose names proclaimed their familiarity with all corners of the globe. Doubtless François de la Tour had his premises here, she thought, as she hurried on towards the wharf beyond. Already, men were stirring, preparing for their daily work. She glanced about, seeing the masts of the many schooners and sloops that lay at anchor or tied up for unloading. How would she ever find the little Baltimore Clipper amongst so many?

The first pier contained nothing she recognized as the *Némésis*, so she hurried back to the streets and down a narrow deserted alleyway to where she had glimpsed another. As she approached the row of vessels she thought she heard footsteps behind her. She turned, but saw no one. Frowning, she wondered if she was letting her imagination play games. No doubt the narrow alley was merely echoing her own footsteps on the cobbles. She continued on her way, then froze as she recognized a most definite second set of feet marching behind. Heart pounding, she stopped and listened. Nothing. Chiding herself for having such an imagination, she shook her head, continuing down towards the small pier that opened at the end of the alley. To Sophie's relief she saw the unmistakable masts of the *Némésis*, raked back at a steep angle. Even though it was still not quite dawn, she could see the vessel was blue and white.

Sophie glanced about her, seeing no one. Quietly she crept up to the ship, grabbed the ropes beside the gangplank and climbed aboard. There was no watch, which seemed strange after the rumours of prowlers, but she was glad, for it made her task the easier. She crossed to the companionway, pausing in the shadows to search the pier and the alley that had spooked her, but there wasn't a soul in sight. Blessing herself for luck, she tiptoed down the stairs.

As she stepped out into the small hallway, a slight movement caught her eye and she turned. Too late! An arm snaked around her throat.

Sophie tried to scream but the sound was cut off by the sleeve choking her. With a desperate cry she kicked out at her attacker, causing him to loosen his hold. She pulled free and swung around to face him, determined not to give him such an advantage a second time. She felt the whoosh of air as his fist smashed into her face, then a blinding light as her jaws snapped together under the blow.

And then night returned.

★ ★ ★

Sophie swam back into consciousness slowly, aware only of an excruciating pain in her jaw and the sensation of having been sat upon by a horse. But worse was to come, for, as she forced her eyes to open, she encountered the thunderous brow of Jean-Michel de Chambois, in the foulest mood she had ever witnessed.

'Wh — ' She tried to speak, but her mouth wasn't responding properly. 'What happened?' She winced, holding a hand to the throbbing flesh of her jaw. 'Ouch! Did you hit me?' she asked in amazement, ignoring the banked fury in his gaze.

'I don't hit women,' he all but snarled in reply. 'I hit a man who was trying to sneak aboard my ship.'

Sophie opened her mouth to object, but the pain in her jaw stopped her. Instead, she tried to take a breath, but couldn't quite fill her lungs. Looking down, she suddenly realized why. Jean-Michel was sitting on her!

'Get off me, you brute!' She shoved at him, and with some reluctance, he released

154

her, getting up sharply. Before she could say another word he had scooped her into his arms, kicked open the door to his cabin and dumped her unceremoniously on the bed.

He stood, glaring down at her, his dark brows drawn together in a furious arch. 'Now, Miss Sophie Lafleur, I think it is high time you stopped all this playacting and told me who you really are and what you want from me. And if you think Jack Morgan is going to waltz in here and rescue you, rest assured, I have a dozen men on the pier and the ship itself, all armed and ready for just such an event.'

'Jack Morgan!' Sophie stared at him uncomprehendingly. 'Why on earth would he — ?'

'Oh, come on, my dear. The time for being coy is well past.' He straightened, stalking about the small room, raking one hand through his hair and talking almost to himself. 'How could I have missed it? It was so obvious, and I never twigged. Dammit, Chambois, you are a lackbrained fool. A gullible dupe for anything in skirts, especially' — and here he cast Sophie a black look — 'one with big blue eyes and helplessness written all over her.'

'I am not helpless!'

He laughed mirthlessly. 'No, so I now

perceive. So, how did you let Morgan know he would find the *Némésis* in Boston harbour? No doubt you smuggled a letter from the house — '

'I did no such thing!' This was too much. Sophie struggled upright in the bed, swinging her legs over the side. She would have stood, but the room swam about unpleasantly, so she satisfied herself with remaining perched upon the edge. 'I came here to tell you what Mrs Otis said, and — '

'Muriel Otis! Why should I give a tinker's . . . never mind . . . about what that addle-pated old — '

'Mrs Otis,' Sophie interrupted him firmly, 'said that Morgan has offered a reward for information about the sinking of his ship.'

He looked at her darkly. 'Yes, well no doubt you'd know all about that.'

Sophie glared at him. 'I thought you should know.'

'And no doubt this beneficence towards me was the ideal way to lead the man right to me, thus saving him considerable time checking out all the Baltimore Clippers in port.'

Sophie rubbed a hand over her eyes, for he was not making any sense. Perhaps if she had been able to sleep a little last night . . . 'What are you talking about, Jean-Michel?' she said, then moaned. 'Oh, but my head hurts.'

Without a word he rummaged in one of the fitted cupboards near the desk, withdrawing a leather case. He flipped it open and withdrew a small silver flask and a tiny glass.

Sophie waved a hand to stop him. 'Please, I do not like strong drink. I think it would make me sick.'

'This is medicine, not brandy, and you will drink it,' he replied without ceremony. He poured a little of the liquid into the glass and handed it to her.

'What is it?' she asked, frowning.

'Only laudanum.' And without so much as a by-your-leave, he wrapped his hand over hers, raised the glass to her lips and tipped the contents down her throat. Sophie gagged, but swallowed, feeling an almost immediate warmth fill her bones. She allowed him to ease the glass from her fingers and did not object when he pressed her back upon the pillows. He lifted her feet and one by one removed her boots, then swung her legs onto the bed.

'Thank you,' she murmured, already feeling drowsy, though whether it was from the laudanum or the effects of a sleepless night and a long walk in the chill air, she knew not.

The last thing she remembered was him

kissing her lightly on top of the head, and promising they would talk when she awoke.

★ ★ ★

It was dangerous, but under the circumstances, Jean-Michel felt he had no choice. He ordered the *Némésis* out to sea, heading down the channel and directly east into the Atlantic. They encountered a heavy mist around noon and hove-to, dropping the anchor to drag in the deep water and maintain their position.

He went below once or twice, only to find Sophie sleeping deeply. Her flushed face and shallow breathing made him wonder if he had perhaps overestimated the dose he had given her, but there was no remedy for that. He stood, looking down at her sweet oval face, pale and innocent in the murky light, marred only by the ugly bruise on her jaw from its encounter with his fist. She had been right to upbraid him. The moment he wrapped his arm about her neck he knew something was amiss. There had been something delicate about the neck he grasped so carelessly, something altogether too light for it to have been a man's. Yet he had not heeded the warning bell that had sounded in his head. Tense from a long night on watch, and furious that a spy should have the gall to walk openly onto his boat, he had lashed out with his fist, knowing that one blow would be enough.

He reached out a finger and stroked her cheek softly. Enough it had certainly been. He didn't think he would ever get over the flood of shame he had felt when he had pulled the battered hat from his victim and recognized Sophie lying in a heap at his feet.

'Who are you, Sophie?' he murmured, knowing she could not hear. Then he shook his head, going out softly and closing the door behind him, for he knew there would be no answers until she was awake once more.

★ ★ ★

When Sophie did awaken, it was to find herself back in her bed at La Tour House with the morning sun streaming around the edges of the heavy curtains. She blinked, disoriented by both time and place.

'So, you are awake at last,' came a soft voice from the corner of the room.

'Jean-Michel? What are you doing in my room? How did I get here? Whatever is the time?'

He laughed as he crossed towards her, bearing a glass of fruit juice in his hand.

'So many questions. Here, drink this.'

She accepted it gratefully, for she was dreadfully thirsty. Then she paused, eyeing him. 'What is it?'

'Just the juice of a pineapple, pressed for you by Madame Marlotte herself this morning.'

Sophie allowed herself a sip. It was delicious and so refreshing she finished it at one go. 'Bliss!' she said, returning the glass to his outstretched hand. 'But I feel so rested. How can it still be morning?'

'Because it is tomorrow,' he replied urbanely. 'You have slept somewhat longer than I expected. Even the swelling in your jaw has gone, though the bruise, I fear, will take a few more days.'

Sophie stared. 'You brought me back to the house! But . . . but what explanation — '

'I told them the truth, to a point,' he replied, coming to sit on the bed beside her. 'I said that you had been unable to sleep and had gone out, ill-advisedly, for a walk, then been set upon by brigands on the common.'

She eyed him cautiously. 'So you said nothing to arouse suspicion concerning Mrs Otis's news.'

'There would have been no point,' he answered quietly, 'would there?'

That this last was meant as a very serious

question, Sophie was in no doubt. His accusations after their violent encounter came streaming back into her mind, and there was no doubt now as to his inference. 'Why do you think I was in communication with Jack Morgan?' she asked.

There was a pause, during which Jean-Michel gazed steadily at her. At length, he replied, 'For the money. You made it plain enough that you resented being kept here any longer than was necessary, yet you could do nothing else without funds.'

'That is preposterous!' she declaimed. 'Why, how could I possibly explain what I knew of Morgan's ship unless I were to admit that I had been a stowaway aboard the *Deliverance*? Were I to admit to such a thing, Morgan would have me in irons in the flick of an eye.'

'You could have concocted a story about overhearing some injudicious talk. He would suspect nothing.'

Sophie gazed at him steadily. 'Jean-Michel de Chambois, can you say before God as your witness, that you truly believe me to be capable of such perfidy?'

She was gratified that he could not meet her eyes. 'I thought not,' she crowed. 'And now, I do believe you owe me one enormous apology.'

He glowered at her. 'I will not apologize! If you expect to take ridiculous risks like that, dressing like an urchin and sneaking about other people's property in the dead of night, then you must suffer the consequences.'

'Is that what you told your sister when she was caught pretending to be you aboard that French naval vessel?'

'Had I been there, I would have tanned her hide!' he said peremptorily.

Sophie blushed. 'No doubt you are right. It was a stupid risk. But how else was I to get the tidings to you? I was afraid the reports of prowlers on the vessel were nothing but a trap to draw you to the ship! As it was, the two events were probably no more than coincidence — '

The sob that was rising in her throat was swallowed up in the warmth of his shirt and he wrapped his arms about her and held her close. She clung to him, relieved that it was over, that he was safe, that he believed her. For a moment, she allowed herself the wonderful luxury of pressing her face into the hard muscle of his chest and listening to the strong beat of his heart. Then he tucked a finger beneath her jaw, and light as a feather so as not to hurt her, tipped her head up.

'Thank you, Sophie,' he said softly.

'*Tant pis*,' she whispered, watching as his mouth descended to brush the softest of kisses across her lips.

'And,' he murmured as he kissed her again, 'I do apologize for hitting you,' — and then kissed her more deeply — 'even though I thought you were a . . . man.'

And after that, there was no more talking.

7

Sophie saw no more of Jean-Michel that day, for he left her then, saying he had business to attend to, and she herself, feeling still quite tired from her ordeal, spent much of the day sitting on the window seat in her room, reading and thinking about all that had happened. But next morning, she knew she must hide away no longer and took herself downstairs to partake of breakfast. When she entered the small dining-room, it was to find not Jean-Michel, as she had hoped, but the duke engrossed in a newspaper, a half-empty cup of coffee at his elbow.

'*Bonjour, mademoiselle*, I trust you are recovered from your misadventure. It is never wise for a lady to venture out alone, most especially at night.'

'N-no, indeed, Your Grace,' she stammered, taking a seat opposite him. 'But, thank you, I feel quite recovered.'

She felt his gaze on her, his dark blue eyes studying the bruise on her chin, but he said no more upon the subject. Instead, he poured her a cup of coffee, and passed it to her without comment. She thanked him, then busied herself with the silver tongs, placing two lumps of sugar in her cup, then adding a little milk. Still, she could feel his scrutiny, yet when she finally looked up, he was once again reading his paper.

She sighed imperceptibly and went to the sideboard to help herself to some eggs from a covered dish, though she had little interest in food.

She returned with her breakfast, glancing at the door once or twice as she attempted to eat.

Finally, from behind the newspaper, came a muttered comment.

'He is not here.'

Sophie paused, fork halfway to her mouth. 'I beg your pardon, Your Grace?'

'Pray do not call me Your Grace, Sophie. My name is François. I never thought of myself as a duke even before the Revolution, much less now. I find it quite peculiar that people in this infant republic so delight in titles.'

Sophie stared, thinking how it would certainly take a man as determined and independent as this to make the unusual Léonie happy. They truly were well suited.

She nodded, giving him a faint smile. 'Very well, sir. But I do not think I can call you by your Christian name, if you do not mind.'

'I do mind.'

'Oh.'

There was a moment of silence, then the duke grinned. '*Tant pis*. It is of no consequence. I can see you are anxious to find my errant brother-in-law. Your thoughts are more upon that than anything else, I'll wager. But he is not here this morning.'

Sophie's face fell, and she was annoyed with herself when she saw that the duke had noticed.

'We have become accustomed to his comings and goings. This is his home, but only after a fashion. He sleeps here when in Boston, no more.' François tossed the paper aside and reached for the half-eaten brioche on his plate. 'Why, I recall a few years ago that he disappeared on a boat to China and didn't return for many months.'

Sophie looked at him in consternation. 'But were you not concerned?'

'I am only his brother-in-law, my dear. Not his keeper. He will return when he is ready.'

Sophie hoped there was no more to it than that, though such a sudden disappearance hot on the heels of Jack Morgan's reward and the unknown prowler on the *Némésis* caused her brow to furrow.

François leaned across the table and patted

her hand. 'Do not alarm yourself, my dear. I am certain he'll return once his business is concluded. I fully expect him for dinner.'

Sophie excused herself from the dining-room, suddenly in need of fresh air to calm her racing thoughts. Wherever he had gone, there was no doubt a reasonable explanation, and anyway, his business was scarcely her concern. She had no right to know his life.

She pressed a hand to her lips, remembering, almost as though it had been a dream, the kisses they had shared yesterday in her bedchamber. How could he behave in such a fashion one moment and then disappear without a word to her? Did it mean nothing to him?

She picked up the new shawl the dress-maker had brought yesterday afternoon and wrapped it about her shoulders as she let herself out onto the colonnade. She hurried towards the vineyard, intent on a brisk walk around the circumference of the extensive grounds, only to encounter Léonie picking yellow daffodils beneath a cherry tree.

'Good morning, *madame*. Are you well? You look very pale. Perhaps you should go indoors and rest.'

Léonie was not amused. 'There is nothing the least wrong with me, Sophie. Unless it

167

is that my girth is becoming almost greater than my height.'

Privately, Sophie reflected that such a thing would be impossible, even if the duchess were bearing triplets, for she was an uncommonly tall woman.

She murmured her apologies and made a discreet escape. She had no wish to further promote the duchess's sharp tongue. She had more than enough on her mind today.

She followed the East Walk, as she had done the previous day in Léonie's company, but this time followed the route around the lake's edge, where it alternately appeared and disappeared in the tall bulrushes that crowded there. She stopped twice to observe the red-winged blackbirds that alighted on the stems and filled the spring air with their melodic warbling. But she met no one, except the old gardener busy at a bed of delphiniums, and all too soon found herself back at the house, her thoughts on the subject of Jean-Michel's unaccountable behaviour no clearer than they had been when she started her walk.

She entered via the terrace only to find chaos and uproar within the house. She was almost knocked down upon the stairs by the twins, pursued, it transpired, by an irate Nanny, whose older legs gave the boys an untouchable advantage. The woman paused when she reached Sophie, though her stream of invective did not.

'Is something wrong?' Sophie asked.

'Wrong? Wrong! *Mademoiselle*, there has been something wrong since the day those two little devils were birthed.' She drew herself up, which still left her several inches shorter than Sophie, and wiped her hands down the sides of her black dress. 'Well, I've had my fill, I can tell you. The mistress may think what she will, but I'll not stand for those two another minute. Nor that wild Christiane. Why, she's the biggest tomboy I've set my poor eyes upon in all my years, and that's the truth. Mind you,' she said with a meaningful glare at Sophie, 'if they had a mother with half an ounce of decency, perhaps 'twould have given them a proper start in life. But what do they have? A woman who wears men's breeches and fights with swords, saints have mercy! What sort of example is that to be setting the poor children?'

Sophie scarcely knew how to respond to the depiction of the twins as devils one moment and 'poor children' the next.

'I am sure they are all a little anxious about the pending addition to the family, *madame*,' she said as soothingly as she could. 'Once the baby has come, they will settle down again.'

'Settle down?' The woman's muslin cap bobbed furiously. 'They've not been settled for a single minute since I got here.' She cast one final glare in the direction in which the twins had disappeared and turned back up the stairs, hoisting her skirts above her booted ankles. 'Well, I've done what I am able, but until those children are made to behave by their father, there's nothing to be done with them, that's for sure.'

'Oh but surely . . . ' Sophie picked up her own skirts and hurried to catch up. 'You can't mean to leave the duchess's service at a time like this, *madame*? She can't possibly manage — '

'She should've thought of that before she allowed those children to run wild without proper discipline. That's the root of the evil in this house, young lady. Spare the rod, I always say. The Bible makes no bones about what's good for children.'

Sophie stopped, watching as the woman slammed the nursery door behind her, while the horrible image of François de la Tour beating his beautiful children filled her mind. How could the woman believe such harshness would be in the best interests of the children? The very idea was repugnant.

She jumped as a scream issued from behind a door. Sophie's blood curdled. The sound came from Léonie's private sitting-room, but she hesitated barely an instant before grasping the handle and entering the room.

'Sophie! Oh dear God, have you seen my husband?'

'Not since breakfast, *madame*.' She surveyed the room in amazement. The duchess, with her gown knotted at the hip exposing a pair of very shapely lower legs, was brandishing an epée, and her eyes darted about in real terror.

A small whimpering sound brought Sophie's attention to the *chaise-longue*, behind which cowered two small girls, their dark heads almost touching and their wide eyes peeking out in fright from their refuge. A sewing basket, its contents strewn about the floor, lay upended on the rug, as did a small table. And the remains of a once elegant lamp littered the far corner of the room.

'Pray, *madame*, set the sword down,' Sophie began, convinced that perhaps Nanny had been right, and the mistress of this house was not quite well in the head. 'You are frightening the children.'

'The children?' Léonie scoffed. ' 'Tis not my rapier that scares them.' Then she shrieked, and moving with astounding speed for a woman so advanced in her confinement, leapt onto a chair, brandishing her sword at the sewing basket.

Sophie frowned. 'What on earth — ?' Then she saw a forked tongue dart from the shadows of the basket.

Without hesitating, she crossed to the basket and in one smooth motion snatched up the serpent, holding it firmly behind the head.

'Aah!' Léonie screamed. The girls wailed in horror and covered their eyes with their little hands.

Sophie regarded them in astonishment, holding the creature out in front of her. ' 'Tis but a garter snake, *madame*. And a perfectly harmless one at that!'

The duchess climbed down from her refuge and untied her skirt with one hand, still keeping the epée clutched firmly in the other. Her eyes were wary and she was clearly terrified of the creature.

Sophie backed away towards the door. 'Perhaps I should take it outside where it belongs.'

'A truly excellent idea,' replied the duchess faintly.

Sophie stopped in the doorway and turned to the little girls, who were now standing behind their mother and staring at her, wide-eyed. 'Would you like to come with me?'

They glanced at each other, then at their mother, then nodded, all without a sound.

Sophie smiled to herself as she led the way down the stairs and out to the woods beyond the driveway. She waited for the children to catch up.

'This is a good place for a snake to live. He needs to find food and a mate so he can have babies, you know.'

'Snakes have babies?' asked the older of the girls, her dark-blue eyes as round as moons.

'Well, not really. They're reptiles, so they lay eggs,' Sophie told them as she bent down and gently released the creature. It slithered away and vanished into the heavy undergrowth.

They watched for a moment, but when it did not reappear, the girls each took one of Sophie's hands and they turned back towards the house.

'Our hens lay eggs,' said the littlest girl, whose eyes, unlike those of her brothers and sisters, were a rich hazel. 'Does that mean they are reptiles too?'

Sophie laughed. 'No, indeed. Reptiles have cold blood. 'Tis why they feel cold on a chill day and warm in hot weather.' She gazed down at their serious little faces. 'Have you never picked up a snake on a really hot day? It feels soft and cosy like a — '

'Ugh!' the girls cried in unison.

'We hate snakes,' the younger one said.

'Like *Maman*,' added the older girl.

Sophie gave up. Clearly they would not be persuaded. She took them around the side of the house and they sat on the grass amongst the daffodils.

'You're very brave,' said the oldest girl. 'Are you Uncle Jean-Mich's lady? He's brave too.'

Sophie felt the heat rush to her cheeks, but made no reply to *that* question. She drew the youngest child onto her lap. 'Tell me your names. I have met Christiane and the twins, but I do believe you must have been hiding away with Nanny since I arrived.'

The older one answered for them both. 'My name's Françoise,' she said proudly. 'I'm named after my father. And that's Rose-Marie. She's only four. I'm five and I have a dog named Bonbon. Would you like to see her?'

'I would. Do you keep her in the nursery?'

Françoise screwed up her little nose. 'Nanny won't let me. She says dogs are unclean. I hate Nanny.'

'Oh dear,' Sophie replied, wondering if that particular problem might have resolved itself while they were busy with the snake.

'And anyway,' Françoise went on, 'Michel and Jean brought the snake inside to scare Nanny. They kept it in a box under their bed. but it got out and hid in *Maman*'s sewing basket.'

'I see. And your *Maman* doesn't like snakes.'

Little Rose-Marie opened her brown eyes very wide and added, 'But she likes spiders.'

'Well, that's good.'

'And she fought a pirate once.'

Sophie suppressed a laugh at the child's serious tone. She stroked the little girl's black hair, enjoying the sweet feel of the tiny body pressed so trustingly against her. It brought an almost painful longing for something she knew she could never have.

'Come,' she said, setting Rose-Marie on the ground. 'Let us go and see if your *Maman* is recovered from her ordeal.'

As they re-entered the house, it was abuzz with activity. Several maids rushed past carrying linens, others followed with vases of flowers fresh from the garden. The flagstone floor in the front hallway was receiving its second scrub of the day and Aileen, the young Irish maid, was polishing the oak banisters as though the housekeeper herself stood at her elbow.

'*Que se passe-t-il*?' Françoise asked, but Aileen merely glanced at her and rolled her eyes.

They hurried up to Léonie's private sitting-room where they found order somewhat restored. The duchess herself was reclining on the window seat gazing out into the garden. She turned as the trio entered and Sophie was immediately struck by how pale she looked.

She hurried to her side. '*Madame*, are you ill?'

Léonie sent her a disgruntled look. 'Are you fussing again, Sophie?' Then she saw the girls and held out her arms. 'Come, my darlings, and tell me how you vanquished the serpent with Mademoiselle Lafleur.'

'Oh, *Maman*, she was sooooo brave!' Françoise enthused.

'She let it go in the woods to have babies,' Rose-Marie added, sliding a small thumb into her mouth.

'*Vraiment*?' Léonie looked curiously at Sophie.

She shrugged. 'It was only a garter snake, *madame*. They are good at keeping pests down in the garden.'

Léonie shuddered visibly. 'Forgive me,

Sophie, but I have never been able to reconcile myself to snakes. Bloodied wounds I can manage, spiders worry me not in the least, and I account myself passably friendly with insects of all colour. But serpents . . . ?'

Françoise giggled, putting her hands together and weaving them snakelike towards her mother.

'Françoise,' Sophie reprimanded her gently, pulling the child's hands away from the dismayed duchess's face. ' 'Tis not ladylike to tease.' She shooed the children out of the room, then paused in the doorway. 'Is there something I may get you, *madame*? Some herbal tea may prove relaxing.'

'Brandy would, too.'

Sophie frowned. 'But the baby . . . '

'Never mind, 'twas merely wishful thinking on my part. Come here, Sophie,' she said. 'There is something I must ask you.'

Sophie obediently closed the door and returned to sit at the other end of the window seat, folding her hands in her lap.

The duchess observed her for a moment before speaking. 'You are a quiet soul. I can see that you would have been an excellent lady's companion. No doubt your previous employer was lucky to have you. Were you with her long?'

'Most of my life, *madame*,' Sophie replied,

wondering where this was leading. 'My mother served in that capacity until she grew ill, then I took over. Madame Guillaume — ' She stopped, one hand flying to her mouth. She had not meant to let the woman's name slip. If the duchess were to check for such a name in Charleston —

'Madame Guillaume what?' Léonie prompted gently.

'She . . . ' Sophie sighed. Falsehoods had never been easy for her. 'She was more of a grandmother to me, I suppose. A dear friend I was happy to serve.'

'Yet you left. In a great hurry — with no belongings.'

'Oh, no! I lost my things, *madame*. And I left because . . . ' How should she explain? What lie was she supposed to tell now? Oh, she thought in frustration, this was entirely too much! The sooner she was away from Boston the better. 'Because my mother died and I wished to return home, to find what remains of my real family.'

'Ah,' Léonie replied, though she did not look at all convinced. Sophie stared miserably into her hands.

She was released from further questioning when a brisk tap sounded upon the door and the housekeeper entered. Sophie had met the unsmiling woman only once and, judging by the expression on her stern face this morning, she was in no better a mood.

'Madame Renault?'

'*Madame la Duchesse*,' came the stiff reply. The housekeeper's eyes flitted from Léonie to Sophie, and Sophie knew that the woman was another who did not believe her tale of having lost her luggage on the journey from Charleston. What Madame Renault actually did suspect, Sophie had not the least desire to find out. She turned away, focusing on the garden beyond the half-open window.

'The rooms are ready for the duke and duchess's arrival, *madame*,' the housekeeper said brusquely. Sophie turned. So that was what had caused the commotion downstairs. 'Cook wishes to know if roast goose would meet your approval for dinner this evening.'

Léonie nodded. 'Goose will do admirably. And ask her to be sure and include some bananas on the fruit platter for dessert. My mother has a most particular preference for the fruit.'

Madame Renault gave her a glance that clearly said what she thought of such extravagance, but she nodded stiffly, and as there was nothing further, let herself out.

'An unpleasant woman at the best of times,' Léonie said on a sigh. 'But there are so few French-speaking staff with appropriate experience one must take what one can get and cling to it.'

Sophie tried to envision anyone clinging to Madame Renault's unyielding form, but it was quite beyond her.

'You had something you wished to ask me, *madame*?' Sophie asked, hoping she could escape to her room before the visitors arrived. If things went as she hoped, she might never have to meet them. She was determined to make Jean-Michel see that she must leave immediately. Until then, she would make do with a tray in her room.

But Léonie had other ideas. 'My parents' ship is in the harbour, Sophie, and they will be here within the hour. Unfortunately I have had to send Nanny packing with a flea in her ear. The woman was utterly impossible. Why, she insisted that the twins had brought that disgusting snake into the house on purpose to frighten me . . . Jean and Michel would never do such a thing. Especially now.' She rubbed her belly absently.

Sophie demurred gently. 'Perhaps it was not their intention to frighten *you* with it, *madame*, but — '

'You knew of this?'

'No, indeed! But Françoise did let slip that

the boys were keeping the creature in a box in the nursery.'

Léonie sank back against the cushion propped at her back. 'Those little rascals. Their father will have their hides. They are always bringing wild animals into the house, no matter how much we forbid it. Why can they not leave the poor creatures where they belong?'

Sophie grimaced. 'It is a natural inclination for children,' she responded, wondering whether she might dare to intercede on the boys' behalf with their father.

'So you think I was wrong to send Nanny away?'

'Oh, no!' Sophie was alarmed that Léonie should think she was criticizing her. 'I would not be so presumptuous. And, to tell you the truth, *madame*, I believe you may simply have struck a second before Nanny herself did.' Perceiving Léonie's confusion, she explained. 'Nanny herself told me that she would be leaving of her own choice, for she found the children . . . ' How to explain without seeming to criticize?

'Incorrigible?'

Sophie nodded. It was as good a description as any.

Léonie laughed. 'So then, I need feel no guilt upon the matter.' She turned to Sophie, her eyes suddenly serious. 'But I cannot let you leave now, you know. It would be unthinkable for you to disappear to Canada and leave me in such a predicament.'

Sophie's jaw dropped. '*Madame?*'

'My mind is entirely made up, Sophie. You shall stay and be the children's new nanny. They clearly adore you, and you are gentle with them. Do not, pray, be too gentle, for they are quite a handful *en masse*. If they are too troublesome, you may enlist help from François, whom they worship as they should, but also fear just a little. Even Jean-Michel can be intimidating if he becomes cross enough. The twins will listen to him. You will do it, will you not? Do please say yes, my dear.'

Sophie swallowed past a lump in her throat. How could she refuse? Yet this was all too much. She felt as though she had somehow tumbled into a fisherman's net and Jean-Michel and his family were inexorably reeling her in.

Acadia. She must remember her purpose and be firm. The duchess's domestic problems were none of her affair. She took a deep breath, looked Léonie straight in the eye, and said, 'Very well, *madame*. I will stay until you can obtain the services of a new nanny.'

She returned to her room, reeling from the shock of having said the exact opposite of what she had intended! How *could* she have given in so easily?

She sat heavily on the bed, clutching the coverlet in her chill fingers. Things were going from bad to worse, with Jean-Michel away who-knew-where and the Duke and Duchess de Chambois arriving.

She rolled sideways onto the bed, covering her face with her hands and willing a few easeful tears to fall.

But they would not. Her eyes remained dry, the ache in her heart unrelieved.

'Oh, Mama,' she whispered in the silence, 'why did they not let me be with you when you were sick? If I had caught consumption, could my situation have been any worse than it is now?'

But there was no answer. Only the gentle pressure of her mother's ring against her heart where it hung on its simple gold chain.

8

Jean-Michel shucked off his jacket, not bothering to change his mud-spattered boots, and went into the small bathroom adjoining his bedchamber. He washed his hands, feeling relieved that his interview with his father was over. His two-day absence from home had unfortunately coincided with the arrival of his parents, and his father especially had felt the slight. Not so his mother, who had always taken her family's comings and goings with equanimity. She had been nothing but delighted to see him, embracing him in a hug and standing on tiptoe to kiss his cheek as though it were not ten years since they had last met. She looks older, he mused as he dried his hands on a thick white towel, but not much, her hair now greying at the temples. His father, at sixty-eight, was becoming an old man, clearly suffering from a stiffness of movement that he would never admit. The old duke was a proud man and the Revolution in France had not been kind to him.

Jean-Michel returned to the bedchamber, picked up three cloth-wrapped parcels, then let himself out of his room.

The door to the nursery was closed, and in deference to his bundles, he knocked with the toe of his boot. The door opened almost instantly, and he drew a breath of surprise as he encountered Sophie's soft blue eyes. Her hair was piled into a loose chignon, a few tendrils escaping to caress her cheeks and shine like gold in the light of the argand lamps. His glance fell to her jaw and he was pleased to see the bruise he had inflicted so mistakenly was now but a faint yellow.

But where he had expected warmth — a faint blush even, in remembrance of their kisses — he encountered only ice. Without a word, she stood back to admit him.

'The children are at their lessons. I would prefer that they not be disturbed.'

He glanced about the long room, noting the twins perched on their bed with a book, the two youngest girls sitting primly at the table with slates and chalk, and Christiane at the harpsichord. All eyes lit up at the sight of him.

'Surely they may be spared for five minutes? I have brought them something.'

To his surprise, though they quivered with excitement and turned their bright eyes upon Sophie, not one moved from their place.

Then she nodded. 'Very well. Five minutes.'

Her further exhortations were lost in the resultant mêlée as five children flew across the room towards him.

'*Attendez!*' he howled as his parcels nearly crashed to the ground. They stood back a fraction. 'That's better.' He passed the smallest parcel to Christiane. 'This is for the girls to share. Pray be careful, for it is easily damaged.' She took the gift, kissed him on the cheek and ran to the hearthrug with the others to squat upon the floor.

The boys were greedily eyeing the two remaining parcels, but he wasn't going to give in that easily.

'I hear you have been excessively wicked while I was away, scaring your *Maman* with all manner of wild creatures.'

Their faces fell and they began an earnest inspection of their boots. Jean-Michel already knew they had endured a tongue-lashing from their father and that he had ordered them to memorize three pages each from Euripides.

' 'Twas not meant in harm,' Michel mumbled.

' 'Twas only a little garter snake,' Jean added.

'Only? Were you forgetting that your mother has an abomination for such creatures?'

They looked up, their young faces filled

with righteous indignation. 'We had not meant it for *Maman*. 'Twas to scare Nanny!'

Jean-Michel eyed them as severely as he could, though he was longing to laugh, for their indignation was nothing if not comical. 'Well, now Nanny is gone and you have Mademoiselle Lafleur to take care of you. I trust tricks of this nature will not be played upon her person?'

'No, Uncle,' they averred, with a quick glance at Sophie.

'Or else,' Jean-Michel said, leaning over so that his face was but an inch from theirs and speaking so softly that only they could hear, 'you shall have me to answer to.'

Their eyes widened momentarily, and he straightened, taking pity on the boys. '*Voilà*,' he said, passing them each a parcel and ruffling their hair to show that he was not really cross, 'there is one for each of you.'

With a whoop of delight, they carried their booty to the large bed they shared at the far end of the nursery and eagerly unwrapped their prizes.

Jean-Michel glanced at Sophie, who was watching him with a strange look on her face. She turned away immediately, going to straighten the music sheets upon the harpsichord.

He could feel the tension in her, see it in the stiff way she attended to the task, the way she folded her hands together afterwards and glanced about her as though looking for some other occupation.

'Sophie?' he called softly.

She looked down at the floor, but did not turn his way.

He crossed to her, feeling the strongest urge to wrap his arms around her and warm away the stiffness in her spine. But he did not, not merely because of the children, but because whatever bothered her would surely not be soothed so easily.

She turned, finally and looked coolly at him. 'Your brother-in-law tells me you are in the habit of disappearing for unknown lengths of time. I am almost surprised to see you back so soon. Was there no boat to be found going to China this time?'

He winced. 'You and François must have had quite some discussion about me.'

'Pray don't flatter yourself,' she replied archly, moving to the table where she picked up one of the slates and inspected it. She made a quick mark with a piece of chalk before setting it down and picking up the other.

He followed her, prying the slate from her fingers and setting it back on the table.

'Are you angry with me because I did not tell you I had some business to attend to?'

'Business! You disappear without a word when there are rumours that Morgan is out for your blood. How is anyone to know that it is no more than business that occupied you? Perish the thought one might be concerned for your safety.'

Jean-Michel could not stop the smile that spread across his face. 'Why, little mouse, you were worried about me!'

She glared at him and turned smartly on her heel, but he grasped her arm and pulled her towards the window.

'Forgive me — '

'There is nothing to forgive. One cannot alter one's nature,' she replied archly.

That stung, and he loosened his hold. They stood there, facing off like two dogs in a ring. He was touched that she should care so patently, more so that she tried so hard to deny it. 'I shall endeavour to behave better next time, *mademoiselle*. There now, am I forgiven or must I write lines on my slate all afternoon as penance?'

She tried to look offended but he could see the corners of her mouth curl slightly. He reached out a finger and stroked it across her lips, suddenly remembering where they

189

were when he saw her glance quickly at the children.

They were fully absorbed by the gifts he had brought, but Jean-Michel dropped his hand anyway. How he wished they could be alone. The memory of the kisses they had shared in her room had scarcely left him for a moment since, and his loins tightened at the thought of repeating the experience.

She looked up at him nervously, as if the same thought were in her mind, then her pink tongue darted out to lick her lips. Jean-Michel almost groaned aloud, swamped by an overpowering urge to close the inches between them and taste those sweet lips once more.

He heard his name being called and, like a siren, it brought him back to the present. He coughed and turned abruptly away.

'Uncle Jean-Mich! Look, we can have a jousting match on our steeds!'

He swore under his breath as he heard Sophie gasp and storm across the nursery to the twins, who each held a fire iron in one hand and their hobby horse's reins in the other and were about to embark on a battle which could do serious injury.

'Give me those at once!'

Jean-Michel's brows rose. Was this his

meek and mild Sophie? He watched in amazement as she removed the weapons from the boys' hands and restored them to the hearth, and wondered at his effortless use of the word 'his'. Was that how he thought of her now, as 'his' Sophie?

The idea troubled him. He liked her, enjoyed her company, found her intriguing, and enjoyed kissing her more than he should, but he had no desire to entangle himself in any relationship. The time for that was past. Years past.

When order had been restored, he had a sudden idea.

'Sophie, how would you like to come riding with me? You have still to hear my explanation for my absence, and I demand a chance to vindicate myself.'

'Riding?' She waved a shaky hand towards the window. 'On a day like this? Why it might even come on to rain, and anyway, as you can see I have promised your sister that I will look after the children until she has engaged a new nanny. I could not possibly leave them.'

'I shall fetch Danielle. She can keep them amused for an hour.' To stem any further objections, he placed a finger on her lips. 'Come, you are only helping Léonie as a favour. I shall not let you relegate yourself

191

to the role of servant in this house, nor do François and my sister expect it.'

'But I do not know how to ride,' she admitted weakly.

'*Vraiment*? Well, no matter. I shall find the gentlest mare in the stable and teach you myself.'

★ ★ ★

Twenty minutes later, dressed in a wool gown with a heavy pelisse and boots — in deference to the unseasonable weather — Sophie found herself seated on a horse for the first time in her life. The only other occasion had been as François de la Tour's prisoner, and she had no wish to recall that embarrassing experience!

Settling into the strange twisted position on the lady's saddle was one thing, but when Jean-Michel took the reins of the beast and it began to jolt along the lane, Sophie knew she was doomed.

'I shall never stay atop this creature's back!' she cried out in real alarm, clinging to the saddle as though to life itself.

She heard him chuckle. 'Relax, Sophie. Let your body move with the horse rather than fighting against it.'

That was easy for him to say, she thought,

as she tried to soften her ramrod-stiff spine. He'd probably been riding since he was an infant.

Thankfully, he kept the horses at a snail's pace and gradually Sophie began to feel less as though she were in imminent danger of tumbling off. Jean-Michel sat with enviable comfort astride his own horse, a huge black beast that towered over the little mare he had chosen for her. She was named Arabella and appeared entirely indifferent to the awkward package she bore.

After what seemed a lifetime, they crossed Beacon Street and entered Boston Common, passing through a row of budding trees and onto the rough grass. There were few others about, Sophie noted, thinking that very sensibly they had decided to stay indoors rather than venture out for the dubious pleasures of horseback riding on so grey a morning.

They climbed a small rise, the angle of the horse's back alarming Sophie more than she cared to admit, and finally came to a stop upon what Jean-Michel informed her was Fox Hill.

'Shall we dismount for a while?' he asked.

'I would be delighted,' she replied dryly, wondering how she could persuade him to let her walk back. She would rather lead the horse than sit upon it. Her back ached and her derriere was altogether offended by the constant jarring of the animal, though she would never admit *that* to him.

She took his hands, grateful for their support as she slid from Arabella's back. They lingered upon hers for a moment after she reached the ground and she looked up, quickly regretting the warmth she witnessed in his eyes.

For a second, neither spoke, then he turned away and gestured across the common. 'Is the view not worth the ride, Sophie?'

She followed his eyes across the park towards the town and harbour beyond. Even from this distance she could see ships at anchor or bustling up and down the busy waterway.

'Have you been aboard the *Némésis*?' she asked, pulling her hands free and wrapping them tightly around the riding stock she had been holding — as if she were ever likely to use such an item!

He looked puzzled for a moment, then smiled. 'Ah, the little governess is intent upon quizzing me on my whereabouts, I see. Very well, I shall explain myself, if it will ease your mind.'

They walked down the hill a short way, leaving the horses to munch on the new grass. Overhead, a distant rumble of thunder sounded.

'It is none of my affair,' Sophie said quietly, realizing that she had no desire to know Jean-Michel's business, no more than she wished to become further embroiled in his charming but overwhelming family. 'I had merely hoped to ascertain whether you had news for me. Concerning my voyage to Canada.'

'Not yet, I regret. But I am hopeful — '

'That's what you say each time I ask! When will I find a vessel to take me there? I cannot remain in Boston any longer. Your sister is about to bear a child, your parents and your brother are here. I feel . . . ' She stopped, biting her lip.

'You feel what, Sophie?' he asked not unkindly.

She shrugged. 'I dislike the subterfuge, the lies I have told to divert your family from the truth. Falsehoods do not sit well with me. And I am anxious to rejoin my uncle.'

'I am trying to find your uncle. When I do, perhaps we will be better able to plan.'

'No! I cannot wait. If my uncle is not still living in Acadia, then I shall find some other person to help me. But I cannot remain here.'

'And I cannot let you go unless I can be sure of your safety. No more than I could turn my back on Sarah.'

She turned, frowning. 'And who, pray, is Sarah?'

'Sarah is the reason I was occupied upon business. She was a slave.'

'Was?'

'Now she is an escapee, recovering from her wounds. Soon, I hope, she will be free for the first time in her short life.'

Sophie's lips compressed thoughtfully for a moment. 'You helped her escape? But there are no plantations here in the Province of Massachusetts Bay, surely.'

He gave a short cynical laugh. 'That does not mean there are no slaves. Sarah has been abused by her 'owner' for four years. She was a housemaid and skivvy and so poorly fed that she often fainted from hunger.' He paused to admire the view while Sophie absorbed this information. 'Her employer — an upstanding member of society who shall remain nameless — believed her to be faking illness to avoid her duties. So she beat her, quite regularly I understand, with anything that came to hand. Right now she has a broken arm and nose and two missing teeth. The weapon of the day was a poker, I believe.'

Sophie shuddered. 'How can people be so vile?'

'How, indeed.'

'And so you have spirited her away. But what will become of her? Where can she go?'

'For the moment she is in a house many miles from here, resting from her injuries. She will be cared for and taught new skills and, when she is ready, she will take up a new life as an artisan, probably in Upper Canada if she so desires. They abolished slavery last year, so she will be safe enough, especially with the papers I will provide.'

She turned to face him. 'You do this yourself? For others like Sarah as well?'

'Men and women. Children sometimes.' He shrugged, as though such activities were nothing beyond the ordinary. 'A man must do something with his life, mustn't he?'

She nodded softly, feeling a rush of warmth that he would endanger his own life so completely for the sake of the world's forgotten souls. 'I am more accustomed to seeing rich men occupy themselves with nothing more uplifting than gaming and drinking,' she said quietly.

He patted her gloved hand where it rested upon his arm. 'Well, I must confess to spending a considerable amount of time at the tables myself.' When she frowned, he added, 'I think of it as my opponents' way of donating to my cause.'

'You must have a talent for gambling, then.'

'I have my lucky days.'

'And considerable enemies, no doubt.'

He shrugged. 'That does not concern me.'

'Not even if that enemy is as powerful as Jack Morgan?' she asked, sliding him a glance.

'Morgan? I have never played cards with the man, though I would rather like to.'

She gasped. 'You would not dare!'

'*Bien sûr*. I am not afraid of discovery. They are looking for a pirate with a beard and whiskers, remember?' His eyes danced as he said this and she frowned at such levity. They came to a small copse of apple trees in full blossom, and he reached up to snap off a flower-studded twig. He tucked it gently behind her ear, his warm fingers brushing her cheek and causing her heart to do strange little flips.

'I do not believe Jack Morgan's spies suspect the *Némésis*. She is nought but a harmless little coastal vessel in a gay blue-and-white coat. You worry too much, Sophie. Although,' he added, tapping her nose playfully with a finger, 'I am touched by your concern.'

They stood facing each other beneath the canopy of white scented branches. Vaguely, Sophie was aware of the gentle hum of bees amongst the flowers. A petal floated from above and landed on Jean-Michel's hair and she reached up without thinking to brush it off.

'Sweet Sophie,' he murmured, capturing her fingers in his hand. 'Do you know how lovely you are?' He raised her gloved hand to his lips and she felt his warm breath right through the soft leather as he planted a slow kiss on her palm. Her heart almost stopped beating.

'Wh-what are you doing?'

He stared down at her, his eyes dark in the shadowy light. 'I'm not sure. I only know that I would like to kiss you again. Indeed I have thought of little else these past days.'

This cannot be, Sophie thought, willing her rational mind to her rescue. Yet his words were like an echo of her own heart —

'Oh!' she cried out in shock, jolted from the moment by a sudden plop of cold water hitting her on the nose.

They looked up. Beyond the copse of trees, rain was falling, gaining in strength with every moment.

'We shall catch our deaths!' Sophie looked in dismay at how far they had wandered from the horses.

Jean Michel laughed. ' 'Tis only a shower, and the trees will protect us. Come.' He led her towards a small rock, tugging her down to sit beside him, then pulled off his greatcoat and held it above their heads like an umbrella. She could feel the whole length of his body pressed against her, from his arm where it encircled her shoulders, to his hip and knee. A curious warmth spread from the contact until it enveloped her whole being in languid heat.

She knew she must pull away, create some sensible distance between them, yet he was so warm, and the rain was pouring down . . .

His lips at her ear brought all rational thought to a stop.

'I do believe we are the last two souls still abroad on the common,' he murmured. 'Do you think it will stop soon, or shall we be imprisoned here until someone comes searching for us?'

She shivered, as much from the idea of being trapped like this for a lengthy period as from the cold. He was instantly contrite. 'Sophie, you are trembling.' He wrapped his arm more securely around her, pulling her closer so that her head rested against his chest. She could hear the steady rhythm of his heart beating through his jacket, and smell the unique blend of man and sea that she was coming to associate with him.

She pulled back, sitting upright. Chill air snapped into the space between their bodies making Sophie feel as if someone had thrown a bucket of iced water over her.

'What's wrong?' he asked. 'You will get wet.'

She shook her head, trying to rein in her wayward imaginings. She could not continue like this, letting herself slip into some kind of romantic dream. She had made a vow, a bargain, and she must hold fast to it. Not for her the sweet torturings of spring love. She turned away to stare beyond the trees to the common where the rain was showing some signs of easing, and hoped he would not notice the fire that burned her cheeks. Then his gloved hand touched her chin and she jumped up.

'No! Please, you must not!'

She fled through the rain, heeding neither his calls for her to wait, nor the long wet grass snatching at her skirts, until she had reached the horses sheltering under a tall evergreen.

By the time he caught up with her, she was as wet as a drowned cat, gasping for every breath and aching with unfulfilled yearning. Her lips still tingled for his touch and her traitorous body longed to throw itself into his arms. But she pressed her lips together. She had vowed to give her life to the service of God, and she *must* fulfil that vow.

Jean-Michel helped her onto Arabella's back in silence, though the blackness in his face betrayed his feelings all too clearly. They rode back to the house in silence through the steadily falling rain.

Sophie kept her face averted, ignoring the cold rivulets that trickled down her neck and chilled her to the bone. She wondered miserably how she could desire another person so much that she craved his slightest touch; how she could want a life of chastity and yet yearn for the taste of this man's lips upon hers.

I'm lost, she thought forlornly as they arrived at the stables. So utterly lost.

9

Supper was to be served in the banquet hall, for the small dining-room was too snug to accommodate everyone now that Léonie's parents and elder brother were in residence. But first everyone would gather in the parlour for aperitifs. Sophie paused outside the doors for a moment, twisting her fingers uncertainly in her new cashmere shawl. The elegant white silk gown with its gold sash and matching shoes had arrived just this afternoon from Léonie's dressmaker, but it did not bestow inner confidence. She told herself her nervousness was merely fear of the unknown. She had yet to meet the senior members of Jean-Michel's family, for her duties with the children had kept her so well occupied that she had encountered only his mother during an early-morning stroll with the children.

She drew a deep breath and let herself into the parlour, relieved to see that the only occupant thus far was Léonie, who smiled at her from a *chaise-longue* near the fire, lit in deference to the dark, rainy afternoon. She had strings of creamy pearls woven into a bandeau around her vibrant red locks and had disguised her advanced confinement in a pretty Creole gown of palest green silk.

'Come and join me, my dear. You are the first, so we may steal a moment to speak of the children before my stuffy brother Robert arrives.'

She gestured to Sophie, who gladly joined her, pulling up a foot-stool to sit on. But Léonie laughed and waved it away. 'Good heavens, child, don't sit at my feet like a maid. Pray take the other *chaise-longue*. A gown such as yours deserves to be shown to its best advantage.'

'I — I could not possibly, *madame*,' she stammered, colouring at the very notion. However, she eschewed the footstool and instead perched primly on the edge of a *fauteuil*, adjusting her shawl and folding her hands in her lap.

Before Léonie could quiz her about her beloved offspring, however, the door opened and the rest of the party arrived, creating a sudden commotion. Sophie stood, quietly awaiting her turn to be introduced to the Duke and Duchess de Chambois, occupying herself by surreptitiously observing the gentleman whom Léonie had referred to as her 'stuffy brother'. Robert, Marquis de Chambois, favoured his mother's colouring, but had none of the vivacity of the duchess. He was slightly portly, his black hair receding somewhat, and his grey eyes held a somewhat disdainful look. So this was the heir to the Chambois fortune — and its bane, if she surmised correctly. Sophie had heard enough whispers concerning Robert to realize that he had handled the early stages of the Revolution in France rather badly, forfeiting the family estates in the Loire valley in consequence and ruining his own future.

She was startled from these contemplations by the duchess introducing her to her husband. Dressed in a slightly old-fashioned plum faille coat and breeches, with his hair in a queue, he was still a striking man, though like his elder son, not overly endowed with a cheerful demeanour. She curtsied deeply.

'*Monsieur le Duc.*'

'Mademoiselle Lafleur is helping Léonie with the children until she can find a new nanny. Is that not sweet of her, Jean-Alexandre?' the duchess asked, tapping him with her fan.

The duke's eyes flitted with lightning speed over Sophie's attire before he answered blandly, 'Indeed. Most kind.'

Sophie knew what he was thinking as clearly as if he had spoken aloud — what was a children's nurse doing dressed like a lady taking supper with them?

Privately, she agreed with him, though she could not possibly say so. This was a curious family, to be sure. The duke and his eldest son she could deal with. They knew her place, as did she. But the elder duchess, the still-beautiful Eléanor, and her flame-haired daughter Léonie, were as unpredictable as Jean-Michel.

Sophie suppressed a tiny shiver of anticipation as her thoughts strayed to the *vicomte*. She wondered whether he would join the gathering this evening. After their disastrous ride on the common that afternoon, she would have considered it a blessing had he absented himself.

But no sooner had she entertained this calming thought than the door opened and he strode in. His eyes flew across the room to her, as though sensing instinctively where to find her. He stared openly for a second, taking in her elegant chignon and shimmering white gown as if he had seen nothing like it before. She flushed, turning to retrieve Léonie's stole, which had fallen to the floor — but not before she noticed the speculative gleam in the Duchesse de Chambois's eyes as she caught the lightning exchange.

Sophie's heart sank. She had no wish for Jean-Michel's mother to gain the wrong impression. She fancied the woman would make a formidable enemy, and no doubt she was as protective of her son's future as any noble matron. She vowed to set the duchess straight concerning her plans for the future, if the opportunity arose during the evening.

Drinks were offered on silver salvers and the Duc de Chambois raised an eyebrow as he observed the pale wine in his glass. François, who stood a head taller at his side and cut a commanding figure in a suit of dove-grey velvet, held out his own glass and announced proudly,

'*Monsieur, madame*' — this while extending a slight bow to the senior duke and duchess — 'may I present a taste of the New World. Chateau Beligny-Boston, 1793! Not quite a Bordeaux, damn the soil and the winters, but we Americans are nothing if not adaptable, *n'est-ce pas, chérie?*'

Léonie's eyes twinkled with merriment, which, as she watched her father grimace at his first sip, turned to a peal of laughter. 'Now, Papa, you are not going to insult my husband's vintning, I trust?'

The duke glanced at his daughter, then at François. 'I seem to have curiously mistaken the role you would play in my daughter's life,' he said gravely, not caring that everyone in the room was listening avidly. 'I rather fancied you would effect a sobering influence upon Léonie, but I see she has instead corrupted you, Béligny. Or perhaps 'tis just that too many years at sea have dulled your nose.' He raised the glass so that the light from the argand lamps sparkled in the crystal. 'This is undoubtedly the most appalling vintage I have ever tasted.'

Sophie pressed a hand to her mouth to silence a gasp. But François merely grinned.

'You're right, of course, *monsieur*, upon all counts. But luckily my skill as a ship-owner vastly exceeds my nose for wine. As for my wife . . . ' He crossed to Léonie and laid his hand upon her shoulder, smiling down at her with such love that Sophie felt an inexplicable pang. 'My wife has given me more than you could imagine. For that, I would gladly consume the swill from the worst inn in Boston harbour.'

Léonie grinned impishly up at her husband, Eléanor clapped her hands with delight, and Robert frowned. The duke, for his part, appeared unabashed. But the corners of his mouth succumbed to the faintest of smiles. So, he was not as crusty as he liked to appear, Sophie thought.

She glanced across the room, feeling Jean-Michel's eyes upon her. He, too, was smiling, holding a glass of François's wine towards her in salute. Her heart began to beat altogether too fast, but Sophie raised her own glass and took a sip, her eyes never leaving his face. The wine was dry, young and rather harsh, but not as bad as she'd anticipated. She shrugged lightly in response to Jean-Michel's questioning brows, and he grinned, then turned away as his brother claimed his attention.

Sophie stood quietly, observing the man who was both pirate and nobleman. He stood almost as tall as François, in fawn breeches and boots. His dark green jacket covered a white silk shirt topped with an elegant stock that emphasized his broad shoulders and firm jaw. His hair, Titian in the lamplight, was cut just to the collar and curled slightly at his temples. She let her eyes wander over his straight aquiline nose and firm mouth, tilted now in wry acknowledgement of his brother's words, and her thoughts returned to that morning, when they had sheltered together beneath the apple trees on the common. Her lips tingled as she remembered how close they had come to kissing, how much she had wanted it, how the sudden remembrance of her future had poured colder water on their ardour than the greatest downpour could ever have done.

She turned away towards the uncurtained

windows, where heavy rainclouds had brought night early, and was startled to see him staring at her reflection in the darkened glass. She gazed back, her eyes widening with shock as he solemnly winked at her.

She was relieved when dinner was announced a few moments later. She hung back, expecting to follow the family quietly on her own, only to find herself paired with Jean-Michel, he being the younger brother and she the lowest ranked lady present.

Just as they were about to pass through the doors leading out of the parlour, he paused, letting the others continue without them.

She stiffened as he tilted up her chin with one finger. 'You look very beautiful tonight, Sophie.'

She blushed, feeling a sudden ache behind her eyes. 'Please do not say that. I feel all wrong, as though I am acting a part in a play.'

'You look like Aphrodite in that gown,' he murmured. 'But if you are the Goddess of Love and Beauty, what does that make me?'

'With hair the colour of flame, sir, I would say you are Hephaestus incarnate.'

He laughed aloud, resuming their progress towards the banquet hall. 'Well said, little maid. I knew there was more to you than meets the eye. Hephaestus, indeed. Are you so well read, after all?'

Sophie held her head high, though she was not willing to expose a lonely youth spent amongst the dusty tomes of the library at Mon Bijou. 'I read well enough.'

'Even in Greek?' he prodded, as they entered the huge banquet hall where a long table was set for dinner.

'And Latin.'

'But not English,' he added, as he handed her into her seat.

'God speaks French well enough,' she replied, pleased to see he caught the allusion to her reason for running from his kiss that afternoon.

He smiled wryly. 'Then you should have no trouble keeping Him in line, should you?'

She watched him assume a seat opposite her. They were positioned in the middle of the heavy mahogany dining-table, which could easily have seated thirty when all the leaves were inserted, but tonight a mere eight places were set.

Just as Sophie was about to enquire as to the reason for the empty place set beside her, the door opened to admit an elderly cleric dressed all in black. His shoulders were slightly stooped and he walked somewhat stiffly with the aid of a cane.

'Father Cassel!' Léonie cried. 'I am so glad you could come.'

Sophie was surprised to see the priest visit each person, shaking hands with the men and kissing the ladies' fingers as though he were greeting old friends, for clearly he was no stranger to the Duke and Duchess de Chambois, nor to the marquis.

Finally, he reached her.

'*Mon Père*,' Jean-Michel said, having stood to greet the old man, 'may I present Mademoiselle Sophie Lafleur.'

Sophie was grateful he did not add 'from Charleston' to the introduction, for she was not sure she could countenance an outright lie to a man of the cloth. He kissed her hand no less warmly than he had Eléanor's or Léonie's, and then settled himself comfortably into the chair at her side just as the first service was brought in.

As they selected from a choice of cucumber soup or herring, conversation centred around Father Cassel and his life since he had been parish priest on the Chambois estates in the Loire Valley before the Revolution. He described, for the benefit of the duke and duchess and the taciturn Robert, how he had escaped at the beginning of the Terror with Christian Lavelle and his bride aboard a stolen frigate.

Robert was not amused. 'Lavelle had a brilliant career in the navy. Why would he throw it away by turning himself into a pirate of the worst kind?'

Sophie sneaked a quick glance at Jean-Michel through her lashes, remembering how she had accused him of much the same tyranny when they'd first met. But he was concentrating on his soup, only a slight frown betraying that he had even heard his brother's question.

Léonie answered, as boldly as ever. 'He was a hero, Robert. He saved Catherine's life, and that of her father-in-law, the Prince de Charigny. They were all here last year during the terrible yellow fever outbreak in Philadelphia, but they returned once the worst was over.'

'But you remained in Boston, Father?' Eléanor asked, smiling at the old man. She was clearly fond of him.

Father Cassel glanced wryly at his host, seated at the head of the table. '*Madame la Duchesse*, I have spent so much of my life in the service of your son-in-law, it seemed only natural to stay in Boston where I could be of further service to his family.'

François grunted, though his eyes were warm as he regarded the old priest. 'Keep me in order, you mean, Yves.'

213

'Ah, not I,' came the soft rejoinder. ''Tis your beloved wife who does that, François.'

There was general laughter about the table, with much teasing of François for being henpecked, which he took with good humour. Sophie watched the exchanges with no little envy at the warmth and closeness of this family, which somehow surprised her in a group of such elevated aristocrats. What she had expected she was not sure. Quiet *politesse*, perhaps formality, yet they were as comfortable with each other — with the possible exception of Robert — as any commoner family.

They had progressed to the fourth service when Jean-Michel destroyed Sophie's appetite for the evening.

'Father Cassel,' he said calmly as he signalled a servant to refill his glass, 'has Mademoiselle Lafleur informed you that she is on her way to Canada to give her life to the service of God?'

There was a sudden silence in the room, punctuated only by a tiny gasp of surprise from the elder duchess. Sophie felt her cheeks redden. She set down her fork, all thoughts of food suddenly repugnant to her, and folded her hands in her lap.

'Indeed?' the priest replied, his keen gaze burning into her, though she could not quite meet his eyes. She sent Jean-Michel a reproachful glance across the table, but his lips merely turned up in the faintest smile, as though he had tried purposely to annoy her. She stiffened her spine. If he thought she could be dissuaded merely because she was face to face with a man of God, he was much mistaken.

'Is this true, Sophie?' Eléanor asked from the top of the table.

Reluctantly, Sophie turned to face the curious eyes. 'Indeed it is, Your Grace. I am on my way to Acadia. My family comes from there and I wish to be of service to the natives and the poor.'

She saw the duchess glance quickly at Jean-Michel, a tiny frown marring her face, before she smiled. 'That is truly a daunting calling, my dear. You must be very devout.'

'Y-yes, Your Grace,' Sophie stammered, suddenly seeing her decision through their eyes, and the enormous disparity between the way she was living at this moment and the future she espoused.

The conversation turned to other matters and dinner continued, though Sophie did no more than toy with her dessert.

The end of dinner was a blessed relief, for since Jean-Michel's revelation Sophie had felt like some kind of specimen in a museum display. Everything about her, from that moment on, had felt wrong. Who she was, who she appeared to be, who she claimed she was intending to be; none of these images gelled, and the curiosity of the others at the table was palpable.

Except for Léonie and Jean-Michel, who, with the like minds of twins, seemed almost smug in their belief that she would never give her life to God. But she was growing used to that. The Duke and Duchess de Chambois, on the other hand, had seemed utterly perplexed, while Robert clearly thought that she was slightly mad. The priest, with those uncanny eyes of his, made her deeply uneasy, as though she were performing some kind of charade, when in fact she was in deadly earnest. It troubled her that her determination to give her life to God could cause such a reaction in one who had done exactly that himself.

Only François seemed to accept her, and she found a renewed sense of gratitude towards the man. Once or twice during dinner as the others had pressed her for information, she'd found him smiling quietly at her, offering silent encouragement, or taking up the conversation himself and turning it to other matters so that she might be afforded some peace.

Peace was what she sought as she excused herself to see to the children. For the first time since she had arrived at La Tour House, she sought sanctuary in the tiny family chapel. The room was blessedly silent and empty, and she lit a candle on the small wooden altar and knelt before the light, staring up at the golden cross that glinted back at her.

And she prayed; prayed for strength, prayed for relief, prayed for escape, prayed above all for forgiveness.

She felt a little better as she climbed the stairs to the nursery twenty minutes later. The children were all abed, angelic in sleep as only children can be. The twins slept with their little arms flung out above their heads, side by side in the big bed at the far end of the room. She kissed each small cheek, then moved to the younger girls, who shared another bed closer to the fire. She tucked the bedclothes more tightly around little Rose-Marie and retrieved a fallen rag doll for Françoise, who would cry out if she awoke and found her beloved toy absent from her arms. Christiane, the eldest, had her own bed, but she, too, clutched a stuffed horse as she dreamed.

They were so sweet, these children. So innocent and unaware, as Adam and Eve must have been before the Devil tempted them with the fruit of knowledge. She wished she could have remained in that state of innocent bliss.

The nursery was quiet, the dying embers in the grate casting a soft red glow, occasionally sputtering as a log shifted deeper into its blanket of ashes. She let herself out quietly and returned to her own room, her heart deeply troubled.

Danielle was waiting, agog for news of the dinner and Jean-Michel's reaction to her gown and hair. Sophie tried to remonstrate with her, to make very certain the maid understood there could be no possible connection between herself and the viscount. But she was difficult to distract.

Finally, in desperation, she began asking questions of Danielle and her life both here in Boston and earlier. She scarcely attended to the answers, for her mind was far too preoccupied.

Suddenly something about Danielle's manner caught her attention, and she looked up, their eyes connecting in the mirror where she sat so Danielle could remove the ribbons from her hair.

'You are blushing, Danielle.'

'I am, *mamselle*? I'm sure I do not know why.'

'Indeed you do! You were speaking of Zamore and you came over all — '

'I was merely observing what a gentleman he is, *mamselle*. Nothing more.'

'Fiddlesticks!' Sophie was intrigued, her own problems forgotten for the moment. 'Danielle, are you in love with the captain?'

The maid gasped, dropping the brush. 'Why would you say such a thing?'

'You know perfectly well. And why should you not be?'

'Oh, *mamselle*. He'd never take notice of a nobody like me. He's a sea captain, and much respected. I'm nothing but an abigail.'

Sophie smiled at her in the looking-glass. 'Captain Zamore is one of the more admirable, straightforward of men I have ever known. Why, he doesn't have a snobbish bone in his body. He treated me with only the greatest respect, which was more than I deserved considering — '

'You know Zamore?'

Too late, Sophie realized her error. Danielle came around the *poudreuse* so she might face her directly. 'When did you meet him, *mamselle*? I had thought you were aboard the *Lady L*, but Captain Zamore's ship is the *Némésis*, a mail packet that runs the — '

Sophie jumped up from the stool, angry

219

with her own thoughtlessness. 'I know who he is, Danielle. I met him only briefly — '

'But you spoke as though you had some leisure in which to form so strong an opinion.'

Sophie had had quite enough of prying questions for one evening. She turned upon the maid. 'That is quite enough, Danielle. I am tired. If you do not mind, I should like to go to bed.'

Even the stricken look on the girl's face was not enough to appease her vexation. She set her lips in silence, allowed the maid to assist her out of the white silk gown, slipped her night-dress over her head and climbed into bed, twitching the bed curtains closed behind her.

She listened until she heard the maid close the door to the chamber softly behind her, and then she turned her head into the pillow and cried tears of frustration.

She had to leave. Despite the children, despite Léonie, despite Jean-Michel. No, especially because of Jean-Michel, for it was he who was standing four-square between her vocation and her peace of mind.

It was time Sophie Lafleur started looking out for herself, for she was a woman alone in the world, and she could never afford to forget that.

10

Saturday dawned brighter, with sunny skies and a mildness in the air that bespoke the approach of summer. But Sophie could not appreciate the beauty of the day, for she had not slept well, and her drenching on the common the previous day had resulted in sneezes and a slight fever. Another of God's little reminders, no doubt.

She decided to stay in bed awhile, as Brigitte, Léonie's personal maid, offered to take the children for a walk. Danielle brought hot chocolate and a plate of tempting pastries, though Sophie had not the least interest in food.

'I'm sorry I spoke so harshly last evening, Danielle,' she said as the girl adjusted her pillows at her back. 'It had been a trying evening.'

'*Ça ne fait rien, mamselle,*' came the meek reply.

'But it does matter, Danielle. It was quite uncalled for. You were right, I do know Captain Zamore, but I cannot tell you how. All I ask is that you keep my confidence, as I shall keep yours.'

'Yes, *mamselle*.'

Sophie took the cup of chocolate and sipped it, feeling the sweet liquid soothe her raw throat.

'Do you require anything else for the moment, *mamselle*?' When Sophie shook her head, Danielle turned to go, and then suddenly remembering something, delved into the pocket of her apron and produced a letter. 'Forgive me, I had almost forgot. *Monsieur le Vicomte* asked me to give you this.'

Sophie took the letter and waited while the maid left. Her heart pounded as she stared at her name written with a bold flourish on the vellum envelope. Could he have found her a passage to Canada? Was her prayer of last evening to be answered after all, and so soon?

She slid her finger under the seal and withdrew the note.

My dear Sophie, it began. Was she his dear? she wondered with a sudden spark of joy, quickly squashed. *Quelle absurdité*! She had not the slightest wish to be anyone's dear. She read on.

I trust you are feeling rested after a somewhat disquieting evening. I myself have been called away on pressing business, but I shall return as soon as I am able. During my absence, I hope to obtain some news concerning your family's fortunes in Nova Scotia.

Sophie's heart sank. So they were back to that once more. Why would he not just secure her a passage and let her make her own arrangements once she arrived? She consoled herself with the thought that at least he had taken the time to pen her a note warning of his absence.

The note ended in typically blithe Jean-Michel style:

Don't fret, little mouse. Kiss Rose-Marie for me.

It was signed simply 'J-M'.

She lay back against her pillows, clutching the letter and staring up at the pink flowers embroidered on the bed-curtains. An image of the baby of the family came into her mind. Much as she adored the dark-eyed little poppet, she found it strange that Jean-Michel would play favourites when he seemed so devoted to *all* his sister's children.

She resolved that she would mention it to Léonie, if she could find her alone later in the day. And then, feeling strangely reassured by Jean-Michel's little note, she curled up and fell into a dreamless sleep.

★ ★ ★

It was dark when she next woke. Danielle brought some broth and though she intended to get up and at least make an appearance, she found herself too exhausted to do more than make use of the necessary and brush her teeth before collapsing once more into bed.

And so Sunday passed, with Brigitte and Danielle once again in charge of the children, who were forbidden to enter Sophie's bedchamber lest they catch the affliction themselves.

By Monday, Sophie felt a great deal improved. A warm spring sunshine poured in through her uncurtained window and she at last felt its pull. She breakfasted in her room, dressed in a simple dimity gown with a loose shawl about her shoulders, and went downstairs, finding the parlour empty and the French doors open onto the terrace.

'*Bonjour, madame*,' she called as she spied Léonie lying on a wooden *chaise-longue* with her face unashamedly turned into the sun.

'Ah, I am glad to see you better, my dear. Come, sit with me. This sun is heavenly.'

She laughed, waving a hand at Sophie's frown. 'Now, pray don't lecture me on the deleterious effect it is having on my complexion. A pregnant woman must be allowed her eccentricities.'

Sophie smiled. The woman was irrepressible. She settled herself on a wrought-iron chair beside the duchess.

'Are you quite recovered, then, Sophie? The children so wanted to visit you and keep you company, but Brigitte managed to persuade them that it would be wiser to stay away.'

'She was right, indeed, *madame*. But I am considerably recovered, thank you.'

There was a moment's companionable silence, during which Léonie returned to basking in the sun, her eyes closed like a cat. Sophie wondered whether it would be prudent to broach the subject of Jean-Michel. She glanced at the house, wondering whether the other guests were still abed.

'Jean-Mich is not here, *chérie*,' Léonie said without opening her eyes. 'He has some business up the coast, so François says. He might return for supper.'

Sophie cleared her throat. 'Indeed, I had a note . . .'

'Ah!' That caught Léonie's interest. She lifted her head, shading her eyes against the sunlight as she regarded Sophie. 'Then you are most certainly having an effect upon my brother. Bravo, *mamselle*.'

Sophie flushed. 'I do not know what you mean, *madame*. However,' she went on before the duchess could elaborate, since Sophie felt certain she would be delighted to explain, 'I was puzzled by something in his letter concerning the children.'

'How so?'

' 'Twas . . . 'twas little Rose-Marie. He especially asked that I pass on his regard to her.'

'And?'

Sophie frowned. 'I had not perceived favouritism to be among his vices, *madame*. Surely he loves all the children equally?'

The duchess giggled. 'Are you so familiar with his vices, Sophie?' Then as Sophie's face burned scarlet, she tsked. 'Forgive me. That was entirely too wicked for this time of the morning, was it not? And you are quite correct. My twin does not have favourites among my children. But then, Rose-Marie is not my child.'

Sophie was confused. 'Not yours, *madame*?'

The duchess, with some difficulty, pulled herself upright at last and lay back against a large embroidered cushion. 'I thought you knew, my dear. Oh, *nom de Dieu*, how silly.

Rose-Marie is my niece! She is Jean-Michel's daughter.'

Sophie stared stupidly at Léonie for a moment as she attempted to assimilate this intelligence. Her head spun quite dizzily and she grasped the sides of the chair to steady her thundering emotions. Jean-Michel had a child. A four-year-old child. That meant . . .

She was spared the asking.

'His wife, Marie, died when the babe was but two. She never recovered from the birth, poor thing, just faded away. It is why Jean-Mich moved his family in with us, so Rose-Marie could have brothers and sisters — and a 'mother' who was as strong as an ox,' she added with a grimace. 'It was a comfort to Marie — and to François and I, since our own baby boy, Léon, who was the same age as Rose-Marie, died before his first birthday.'

'I — I'm sorry, *madame*. I had no idea. Naturally, I assumed — '

'*Bien sûr.* Who would believe otherwise unless they were told? It was a sad few years.' She sighed. 'My brother has never recovered from Marie's death, and I still miss her myself. She was our dearest friend while we were babes. Then, later, she became my maid, until she married Jean-Mich. A woman misses her only sister, you know, and that was always how I thought of her.'

Sophie sat back, shocked to the core. That Jean-Michel had been married and had a daughter had stunned her, but that his wife had been none other than his sister's maid fairly stole her breath away.

'But *Monsieur le Duc* . . . your parents . . . they accepted the marriage?'

Léonie's gaze was shrewd as she squinted at Sophie. 'Indeed they endorsed it. Marie gave her life to protect the honour of my family, which sadly I was responsible for risking. The wounds she received while trying to protect my reputation were so lasting that she lost three babies before she finally gave birth to Rose-Marie. My brother blames himself, of course, silly man.'

That, at least, she could comprehend. Sophie had always sensed self-loathing in the man, though he buried it deeply. Despite her best efforts to the contrary, she found her heart warming towards him. She knew how great was the pain of losing the person you most loved in all the world, for she had lost both her brother and her parents.

The duchess seemed inclined to elaborate. 'Jean-Mich was wounded in a silly duel. He had accused a man of cheating at cards — quite rightly, of course — and the blackguard called him out. My twin was due to join a naval expedition to the South Seas to search for a lost scientific expedition.' She shrugged. 'He could not go, so I went in his place. Just for fun, really.'

'*You* went, *madame?*' Sophie gasped. 'But were you not the only woman aboard the vessel?'

Léonie laughed. 'They did not know that. I learned a great deal and saw half the world before I was discovered.' Her grey eyes twinkled with mischief. 'I was shot in a battle with Malay pirates and the captain had to dress my wounds!'

'Oh!' Sophie sat very straight in her chair. She was not at all sure she wished to hear another word.

'It was perfectly all right,' she added airily. 'For my captain was none other than François himself, so you see my honour was quite safe in the end.' She sobered slightly, her brow darkening. 'But Marie was less fortunate. She fell from a high window trying to escape the villain who had wounded my brother and was trying to expose my secret to the world. His sole intent was to blackmail my mother, but he misjudged my family sorely. We exacted our revenge on the evil creature. But that did not help Marie, and Jean-Michel could do nothing but watch her pain.' She sighed, lying back upon the *chaise-longue* and rubbing her enormous stomach protectively. 'But we must think of the future, not dwell upon the past. Life is too short to waste upon that which cannot be changed, do you not agree?'

Sophie stared at Léonie de la Tour, seeing her anew, as a woman of great complexity and much courage. And in that same moment, she came to a realization that both warmed and terrified her: she loved this woman's brother. Despite all his dark secrets and his light, teasing ways, Sophie had been inexorably drawn to him from the first moment of their meeting.

And that fateful encounter would surely cause her the greatest pain of her life, for she knew that she could never have Jean-Michel de Chambois, never love him as she yearned to do, and that this was how God would punish her after all, with her own personal hell on earth.

★ ★ ★

Dinner that evening was a rather stilted affair. Jean-Michel arrived late and sat down next to Sophie with only the briefest of formalities towards his parents. Sophie longed to speak with him, but could find no opportunity until

Robert began regaling his sister Léonie with a detailed account of the lands and assets of his fiancée, the stuffy-sounding Lady Alice, eldest daughter of Lord Ashby of Rutledge. The English lady had apparently declined to visit America with her intended, fearing the journey unsuitable for a lady of such delicacy. Léonie's response to that created an ensuing argument that gave Sophie a chance to broach the subject dearest to her heart.

'Have you heard news of my uncle?' she murmured, as she sipped her wine.

He speared a piece of mutton on his fork. 'Possibly.'

Sophie gasped in delight, then looked quickly at the others, relieved she had not been observed, for she had no wish to share this conversation. 'Where?' she whispered, as she too, became busy with her fork. 'Is he well? Can he take me in? Does he have a family?'

Jean-Michel lay his hand atop hers on the table. 'Stop. I shall tell you what little I know.'

Sophie's heart beat a little faster, whether from the pressure of his fingers or the excitement of hearing something at last, she wasn't entirely certain. He grinned, then released her hand and once more turned his attention to his meal. 'Firstly, I know only that he is called Dalibar.'

'You did not meet him then?' Her face fell.

'No. I heard this from an agent who trades in furs along the Saint Lawrence.' He took a sip of wine, making her want to scream in frustration as she waited. 'There is a Monsieur Bernard Dalibar who works as a notary of some repute in the town of Québec. He has done well for himself by all accounts, with a wife and family, so I am told. And he is an elected member of the *Assemblé*, which is why 'twas simple for my man to gain news of him.'

Sophie let out a sigh of relief. 'Thank heavens. So, now, I trust you are satisfied and will let me return to my family?'

He paused in the process of wiping his lips upon his napkin. 'Sophie, the man may not be your uncle. It is not inconceivable that they simply share the same name. Did you not tell me that his family were fishermen from the Île Saint-Jean?'

'That is true,' she mumbled, setting down her fork. 'But I feel so certain it is he. Mama said he was a most ambitious and capable boy. Does it not make perfect sense that he would have escaped the English by moving to a French settlement further inland?'

He was silent for a moment. The

232

conversation at the other end of the table had moved to other matters and was becoming somewhat desultory. Clearly, Robert had been on the receiving end of his sister's sharp tongue and a somewhat awkward impasse had resulted.

'Well?' Sophie prompted under her breath, certain that Jean-Michel had indeed located the last of her family. She herself was too elated to believe he could harbour any further reservations on her behalf.

'Are you so anxious to be gone?' he asked.

She opened her mouth to affirm that she was, but something in his eyes stopped her. 'I . . . naturally, I am eager to begin my new life, to see the home I have always dreamed of, but I shall miss you . . . all of you,' she hastened to add.

A simple dessert of fruits and sherbet was served in the conversational lull that followed. Léonie sat silently toying with the strawberries that François had imported especially for her, while her brother and father sat stiffly watching the elder duchess endeavouring to do justice to her lime sherbert. Clearly, tempers were being held in check by the merest thread.

Jean-Michel had had enough. He was tired from his journey and had no interest in the quarrel between his older brother and his twin. He pushed back his chair and stood.

'*Je m'excuse*,' he said shortly, addressing his apology to his brother-in-law and sister.

'Oh, Jean-Mich,' Léonie replied with a touch of resignation and a quick glance at her father's blank visage. 'Must you go to the tables tonight?'

He regarded her gravely, knowing she was pleading not to be abandoned without his support when tensions were high, but he had no desire to spend any longer in such an atmosphere. And she had her husband to keep the peace.

'You know me, sister dear,' he said with enforced jollity. 'Have to earn my living somehow.'

The instant the words left his mouth, he wished them back. But it was no use. He felt his father stiffen, saw from the corner of his eye that he had raised his head and now turned the full force of his intimidating stare upon his youngest living son.

'I gather you play better than you once did,' the duke said coldly. 'I am told you ruined a man recently, took everything he possessed, from his farm holdings to his slaves and cattle. Does that help you sleep soundly in your bed at night?'

Too late, Jean-Michel realized he had created an outlet for his father's frustrations. Himself.

'I left him his Boston town house, *monsieur*. And the man didn't deserve to own slaves.'

'Perhaps you won that Baltimore Clipper you own, too,' Robert interjected, pleased to vent some of his own anger. 'Hardly the vessel of an honest man — more like something a pirate might sail.'

Jean-Michel clenched his jaw, leaning over the table so that he could stare at his brother full-face. The marquis backed away.

'I bought the *Némésis* at auction because she is fast and deep-keeled, Robert. She can run like the wind yet she needs only a small crew, which suits the business I am in. Perhaps you'd like to see the receipts?'

His brother waved a hand dismissively. 'I have no interest in your petty little mail boat. You cannot possibly expect to make a living from it.'

'I do well enough. Better than you.'

This unveiled attack on Robert's mishandling of the *cahier de doléances* early in the Revolution caused the old duke to bristle. Jean-Michel didn't care. He was used to Robert's failures being defended by their father, no matter how much they might have cost him personally. A first son could do no wrong.

'At cards, perhaps,' the marquis blustered, picking up his glass and taking a sip as though he needed something to occupy his hands suddenly. Jean-Michel contemplated tossing the lot in his lap, but thought better of it. He turned to go, but his father's voice stopped him.

'I see the years have not improved you, Jean-Michel. I had rather hoped America would show you that there was more to life than pleasures of the flesh and idle self-gratification. Clearly an error of misguided optimism on my part.'

He turned, seeing his sister's face take on a dangerous tint and her husband lay a restraining hand upon her arm.

'Jean-Michel does a great deal more than play at cards, Chambois,' François said quietly.

'Indeed? And pray, at what else does my son excel apart from delivering mail? Womanizing, perhaps? He was never as good as his sister at duelling, if I recall.'

Jean-Michel gritted his teeth, stung by this crack at the reason for his untimely removal from the list of naval officers. He reminded himself that his father had always enjoyed finding fault.

'How dare you!' Sophie stormed, her voice breaking as she leapt from her chair. Jean-Michel and everyone in the room turned in astonishment as the girl confronted his father, a man so far above her station she was honoured even to sit at the same table with him. 'You do not know your own son, have not seen him in almost ten years, yet you dare to accuse him of these things without a drop of evidence. Well, I know your son, sir, and he is none of the things you say. He is neither idle, nor self-indulgent. He is a fine seaman, and as to his skill with a sword, I have witnessed none better!' She glanced quickly at Léonie. 'Although, you, *madame*, are also much gifted.' Then she turned her attention back to the duke, suddenly realizing what she had done. With a cry of dismay, she clapped her hands to her burning face, brushed past Jean-Michel and ran from the room.

For a moment perfect silence fell over the table. Jean-Michel stood stupidly staring at the still-open door from whence Sophie had disappeared, not quite believing what he had heard.

Then Eléanor spoke, her voice touched with the slightest hint of amusement.

'I see you have found yourself a girl of unusual spirit, Jean-Michel. Does she come from a good family?'

'*Quoi*?' He turned to his mother, frowning. 'She is not my 'girl' as you put it, *Maman*, and I know very little of her family.'

'That's why he is keeping her here,' Léonie added, grinning now that her mother had released the tension. 'Jean-Mich cannot abide a secret to which he is not a party.'

'Is this true?' the duchess demanded. Jean-Michel's heart sank. Thank you, *ma soeur*, he said silently.

'I am attempting to locate her family, so I may reunite her safely with them. There is nothing more sinister in my intentions than that.' Since his return from New York, that was not entirely true, but it would serve.

'I should hope not,' inserted the duke, apparently recovered from having been chastized in front of his family. 'I will not have you bringing your concubines into my house.'

'*Your* house, Father?' Jean-Michel was enraged by this slight upon poor Sophie. 'If I am not greatly mistaken, this house belongs to Monsieur le Duc de Béligny. I live here as his guest, and I do so by *his* rules. As' — he added dangerously, for he well knew how unwise it was to cross his father, 'do you.'

He strode through the open doors before

another word could be uttered, and before he could stop himself, slammed them shut behind him. 'Damn!' he said as he crossed the hall. He had given his father all the satisfaction he needed, by demonstrating that he could still make him lose his temper in an instant.

Perhaps he was a little more like the old man than he cared to admit.

* * *

He found Sophie in her bedchamber, which he entered with only the most cursory knock, since he could plainly hear her sobs from the passage. She lay on the bed, face down, her golden hair half-tumbled from its Greek chignon and falling about her like moonspun silk. She took his breath away.

'Sophie.'

She sat up with a little gasp of dismay. 'Jean-Mich? Oh, can you ever forgive me? I must leave here immediately. Your father will have me horse-whipped if he ever sets eyes upon me again.'

'Stop, my sweet!' he murmured, closing the space between them and gathering her up in his arms. 'He will do no such thing. Oh, Sophie, my little mouse, you were so brave.' He stroked her hair, loosening the remainder of the locks from their pins so they tumbled about his fingers. 'You positively roared at *Papa*, and *Maman* was greatly amused.'

She lifted her head from his jacket. 'She was? But how is that possible, when I had just insulted her husband? A duke. *A duke!*' she repeated, in awe at the unspeakable audacity of it.

'It did him good. You merely saved me the trouble. And anyway, he is right: I am a pirate and I do make my living from other people's misfortunes. They just happen to be people who deserve misfortune.'

'Then why didn't you say so, in your own defence?'

He laughed, stroking the last of the tears from her upturned cheeks with the ball of his thumb. 'That would really have made Robert happy!'

She grimaced. 'But it seems so unfair.'

'Life often is, *ma petite*.'

He stared down at her, still trapped in his arms with her face turned trustingly up to his and her beautiful blue eyes wide, and something cracked deep within his heart. Slowly, he lowered his head until his mouth touched her lips, brushing against them like a breath of air. She tasted sweet, of wine and the strawberries she had sampled at supper, and he moaned, knowing he was lost.

'Dear God, Sophie,' he murmured, then lowered his head once more, this time taking only his second real taste of her since aboard the *Némésis*. Kissing her seemed so different now. When he had plundered her mouth aboard ship, she had been a stranger, a woman strayed at the hands of Fate into his all-male world. But he knew her now, had seen her strengths and her weaknesses, her gentleness and the love with which she cared for another woman's children. And he desired her almost more than he could bear.

Sophie thought she could gladly drown in that kiss. She entwined her arms about his neck, revelling in the feel of his fingers winding through her hair. He slid one hand down her back, grazing the fine silk of her gown. His touch burned her skin through the thin fabric, scalding her as though no such barrier existed. His mouth plundered hers and her lips opened eagerly in response, her tongue meeting his in an intoxicating dance that set every nerve atingle. She moaned as his fingers dug into her scalp and he deepened the kiss, eliciting a fire deep within that made her press against him with wanton disregard for all that was right and proper. She had never felt like this, never dreamed she would want to open herself to another so completely. She brought her hands to his face, holding him as if to assure herself he was real.

At last they broke apart, pausing breathless to stare wide-eyed at each other.

'Send me away, Jean-Michel,' she whispered brokenly. 'For my vows are not safe near you.'

He rested his forehead against hers, stroking his hands over her hair. He, too, was breathing hard. 'Ah, sweet Sophie. I am not sure my heart is safe around you, either. You are far too tempting. Far too tempting.'

11

Tuesday was pleasant and warm, with a gentle breeze wafting through the open windows of La Tour House. Sophie, having heard no further news concerning Jack Morgan, and secure in the knowledge that Jean-Michel would soon find her a vessel upon which she could travel north, felt the promise of the day and went happily about her duties in the nursery. She had marshalled the children to their studies and was reading fairy-tales to the two youngest while Léonie, whose boredom with her confinement grew greater with each passing day, helped the twins and Christiane to shape letters on their slates.

Sophie glanced up as she turned a page, smiling a little wistfully to see the duchess in a voluminous gown, kneeling beside her boys, her eyes sparkling with delight as they laboriously spelled her name in chalk. It was clear the children were among her greatest joys, and Sophie wondered what it must be like to live surrounded by the love of this noisy affectionate brood.

'*Mamselle*,' Françoise tugged on her sleeve.

'What happened? How will Cinderella ever see the prince again?'

Sophie looked down into the girl's worried blue eyes. 'Let's see,' she said, settling the child more firmly on her lap. There was scarcely room enough for the heavy book, with both Françoise and Rose-Marie sitting on her as well.

They continued with the story, the girls exclaiming over the illustrations and sighing with pleasure at the final happy ending.

Just as they finished, there was a gasp from across the nursery. Sophie glanced up to see the duchess gripping the table, her eyes wide and her face ghostly.

'*Madame!*' she cried, setting the children down and hurrying across the room. The boys were staring in fright at their mother's ashen face, and Christiane had wrapped her little arms about her mother's shoulders.

' 'Tis nothing, my love,' Léonie said, putting a smile on her face with effort. She tried to stand, but then stopped again, gasping as another pain hit.

'Christiane, run and fetch Brigitte! Tell her to send for the doctor immediately,' Sophie told her. The child flew to the door and her footsteps echoed down the passage as she made for the stairs.

Sophie helped the duchess to her feet.

Léonie gave a breathy laugh. 'I think this baby has decided it is at last time to come into the world,' she said. The spasm passed and she stood, looking down at her soaked gown. 'Oh dear.'

'*Maman*, you peed on the floor!' Michel said, his eyes round as saucers.

Sophie was not about to explain, but the duchess said easily, 'It is the waters, my precious. It just tells *Maman* that the baby is coming. Soon you shall have a baby sister or brother, but for now, be my angels and take the girls outside to play *cache-cache*. And behave yourselves,' she admonished them as the four small children ran eagerly from the nursery.

Sophie helped Léonie to her room, with the assistance of Brigitte, who arrived breathless from the kitchens. Another spasm made the duchess cry out, but she allowed her maid to help her from her gown and into a clean night-shirt.

Sophie suddenly noticed that Christiane was standing by the door, watching her mother with wide, frightened eyes. Since Sophie was not needed for the moment, she took the eight-year-old's hand and went in search of the children.

'Will *Maman* be all right?' Christiane asked with a quiver in her voice.

'Of course she will,' Sophie replied briskly, for she did not want to alarm the child. 'She is strong and fit and she's had babies before. It will all be over soon enough, you'll see.' She surprised herself by the conviction with which she made this assertion, for she herself had never assisted any woman to give birth, and she knew precious little about the risks. But she knew Léonie, and if anyone could give birth bravely, it would surely be she.

Christiane clutched her hand tightly as they went out the side door to the garden. 'Our last baby brother died, you know. He was always sickly. *Maman* said he couldn't feed properly and the doctor thought it was his heart.'

'But you are healthy,' Sophie said, giving the girl a quick hug. 'And so are the others. I'm sure by day's end you will be able to hold a healthy baby and then you will see how natural it all is. Have you told your papa?'

She shook her head. 'He wasn't home, but I asked Maurice to fetch him from the shipping office.'

'Good girl. Now let's see how well you children play hide-and-seek.'

It took only a few minutes to locate the others, for the young ones, impatient for the game to continue, would call out from their hiding places within a minute if they had not been discovered.

Sophie and Christiane joined in the game, but after several turns, no one could find Rose-Marie. Finally she was located by the stables, watching the doctor's black carriage pull up in front of the house. The tall gaunt man stepped down, his clothes as sombre as his conveyance. He strode into the house with a heavy black bag clasped in his hand.

The children watched in silence, then Jean spoke. 'That's Doctor Martin,' he said. 'I don't like him.'

Sophie felt a frisson of fear, for the sight of the man had not given her confidence either. She hustled the children to the back of the house. 'I'm sure he's a wonderful doctor, and your mother will be well cared for.'

Then Rose-Marie began to cry and, like an echo, Françoise joined in.

Oh dear, Sophie thought. Then she had an idea. 'Come, how would you like to take a picnic lunch to the Common?'

This evoked whoops of joy and the moment of anxiety passed. Everyone trooped into the house in search of bonnets and wraps, though they scarcely needed extra warmth, and the twins rushed off to find Madame Renault, for only the housekeeper could order the cook to prepare a picnic at a moment's notice.

When finally the basket was packed and everyone was ready, Jean-Michel appeared and asserted his intention to join the party, so with considerable noise — which fortunately cloaked the occasional cry that issued from upstairs — they set off on foot down the lane.

They crossed the street and entered the Common, but in order not to be too far from the house, made their way to the top of a nearby grassy slope from which they gained a panorama of the sea. The tide was out, leaving the river flats exposed, a wide ooze of sticky mud which delighted hoards of gulls and wading birds.

The children ran off to play while Sophie spread out the blanket in the shade of a giant maple and began to unpack the basket.

She glanced up, only to find Jean-Michel watching her, leaning with one hand on the rough bark of the old tree. He looked so smart in his dark-blue coat, with his long legs encased in tan breeches, that her heart gave a little flip. She smiled uncertainly, remembering the kisses they had shared the previous night. Her insides warmed just at the thought of his lips on hers, and she made a determined effort to turn her thoughts to purer pathways. She busied herself with the picnic.

She sensed him sit on the red wool blanket, even though she gave no sign, but when his hand covered hers, she jumped.

'What are you doing?' She licked her suddenly dry lips.

'I could ask the same of you.'

She blushed. 'I don't know what you mean.'

He smiled, touching her nose with one finger. 'You're avoiding me. Perhaps you're afraid I shall lay you down upon this rug and finish what we started last night.'

Sophie gave a little squeak of outrage and pulled her hand back sharply. 'Jean-Michel de Chambois, how dare you speak like that!'

'Forgive me, little mouse. I was merely remembering . . . ' His glance fell to her lips and she felt herself colour deeply. Then he sighed. 'I know, I know. 'Twas a mistake, though a damned nice one, but I promise not to repeat it, so you may rest easy.'

He turned away, stretching his booted feet out before him, and changed the subject as though there wasn't a thing more to be said. 'I love this spot. You can smell the sea and the river and the grassy meadow all mixed together like an exotic beverage.

Look, there's a goose with a batch of young ones.'

In a flash he was on his feet, calling to the children to come and see. They broke off their games and trotted across the grass to watch the goslings, not much more than bundles of yolk-yellow fluff, trundling after their mother towards the pond at the bottom of the hill.

Sophie was grateful for the reprieve, for her mind was whirling. That Jean-Michel should regard their kiss as an error, fitted perfectly into what she knew to be right and proper: young single ladies simply did not allow gentlemen to enter their bedchambers and kiss them. And she had done so not once, but twice. Her cheeks flamed at the memory of her own wantonness. Yet her heart, traitor that it was, didn't care. She was pained more by the notion that he regarded their embraces as a mistake than by the knowledge that he was right.

She returned her attention to the picnic basket, setting out napkins and plates with a vengeance. So she had lost her heart to Jean-Michel de Chambois. So what? For his sake, she must never let him know. For her sake, she must learn to un-love him.

Everyone she'd ever loved had died, she thought with uncharacteristic bitterness as she unwrapped a red-chequered cloth to find fresh crusty rolls.

The children returned, ravenous after their exertions, and soon the blanket was so crowded, Rose-Marie had to perch on Sophie's knee — a place she was apparently coming to consider hers by right. They devoured pastries and fruit, chicken and rolls, until little remained but crumbs. Christiane threw tiny pieces of bread to the gulls who had gathered hoping for a share of the bounty, until Jean scared the seabirds by running at them, arms outstretched.

Soon, all but Rose-Marie had run off once more, eager to join in a game of ball with their uncle, and Sophie was left with Jean-Michel's little girl and a mess to tidy. She glanced once or twice at the child. Her dark eyes were solemn as she played with a daisy, methodically pulling off the white petals, one by one.

Sophie set the last of the dishes back in the basket and knelt beside the child. 'Are you sad about something, *chérie*?'

She was shocked to see that the child's eyes were awash with tears. 'Oh, dear heart, whatever is the matter?' She gathered her into her arms and sat on the blanket rocking the infant as the little mite sobbed into her blue dimity gown. Sophie crooned into her hair, feeling the sobs pass and the tiny body relax at last.

She dug in her pocket for a handkerchief and mopped the child's face.

'Is that better?'

Rose-Marie nodded, though her bottom lip still poked out and she would not raise her head.

'Are you worried about Tante Léonie?'

Again, a nod.

'There is no need, *petite*. Having babies is natural. It hurts a little, but soon that is over and you will have a new baby cousin to play with. Won't you like that?'

The dark head shook in a vehement 'No!'

Sophie raised the girl's face to her gently. 'Are you afraid you won't be the baby any more? Everyone will still love you just as much.'

'I know.'

This was getting harder by the minute, Sophie thought, wondering what on earth ailed the child. But Rose-Marie took a great heaving breath and said, 'Babies make mummies die.'

Sophie's heart twisted with the pain in the child's eyes. 'Not always,' she replied gently. 'Tante Léonie has had lots of babies and she's fine. She's strong and healthy.'

There was a pause while Rose-Marie contemplated this, then she sniffed sadly. 'My mummy died 'coz of me. I don't have a mummy.'

'*Ni moi, non plus,*' Sophie replied, hugging her tightly.

'You don't either?' The dark eyes were wide with surprise. 'But you have a daddy.'

Sophie shook her head. 'He died when I was little.'

As soon as the words left her mouth, she wished them back. The child's eyes widened with fright and Sophie turned, quickly scouring the Common for sight of Jean-Michel. She clutched the child to her breast, murmuring words of reassurance that sounded hollow, coming as they did from her own empty heart. But they seemed to calm the child, and after a while the little girl's body relaxed and her deep even breathing told Sophie that she had fallen asleep. But still she sat, rocking her, to and fro, ignoring the ache behind her own eyes that told her she could never have a child like this of her own, no matter how much she might wish it.

* * *

Jean-Michel watched Sophie and his daughter from across the waving sea of grass as he played with the children. He saw Rose-Marie's pain as clearly as if he had been the one holding her, and he could guess what troubled her without hearing a single word spoken. Deep down, he had always known that the child associated her mother's sickness with her own birth, yet he had never found the words to correct the notion. How could you tell a four-year-old that her mother had suffered mortal injuries while escaping a rapist?

He shook his head, snatching up the ball as it came his way and firing it back across the grass to one of his nephews. The truth was, he doubted if he would ever tell her. Ugliness of that magnitude she need never hear, especially when it related to her own mother.

He knew he had left her alone too much, relied too heavily on his sister's beneficence in providing a home for Rose-Marie. To be with the child at first had only added to his pain, for she was the image of her mother, with the same dark straight hair, chocolate brown eyes and soft red mouth. Her serious little nature and the way she hung back — all reminded him of his beloved wife, and in those first months after her death, they had also served to fuel his anger.

So he had been relieved — or so he told

himself — of the need to offer physical and emotional support to his daughter when Léonie had taken over that role. And his sister adored the child, lavishing the same affection upon her as she did upon her own brood. Rose-Marie had thrived, and yet there remained something . . .

She needed her father. She had pretend brothers and sisters, and a substitute mother, but *he* was her father — and he had faded into the background of her young life, expending his energy elsewhere to avoid facing his duty.

He tossed the ball back to the boys one last time and turned up the hill, suddenly badly needing to hold his little daughter in his arms, to tell her how much he loved her. His eyes connected with Sophie's as he approached, and she smiled. He was struck by how entirely different she was from Marie, from her wheat-blond hair to her sky-blue eyes and milky skin. Even her mouth was delicate, a soft pink that stirred his body with thoughts of strawberry kisses.

'Is she asleep?' he murmured, squatting in front of them.

Sophie nodded. 'Would you like to hold her?'

He settled himself beside her, leaning his back on the maple tree and held out his arms. Sophie gently passed him the child, and they sat in companionable silence for a few minutes watching the older children at play, until Rose-Marie awoke.

'*Papa!*' she chirped happily, giving him a wet kiss on his cheek.

'Did you sleep well, *petite?*'

'*Oui, papa.* Are we going home to see the new baby soon?'

'In a little while. I'm glad you're looking forward to it. Do you hope it will be a baby girl or boy?'

The child's brow puckered for a moment. 'A girl, I think. So Françoise and I can dress her in our old clothes like we do our dolls.'

They laughed. Then Rose-Marie became serious. 'Will you have a baby, too, Mamselle Sophie, so I can have a real sister? I should like that.'

Sophie flushed. 'No, Rose-Marie. I do not have a husband. You must be married before you have children of your own.'

'But you can marry Papa. He loves you just like I do.'

Sophie gasped, her eyes flashing to Jean-Michel in an instant of utter mortification. He seemed as startled as she was, his storm-grey eyes dark with some emotion she could not read. Could it be true? Had the child seen something to which she herself had been blind?

'I'm sorry, dearest,' she said when she could once more speak, 'but I have chosen to give myself to God so that I can help others. I cannot do that as well as be a mother.'

To her dismay, Rose-Marie's eyes filled with tears and she wailed. 'But I want you to be my mummy!'

★ ★ ★

They returned to the house to find that the baby had not yet made an appearance, and that the doctor had left Léonie in the care of her midwife with promises to return later. One look at François's face and Sophie knew things were not going well.

The old duke and duchess took it upon themselves to entertain the children with a lavish dinner and dancing in the huge dining-room, keeping their minds off whatever was unfolding upstairs. They insisted that Jean-Michel and Sophie join in, without the least antipathy concerning the scene the previous night.

The children were disappointed that the baby had still not come into the world when it came time for them to retire for

257

the night. The duke led the way, singing an old French peasant song all the way to the nursery, and then commanding Christiane to play the harpsichord while the younger children prepared themselves for bed.

Finally, all was quiet, the children asleep in minutes after the excitement of the day. Sophie kissed each child on the forehead, tucking their rag dolls about them, and let herself out of the nursery, leaving Aileen, the Irish maid, to sit with them for a while.

The Duc de Chambois had retreated with his son-in-law to the study, where no doubt they were enjoying some of François's best cognac. They both deserved it, in her opinion.

A lamp burned in her room and the bed was turned down, but although Sophie was physically exhausted, her thoughts were entirely focused on Léonie. She was desperately worried, for if the young duchess were to die, François and Jean-Michel would be left with a large motherless family between them.

She forced her thoughts to stop right there. It was unthinkable that the duchess would not survive her ordeal. Sophie recalled the woman in her manly attire, sword in hand as she strode across the lawn on the morning of Sophie's arrival in Boston. No, Léonie de la Tour was made of stern fabric. She would weather this storm.

But still Sophie couldn't go to bed. She left the room and went down the back stairs, passing Léonie's chamber as she went. No sound came from within, so she prayed the woman was resting. At the ground floor, she let herself out onto the colonnade and crossed quietly to the kitchen and adjoining servants' quarters, hoping to find Danielle or Madame Renault and enquire about the duchess's health.

The door to the kitchen was open, in deference to the mild evening and the huge fires that burned almost constantly within, and Sophie could see several figures seated about the giant wooden table. She hesitated, loath to disturb them, until she heard a low laugh that caused her heart to beat a little faster.

She stepped across the stone portal, and three pairs of eyes turned her way.

'F-forgive me,' she stammered, suddenly feeling like an intruder. 'I merely wondered . . . that is, I wanted to know how *Madame* is doing, and I could not find Danielle.'

'Come in and sit yourself down, *mamselle*,' said an elderly man with a pronounced stoop whom Sophie had seen busy about the gardens and the vineyard from time to time.

She thought his name was Bérard.

'*Merci*,' she said, smiling as he held a chair for her. She looked about, trying not to notice how Jean-Michel was staring at her, and then realized that he was looking at her hair, which she had brushed out around her shoulders ready for bed. She accepted a glass of house wine from the cook, Madame Marlotte, who beamed at her across the table and passed her a plate of petit-fours.

'No news yet, *mamselle*,' the woman said, 'but Brigitte is just gone to see if she is needed. Her Grace is managing as well as she ever does, which,' she added with a guffaw, 'is not as well as she'd handle a bunch of marauding vagabonds, but no worse than most women with a babe who's in no hurry to come into this world.'

'Will she be all right?' Sophie asked quietly.

' 'Course she will,' the cook replied, waving a plump hand. 'It is not so many hours gone, and the doctor says the babe's facing the right way — towards Hell, as Her Grace put it.'

Everyone laughed, even Jean-Michel, who was looking a little tense. He caught her eye and smiled fleetingly. Sophie smiled back, wishing there was no one else in the kitchen with them, but at the same time relieved not

260

to be alone with him after little Rose-Marie's pronouncement at the picnic that afternoon. The memory still made her cheeks flame, and she ducked her head, raising her wine goblet to her mouth to cover her discomfiture.

At that moment Brigitte returned. '*Madame* is resting,' she pronounced as she dropped into a chair and put her feet up on the table. The cook summarily shoved them down again, which Brigitte seemed scarcely to notice. She looked at Jean-Michel. 'Your sister has a message for you, sir. She said to tell you — and these are her words, so you'll excuse me the telling of them — that 'tis clear God is a man, for He would never have the gumption to do the birthing Himself!'

Jean-Michel grinned. 'She's feeling better then. She always blames François when it's bad and me when she's got herself more under control.'

Bérard the gardener harrumphed. 'Least-ways you didn't have Monsieur Robert under your feet all day, sir, if you'll pardon the disrespect. Says the garden is nowt but wildness and disorder.' He sniffed. 'Told me Their Graces ought to set the place to rights and put in some nice regular paths. Mumbled on about squares and rectangles and points of the sun. I didn't understand the half of it.'

Jean-Michel snorted. 'My esteemed brother thinks everything should be under control at all times, women in childbirth or grass and trees, it makes no matter. He was never a Rousseauist.'

Sophie laughed, trying to imagine the starchy Robert communing with nature in all its rambling glory.

'Well, I don't know about that,' complained Bérard morosely. 'Only thing met his approval were the vines, 'cause they was all lined up nice and straight. But then he told me what he thought of the wine, and I weren't properly disposed to pass the time with him after that.'

Sophie caught Jean-Michel's eye and had to suppress a giggle. The conversation turned to other matters, and Sophie was content to sit in the comfortable room and let the chatter flow over her, enjoying the brusque wine and the chance to observe Jean-Michel in the company of ordinary people. He was relaxed with them, joking and laughing and calling them all by their first names as though he'd known them all his life. Indeed, he seemed more at home here in the huge kitchen with its flagstone floor and heavy beamed ceiling hung with kettles and herbs than he ever was in the fine rooms of the house.

Eventually, Brigitte returned to sit with the midwife in case she was needed, the old gardener shuffled away to his quarters, and the cook, after a cursory tidy up, left for her bed, wishing them both a good-night.

The fire stirred lazily, sending out a few sleepy sparks as Jean-Michel emptied the last of the wine into their goblets. Somewhere outside a fox yapped into the night, and the soft beating of nocturnal wings was heard just beyond the open door.

'You should get to bed,' he said, his voice making her jump in the silence. 'There's nothing to be done but wait, and the children will need us more than ever tomorrow.'

'You were wonderful with them today,' she replied quietly. 'And so was your father. 'Twas a stroke of genius to organize a party like that.'

He chuckled. 'I never knew my father to display such a wild streak. Shows we didn't just inherit our unconventionality from our mother after all, though it is what he's always claimed.'

She smiled. 'He adores his grandchildren. It's good that he is here at such a time.'

'It's good that you are here, Sophie Lafleur,' he answered, suddenly reaching across the table and covering her hands with his. 'You have been a tonic for my sister, and for . . . '

She held her breath, certain he had been about to say she had been a tonic for himself, too, but he simply coughed and withdrew his hands.

'I am glad I was able to help. No, truly,' she protested as he looked askance. 'I know I was displeased at first, but I have enjoyed my stay, although now you seem to have found my uncle, I am anxious to depart.'

'I envy you,' he said sombrely.

'Me?' She laughed. 'What on earth do I have that could possibly cause anyone the slightest envy? I am almost entirely alone in the world, I have no means of supporting myself, an uncertain future, and — '

'And a secret past,' he finished for her.

She shifted uneasily in her seat. 'There's nothing to be gained by looking back, so your sister says.'

'Isn't there? Don't you think understanding where we've been is the key to understanding the journey that lies ahead?'

She laughed lightly. 'You sound like a tutor trying to drum history into a dull brain.'

'But you have learned from your experience.'

She looked up. 'How can you know that?'

'Because you left. Whatever happened to

you in the Caribbean was enough to cause you to flee your home without a penny to your name and seek out a completely new life thousands of miles away.'

She shrugged. 'I told you, 'twas nothing to be envied.'

'Perhaps not,' he said on a sigh as he drained the last of his wine. 'But at least it has given you a plan, some notion of your future.'

She was puzzled by his strange mood. 'Jean-Michel, you have your ship and your daughter, isn't that enough? You will build up your business and I know you will do well, just as François has done — '

'*Jamais*,' he retorted sharply. 'I have neither his drive nor his ambition in business. I do it out of hate; he does it because he loves it.' He stood up, pacing the length of the room, his boots loud on the stone floor. 'You have never quite understood what it is that I do, but since you are leaving, and since you already know enough to hang me, I shall tell you, then you will know me for the man I am.'

Her eyes widened. She was not at all sure she wished to hear this, yet he did not appear to be offering her any choice in the matter. She settled her hands in her lap.

'My wife died from terrible injuries sustained many years ago while trying to protect my family name. When we came to America as man and wife, we were full of hope for the future. She became pregnant, three times, and each time her damaged body expelled the child before time. Three times we buried our babies because they were too small to breathe on their own. Finally, a miracle — little Rose-Marie came into the world, whole and complete and looking every bit the image of her mother. But Marie — ' He paused, running a hand fiercely through his russet hair. 'Marie was too weak to recover. She became utterly exhausted, sickly all the time, until one day she simply lost interest in life. She died when our daughter was barely two years old, and I made a vow the day I buried her that I would devote the rest of my life to destroying people like the blackguard who cost her her life.'

Sophie breathed out, 'So that's why you destroyed Morgan's ship.'

Jean-Michel waved a hand. 'He's only one of many. My father was right about the man I bested at the gaming tables. I took everything except the house his wife and children need to live in. He dealt in human misery, and I freed his slaves and gave his farm away. One day I shall explain it to him, but not yet.'

'And the *Némésis?*'

He gave a self-deprecating laugh. 'She really is a mail boat, when she isn't needed for more nefarious work. Then we paint her black so she may be better hidden — with the sails down she becomes almost invisible at anchor. All her decks are steel-braced so she can carry the recoil of the heavy guns, so she's a match for many ships twice her size, and with her speed, she can outmanoeuvre all but a few.'

'Why are you telling me all this?' Sophie asked, when it appeared he had become lost in his thoughts.

He turned to her, coming to lean his hands upon the table so he could look straight into her eyes.

'So you will not go away from here thinking me some kind of hero. So that you will see what a worthless wastrel I am — God knows, I am even losing my taste for vengeance these days, and if I do, what then shall I occupy my time with? My daughter loves me, but I have no right to her love, and one day she will see that for herself. She will need her cousins and her aunt and uncle then.'

Sophie was appalled. 'Rose-Marie loves you because you are her father — and because you love her. And that's *all* she needs. She does not require a father who owns a shipping company or who trades in silks or spices, much less one whose wealth is obtained on the backs of slaves.'

He shrugged, wandering over to poke a toe at the fire. 'I just wanted you to understand, after what she said this afternoon.'

'Oh,' Sophie replied, surprised that he should have brought the subject up. 'She's just a little girl. She doesn't understand what she is saying.'

'Even so,' he continued, turning to look at her. 'If I were the marrying kind — which I'm not — I could never offer myself to a woman like you. You need a proper husband, one you can respect.'

Sophie stared, a thousand thoughts whirling in her head, not one of which she would dream of uttering.

'You — ' she began. 'I — ' But the words would not come. How could she respond, how could she even start, when he had been so open, so honest with her? She slumped back in her wooden chair.

'You need have no fear of me, Jean-Michel, for I am as little in search of a husband as you are of a wife. But since

268

you have been so open with me, 'tis only fair that I honour you equally. As a friend,' she added hastily. 'I should not like you to hold any opinion of me that was in any way superior to that which I deserve.' A sudden calm came over her, a cold certainty that from this moment on, her life would be forever changed, perhaps even endangered. 'What you have done is not as terrible as the sin I have committed,' she said quietly, and then the words began, hesitantly at first, and then pouring out like water from a broken dam. She described her life as the child of exiled parents, her father's disappearance, and her time in Guadeloupe after her mother fell ill. Finally she related the events of that fateful night at Mon Bijou.

Through it all, Jean-Michel stood quietly, looking into her eyes yet showing no flicker of emotion. Until the end. Until she described the blood and the fear and the terrified dash from the only home she had ever really known.

Then he came around the table, pulling her off her feet and into his arms, enveloping her in a massive hug that blocked out the whole world and left her feeling so whole again, so free, that she began to cry from sheer relief.

She let the tears come, relishing the blessed release even as they washed her soul clean. And all the while, Jean-Michel held her tightly in his arms as though he would never let her go.

12

The door burst open a few minutes before seven next morning. Sophie sat up in bed, blinking the sleep from her eyes as the twins tore into her bedchamber.

'*Mamselle*, she is here! The baby is here!'

Relief filled her, and she hugged the boys. 'And your *maman*, is she well?'

'Papa says she's tired and we are only to visit for a minute,' Michel said excitedly, 'but later we will be able — '

'To hold the baby — ' Jean finished for him.

'So, can we?' This in unison.

Sophie laughed. 'Soon. So you have a new sister, after all?'

They looked ever so slightly crestfallen. 'Yes, but that's all right. Us boys have got each other.'

'Indeed you do,' Sophie replied. 'Now run along and play quietly until I am ready and then we shall see about visiting your mother.'

They scampered off, their little voices high with excitement.

Sophie lay back upon her pillows, truly

glad for Léonie that her ordeal was over. As for herself, she had spent a restless night after her confession to Jean-Michel, trying to decide what she must do. It was clearly imperative that she vacate the house as soon as possible, and yet the de la Tours had not yet found a new nanny, nor would they until Léonie was herself again, for François could scarcely be expected to deal with the matter.

She chewed on her lip as she contemplated the situation she found herself in. Although she was oddly relieved to have shared her terrible secret, she felt more in danger than ever. And she did not think that he would tolerate her continued presence in this house.

She dragged herself from the bed and set about her ablutions, not expecting to see Danielle with all that was to be done this morning.

She breakfasted with the children in the nursery and then tidied them so they might visit their mother.

Léonie lay in the middle of a huge canopied bed, looking pale in contrast to her vivid red hair spread about her on the snowy pillows.

She smiled, holding out her hands to the children, who threw themselves at her — to the consternation of the nurse hovering nearby — all talking at once.

'What does she look like, *Maman*?'

'Does she have daddy's blue eyes?'

'Does she like to play with dolls?'

'Can she talk yet?'

Sophie hushed them, lifting the boys off the coverlet to stand at the side of the bed.

'I'm not sure, *mes petits*,' the duchess replied softly, stroking their heads one by one. 'All babies are born with greyish-blue eyes, but she has a tiny thatch of red hair, so perhaps she will favour her *maman*. And as to talking and playing, it will be a little while before such things occupy her. You must be patient.'

The younger ones groaned. Patience was not one of their favourite words.

'May we see her, *Maman*?' Christiane asked, after casting a disdainful look at the younger children for their silliness.

Léonie nodded to the nurse, who bent over a straw bassinet and withdrew a tiny bundle swaddled in white. Holding her finger to her lips to warn the children to be quiet, she carried the baby to the bed and laid her in her mother's arms.

'Oh, she's beautiful,' Christiane said.

'Kind of wrinkly,' Jean added, screwing up his nose.

Léonie laughed. 'All babies look like that

273

at first. In a few days she'll be all plump and round, you'll see.'

'What's her name?' This from Rose-Marie.

'We have decided to call her Aimée, because it means 'loved'.'

Léonie was clearly fatigued after her long labour. She passed the baby back to the nurse and Sophie ushered the children away, sending them outside to vent their energy on the garden. She followed Christiane to the stables and having ensured that the groom would stay with her at all times, allowed the child the special treat of spending the morning riding her pony, Mathilde.

The boys had taken their toy boat to float on the pond, and the two younger girls were keen to make daisy chains. By the time they had invented a game of make-believe and were dancing about the flowerbeds like little fairies in their garlands, Aileen had come out to watch them, and Sophie was free to return to the house.

She planned to go immediately to her chamber and commence packing, for thanks to the money Jean-Michel had advanced her on her arrival in Boston, she now had a few simple outfits suitable for her new life. The beautiful gowns Léonie's dressmaker had sewn for her would be left behind. She would have no use for those.

But as she entered the house, she realized that more important than fitting her few belongings into her new valise was the task of obtaining passage on a boat heading north. She still had some money left, and hoped it would be enough, so she went to her room, put on her straw bonnet and tied it tightly about her chin, then taking her wrap and parasol she set out in the direction of the harbour.

She followed the same route she had taken before, finding it easier in the daylight. The marketplace was in full swing as she passed through, and she almost tripped when a squealing piglet, hotly pursued by its young owner, shot from between two stalls directly into her path. She reached Merchant's Row, finally, enjoying the relative calm of the businesslike street after the chaos of the market. But where to begin? The most likely source of information was the wharf itself. She would surely find someone there who could direct her.

Long Wharf was busier, lined with buildings that finally gave way to tall ships at anchor. Crowds of stevedores hurried about, loading and unloading, and she was about to question one who seemed to be in the way of a supervisor, when a voice called her name.

Sophie froze, pulling her parasol sharply down to obscure her face. Her pulse raced. She glanced about, deliberately not turning towards the voice, even as her name was repeated more loudly.

There was no escape. Long Wharf ended in the sea and her accoster stood between her and the town. She contemplated throwing herself on the mercy of the burly stevedores, but before she could formulate a plan, she became aware that a very large horse was standing almost at her shoulder.

She glanced up, both relieved and dismayed to see François de la Tour staring down at her. He swung a leg over his saddle and dropped to the ground, raising his beaver hat in greeting.

'Sophie, what the deuce are you doing on the wharf all by yourself? I thought you were at home, looking after the children.'

She flushed, making no demur as he took her elbow and began to steer her back towards dry land. How could she explain herself? What possible excuse could she offer?

'I-I merely felt like a walk, Your Grace . . . '

'To the harbour?' He looked at her sceptically, pulling his horse along behind them as they walked. Sophie could hear the beast snorting as smoke drifted across the road from a pile of old rags someone was burning.

'Jean-Michel has found a man he thinks might be my Uncle Dalibar, living in the town of Québec on the St Lawrence River,' she explained desperately. 'So as soon as I am no longer needed by your wife, sir, I shall be able to leave.' She glanced at his impassive face, wondering if she would be believed. 'I was anxious to discover how often vessels travel to the north and how much I might require for my passage.'

Not a lie, exactly. Sophie felt a little better.

François made no reply, touching his hat in recognition of a friend as they turned back onto Merchants' Row and stopped outside a two-storey brick building. The brass plate over the door proclaimed it the Massachusetts Bay Trading Company.

'My office,' he explained, as he tied his horse to the railing. He escorted her upstairs, to a pleasant room panelled in oak. A huge terrestrial globe sat in a stand next to a walnut secretary with an inlaid leather top, and a glass-fronted bookcase covered most of the far wall. In the centre of the room stood a worn but sturdy table bearing numerous maps and papers. Several wooden chairs completed the furnishings, giving the whole the look of a place where function, rather than comfort, was the rule.

'Pray be seated, Sophie,' the duke said, going to an adjoining room to speak to someone concerning refreshments.

But Sophie did not sit. 'Please, sir, do not trouble on my account. I have no wish to take up your busy day.'

'I am not in the least inconvenienced. I merely came to the office in search of some papers, and was planning to return to the house at once. I thought my wife might have need of my company after her ordeal.'

Not for the first time, Sophie marvelled at the closeness of their relationship. How many men would do other than stay clear of such a domestic scene as a day-old baby and an exhausted wife?

'I shall order a carriage for you after you have had some refreshments,' he added, and so Sophie sat, for not to do so would be ungracious.

A moment later, a clerk entered carrying a wooden tray, bearing — to Sophie's astonishment — an elegant porcelain *cafetière* and three cups. Matching cups and saucers and a plate of wafers accompanied the offering. He set it upon the table and disappeared again.

'My wife's idea,' François explained as he

saw her surprise. 'She likes to visit me here from time to time and insists upon the comforts of home. When we do not have ladies to entertain, Arbousset and I usually make do with tin mugs and ale.'

'I am honoured,' she answered with a smile, hoping the refreshments would not take long. She accepted a cup of coffee, which was every bit as good as the excellent beans his cook served at La Tour House, and sipped quietly at the hot brew.

'So, you are leaving us,' he said, when he had downed a hearty mouthful of the strong, black liquid. 'You had no need to go skulking about the wharf seeking a vessel. Either Jean-Mich or I could have furnished you with a dozen names. He could take you himself, come to that.'

She frowned. 'He could? But I thought it would take time — '

François's dark-blue eyes twinkled. 'After your spirited defence of my brother-in-law a few nights past, I'm not surprised he told you that. He's probably hoping you'll change your mind and stay.'

'Oh, I couldn't possibly!' she sputtered, choking on the coffee. She set the cup down, splashing a little in the saucer. 'I must leave, as soon as a berth might be found.'

He was silent for a moment, regarding her solemnly.

'My wife and I would deem it an honour if you were to remain a few more weeks — at least until she is fully recovered.'

'Weeks?' Sophie repeated faintly.

There was a knock on the door, and François got up to admit a portly man wearing a tall hat. He bowed to her, was introduced as one Claude Derouliers, and passed some papers to the duke.

'Since you have company, François, I'll just leave these bills of lading. Arbousset knows what they're for. I have some furs coming in from the Northwest in a week or so if you're interested — top quality, should fetch a pretty penny in the Orient.'

François nodded, casting a quick eye over the documents. 'I would be, Claude, but I've lost a ship recently and until I can get a replacement at auction, I'll have to delay the next voyage to Shanghai.'

'Lost?'

François grimaced. 'Jack Morgan has her. She'll go to the Court of Vice-Admiralty in Halifax, but I'm not sure I'll give him the satisfaction of buying back my own vessel.'

The other man let out a whistle. 'Morgan,' he said. 'Ain't that the fellow who's put signs up all over the province for information on the sinking of the *Deliverance*?'

Sophie stiffened, then glanced quickly in François's direction and was dismayed to see that he had noticed.

'*Eh bien*, best be off. *Enchanté mamselle*,' he added, touching his hat once more.

She heard the man's footsteps descending the wooden stairs to the street, and tried not to let the silence in the room unnerve her.

'Pray, don't upset yourself, Sophie,' the duke said softly from behind her. 'I already knew you were aboard the *Deliverance*.'

Sophie gasped, jumping up and turning to face him.

'Jean-Michel told me,' he explained. 'The night you tried to sneak away from the house.'

She felt herself pale. If he had told François, perhaps he had told others. And now that she had told Jean-Michel the whole truth . . .

'I must go at once,' she said, gathering up her parasol. 'I am sorry to have wasted your time, Your Grace, but I simply must leave Boston with all haste. To wait any longer would be foolhardy.'

He stared down at her. 'I am quite certain Jean-Michel has told no one else, and I for my part never betray confidences. You are as safe now as you ever were.'

She shook her head. 'No, sir, I am not.'

'And why is that?'

She waved a hand in supplication. 'I cannot truly say. It is just a feeling, as though the world were closing in. Boston is beginning to feel like a prison to me.'

The vehemence of her feelings seemed to surprise him. 'I am sad to hear it. I should certainly not wish to be responsible for such discomfiture. But I would feel happier if you would honour me by allowing me to speak with Jean-Michel. His mail boat under Captain Zamore makes regular runs to Halifax and could no doubt accommodate you, though I believe it does not go north again for a few days.'

Sophie stared at him, struggling to absorb this extraordinary statement. The blood began to pound in her ears as fury, white-hot in its intensity, filled her. 'The *Némésis* sails to Halifax!' Her voice shook and she took a deep breath to steady herself. 'May I ask how often it makes this journey, sir?'

He shrugged. 'Every ten days or so, I believe. Why do you ask?'

'Then it has made the journey at least once since I arrived in Boston?'

'Of course.'

Lies, lies and more lies, Sophie thought bitterly. All this time, while she had been desperate to escape, while he pretended he needed time to find her a passage on a ship, his very own vessel was making the voyage. Well, she would show Monsieur le Vicomte de Chambois that he could no longer keep her prisoner!

'I regret that I cannot accept your offer of further hospitality, Your Grace. I shall not impose myself on your family a moment longer. Danielle can pack my things easily enough and I shall procure lodgings until I can board a vessel — any vessel — travelling north. Kindly give my best regards to your wife and children.'

She purposefully did not mention Jean-Michel, for what she thought of him at this moment was not something a lady could express.

She snatched up her parasol and stormed from the room, grateful when she reached the street to realize that the duke had not tried to stop her. With her eyes brimming, she hurried back towards the centre of the town. She entered the Old State House and made enquiries at the post office — in her anxiety, not giving the least consideration to the fact that she could speak barely a word of English. To her immense relief, the clerk was an elderly gentleman whose knowledge of her own language was more than satisfactory, and she was not only given direction to a modest house close by, but was furnished with the services of a note in English explaining her requirements. Thus armed, she was shown a serviceable room for a modest amount. Parting with the coins was hard, for she knew she must hoard her precious funds, but she felt such relief to be finally 'on her way', that she did so graciously.

She left the room almost immediately, descending to the street and retracing her steps to the post office for further directions. This time she was sent to the somewhat rundown offices of one Josiah McCudden, Purveyor, whom, she had been assured, owned a small fleet of schooners for trading up and down the east coast.

Her business concluded satisfactorily, Sophie made her way back to her lodgings, entirely failing to notice the man who trailed a few paces behind her.

★ ★ ★

Jean-Michel was incensed when François related the events of the afternoon. 'How could you just let her go?' he stormed at his brother-in-law. 'Dammit, François, the girl has no money, no family, no chaperon — '

'I did not 'just let her go', as you put it,' replied François mildly, as he took two glasses from the sideboard and picked up a crystal carafe. They were in his library, his sanctuary in the busy house. 'I had her followed, and I know exactly where she is and how she spent the remainder of the day. I must say, I was quite impressed by her single-mindedness.'

Jean-Michel rubbed a hand across his eyes. 'Oh, dear God. Tell me she hasn't sailed already?'

'Tomorrow, according to Mr Josiah McCudden, who seemed only too pleased to tell me about his unusual passenger.'

'McCudden! She can't travel on one of his salt-fish buckets, she'll never get the smell out of her skin.'

'I doubt that will faze the lady,' François replied, calmly passing him a glass of Madeira. 'Funny,' he said mildly as he took an appreciative sip, 'I rather thought you would be pleased to be rid of her.'

Jean-Michel frowned. 'Not at all.' Then he thought about how she made him feel, as though he was a normal man, who could find happiness in ordinary things, in marriage and family, and sensible work. But he was not. He was a spoiler, a wastrel, and she was better as far away from him as she could get.

'You're probably right,' he said morosely. 'But I still wanted to take her myself.'

François looked up at him from the chair he had settled into by the fire. 'You still could,' he said mildly.

Jean-Michel considered it for a moment, then shook his head. 'Why should she believe me if I tell her I can take her myself on the *Némésis* in three days' time? If she thinks I lied before, she'll scarcely trust me to keep my word again.'

François shrugged. 'No doubt you are right.'

But later, as Jean-Michel lay in his bed, he knew he would have to try. He couldn't just let her disappear like that. He told himself it was no more than the concern any gentleman would have for a lady he felt responsible for. But then, he wasn't a gentleman.

He tossed and turned, trying not to think about Sophie or the tears Rose-Marie had shed when she heard that her beloved '*mamselle*' was not returning.

If he had ever felt like a worthless scoundrel, it was this night.

* * *

Dawn broke windy and cool and Sophie was glad of the warm cloak that had been among her belongings delivered late the previous evening. She partook of a simple breakfast, knowing that the seas would probably be rough, and the less she had in her stomach the better, then repacked her bag and left the room. She had been greatly relieved when Mr McCudden had agreed to take her the very next day, for the less money she spent in Boston the better.

She had further to walk this time, following Fish Street to Hancock's Wharf. Just as she reached it, a black-painted gig pulled by a lively grey pony drove directly into her path. With a cry, she jumped backwards, dropping her valise.

A figure jumped down from the gig and grabbed the bag before she had gathered her wits sufficiently to retrieve it. It was then that she recognized him.

'Jean-Michel de Chambois, give me that at once.'

'Climb up and get it!' he replied smugly, bounding back into the cross-seat and setting the bag beneath the buck.

Sophie regarded him severely, for she was still furious that he had lied to her, but it was hard to hold on to that anger when he was smiling down at her, looking as dashing as any man she'd ever set eyes upon. This was definitely not fair! His mouth was turned up in a quizzical smile, and his felt hat perched at a rakish angle on his head.

'Please, Jean-Mich. Mr McCudden assured me he will not wait if I am late, and I trust you would not have me arrive in Canada without a change of clothes to my name?'

'Definitely not.'

'Don't be smug! Hand me that bag at once, or I shall summon help.'

'The authorities, perhaps? And will you tell them *why* you are in such a hurry to leave Boston?'

She glanced about nervously, wetting her suddenly dry lips with the tip of her tongue. 'Don't do this, please. You lied to me so you could keep me here against my will. All I want is to be on my way.' When still he didn't move to return her belongings, she sighed in exasperation. 'You are not the only one with dangerous secrets to share, *monsieur*. As you pointed out, Jack Morgan is offering a fine reward for information on the sinking of the *Deliverance*.' She was mollified to see a shadow darken his features, and continued airily. 'Perhaps you were right. I shall certainly be in need of extra funds when I reach Halifax.'

She peeked up at him, almost grinning with satisfaction when she saw his brows draw together and his lips set tight.

But just as she was about to take advantage of his distraction and sneak a hand up to snatch her valise, he reached over the side of the seat and lifted her bodily into the gig.

'You are going nowhere without me, Mademoiselle Lafleur.'

Before she could even sit, he flicked the reins and the pony trotted sharply away up the street. Sophie grabbed for the seat before she was tossed bodily into the mud!

'You cannot do this, Jean-Michel. You have no right!'

'*Au contraire*, Sophie. When you threw yourself on my mercy aboard the *Deliverance*, you gave me every right, and every obligation. I may be a blackguard and a pirate, but I take that responsibility seriously.'

'I absolve you of that responsibility,' she replied heatedly. 'Now take me back to Hancock's Wharf on the instant!'

'The *Némésis* sails for Halifax in three days. You may have my cabin, as you did before.'

'Three days!'

'Three.' He glanced at her as they trotted up Hanover Street. 'Is that so long to wait?'

She gave a short disbelieving laugh. 'It was long to wait all this time since your ship last made the journey.' Suddenly infuriated with his deception, she thumped him fiercely on the arm, making him wince. 'You lied to me right at the start. You knew perfectly well that you could take me to Acadia from the moment I told you of my plans, yet you pretended that it would be difficult to obtain an onward passage for me.'

'I did so with the best of intentions. I needed to find out — '

'About me, I suppose? No doubt you sent some spies to Guadeloupe when I wouldn't tell you what you yearned to know. Well, now that I have shared my past with you, you have absolutely no reason to detain me further.'

'I was going to say I needed to find out about your uncle,' he answered when she had finally finished.

She looked at him uncertainly. 'Oh.'

'So will you wait?'

She tugged her cloak over her lap, for the morning was cool. 'What choice have you given me? I paid for my berth aboard Mr McCudden's vessel in advance. I do not have sufficient to cover a second fare.'

'Damn the money, Sophie! I'll see that you have funds, and before you start talking about promissory notes, I don't want it back.' He turned the gig into the lane leading up to La Tour House. 'You've earned every penny helping with the children and my sister.'

'That was no chore,' she replied, realizing how true that was.

'Rose-Marie cried, you know.'

She turned to study his profile, noticing a bleakness in his eyes. 'For what reason?'

'For the reason that you left without so much as an *adieu*! Did you think the children wouldn't notice? They were all upset, and I did not know what to tell them.'

'I'm sorry,' she said in a small voice, as the gig rolled to a stop outside the front steps. 'I shall beg their forgiveness.'

She climbed down, but as she started for the door, he asked, 'But will you ask mine?'

She turned, smiling sadly at him. 'You were the reason I left, Jean-Michel. Perhaps I should tell that to the children and leave you the explaining.'

★ ★ ★

Sophie's final evening in Boston was overcast, the day having surrendered to rain several times already. Summer, she was assured, would commence in another month or so, but spring was a fickle friend, sometimes hot, sometimes almost winterlike in its blasts of cool air.

She hoped this year spring would tend to the warmer side, for she found she was not yet accustomed to northern climes. She dressed for dinner in her classical white gown and Danielle wound gold ribbons through her elegant chignon. She held out her white cashmere shawl.

'You look like a princess,' she said with a wistful smile, as together they observed her handiwork in the cheval glass.

Sophie sighed. 'An illusion entirely of your making, Danielle. But I shall try to remember this night, for I doubt I shall experience another like it the rest of my days.'

'Oh, *mamselle*,' the maid said sadly. 'Must you go off and live among the savages and dress like a farmer? The children will miss you so.'

Sophie refused to think about that, for she knew if she did it would be her undoing. 'They have their new nanny,' she replied briskly. 'Madame Arquette will arrive upon the morrow. She's a kindly woman who's had children of her own, and the little ones will be perfectly content, I am certain.'

'If you say so,' came the unconvincing response.

Léonie, having accepted the fact that Sophie was truly leaving at last, had agreed to find a replacement nanny — with Sophie's help — and they had interviewed a number of candidates, choosing a firm but loving Frenchwoman recently widowed.

Sophie glanced at the gold hands of the ormulu clock upon the mantel and braced herself. She could delay no longer.

She descended the stairs, trying to shake the sense of doom that had overtaken her today. No doubt she was just feeling nervy over what she might find in Canada. The Baltimore Clipper would convey her to Halifax, but once there she would be obliged to obtain passage on another vessel plying the great St Lawrence for her journey up the river to the town of Québec, where she hoped against hope that Monsieur Dalibar would indeed turn out to be her uncle. If he did not, then there was a company of nuns in the town upon whose mercy she would throw herself. In the end, the result would be the same. But in her heart, more than anything she wanted to discover some remnants of family, to find that there were at least a few other souls in this world connected to hers.

Dinner was served once again in the banquet hall, for it being Sunday Father Cassel had remained in the house after saying midday mass in the chapel, and they would be eight at table.

She was the last to enter. She curtsied to Their Graces, and smiled delightedly to see Léonie once again at table, looking beautiful in a lemon silk gown belted high at the waist.

As she slid into her place, she ventured a glance across the table to Jean-Michel, but he sat with his head averted, toying with the stem of his glass.

With heavy heart, she acknowledged the old priest, accepted a glass of white wine from one of the servants, and the meal commenced. They began with soup and fried mutton feet, and were awaiting the second service when the sound of carriage wheels and horses crunching on the gravel beyond the windows created a pause in the conversation.

'Are we expecting visitors?' Léonie asked her husband.

'No, my love.'

In a few moments, the doors opened and Maurice hurried to François's side.

'*Monsieur le Duc*, there is a lady at the door who demands to be admitted. She says her name is Madame Guillaume.'

Sophie cried out in horror, spilling her wine all over the fine tablecloth as she leapt to her feet.

All eyes turned to her. Her cheeks flushed

deep red as she stood frozen in place. She stared at her host, eyes wide with fright, but not a sound issued from her throat.

'You know this woman, Sophie?'

She felt Jean-Michel's arm wrap about her shoulders, but resisted the desire to turn to him and bury her head in his chest.

'*Oui, monsieur,*' she whispered through lips as dry as parchment.

François signalled to Maurice. 'Tell the lady I shall see her in the parlour immediately,' he said, rising.

But it was not to be, for even as Maurice turned to go, a small birdlike woman in her sixties wearing a grey travelling gown and fur tippet walked briskly into the room. Her sharp eyes scanned the group and came to rest on Sophie.

'Ah, there you are, girl,' she said. 'A pretty chase you've led me.'

'*Madame*!' Sophie was too stunned even to offer a curtsy. She pulled away from Jean-Michel, distancing herself. He could not help her now. He had done what he'd thought was best by keeping her here in Boston for so long, but now she would have to pay the price. Her past had caught up with her, and her life, her future, her chance at finding her family, all were gone.

'Well, don't just stand there staring like

you'd never seen me before in your life, girl. Introduce me!'

Sophie snapped out of her dismal reverie, licking her dry lips. Madame Guillaume clearly had known who she would find living in this house, so she was not surprised to find her host was a duke, but to find another duke and duchess took her aback. Robert, however, who looked down his nose at the woman, was stunned when she surveyed his evening attire of embroidered blue coat, scarlet waistcoat and gold breeches.

'A marquis, eh? You'd not be out of place among my flock of peacocks in that garb!'

There was a smothered giggle from Léonie and an insulted gasp from Robert, who promptly sat down and signalled angrily to his servant to refill his glass.

She inspected Jean-Michel a little more shrewdly, allowing him to kiss her hand. 'So this is the fellow who owns that little black whippersnapper of a boat. You'd best rid yourself of the beast, sir, if you value your life.'

Jean-Michel's glance flew to his brother-in-law, whose brows were creased in perplexity at this comment.

Then Léonie spoke. 'I believe you are mistaken, *madame*, for my brother's vessel is blue and white, and quite a pretty thing, if I say so myself.'

Madame Guillaume considered this for a moment, then shrugged as if it were of no import. 'Good a way as any,' she replied enigmatically, before graciously accepting François's offer to join them for dinner. She sat at the end of the table, which to Sophie's dismay gave her as dominant a position as that held by François, for from there she could been seen by all and do her worst.

Sophie wanted only to slink away to her room, but Father Cassel laid his hand upon her arm.

'Pray, be seated, my dear,' he said *sotto voce* so that only she could hear. 'Running away will no longer serve, do you not agree?'

'*Oui, mon Père,*' she answered on a sigh.

Silverware was brought, and since the gathering was ready for the second service, the meal continued from that point. A silver platter bearing an enormous lobster was placed in the centre of the table, from whence its reproachful eyes seem to gaze at Sophie, making her feel more than slightly sick. She confined herself to a small helping of duckling, which attracted her appetite little better.

'Have you journeyed far, Madame Guillaume?' Eléanor asked as they began eating.

'Indeed I have, Your Grace. All the way from Mon Bijou in Guadeloupe. And an unpleasantly long voyage it is, to be sure.'

'Ah,' replied Léonie with interest. 'I had thought you might have ventured from Charleston.'

'Charleston?' the old woman said, frowning. 'Now why for all the saints would you think such a thing?' She stabbed a morsel of lobster, and then looked sharply at Sophie, but made no comment, merely pulling the white meat off her fork and chewing upon it as if she hadn't eaten for a week.

'So how is it that you are acquainted with Madame Guillaume, dear?' Eléanor persisted.

Sophie looked up miserably, seeing the duchess through a sheen of tears. 'She was my employer, Your Grace.'

'In Guadeloupe?'

Robert snorted. 'So, our little nursemaid must let free her precious secrets after all? Come on, then, Sophie, the priest is here. Make your confession, and let us all have our dinner in peace.'

'*Tais toi*, Robert,' said his father brusquely. Then, with more kindness than Sophie could have believed, he said, 'Come, my dear, so you decided it would be more suitable for you to tell us you were from Charleston. I'm sure there's no harm done by it.'

'But that is where you are wrong, Your Grace, for I have indeed done great harm, and Madame Guillaume has come to exact her revenge, as she is richly entitled to do.' She set down her napkin and rose from her place, standing at the table, and looking the elder duke straight in the eye. 'You see, I escaped from Guadeloupe fearing for my life after I committed the greatest sin of all — I killed Madame Guillaume's only son.'

A profound silence filled the room, stilling the diners' hands with forks raised halfway to their mouths. Only the fire snapped and spat without concern. And the rain, that until now no one had noticed, began to sound uncommonly loud against the glass of the tall palladian windows.

It was Madame Guillaume who finally broke the spell.

'Sit down, Sophie, for goodness' sake. Your food is getting cold.'

13

Sophie stared at the woman, not quite comprehending the command.

'Sit, girl, sit! Do you want *Monsieur le Duc* to think his table is lacking? Why, this is the finest lobster I've had in many a year.'

Sophie sank into her chair, open-mouthed.

Robert stood. 'Well!' he said vehemently. 'I for one won't sit at the same table with a confessed murderess. And to think,' he said, as he glowered at his sister, 'that you allowed this . . . this *criminal* to care for your children!'

'Oh, do shut up, Robert,' Léonie replied bluntly. 'She's not the only woman in this room who's killed a man.'

Robert's mouth began to open and close like a beached fish. He looked from Léonie to François, then to his mother and father, and lastly to Jean-Michel, but it was abundantly clear that his entire family were fully aware that his sister — his very own sister — had also taken a man's life.

He sat, looking rather grey, Sophie thought. She glanced at Léonie, who smiled back, giving her a tiny spark of hope. If the duchess had committed such a sin without impunity, then . . . But no. She risked a look at Father Cassel, only to find him regarding her blankly but without the slightest sign of repulsion. She wished now that she had had the courage to confess to him. He would have known how to advise her.

'Why don't you just tell them what happened,' Jean-Michel said quietly from across the table.

She looked at him, seeing a light in his eyes and a determined tilt to his jaw that clearly said he would not let anything happen to her. She was touched, though she knew he could not save her. Her avenue of escape had closed the moment Madame Guillaume had entered the room.

Nevertheless, she began, explaining how she and her mother had come to live at Mon Bijou, how she had grown up there and been educated at her mother's knee. How when her mother had developed consumption she had been taken away to a hillside sanatorium, from whence she had never returned, and Sophie had taken over her duties as lady's companion.

Madame Guillaume did not interrupt, merely nodding here and there as she continued eating.

'Then one day, Madame Guillaume's son, Louis, came home. He was most often away from Mon Bijou — '

'I made sure of it,' her erstwhile employer interjected.

Sophie frowned.

'Louis thought he should run the plantation,' the old lady explained, allowing a servant to remove her plate. 'But he was a poor master. The slaves hated him and when he was at home, there was less work done and constant bickering between himself and my foreman. Louis was a little above himself,' she explained to the company. 'He thought that when my husband died, he should be given free rein about the place. But while I am a slave owner — indeed, I could not run the plantation without the Negroes — I am not an insensitive woman.' She pursed her lips together and her eyes looked sad. 'But Louis treated his horse better than my slaves.'

There was a pause, and when it was obvious *madame* was finished, Sophie continued. 'When Monsieur Louis came home, it was after a break of several years. I . . . ' Here, her voice faltered a little and she lowered her eyes. 'I suppose in that time I had changed, grown up — '

'Grown extremely attractive, if you are

being honest,' Madame Guillaume interjected with a harrumph.

The servants set out the next service: four trussed-up capons, jugged hare and a stuffed turkey. Wine glasses were refilled, and Sophie struggled on with her confession.

'I found him sometimes looking at me strangely. Sometimes — ' She glanced uneasily at Madame Guillaume, but the woman seemed unperturbed. 'Sometimes he would wait for me in the parlour after *madame* had retired and would make . . . improper suggestions. Naturally, I refused his advances. I had never much liked him as a child, and his attentions were not at all to my liking. I suppose in his eyes I was merely a servant, and should be pleased to fulfil his every wish.'

Here there was a snort from Robert, and Sophie knew she was reinforcing every one of his negative ideas about her. But she could not concern herself with the opinions of the marquis. Her life was at stake.

'One night — April 4th, to be exact — I had gone down to the kitchens to fetch *madame* a glass of hot water and lemon, laced with rum. She finds this easeful when her arthritis keeps her awake,' she explained. 'As I was preparing the beverage, Monsieur Louis came into the room and closed the door. I don't know what it was, exactly, but something about him that night convinced me that this time he would not accept rebuttal.' She paused, clasping her hands tightly in her lap. 'I was greatly afraid. All the house servants were gone for the night, and the kitchen was separate from the house. I knew that were I to call out, *madame* could not possibly hear.'

She glanced up, to see the old lady's eyes looking suspiciously moist. 'Do you wish me to stop, *madame*? This can only be distressing you.'

'Certainly not, child. I am perfectly all right.'

Sophie sighed. 'Very well.' She took a sip from her water glass, unable to stop the trembling in her hand. 'He began to pull at my clothing, tearing my gown in his eagerness. I yelled at him to stop, but he just laughed. 'Twas then I smelled the liquor, and I knew I was doomed.

'But I was still holding the paring knife with which I had been slicing lemons. Without thinking, I plunged it into his neck — ' She dropped her face into her hands, sobbing with the ghastly memory. ' 'Twas only a small knife, but sharp,' she said through her fingers, 'and it penetrated his artery. He screamed at me to staunch the blood, and I ran for a cloth, but he came at me, and I stabbed him again in the chest. Again and again, until finally he fell to the floor.' She looked up, desperate for Jean-Michel's strength, for she knew he alone understood. But he was no longer at his place across the table, and she cried out with relief when she felt his arms close around her, holding her tight.

'Ssh, my love. Hush. You have said more than enough. Be at peace.'

She turned to him, letting the glorious warmth of his chest be her haven, if only for a moment. Sobs racked her, stronger than she, but not cleansing, for deep in her heart she was crying from self-pity in the certain knowledge that her only future now was the hangman's noose.

Her tale achieved one result: it put everyone entirely off eating. The magnificent dinner was removed and the party retired to the parlour in search of brandy.

Sophie, still wrapped in Jean-Michel's strong embrace, remained behind, as did Madame Guillaume, who sat at the table with her head bowed.

After the others had gone and the servants had disappeared, she got up with the help of her cane and came to Sophie.

'Child,' she said, gently easing Jean-Michel's arms away, 'I do not blame you for what you did to Louis. He was my son, but I always knew what he was, 'Tis why I kept him away so much. I paid him to stay away from Mon Bijou, for he despoiled the place.' She smiled sadly at Sophie, grasping her hands in her own arthritic ones. 'My dear husband, Marie-Paul, bought the plantation for me as a wedding gift in 1750, and we called it Mon Bijou because that was his pet name for me.'

'My jewel, my love,' Jean-Michel murmured.

'We always knew, from the time Louis was born, that he was not quite right. We had all manner of doctors to see to him — even sent him to Paris for treatment — but nothing worked. My son enjoyed seeing others in pain,' she said, deep sadness in her eyes.

'Oh, *madame*,' Sophie cried, hugging the woman. 'Please forgive me. I am so truly, truly sorry for what I did.'

Madame Guillaume extricated herself from Sophie's arms, tugged her black tippet up her arms and grunted. 'Come, child. It is enough that we've ruined a magnificent dinner with our gruesome tales. Let us join our hosts and be civilized for the rest of the evening, at least.'

Sophie nodded miserably, and returned to her chair to pick up her cashmere shawl which had fallen to the floor during all the excitement. She followed Jean-Michel, with the dowager on his arm, out of the banqueting hall and along to the parlour, wiping her eyes with a kerchief as she went.

Well, now it was out. Everyone knew who and what she was, and there was no further purpose in deceit.

It should have offered comfort, yet it did not.

The room fell abruptly silent as they entered, and Sophie was not surprised they had been discussing her hideous news. Nor could she blame them for their awkwardness in her presence.

She paused, looking about her at this group of people who had almost come to feel like family to her.

'It would be best if I were to retire for the night,' she said quietly, bobbing a curtsy. 'If you will excuse me.'

'Nonsense, girl,' said Madame Guillaume. 'I haven't said what I came all this way to say, yet, so you'd best be taking a glass of *Monsieur le Duc*'s cognac and strengthen your nerves.' She turned to François and said in a loud conspiratorial whisper. 'Never could abide women who faint, you know. Praise the Lord, neither Sophie nor her dear mother were like that, but one can never be too careful.'

François's mouth twisted into a rueful smile. 'I believe I know exactly what you mean, *madame*,' he replied with a grin at his wife. Léonie twinkled back, and Sophie envied them so much at that moment it was almost more than she could bear.

She took the brandy and perched upon a chair near the fire, looking about her, as if in an effort to imprint this beautiful house on her memory. As if memories could appease her desolation.

'Perhaps I am misunderstanding something here,' Robert complained loudly. 'But as if it were not bad enough that we have abandoned a perfectly good dinner, are we now expected to behave as though Mademoiselle Lafleur was just another guest? Perhaps she will play for us at the pianoforte, or enjoy a game of whist? Perish the thought that she should be taken away in irons.'

'Robert!' Léonie called in shocked tones. 'I will not have you speak that way to Sophie!'

'Indeed, dear Sister? And pray in what manner would you choose me to behave in the presence of a woman who slaughters an innocent man with a kitchen knife because of what she *perceives* he might intend upon her person?'

Jean-Michel, who was standing at Sophie's

side, stormed across the rug to his brother. He was a good three inches taller than the marquis, and his fine physique made him clearly intimidating. 'You will apologize to Sophie for that nefarious remark, Robert, or I will personally — '

'Come now,' said Eléanor, stepping directly between her sons. 'I will not have bickering. Jean-Michel, you should be used to the fact by now that your elder brother does not mean to be pompous. It comes as naturally to him as breathing. Now kindly return to your corner and let us enjoy a little peace. Perhaps dessert' — she looked enquiringly at her daughter — 'might be served in here?'

Léonie signalled to a servant who stood by the door, then turned her attention to the dowager, who was accepting a glass of brandy from François.

'Madame Guillaume, you will forgive me, but I am curious as to your plans. Is it your wish to take Sophie back to the Caribbean to stand trial?'

Sophie's heart stopped. She turned to the old lady, her eyes hot with unshed tears. She felt Jean-Michel's hand on her shoulder and prayed for strength.

'Indeed it is not, Your Grace.' Madame Guillaume frowned at the group scattered about the room, some sitting, some standing.

'There are far too many 'your graces' in this room for my liking. My father, God rest his soul, was one himself, but we left all that behind when we sailed for the New World. I trust you are aware that America is a republic now?'

Sophie gasped. 'You are a duke's daughter, *madame*? But why did you never tell me that?'

'Doesn't signify, that's why,' replied the dowager smartly. 'Who's to care in a place like Guadeloupe, anyway?' She looked up at Robert, pointing a no-nonsense finger at him. 'As for you,' she said in a peremptory tone, 'just because you've got blue blood doesn't make you a paragon.'

Robert turned away, his cheeks red, and Sophie felt sorry for him. It was clearly not every day that he was dressed down by a total stranger twice in one night — or accused of being stuffy by his own mother.

Madame Guillaume leaned towards François, who sat at the other end of the *chaise-longue* from her. Clearly, she had taken a shine to the man. 'Very good cognac, sir, if I may compliment you.'

He refilled her glass with a smile. 'You were about to divulge your plans, *madame*.'

'Was I indeed? Very well, since you are all so hang-dog about this.' Sophie wished she'd used some other expression, but Madame Guillaume sailed blithely on through her blunder. 'As I explained to Sophie and her young man here,' — at this Sophie's cheeks flamed — 'my husband and I had tried to get treatment for my son, to no avail. He was not well up here,' she said, tapping a finger to her silver hair, 'and I always knew that one day he would go too far and come to a messy end. Of course, I never expected it to be in my own house, but there, that was God's will, wasn't it, Father?'

Father Cassel merely raised his eyebrows at this interpretation.

She continued. 'I did hear the commotion that night, for I'd decided that I was hungry as well. I've always had a prodigious appetite, even though I'm not above eighty pounds. Hard work and honest living, that's what I say. So I came down to the kitchen to find Sophie. Instead I found my son.' She stared into her glass, obviously revisiting the abominable scene in her mind. 'There was nothing to be done for him. I knelt on the floor and closed his eyes, picked up the knife and set it on the table, and went to the open door. I saw Sophie running across the lawn in the dark, and I called to her, but she was too far away.

'When I turned back, I saw how much

blood was on my nightgown and hands, and I knew what I must do. I summoned the servants and told them my son had gone mad and that I had killed him to save myself.'

Sophie gasped.

'They believed me, of course, and so did the authorities. Why would they not? I was drenched in blood, and they all knew Louis was quite capable of fits of dementia.'

She glanced across at Sophie, who was crying softly into her handkerchief. 'We buried him in the family plot, next to his father, and I mourned him, Sophie, because he was my son, because of the tiny babe he had once been, innocent and sweet. But I have never mourned the man he became, nor have I ever blamed you for his death.'

Sophie jumped up from her chair and ran to the woman who had been the second most important person in her life after her mother. She threw herself into her arms and hugged her till the breath stopped in her breast.

'There now, that's quite enough. If you hadn't been so quick to sneak aboard the *Deliverance*, I should have found you sooner and put your mind to rest. My agents have had the devil's own job to find you.'

Jean-Michel was staring in astonishment at her. She grunted. 'It was you, wasn't it, who sank Jack Morgan's ship?' He made no reply, but Sophie saw the muscle clench in his jaw. 'Bah. I found out easy enough, while I was searching for Sophie. You should have been more careful, young man! You could have blown my Sophie to kingdom come! What did you want to do a fool thing like that for, anyway?'

Jean-Michel sent her an incredulous look. 'I — er . . . it's a long story.'

'Hmm. Well, I expect we've had quite enough of those for one evening,' the dowager acknowledged.

But the Duc de Chambois was not willing to let it pass. As a tray of sweetmeats was brought in and offered around, he crossed to his son. 'What's this about you and this ship, Jean-Michel? I didn't know you were a privateer?'

'You blew the ship up?' his mother, who was quickly at his elbow, further enquired. 'For what purpose?'

He held up his hands in defeat. 'As I said, 'tis a long story. And no, I am not a privateer,' he added, lowering his voice so that the servant with the tray might not overhear; fortunately he was on the far side of the room, occupied with Madame Guillaume and her efforts to ply Sophie with custard tarts.

'Well,' replied his father, clearly not pleased

by the turn of events, 'you'd best stop carrying on like that, or it will be you who will feel the hangman's noose about your throat.'

Jean-Michel grimaced. 'You may rest easy, sir. I do believe these last weeks have made me lose my taste for the sport anyway.' He caught François's eye and excused himself from his parents.

'So,' murmured his brother-in-law, as he twirled the cognac in his goblet, 'perhaps it was not Morgan after all whose spies were making enquiries about the *Deliverance*.'

'Yet you heard he had posted a reward? Surely it could not have been — ?' They both looked at Madame Guillaume, now smiling and chatting animatedly to Léonie, with Sophie sitting on a stool at her feet demurely munching on a tart. Jean-Michel's heart went out to her, his relief that she would not be held to account for her moment of panic almost overwhelming. It came to him then that he loved Sophie, that he couldn't bear the thought of letting her go.

'I don't know,' he said. 'But I think I might ask her when I can get her alone.'

He crossed to the ladies, patting his sister on the shoulder. 'Léonie, I think we could all use some entertainment. Why don't you sing for us?'

'Me? Jean-Mich, are you quite gone mad? Was it not you who accused me of being able to sing in any key as long as it was Cacophony Major? Oh, very well,' she grumbled, seeing that he wished to be left alone with the others. 'I shall see if Mother will do the honours. I can safely be trusted to play an accompaniment, I think.'

Jean-Michel took the place she had vacated and smiled down at Sophie, his heart feeling so full when she timidly returned his gaze that it almost pained him. Tomorrow. Tomorrow he would speak to her. Meanwhile, he engaged Madame Guillaume in conversation, gradually edging towards his question concerning the *Deliverance*. His face fell when he discovered it was indeed not the Caribbean dowager who had posted the reward.

So Jack Morgan *was* out for his blood after all.

14

Sophie felt a great calmness spreading through her as the evening wore on. Just to see Madame Guillaume again and hear from her own lips that she had been forgiven, lifted an extraordinary weight from her shoulders. She felt almost giddy with it, although her relief was tempered by the knowledge that *madame*'s assumption of the guilt did not free Sophie from the actuality of the crime.

While she might be free to continue with her life, she would forever have the stain of murder upon her soul. It was a sobering thought.

Jean-Michel joined her after the entertainments were concluded. She smiled at him sadly. 'Thank you for your support during dinner. I thought I was actually going to faint and disappoint Madame Guillaume hopelessly.'

'I think she was proud of the way you explained yourself. She certainly found no fault with your narrative — except perhaps a little unwarranted modesty.'

Sophie blushed, quickly turning the subject to more practical matters. 'At what time must

I be ready, tomorrow?'

He frowned, his grey eyes dark. 'You still wish to go to Nova Scotia, even though there is no longer any need?'

'Of course. What else would I do?'

He made a gesture of frustration. 'Why, stay here, of course. Or return to Guadeloupe. Madame Guillaume has said she would be delighted to have you return with her.'

Sophie shuddered. 'I could never live there again, especially in that house. It would be too painful. All those reminders . . . '

'Very well,' he said impatiently. 'I understand that, but surely you have been exonerated. You are free to do whatever you wish now.'

'What I wish,' she said, tilting her face up so that she could look fully at him, 'is to create a new life as something more than a lady's companion. Something useful, whereby I might shrive my sin.'

'But that's ridiculous!' he exploded, running a hand through his hair. ' 'Twas not your fault! The madman would have done heaven knows what and — '

'And 'thou shalt not kill',' she answered firmly. 'I do not recall the Commandments containing any marginal notes explaining under what circumstances breaking the rules might be permitted.'

Jean-Michel opened his mouth, started to speak, and then snapped it shut in frustration. He turned, looking about and then calling to Father Cassel, who stood at the window leaning on his cane and gazing out into the rainy night.

'Yves, may we speak with you a moment?'

The old priest hobbled across the carpet with a smile on his face. 'If I may be of service, Jean-Michel.'

'Indeed, I hope so. Sophie says that if she doesn't traipse away into the wilds of the north and save a few heathens then she will burn in Hell. Tell her she's being an addlepate, will you?'

The old man's brows rose. 'Are you quite sure those were her words, young man?'

'Indeed, they most certainly were not, *mon Père*. Jean-Michel simply believes I can remain here as the children's nanny as though nothing ever happened. Please make him understand that tonight's events change nothing. I am as determined as ever.'

'Are you determined?' he asked.

'Now do you see, Sophie?' the *vicomte* asked, clearly exasperated. 'Even Father Cassel doesn't think it's necessary.'

'I don't believe I said anything of the kind,' the priest answered in his own defence. 'Perhaps, Jean-Mich, you are only adding to

318

the confusion. Sophie has had a difficult day, a day during which much in her life has changed. She must decide for herself what is in her heart and act accordingly.'

Sophie looked triumphantly at Jean-Michel, who stood staring down at her, his expression thunderous in the lamplight. 'At least Father Cassel understands,' she replied.

'Mmm. Perhaps,' the old man answered, adding with a mischievous gleam in his eye, 'but of course, staying at La Tour House may well be a form of purgatory in itself. Should that fail, perhaps I could check my attic for a hair shirt you might borrow.'

And with that enigmatic rejoinder, he shuffled away to speak to François, leaving Sophie staring at him in dismay.

★ ★ ★

Sophie awoke to a beautiful spring morning entirely at odds with her mood. She had lain awake much of the night, reliving the horrible scene in the banqueting hall last evening, over and over in her mind, until she found herself trembling in a cold sweat.

Now she was exhausted. Yet she knew that she must be ready for her departure by noon.

She was lying in bed, staring up at the

floral bedcurtains and trying to imagine what her new life would entail, when Danielle entered the chamber bearing a silver tray.

'*Bonjour, mamselle,*' she said a little breathlessly, setting the tray down on the night stand. Her dark eyes were wide as she helped Sophie sit up, plumping the fat pillows behind her, and then silently — warily, almost, Sophie thought — passing her a cup of hot chocolate.

'Danielle, is something amiss?'

The black maid shook her head swiftly, lowering her eyes. 'Nothing, *mamselle.*' She turned away and began to fuss about the room, opening the curtains and spending an age over the ties, then going to Sophie's new trunk to remove clothes, folding and refolding them while she babbled on about the weather and various inconsequential topics.

Finally Sophie could stand it no more. 'Danielle, pray do leave those poor garments alone and tell me what is bothering you. Why, I have never seen you so agitated. Has something happened?'

The girl dropped her hands to her sides as though burned. 'No, *mamselle.* Not yet.'

Sophie frowned. She patted the coverlet. 'Come,' she said softly. 'Sit here and tell me what has you so flustered.'

The maid crossed to the bed, but she did

not sit. Instead, she stood staring down at Sophie with her eyes like black moons.

'I — I may not speak of it, *mamselle*. No one may. Else we shall all be let go.'

'Let go?' Sophie was becoming alarmed. 'Who says such a thing? And speak of what? What is it you are prevented from speaking of?'

'You, *mamselle*,' came the whispered reply. '*Monsieur le Duc* said we were none of us to speak a word or we should all be sent off without a reference.' Tears filled the girl's eyes. 'What would become of us, *mamselle*? Where should we go?'

'Speak of me?' Sophie repeated. Then comprehension dawned. 'Oh, dear,' she said with a sigh.

'Is it true, *mamselle*?' Danielle whispered, leaning closer. 'Did you truly kill a man with a knife?'

Sophie closed her eyes, willing this conversation away. But when she opened them, Danielle was still standing over her. 'Yes, Danielle, I did kill a man, but not intentionally and only to save myself in a fit of terror.'

'*Nom de Dieu*,' the girl said, standing back and blessing herself. 'So it was true. When Maurice and the others came back from the banqueting hall last night with their tales, we could scarcely believe such a thing. Why, not our Sophie, we all said. Madame Marlotte dropped an entire capon on the floor and the head gardener's dog made off with it without so much as a scolding. Then this morning, we were all summoned to the kitchen, every last servant — even those who don't work in the house — and *Monsieur le Duc* came. We were all terrified.'

'François came to the kitchens?'

'Indeed. And he told us that he knew we were all prattling about what had been said last evening. We never said a word, but our faces were as red as Madame Marlotte's best lobster, so he knew. Then he told us that if ever a single word of it leaked out from the estate, he would know 'twas one of us, and we would *all* be let go without a commendation. No exceptions, he said.'

Sophie sank back against the pillows, touched that François would come so strongly to her defence. 'Whatever must you all think of me,' she said tiredly. 'I am so sorry to have caused this trouble. Please tell them that. At least I shall be gone today, so you can rest easier.'

She was surprised when Danielle grasped her hand. 'You have not caused us trouble, *mamselle*, and we none of us want you to go.'

'That is kind, but I must. My life is not here. And now you must help me get ready. I dread goodbyes, and I have so many to make this morning.'

So Danielle helped her bathe and dress and then packed the last of her things into the trunk that François had given her as a parting gift. Léonie had insisted she take every last gown and shawl and frippery she had been given during her stay as payment for her work with the children, and then François had paid her handsomely in gold as well and would hear no objections concerning the money.

She had made her farewells to everyone except Léonie, whom she found resting in her private parlour with baby Aimée in her arms.

'Come in, Sophie!' she called softly. 'We have been waiting for you.'

Sophie bent over the tiny bundle in the duchess's arms. The baby was awake, staring up at her with solemn grey-blue eyes.

'Take her,' Léonie said, offering the child, but Sophie stepped back quickly.

'I would not wish to harm her. She is still so tiny.'

'Indeed she is,' came the somewhat disappointed reply.

Sophie wondered why the duchess should

323

wish her to hold her baby. 'If you are tired, *madame*, I can call the nurse.'

'Not at all,' Léonie replied brusquely, swinging her legs down to make room for Sophie. She patted the seat beside her. 'Sit down, my dear. I have had no chance to speak to you about your plans since last night's extraordinary events. Have you decided to stay with us now that you are free?'

Sophie swallowed. 'Er, no, *madame*. I — I am leaving at noon.'

'*Quoi*! But for what possible purpose?'

'Just because Madame Guillaume herself forgives me for what I did, does not reduce the fact that I took her son's life. 'Tis I who must make amends as best I am able, *madame*.'

'But as a *réligieuse*?' Léonie seemed faintly appalled. 'Oh, Sophie, I beg you to reconsider. Such a life . . . such deprivation . . . such, such . . . ' She waved a hand as she sought the appropriate epithet. 'Such *quietness*!'

Sophie laughed. 'Is not for everyone, I agree.' She understood how a woman of such boundless vivacity would quickly suffocate under the regime of the cloister. 'But for me, who is used to my own company — '

'And Jean-Mich!' Léonie continued as if

Sophie had not spoken. 'How can you just leave him like this? He will be heartbroken.'

'*Madame*! Your brother and I are . . . ' She sought a description that was at once honest and discreet. 'That is, we are . . . friends, perhaps, though he may consider me no better than a nuisance after all the trouble I have caused.'

Léonie let forth a peal of laughter that caused the baby to squirm. 'Methinks you have had your eyes too much in your Prayer Book, my dear, if you think that.'

'No, *madame*. And even if it were more than that — which it is not — after last night he would not wish to have me close at hand, most especially not where I might contaminate the children's minds.'

'Bah!' Léonie retorted inelegantly. 'You are beginning to sound like my brother Robert. You forget, dear heart, that my twin brought his only daughter into my care when his wife died, knowing full well that I had killed a man. More than one, actually.'

Sophie paled. 'But that was in battle, *madame*.'

'From your description of events in Guadeloupe, it sounded rather as though you were engaged in a battle yourself.'

Sophie hung her head.

'Sophie, are you sorry you killed Monsieur Guillaume?'

Her head shot up. 'Of course! How could I be otherwise?'

Léonie shrugged, moving the baby to rest in the crook of her other arm and stroking her velvety skin with a finger. 'I am not sorry.'

Sophie was horrified. 'But the taking of a life — '

'Is sometimes necessary,' came the simple reply. Léonie turned her attention forcefully upon Sophie then. 'Have you never considered, Sophie, what might have been if you had not been holding that knife? He would have done whatever he wished, you know. And not just once. Men like that — ' She shuddered, clasping Aimée more tightly to her breast as if to protect the babe. 'They enjoy the misery they inflict, and once is never enough. Had you not stopped him, he would have used you again and again, until the only freedom left to you would have been to take your own life for the shame of it. And then you would not have been able to do your good works and shrive your sin, would you?'

Sophie's cheeks were burning, her eyes wide with horror as she absorbed the ghastly picture the duchess presented. That a lady should even be able to imagine such horrors amazed and disturbed her.

'You have seen so much, *madame*. I had not thought — '

'Don't be sorry, Sophie,' she added, patting her hand. 'Unless that sorrow be for the necessity of defending yourself. I am not in the least sorry for the men whose lives I took. They would have killed me, and maybe even my beloved François had I done otherwise, and then my beautiful children, even little Aimée, here, would never have been born.'

'But do you not fear eternal damnation?' she asked on a whisper.

Léonie considered that, stroking the baby's tight red curls. 'No. I would kill any person who tried to harm one of my children, and while I would regret the necessity, I would never deplore the action.'

Sophie reached out to stroke the baby's hand. Her tiny fingers instantly gripped her index finger, surprising her with their strength. 'I am not sure I quite see the world that way,' she replied. 'But then I have never been a mother.'

'Nor will you,' Léonie replied smartly, 'if you give all of yourself to God.'

'Why do you hate the idea so much?' Sophie asked, as Léonie got to her feet.

'Because there is something about you that makes me feel you have other gifts. Your talent with children, for instance, and the way you have brought the spark back into my brother's eyes. Now, I must make use of the necessary. Hold Aimée for me, will you?'

Without awaiting an answer, she dumped the child in Sophie's lap and hurried through to the adjoining bedchamber where her private bathroom was.

Sophie clutched the precious little scrap of life to her, finding she enjoyed the milk-sweet scent of her skin and her soft breath on her neck. The baby began to fuss, so she stood, walking about the sunny room with the baby against her shoulder, rubbing her back gently and murmuring. Soon, the grizzling stopped. Sophie brought the child into her arms again and smiled down at her. Aimée stared back, her little mouth slightly parted in what Sophie almost imagined was a smile.

Her eyes filled with unbidden tears as she understood what the duchess had said. Perhaps she *would* give her life — or even take another's — to protect this innocent God-given trust, this unspoilt, perfect human life.

A deep longing filled her as she stood in the silent room holding the baby with the sun warming her back. She stared into the face of the tiny infant, then bent and kissed the petal-soft skin. Aimée seemed to smile at her, emitting a contented gurgle through her tiny pink mouth, and Sophie laughed back.

When Léonie returned moments later, she took the child without a word, but the knowing smile on her lips made Sophie wonder if perhaps she had designed her absence with a purpose.

* * *

Sophie arrived at the harbour in François's coach, a few minutes before noon. The *Némésis* stood at the wharf, resplendent in her gay blue and white, with the American flag flying high in the cheerful breeze. So different was the picture from the dangerous vessel painted entirely black, that Sophie could scarcely credit it was the same boat.

She was greeted on board by Captain Zamore and taken to Jean-Michel's cabin. A curious sense of *déja vu* overtook her as she lay her wrap and hat upon the narrow cot. Everything was the same, as real as the image engraved upon her mind. Except there was a heavy vase of spring daffodils, set on a thick rubber mat, brightening the desk.

She turned as a knock sounded.

'*Entrez!*'

Sophie held her breath as Jean-Michel

entered. She had not seen him since the night before. He glanced about, his eyes taking in her trunk stowed at the bottom of the bed, her valise, straw hat and wrap.

'So,' he said at last, his face a mask, 'you are still determined to go.'

'Yes.'

He clasped his hands behind his back, his eyes dark as he looked down at her. She thought he would speak again, try once more to dissuade her from her path, but instead he turned sharply and left, closing the door behind him with controlled precision.

Sophie sighed. She had hoped he might make this easy for her, but clearly he was furious that she would not stay. She found herself feeling angry also, for why was it that Jean-Michel de Chambois believed he knew what was right for her more than she herself did?

It was not as though there was any reason for her to stay. The children had a new nanny, whom they seemed instantly to like, and Léonie's baby was safely born. She had no right to impose herself upon their family a moment longer.

Somehow she had not been able to persuade Jean-Michel that she needed her own life — her own family, and her own purpose. Sophie had to feel she had been put on this earth for a reason, and unless she discovered that purpose she knew she would never know a moment's peace.

She went up on deck as she heard the ropes being cast off. Zamore was standing beside the helmsman, talking in low tones, and the crew were busy with their duties. The boat was being towed away from the wharf, out into clear water, then the line was cast off and the dinghy pulled away. Moments later the first sails were hoisted. She looked up watching the sailors scuttling about in the rigging like a bunch of sure-footed monkeys in a tree.

The light breeze caught the heavy canvas, snapping it into fullness like a crisp bedsheet on washday. The boat responded, the hull feeling the resistance of the water as it was pulled into the roadstead. They sailed thus down the waterway until finally Massachusetts Bay opened before them, then more sails were raised and the vessel began to weave earnestly through the waves.

Still Sophie stood at the rail, watching the green and gold countryside slip away behind, feeling both sadness to be leaving so beautiful a place, and excitement at what lay ahead.

Evening brought a rich swell to the Atlantic coast, and Sophie's land legs got the better of her. She declined dinner and took to her bed, finding sleep a welcome respite from the unaccustomed motion of the boat.

She arose gingerly next morning, but discovered that her stomach was more settled. The rest had clearly done her good.

She breakfasted sparingly on crusty rolls and preserves brought to her by Pierre, the cabin boy, whose music had so entertained her on the voyage from Guadeloupe. He seemed delighted to see her and fussed about, trying to discover ways to make her more comfortable for the short trip to Halifax. She sent him away with a smile, asking only that he return that evening with his hurdy-gurdy.

The day was as mild as Monday had been, and her spirits lifted as she went above, tying the ribbons of her straw bonnet as she went. Zamore greeted her as soon as she reached the deck.

'*Bonjour, mamselle*. I trust you are feeling a little better this morning?'

'Indeed, I am, thank you,' she replied with a smile, pleased to see the blackamoor again.

She joined him at the railing, gazing out at the iridescent blue waters and the endless blue bowl of the sky with nary a cloud to be seen.

She looked about, surprised to see they were beyond sight of land. 'I thought we would not be so far out to sea,' she told the captain.

'Not above a hundred miles,' he replied. 'You know *Monsieur le Vicomte*'s favourite rule.'

She laughed a little awkwardly, for she had not seen Jean-Michel since they had quarrelled in her cabin, 'Concerning a straight line being the shortest route?'

Zamore nodded, grinning.

Sophie glanced at him, wondering if this might not be a suitable time to approach a rather personal subject.

'Captain,' she said somewhat hesitantly, 'you will forgive my impertinence, but I cannot help but wonder . . . '

'*Oui, mamselle*?'

She flushed, thinking that it was after all none of her concern. She should not interfere.

'Never mind,' she said with a shake of her head. ' 'Tis none of my affair.'

He looked down at her, his lips turned up slightly at the corners. 'Perhaps it is none of *your* affair, *mamselle*, but it sounds to me as though it may well be mine. Pray, do not be shy. I have sailed over the seven seas and seen and heard most things.' He leaned down, his dark eyes teasing, and she thought what a very handsome man he was. 'I do not blush easily.'

She grinned. 'Very well. I merely wondered whether you have ever considered marrying.' There, it was said.

His brows lifted, and despite his proclamation, he flushed deep crimson. 'Well,' he replied after a moment. 'Yes, I suppose I have, like most men. But I mind what *Monsieur le Vicomte* says — we mariners are a bad risk. We are scarcely at home, and with all the dangers of the oceans, what kind of husbands do we make?' He shrugged, looking out over the crystal blue of the Atlantic.

'*Quelle sottise!*' Sophie replied spiritedly, borrowing the expression from Léonie without a moment's thought. 'A woman who marries a sailing man knows the risks. That does not prevent her falling in love.'

Zamore's expression became puzzled and he turned to look at her.

'You will forgive me the indelicacy, *mamselle*, but is this purely a hypothetical conversation, or are you speaking of someone

334

specific? Yourself, perhaps?'

Sophie hastened to dispel any such notion. 'I speak of you, Captain, and a . . . certain young lady who holds you in considerable esteem.'

'Really?'

'Surely you know of whom I speak?'

Now he looked discomfited. 'Perhaps you should tell me.'

'Very well. During my stay at La Tour House, it has become abundantly clear to me that Danielle is in love with you, sir. I cannot believe you are entirely blind to her admiration.'

The captain stared at her, seemingly lost for words, his mouth opening as if he meant to speak, and then closing again without a sound.

'Well, Captain? Do you mean to tell me you have no feelings for the girl?' Sophie was enjoying herself, for she could clearly see the emotion that filled his eyes. She sighed pretentiously. 'Obviously Danielle was right. A man in your elevated position would never notice a simple soul such as she.'

'Danielle is not simple!' he replied, blustering with indignation.

'Ah, then you do recall her?'

Zamore turned back to the ocean, mumbling.

'I'm sorry, Captain. I do not believe I caught that?'

'I said she would never look at me,' he replied without turning.

Sophie harrumphed. ' 'Tis precisely what she said of you, sir. Why do you not ask her?'

He turned then, an expression of such bashful hope in his eyes that Sophie almost laughed.

'It would be the best way to ascertain her feelings, do you not think?'

'Mmm. Perhaps.'

'Of course,' Sophie added airily, 'if she were to think there was no hope, she might set her sights elsewhere.'

'Elsewhere? You mean she'd go after some other — '

'Time is passing, Captain, and Danielle is a very beautiful girl. No doubt she has had her share of offers.'

That rattled the man. She saw his jaw clench, and deeming the fish to have taken the bait, she bid him good morning and left him to his empty ocean.

But she felt certain that when the *Némésis* returned to Boston harbour, Danielle would be receiving a gentleman caller.

★ ★ ★

Zamore did not come to the *grande chambre* for dinner, but Jean-Michel did. Sophie greeted him cordially, but with Pierre present all the time, at first serving them and then staying to entertain them with tunes on his hurdy-gurdy, there was no opportunity for conversation of a personal nature. Sophie enquired as to their sailing time to Halifax, and was told they expected to make harbour on Thursday. Jean-Michel enquired as to whether her cabin was comfortable and if she needed anything, and she replied in the positive and the negative respectively.

Finally, he dismissed Pierre, and Sophie found herself alone with him, not at all sure the situation was to her liking. She knew there was nothing further to say. She loved him, but that was her secret burden. She could not break her vow to devote the remainder of her days to the service of others; indeed, she felt the responsibility doubly now that she had been spared the pain and humiliation of paying for Louis's death here on earth.

She set her napkin down upon the table and rose, only to find a restraining hand on her arm.

'Stay,' he said. 'Please.'

Sophie suppressed a sigh, but she sank back into her seat.

'There is something I would say to you before we reach Halifax, and I may not get another chance.'

From the expression on his face, Sophie knew that whatever it was, Jean-Michel was having considerable difficulty phrasing it.

'I hope you are not going to waste time on further entreaties to me to return to Boston,' she stated, 'for it would be entirely pointless. My mind is made up.'

He glared at her, his eyes storm grey. 'I have exhausted that avenue, clearly,' he said. 'But I believe I may know the reason. And while I would not perhaps have chosen this path otherwise, you have forced me to it.'

Sophie's mouth fell open, wondering whatever he was plotting now.

'You must marry me,' he said abruptly, 'and then you will have the family you so want to find. Rose-Marie wants it, as you know, and it makes perfect sense from every angle.'

'Perfect sense!' Sophie jumped up, tipping her chair backwards onto the floor in her outrage. 'How dare you?' She spread her arms, her mouth agape with a thousand objections to such a bald proposal. 'There is no 'must' involved here, *monsieur*. I do not have to marry you, and I seek my *own* family, not someone else's. And let me tell you,' she added, bending across the table and jabbing him in the chest with one finger, 'I would never marry anyone unless it were for love. Your daughter has a wonderful substitute mother already, and your attempt to bring her into this is utterly deplorable!'

She stormed around the table and headed for the door, coping effortlessly with the rising and falling deck in her outrage. 'You cannot bear that I should have my own life to lead, Jean-Michel de Chambois, but I am happy with my choice, I — Oh!'

She gasped as his mouth descended on hers and his arms encased her in steel bands. His kiss was urgent, punishing, and tasted far, far too intoxicating. Sophie felt her temper subside momentarily with the delicious torment, and then return with the force of a gale as she realized what he was doing.

She pushed him away. 'No! You shall not — '

'Tell me you do not love me, Sophie Lafleur,' he said, his voice dangerously low and his face scant inches from hers. 'Go on, say the words before God — if you can!'

She gazed at him, feeling something tearing deep within her heart. Oh, how she wanted to agree, to speak those precious three words, but she could not. Too many things prevented it. Her eyes slowly filled with tears, but her lips remained mute.

He softened his grip slowly, setting her away from him, his eyes betraying a mix of desolation and frustration. 'So, you are still determined. How skilled you have become at falsehood, Sophie. I doubt you even recognize the lies you tell.'

'Indeed I do,' she whispered brokenly. 'I detest lying, nor am I the least bit good at it. Why even you saw through my story in the Caribbean.'

He stepped away, running both hands through his dark red hair. '*Au contraire*, my dear. You practise your deceits until they become your reality.' He gave a short bark that wasn't quite a laugh, turning to look mockingly at her. 'Every time you say you want to be a *réligieuse*, you lie.' He pointed a finger at her. 'I know you. I know what you want.'

'And pray, what is that?' Sophie replied, her voice as shaky as her knees.

'You want to be a woman. A *whole* woman.'

She gasped. 'And what makes you think a nun is less than a whole woman?'

'I do not speak for others,' he stated. 'But God gives us all special gifts, gifts that cannot be denied if we are to be whole. Yours are many, but they include love — love for children, love for beauty and life. You are trying to convince your heart that you love only duty and obedience.'

'Duty to God *is* a part of love.'

'You know what I mean,' he replied, coming to confront her again. 'You are not meant for that life, Sophie. It will not suit.'

'And you think I should marry you instead, 'because it makes sense'?' she replied archly. And before she could lose her temper again, she turned quickly and marched from the room.

15

He did not speak to her again. Sophie found her outrage quickly replaced by sadness that Jean-Michel should offer marriage as a last resort. Did he think the prospect of life in mission work was so dismal that she would accept any way out — even a doorway into a loveless marriage, for that would surely be what it was? *He* had not spoken of love after all, and despite her own deep feelings for him, she would never put herself in such a heart-breaking position. After all, had Sophie believed that Madame Guillaume's assumption of guilt freed her from blame, then she would surely have been eager to accept the woman's invitation, and return to Guadeloupe.

But no, Jean-Michel had resorted to a virtual order to marry! The effrontery of his proposal left her breathless with astonishment every time she recalled his words — which was far too often for her peace of mind during the course of the next day.

As the dinner hour approached on Wednesday, Sophie deemed it expedient that she remain in her cabin. The ship would dock the next day, and she had no desire to engage in any further battle of words with Monsieur de Chambois. She told Pierre she would eat in her cabin.

But Jean-Michel's thoughts were not on dinner. Nor did he have the leisure to dwell any longer upon the unpleasant scene that had transpired the previous evening. He and Zamore were at the rail, spyglasses in hand.

'What do you think?' the captain asked.

Jean-Michel felt a creeping sensation run up his spine, but shook it off. 'A slaver, perhaps. 'Tis too far away to tell.'

The object of their curiosity was a clipper — like theirs, of Baltimore design — making slow progress in a south-westerly direction not half a league from their port side. She appeared to have some trouble with the square sail on her foremast, though from such a distance they were unable to ascertain the nature of the problem.

'She's not signalling distress,' Zamore concluded. 'We'll be able to tell as we get closer.'

'I don't like it,' Jean-Michel said, glancing at the low band of coastline that lay clearly visible to the west now that they had reached the southern tip of Nova Scotia.

The *Némésis* was tacking, in order to make use of the sweet wind that had blessed them since their departure from Boston, and it pulled away from the ailing vessel for a time. But when the ship turned about and came back along its zigzagging path north, the distance to the other Baltimore Clipper was halved. Now, several of its sails were down, and they could see the crew scrambling about.

Suddenly, Jean-Michel swore and he pulled the spyglass from his eye. 'Dammit, Zamore, can you smell that?'

The captain frowned, lifting his nose to the wind. He set his mouth in a grim line. 'I can hear it, too.'

It was true. As the sun slowly settled behind the headland, they stood side by side and contemplated the low keening of human voices that carried in the breeze, bringing with it the unmistakable odour of unwashed bodies housed in cramped quarters. They had each of them smelled that stench before, and neither had a wish to repeat the experience. The two men glanced at each other.

'Well?' Jean-Michel said.

Zamore frowned. 'They have the advantage. They know we are here.'

The *vicomte* nodded. 'We could pass by — return after dark.'

'They would still see us. We are too pretty for stealth.'

Jean-Michel grimaced. He'd forgotten the *Némésis* was wearing her elegant suit of blue and white. What he would give for a quick repaint in obscuring black, he thought savagely, for if there was one thing in this world that fired his anger it was slavery. And he was now quite certain that the disabled vessel carried a cargo of human ballast.

'*Un moment*,' Zamore growled. 'They're travelling south!'

'From whence, do you suppose?'

The captain shrugged. 'But if they are coming south, I'll wager those are not black men in the hold.'

Jean-Michel supplied the word. 'Indians,' he said, then let loose an expletive that would have done the lowest of his matelots proud.

By now the distance between the vessels was at its minimum. In another moment the helmsman would turn the wheel and tack back out to sea. Jean-Michel hesitated a moment, and then said quietly, 'We'll take her, Zamore. Order the men to their battle stations.'

★ ★ ★

Sophie became aware that something was amiss when she heard the grating sound of hatches being dragged about, and the

345

patter of feet on the deck above. She peeked out her door, finding the short hallway empty. She tiptoed to the open door at the end that led into the men's quarters, and stopped abruptly, pressing a hand to her mouth. Where before there had been plain bulwarks were now two open hatches gaping onto the sea on the port side, each brandishing a heavy cannon. Each cannon occupied a crew and each crew was busily engaged in loading the great iron guns.

Before Sophie could flee, the order was barked and the fuses lit. The deafening roar almost knocked her senseless, followed closely by a pall of acrid smoke that stung her eyes.

Coughing, her eyes blurred with tears, Sophie scrambled for her cabin at the back of the ship, reaching it only seconds before she heard the retort of an even larger-sounding cannon from the deck above. That gun she had seen, but she had not until now realized just what Jean-Michel had meant when he'd explained that the *Némésis* was outfitted with a few nasty surprises.

As the next volley was fired, she felt the small vessel tremble, and wondered if the special steel reinforcing of which he had spoken would prove sufficient to prevent the ship being torn apart by the recoil of its own secret weapons.

Sobbing with fright, she peered from the open window of the cabin. A vessel lay bare yards from the *Némésis*, its grimy hull miraculously undamaged, but some of the rails and decking torn away, and the foremast toppled. Some of the sails were alight, and sailors were desperately cutting them loose and pushing them overboard before the fire spread through the wooden ship.

Why would he stop to engage in battle? she wondered in frustration. From her vantage point, she could see only a couple of much less sinister carriage guns mounted on the other vessel. She doubted if they even carried any cannon. It hardly seemed a fair fight.

Suddenly, the pounding stopped. The sudden silence — of guns on both sides — was almost more unnerving than the din of battle. But more chilling still was the voice that carried across the narrow strip of water.

'Hold your fire, Chambois. 'Tis no use. I know it was you who sank the *Deliverance*, and I'll see you hang for it!'

Sophie blanched. It was the same voice she had heard the day she escaped from Guadeloupe — the captain of the *Deliverance*: Daniel Blackthorn. She pressed her fingers to her lips to keep from crying out as she heard

347

him laugh. 'Sink this accursed vessel if you will, but I have a hundred and twenty slaves aboard who'll go down with her!'

There was a shout from above and Sophie recognized Jean-Michel's voice as he replied. But his demand that Blackthorn surrender his ship was met with laughter, followed by a gigantic explosion. Sophie screamed. There was a tearing crash and part of the ceiling of the cabin ripped away above her head. Splinters of wood flew all about, raining down on Sophie, who dived for cover beneath Jean-Michel's desk.

As the dust cleared, she crept out, seeing daylight where there had once been beams in the ceiling. The hole was not large, but the cannonball — for that must surely have been the cause of the destruction — had not come from Blackthorn's slaver, but from the other side of the ship. And as she gazed up through the hole, she saw why. A much larger vessel towered over them to starboard, having presumably crept up on the *Némésis* while she was otherwise engaged, and its cannons were aimed broadside at close range.

She heard Jean-Michel surrender and then the sound of grappling hooks digging into the deck as the enemy prepared to board.

Sophie pulled back from the hole, looking about her in desperation. She had no desire to be captured by a load of cut-throat privateers defending their rights as slavers. She glanced about, considering hiding herself in the lockers beneath the bed, but knowing that it would be a likely place for anyone searching. She tried the desk, but it was too small, and finally turned to the quarter-gallery. The washstand! The small cabinet had two doors with brass handles. It was tiny, too small for any man . . .

But not for a slightly-built woman.

Quickly and quietly, Sophie squeezed her body through one of the doors, pulling her gown carefully after her. Just as she was about to close the door, she realized that anyone entering the cabin would see evidence of female occupation and would search in real earnest if she were not apprehended. With a whimper of fright, she untangled her limbs and climbed out, going swiftly to the other room to remove all traces of her stay. She jammed everything into her small wooden trunk, willing her hands to stop shaking, then with some difficulty hoisted the box onto her shoulder and pushed it out the window. It stuck momentarily, and she was obliged to give it a firm shove with her shoulder, then it splashed into the water below.

She could only trust that no one had

observed the action, for they would certainly deem it worth exploring, but once it was bobbing about on the water, it would be just one more piece of detritus let loose by the cannon fire.

No sooner had this been accomplished, than she heard heavy footsteps descending the stairs from the deck. She hurried back into the quarter gallery, shutting the door silently and jamming herself into the washstand cupboard without a care, banging her head and her elbow in the process. She yanked her gown in and tugged the door closed just as the door to the outer cabin was wrenched open.

With her fist pressed against her mouth and her eyes wide in the darkness, Sophie listened without understanding to the invaders' mocking tones. They ripped open desk drawers and dropped them to the floor, searching the lockers beneath the bed, just as she had expected. She held her breath as the door to the quarter gallery slammed back on its hinges.

'Huh!' said a rough voice in English. She did not understand their exact words, though their meaning was obvious as they took in the little bit of luxury. She heard the word 'aristos', though, and shuddered for Jean-Michel.

Then they left, their boots heavy on the

planking as they repeated the exercise in other cabins. She heard one or two hapless souls being discovered and taken away with much shouting in both English and French.

Still she remained in her tiny hiding place, trembling with fright lest they return. Her neck ached from being bent double, her legs and arms burned with pins and needles, but she would not come out. For what seemed like hours she remained there, praying and listening, until the ship fell silent. Then she heard a new crew coming aboard and within minutes the *Némésis* was once again under sail.

Eventually, when nature would simply be denied no longer, she crept from her hiding place, suffered the agonies of returning circulation while she used the necessary, and then sat on the wooden floor, listening to the rise and fall of the vessel and wondering where they were going and what would become of Jean-Michel, Zamore and their crew.

Eventually, exhaustion and the gentle rise and fall of the boat made her sleepy and she fell into a fitful doze full of dreams punctuated by loud noises and heavy boots. Jean-Michel was calling out to her, shaking her —

She jumped, stifling a scream as a hand

came down on her mouth.

'Hush, *mamselle*. Make no sound!'

Eyes wide, she stared up at Zamore, wondering whether he, too, was part of her dream. But the captain was as real as the creaking ship, and she felt a flood of relief so great that she hugged him.

'Zamore! I thought for certain you had been taken prisoner, too!'

He smiled grimly. 'I was below with the cannon crews when the second ship appeared. I decided I could do more good if I remained hidden. I have one other with me, but he is slightly wounded. Are you well, *mamselle*? How did you avoid capture?'

Sophie scrambled to her feet, steadying herself on the side as the ship plunged into an unexpected trough. 'I hid in the washstand.'

The captain looked dubiously at the tiny space. 'I could scarcely fit a dog in there.'

' 'Tis why they did not bother with it, for they searched the lockers and cupboards in the cabin most thoroughly.' Quickly, she explained how she had disposed of her belongings to avoid suspicion, and his eyes lit up.

'That was most resourceful, *mamselle*,' he said, speaking in low tones so his voice would not carry beyond the room. 'But soon you will be tested even more, for we are even now nearing Halifax harbour. The slaver is gone. I suspect the fault that caused them to heave to off the coast was merely a ploy, a decoy planted to distract us from the second ship that escorts us now.'

'They knew the *Némésis* was coming,' she agreed, 'for it was Blackthorn's voice I heard, threatening to hang Jean-Michel for the loss of his ship in the Caribbean. Oh, Zamore — ' Her voice broke, and she buried her face in her hands. 'What is to become of Jean-Michel and the others?'

He patted her back a little awkwardly, and she drew a deep breath, forcing away the useless tears. There were but three people free of the privateer's shackles, and one was injured. That meant it was up to her and Zamore to help the prisoners. To fail could mean their deaths.

'What can we do?' she whispered determinedly.

'You must remain here, where you can be safe. But be prepared at any moment to return to your bolt-hole, for Blackthorn is at the helm and who knows if he will decide to search the ship again. After we drop anchor, I shall go ashore and try to gain access to the brigantine. She is carrying some cannon like our own, which I shall spike in case we can make good our escape in the *Némésis* — we are seaworthy still, but another broadside and she could not make the journey home.'

'But I can't stay here!'

'Please. You must. I cannot protect you in the town if I am to make haste.' His dark eyes were so earnest, that she felt her opposition crumbling.

'Very well,' she agreed at last, sinking back upon the wooden floor, and wishing, uncharacteristically, that she had been born a man.

★ ★ ★

'Damn you to hell, Morgan,' Jean-Michel de Chambois said as he was led along a darkened hallway in what had to be the scruffiest most disreputable inn in all the town of Halifax.

The man who walked in front of him merely laughed, responding easily in French. 'I went to hell years ago, Chambois. Your curses don't frighten me.'

He opened a door and entered a room. Jean-Michel felt the sailor at his back press a pistol into his spine and knew he was in no position to argue. He followed.

They were in what probably passed for a parlour. The walls were grimy, the ceiling

354

hung with sooty cobwebs, and the fireplace sported a mean little flame that scarcely raised the temperature above the chill damp outside. Summer was slow to arrive in Nova Scotia.

Two wooden chairs sat by the hearth. Across the room, a rough table supported a single candle long-since burnt down to the stub, and the remains of someone's meal of the previous evening.

It was not long past dawn, and Jean-Michel was hungry, but one look at this establishment robbed him of his appetite most effectively.

'You cannot hold me, Morgan,' he said in passable English. 'Britain is not at war with America.'

Morgan, for his part chose to speak to his prisoner in French. '*Mais vous êtes Français, Monsieur le Vicomte!*' he said vehemently. 'And a pirate into the bargain!'

Jean-Michel fidgeted with the bonds that tied his hands behind his back. 'I am an American citizen, have been for years, and the *Némésis* flies the flag of the United States, as well you know.'

Morgan's blue eyes gleamed. 'Ah. So you are a privateer licensed by the American Government, then?'

Jean-Michel knew he was cornered. He

clenched his jaw for a moment. 'No.'

'By Monsieur Genet, perhaps?' he asked, referring to an errant French diplomat who had licensed American privateers by the hundreds under George Washington's very nose.

'No.'

'I see.' Morgan strolled to the grimy window, staring out with a half-smile on his lips. He was a handsome devil, Jean-Michel thought. A pity he would have to kill him if he were to get out of here alive. He glanced over his shoulder at the matelot whose pistol was still inches from his spine. He hoped the damn thing wouldn't discharge of its own accord.

'So, *monsieur*,' Morgan said, turning to regard him coolly from the other side of the room. 'You are just a common pirate on the high seas, after all. A strange occupation for a gentleman not in need of money, wouldn't you say?'

'I make no profit from my activities.'

An angry frown flitted across Morgan's face, but was gone in an instant, replaced by that bland smile again. 'That, I confess, is the part that has most confounded me. Most men, whatever their villainy, have simple motives.' He began to count them off on his fingers as he paced slowly in front of the fire. 'Greed, possession, revenge, self-aggrandisement. But you . . . ' He pointed one finger at Jean-Michel. 'You take a man's ship, set the crew free and sink the vessel, keeping not one sou from the cargo. And then' — here, his eyes glittered and Jean-Michel felt a moment's unease — 'and then you have the effrontery to send my creditors the bills of lading so that I am obliged to pay for the goods, and to write *me* a civilized — but unsigned — letter explaining exactly where this treachery took place. Did you expect that I would somehow find a way to raise the vessel from the abyss, or was your intention merely to add insult to injury?'

Jean-Michel shrugged, moving experimentally a few steps to one side to discover how the pistol-bearing guard would respond. The jab of steel against his ribs answered his question promptly enough.

'You took exception to my cargo, if I recall your note. You dislike first-quality Caribbean rum? Or perhaps it was the pineapples or the molasses in the hold that troubled you?'

'I took the *Deliverance*,' Jean-Michel replied as blandly as Morgan, for he would not give him the satisfaction of enjoying his undoubted disadvantage, 'because both the ship and its cargo were worth a small fortune.'

This was greeted by a moment's incredulous silence. Then Morgan jumped to his feet and began pacing the damp stone floor, his voice now rich with fury. 'Yet you did not sell the goods yourself, but sent them to the deep like a load of putrid fish heads?'

'I am in the mail business, sir. I do not sell merchantable items.'

'No, of course not,' Morgan replied sarcastically. 'You only sink those.' He sighed, perching himself on the edge of the heavy wooden table. 'Perhaps you would care to explain it to me. I should so hate to hang you before I have understood the reason for your hatred of me.'

Jean-Michel gazed at him, taking time before answering. He knew that Daniel Blackthorn would be here at any moment, and then it would be three against one. Right now, with Morgan so intent on solving his mystery, and the guard becoming a little bored with his duties, it might be Jean-Michel's only real chance. He contemplated the problem of his bonds, and the very real possibility that even if he were able to disarm the matelot, Morgan would almost certainly have a weapon about his person. And there was not the slightest reason to doubt that he would use it.

★ ★ ★

Sophie watched the lightening of the eastern sky above the hills that surrounded the harbour. Dark clouds covered much of the sky, so the sunrise was not as swift as it might have been and she wondered whether Zamore had been able to slip away in the gloom.

She could not see much of Halifax harbour from her vantage point in the cabin, for the rear of the *Némésis* faced away from the town. Yet she could discern enough to know that they were docked at the end of a wharf.

This was Canada. She stared out at the silhouette of hills, waiting for the expected exhilaration to hit. Yet all she felt was a nagging emptiness. No sense of homecoming. No delight in the possibilities of the future.

Jean-Michel, her traitorous heart whispered, where can you be?

She twisted her hands in her soft cotton gown, wishing she still had at least one of the beautiful shawls she had been given in Boston.

Unbidden, images of apple blossom and the smell of clover came to mind, and she smiled sadly as she remembered that day on the Common. How the light of laughter had lit Jean-Michel's eyes. How he had enjoyed teasing her, testing her determination. And Rose-Marie, her tiny arms clinging to Sophie's neck as she gave way to her fears about losing Léonie to childbirth.

Sophie's heart ached. She knew these things were not for her, and yet from this vantage point, imprisoned on a damaged ship in the middle of a strange harbour, they seemed dear indeed.

She sat up. She could not possibly sit here like a rag doll while Zamore went alone to try and rescue Jean-Mich.

Sophie Lafleur was no shrinking violet. Sophie Lafleur had killed a man. Perhaps this time, she could save one from death.

She got up quickly and left the cabin without the slightest idea of how she was going to escape the ship — but escape was exactly what she must do, promise or no promise. Zamore would understand.

She loved Jean-Michel de Chambois. Though she had done her best to deny it, she had known for a long time how much she cared for him. And it was her fault that he had been trapped by Blackthorn. And now, doubtless Jack Morgan had his evil hands on him.

She cringed at the thought of the retribution

Morgan might exact for Jean-Michel's campaign against him. Time was of the essence. She inspected the sailors' quarters, finding the vessel apparently deserted. From the floor beside one of the six-pounders, she retrieved some kind of an iron rod, which she secreted in the folds of her skirt.

Cautiously she tiptoed up the companionway steps, stopping as her head reached the upper deck. Two guards lounged beside the gangplank on the starboard side, their muskets leaning on the railings as they shared a pipe of pungent tobacco.

Slipping down out of sight, she pondered her options. She knew she could not take on two armed men, but what if . . . ?

She ducked back down the stairs and hiding behind the door to the *grande chambre*, withdrew the iron bar from her pocket. She raised it above her head and dragged it slowly across the planks of the ceiling.

She listened. The soft talk stopped, then began again, more volubly. She held her breath, knowing she did not have the advantage of understanding their language, but hoping that they would not both abandon their posts to investigate at the same time.

She was rewarded by the sound of a single set of footsteps crossing towards the companionway. She gripped her weapon more tightly, reminding herself of Léonie's claim that one must sometimes kill or be killed.

The sailor's footsteps came below and then stopped as he observed the slightly open door. She heard him curse — words that needed no translation — and then his fingers appeared around the edge of the door. Sophie held her breath and raised the iron bar silently, willing him to step into the room. Just as she was afraid her lungs would burst, he walked forward. Shutting her eyes, she slammed the bar down on his head, hearing his grunt as he fell.

Feeling suddenly nauseous, Sophie stared down at the man. How could she be doing this again? Had she not learned her lesson the first time? And yet she felt none of the terror of the night she had murdered Louis Guillaume. She inspected the body. There was no blood, and the man was breathing and moaning softly, so he was not dead. She blessed herself in a gesture of thanks, then stepped quickly past him out the door, concealing herself once more, this time behind the door of Jean-Michel's cabin.

A shout came from above. Clearly, the remaining guard had heard the fall and was concerned. Sophie closed her eyes, sending up a fervent prayer of thanks when she heard his much heavier tread upon the stairs.

Fortuitously, the injured man on the floor of the *grande chambre* groaned at that instant, drawing his companion's eyes away from Sophie's hiding place. He hurried to his aid, bending over just as Sophie crept up behind him and dealt another firm blow with her weapon. The big man crumpled onto the first without a sound, falling to the side.

Sophie did not wait. She dropped the iron bar and made for the deck. Without hesitation, she slipped down the gangplank just as the sun broke through the heavy morning cloud. With its welcome early warmth on her back, she hurried along the wharf. There seemed to be English soldiers everywhere, reminding her that this was a colony at war, but she kept her eyes down and ignored their lewd glances, praying that she would not be challenged — her French would tag her an enemy in an instant. Finally she slipped away into the safety of the streets, turning left and right at random along roads and alleys that seemed to be laid out with the most astonishing symmetry.

The way climbed, and she followed the grid of streets without any idea where she was heading. She paused on a corner, waiting while a coach and horses passed, the wheels sending up splatters of mud from the deep ruts in the roadway. A couple of young women were approaching, coming down the hill with their baskets of bread covered in red chequered cloths. They stared openly at Sophie, and she was just about to speak to them and ask directions, when she froze.

English! she thought stupidly. You do not speak English, Sophie! A stranger speaking only French here could easily be taken for a spy.

She turned away, tears in her eyes, and rubbed her chilled arms with equally cold fingers.

With no other choice, she hurried on, though her steps grew increasingly aimless as she considered the hopelessness of her situation. The streets became poorer, the houses smaller. At one crossroads, she stopped to get her bearings only to become aware of a conversation that she could actually understand taking place on a doorstep. A young man and a pretty girl in a much-mended gown stood flirting in the morning sun — speaking French!

With a sense of real relief, she approached, explaining that she was new here and did not speak English. She asked if they knew of an English privateer name Morgan. When they seemed mystified, she mentioned Daniel

Blackthorn, drawing an instant grunt of disgust from the girl.

'I know him, all right. Everyone knows Blackthorn.'

'Do you know where I might find him?'

'Stinking rat spends his time down at the Grey Goose Inn. Likes his beer with a few side orders, if you know what I mean. And he don't care if you're willing, neither.'

Sophie swallowed. 'Could you take me there, do you think?' she asked, knowing that she had no money to pay the pair, for she had not given a moment's consideration to the fact that her precious store of wages was stowed in the bottom of the trunk she had so carelessly tossed into the sea.

She would deal with that difficulty later. First she must find Blackthorn, for she was certain Jean-Michel would not be far away. Somehow, she would force the Englishman to set him free.

That this was a fantasy in the truest sense of the word, Sophie was fully aware, but just at present, when she was finally getting close to locating him, she had no wish to be that sensible. God would help her find a way.

'*Pas moi*,' the girl said. '*Maman* will skin me if I leave the house before I've done my chores.'

Sophie turned her eyes upon the young

man. 'Please. It is most important that I find him.'

'What do you want with the likes of Blackthorn, then?' the youth asked suspiciously. 'You don't look his sort, and he don't like the French.'

'He has stolen something very precious from me,' she said, knowing it to be true. 'And I intend to get it back.'

The young man's brows rose. 'You be a brave one, then,' he said. 'Come on, I can take you.'

He gave the girl a cocky wave and sauntered off, hands in pockets, as though he had not a care in the world. Sophie ran to keep up with his long easy stride, her heart pounding with a mixture of excitement and dread.

* * *

Daniel Blackthorn entered the parlour of the Grey Goose, followed by a pretty young girl in a filthy apron bearing a tray. She crossed the room to set the tray upon the table, glancing at Jean-Michel's bonds, then apprehensively at the pistol in the sailor's hand.

'Get off with you, girl,' Blackthorn muttered, giving her a swift kick as she darted from the

366

room, evidently too slowly for his liking. He grabbed one of the mugs of ale from the tray and began drinking thirstily, a bubble of froth trickling down his chin.

Jean-Michel's heart sank. Now he was truly outnumbered, though he noted with interest that Morgan's lip curled disdainfully at the sight of his partner. Clearly, Blackthorn was already drunk, despite the early hour.

'So, Daniel, you have caught my nemesis — pardon the pun, *Monsieur le Vicomte* — and delivered him to me. A pity you are not sober enough to tell me how you achieved it. No matter, you shall have the reward money, as promised. No doubt you had help?'

Blackthorn nodded, setting his tankard upon the table with a bang and wiping his mouth on his sleeve. His colourless eyes betrayed a gleam of satisfaction as he studied Jean-Michel.

'Herbert Wilkins. He was hiding in the *Kestrel II* in the Shelburne estuary. That is, until Captain high-and-mighty Chambois, here, took the bait and tried to steal the *Doubtless.*'

Morgan glowered. 'You never give up, do you, Chambois?'

Jean-Michel shrugged, twisting his wrists gingerly to ease the circulation in his hands. 'I seldom lose, either. Let's just say I was distracted.' He wasn't going to admit that he was not the captain of the *Némésis*, but merely its owner, for he had no wish to implicate Zamore in all of this. He was well aware that his captain had escaped capture, as, to his immense relief, had Sophie, though how that had happened was unclear.

If he was going to hang, so be it, but he was fairly certain that it would not occur as a result of a court of law. Otherwise, why would these brigands have brought him here to this filthy inn rather than straight to the town jail?

'Sir?' All three men turned to the sailor who was holding the pistol on Jean-Michel, albeit in a more relaxed fashion now that there were two other Englishmen to guard him.

'What is it?' Morgan asked.

The man's cheeks stained deep red and he indicated the door with his head. 'Nature, sir, if you wouldn't mind, sir.'

'Get out,' Morgan barked. 'And stay out. We can take care of the prisoner.'

The sailor relinquished his pistol to Morgan and scurried off to relieve himself. Jean-Michel wasn't averse to such an idea himself, but he could wait. Perhaps later . . .

As the sailor left, a different girl came in, her face averted shyly, carrying a tray laden with food. Jean-Michel glanced at her without interest, and then froze. Sophie! His heart began pounding fit to burst and he looked away, hoping he had not drawn attention to her by his reaction. She herself kept her head down, fussing over the table until Daniel Blackthorn bellowed at her. 'Begone, vixen, before I find some real use for you!'

She jumped, but still with her head averted crossed to the door, going out without a word. But just before it closed, she opened it again and walked calmly back into the room pointing a flintlock pistol directly at the two Englishmen.

'What the devil . . . ?' Blackthorn spluttered, his mouth once more awash with ale. Jean-Michel's eyes flew to Morgan, in whose hand the sailor's pistol hung loosely. If he raised it, he could undoubtedly kill Sophie long before her finger squeezed the trigger. Yet he made no move, staring at Sophie with an extraordinary expression on his face.

'Put that down instantly,' she told Morgan, her voice betraying only the slightest tremble, 'or I shall kill you.'

16

Sophie held the flintlock in both hands, surprised that they shook much less than she expected. Her knees trembled beneath her gown, but they were not to know that. Her rage at seeing Jean-Michel in their clutches was beyond both her comprehension and her control. All she truly knew at that moment was that she would happily kill both these Englishmen to have him safe.

I love you, Jean-Michel de Chambois, she thought, knowing that for now, nothing else on earth mattered. She could no more crush her feelings for him than undo the murder she had committed so long ago. Call it fate or weakness, either way she was no longer in charge of her destiny.

'Set it down,' she ordered the older of the two men, the one she assumed to be Morgan. To her relief, he did as she ordered, tossing it across the room so that it hit the wall and slithered to the floor.

Blackthorn laughed. 'Lucky for you he speaks French.'

Sophie ignored the comment, though she, too, was relieved. 'I will shoot you, if either one of you moves,' she stated, wondering which of them to trust the least. Her eyes flickered over Morgan's features again, an image passing through her mind that she could not quite grasp. There was something about the man, something almost familiar . . .

Blackthorn laughed, displaying a row of tobacco-stained teeth.

'I have killed a man before,' she said, gripping the weapon more tightly. Then she moved to the side of the room where she would be well beyond reach if one of them decided to lunge for her weapon.

'This becomes more interesting by the minute,' Morgan stated, resting his back against the window. 'Pray, tell me how you come to be here, rescuing this aristocratic pirate who has been trying to lay waste to my business.'

'Business?' Sophie voice was high with indignation. 'What kind of man are you that you dare to call trading in human flesh a 'business'? No, sir, do not answer that, for I know what you are, you and your Captain Blackthorn here.' She looked Morgan straight in the eye. 'Now untie Monsieur Chambois this instant.'

There was a hushed silence, punctuated only by a growling burp from Blackthorn as he staggered to his feet.

'Damn you, you young — '

'Enough! Hold your tongue, Daniel.' Morgan's sharp tone lightened as he returned his attention to Sophie. 'Pray enlighten me, *mamselle*. I believe I may at last be gaining some understanding of Monsieur Chambois's dislike.'

'You flatter yourself if you think 'tis so gentle an emotion, sir,' she replied. 'I have spent my life among slaves. I know what befalls a man or a woman stolen from his home and forced into the service of another. I have seen them die of hunger and disease, while their masters enjoy every luxury. Are you so conceited as to think no one condemns you for your despicable trade?'

Blackthorn was looking distinctly uneasy. 'She talks in riddles, Morgan. Stupid chit. Making up any old thing — '

'Silence!' Morgan's roar made Sophie jump, and Blackthorn pale. He continued, his voice now dangerously low, but his question was addressed full-face to his junior partner. 'Pray explain to me, Daniel — what precisely was the nature of the cargo aboard the *Doubtless*?'

Blackthorn waved a broad hand, then ran it through his rough-cut black hair. 'The usual,' he replied noncommittally.

'Indians,' Jean-Michel supplied. 'Micmacs, *sans doute*.' He was enjoying the way this was going. Sophie was behaving like a perfect little viper and his heart swelled with pride at the way she was standing up to this pair of bullies. His sister could have done no better.

Morgan regarded Jean-Michel for a moment, then turned his attention to Blackthorn. 'Indians?' he repeated softly.

Blackthorn began to bluster. 'Damn Godless heathens! We fetch a good price for them at auction. You've never complained about the profits!'

Sophie looked from one man to the other, realizing that she had unleashed something here. Clearly there was no love lost between these two men, and she could see why. For Jack Morgan seemed almost a gentleman, his clothes plain but clean, his hair neatly trimmed and his face clean-shaven. Blackthorn, on the other hand, smelled like he lived at this disgusting inn, and his face hadn't seen a razor in many a day.

But that was their affair. She had no interest in the business quarrels of two cut-throats. She waved the pistol that was becoming like a lead weight in her hands and repeated her order. 'Untie Monsieur

Chambois, Morgan. This instant, if you please.'

Morgan turned from Blackthorn to stare gravely at her, seemingly unconcerned by the pistol. For a moment he examined her face, her hair, even her body, yet she felt not the least threatened by him as she endured his unhurried scrutiny. Then he tipped his head to the side.

'As you wish.'

She was puzzled by his casual acceptance. It was as though he had suddenly lost interest in the man who had destroyed his beautiful flagship and almost captured another. Keeping most of her attention focused on Blackthorn, she watched Morgan take a knife from his boot and slash the ropes that bound Jean-Michel's hands. She sighed with relief as she saw him rub his wrists, a faint smile playing across his lips.

She smiled back, and in that instant, with her attention distracted for but a heartbeat, Morgan moved, so quickly she barely caught the flick of his wrist or the glint of the flying blade.

Sophie screamed.

Daniel Blackthorn made an odd gurgling sound through a throat that suddenly flowered scarlet with his own blood, and eyes wide, fell face-first on the floor at her feet.

She stared stupidly down at him, still training the flintlock upon his inert form as though he might leap up and grab it from her limp fingers. But he made no move. Only the pool of blood widened like an inkstain on the polished floor from the knife embedded in his neck.

There was a long silence broken only by the sound of a slop bucket being emptied into the street beyond the window.

Sophie looked at Jean-Michel. Then at Morgan.

'Why did you kill your own partner?' she whispered.

Morgan smiled. It was not an unpleasant sight, in fact it brought another curious twinge of recognition into Sophie's mind.

'You said you had already killed one man. I could not let you kill a second, could I? Anyway, 'twas the merciful thing to do. They would have hanged him — or worse, handed him to the Indians to deal with. He was lucky.'

'Lucky!' Sophie straightened the pistol once more. 'You kill a man in cold blood and then say he was lucky? What kind of monster are you, Jack Morgan?'

He shrugged, turning away a little, avoiding her eyes. Then he raised a hand and rubbed it across the side of his jaw.

Sophie frowned as an image flashed suddenly across her mind, like a painting on a gallery wall. She gasped.

'Jean-Mich!' she cried. 'His ring! Make him give his ring to me!'

Jean-Michel grimaced. 'Not while you're holding that thing. Who knows which one of us will get the bullet!'

She frowned. 'Then I shall take it, if I have to blow off his hand first.' She stormed across the floor, side-stepping the inert form of Daniel Blackthorn, until she stood directly in front of Morgan. Jean-Michel stepped forward, horrified that she would place them in danger so thoughtlessly.

Too late. Morgan was closer to the weapon than he was.

The Englishman smiled. 'So, you recognize my ring.'

'*Your* ring!' Her face was purple with rage. A bad sign, Jean-Michel knew. If he were Morgan, he'd relieve her of the pistol instantly, so abstracted was she by her fury.

'That ring belonged . . . ' she began, but then frowned, as though some strange sentiment had passed through her. 'Belonged . . . ' She turned, and Jean-Michel was amazed to see Morgan calmly allow her to pass the pistol to him. He grasped it quickly, for her gesture had been impatient and careless, and such weapons were less than trustworthy. But he felt better for having it, even if Morgan seemed not the least concerned.

What the devil is she up to now? Jean-Michel wondered as he watched her poke about in the neck of her gown. Then she uttered a most unladylike epithet, blushed furiously, and turned her back.

He exchanged a puzzled glance with Morgan, who smiled enigmatically. When they turned their attention back to Sophie, she was holding out her hand. It held a ring still attached to a long gold chain that hung about her neck. The ring was identical to the one Morgan wore, but smaller.

'Ah,' he said sadly. 'So Anne is dead after all.'

Sophie stared at him, her mouth open. 'What did you say?'

He slid off his own ring and laid it on her palm. 'Perhaps it is right that you should have them both.' He looked so sad, Sophie felt a numbness growing around her heart, spreading to her limbs, her tongue. She could not move. She could not speak. He continued, looking down at her with a bleakness that chilled her to the very soul. ' 'Tis the first time I have taken it from my finger since the day she gave it to me. But since she is gone . . . '

There was silence for a moment, then Sophie opened her mouth to speak.

'You . . . you are . . . ' She licked her lips, but her throat was so dry she could not utter the words.

He did it for her. '*Oui*, Sophie. I am your father.'

17

The silence that enveloped the room at that moment was absolute. For an endless minute that surely lasted a lifetime, no one either spoke or moved. Then a dog barked outside, breaking the spell.

Sophie grabbed the ring from her palm, inspecting it through the tears that filled her eyes.

No, it could not be.

It could *not* be!

She wiped the back of her hand savagely across her eyes and stared up at Jack Morgan.

'How can you be my father? My father is dead. And you are an Englishman. And a privateer. And a . . . and a slaver!' She all but spat the word through her lips, so disgusted was she with this impostor.

Morgan stood his ground, looking down at her without flinching. 'Firstly, I am no slaver. Nor did I have the slightest knowledge that any such business involved my ships. That was his concern entirely,' he added with distaste, pointing to the body of Blackthorn. 'Had I known how he was using my vessels, I would have dealt with him far sooner.

Secondly, I became a privateer for the sake of my family — for Anne and for you, Sophie. And, though you may struggle to comprehend the reason, I became an Englishman out of the same necessity.'

Sophie let out a short bark of disgust. '*Vraiment*? Some father! How is it there are not more fathers running off to change their identities and steal from the innocent for the sake of their families?' She turned away sharply, clutching both rings so tightly the gold cut into her palm. She was angry. So very angry, she could barely contain herself. She marched across the floor to Jean-Michel, snatched the flintlock from his hand and turned it upon Morgan.

'No!'

She heard Jean-Mich's cry of dismay at the same moment as the weapon discharged. Morgan crashed to the floor, spread-eagled across the body of his captain, and a burst of plaster seemed to explode from the far wall of the parlour.

She gave a cry of horror. 'Oh, God have mercy, I have done it again!'

Then she felt Jean-Michel pry the pistol from her fingers and push her onto a hard wooden chair.

'My love,' he said, his voice shaky, 'you are a danger to have around sometimes.'

She stared at Morgan, and then realized that far from his eyes seeing only the hereafter, he was looking straight at her.

A grin spread across his face and that grin became a laugh, a deep, sonorous, breathtakingly familiar laugh. A laugh that Sophie could remember so plainly it took her breath away with the suddenness of the memory it provoked — herself, aged no more than three or four, sitting upon her father's knee, her brother Pascal on his other, playing peekaboo through their father's fingers.

'*Sainte vierge,*' she whispered as she watched him clamber up from the floor and brush down his pants, still chuckling. How could she forget that laugh? She had never forgotten it, merely let it be swamped by later images — images of a beaten man, a man who could not provide well enough for his family to prevent his children dying. A man who had run away . . .

And taken that laugh with him.

She looked down at her hand, unfurling her palm and staring at the two rings, side by side. She reached around behind her neck and unfastened the gold chain, sliding off her mother's wedding ring. 'Here,' she said quietly, holding them out. 'They are both yours, now.'

Morgan stood up, silent for a moment.

Then he nodded, stepping across the room to her. He lifted the smallest band first, holding it in his hand and turning it this way and that to catch the dim light. Moisture dampened his eyes. He placed the ring back in her hand, then took the larger one and slipped it back upon his own finger.

'Keep it, Sophie. For your mother, and for me.'

She could not reply. Her throat was too choked to admit the slightest sound. She tucked the precious gold band — her only tangible reminder of her mother — into her pocket with the chain, pressing her hand against the cloth as if fearful that it might slip out and be lost.

She felt Jean-Michel's hands on her shoulders, warm and reassuring, yet she could not take her eyes from her father. Now that she knew who he was, she was drinking in every detail, each part of him, comparing it all to memories lost in the mists of childhood. There were so many things that she now realized she could and did recall. The way his mouth curved when he was amused, the way he rubbed his jaw with one hand when trying to think what to say. He was doing that now.

'Why did you leave us?' she asked softly.

He glanced at her, then sank into a chair.

'I've asked myself that a thousand times.' He spread his hands, glancing from Sophie to Jean-Michel, who still stood at her back, his hands comforting against her shoulders. 'At the time . . . after your brother died . . . Damn, I don't know, Sophie. I was young and mad at the world for the hand it had dealt us. There had to be a way I could get us home, back to Acadia and our old lives.' He laughed harshly. 'Some cruel joke, that, eh? By then there was nothing to go back to. But I didn't know that.'

'So you tried to return to Canada?' she asked dubiously.

He shook his head. 'Not at first. I needed money. For us all. I had no wish to return unless we could all do so together. I had heard tales of young men making their fortunes from privateering, even young boys doing no more than getting their share of the bounty while serving as cabin boys. It was too enticing.'

Sophie frowned. 'But why did you simply disappear? Am I to believe that you did all this out of a sense of honour, yet you could not share it with your wife? As far as my mother was concerned, you simply vanished, leaving her with nothing. One cannot eat honour, sir!'

He swore. 'I know that. But what else

could I do? I barely made enough as a fisherman to put food on the table, with no hope of ever improving our position. Had the English not intervened — '

'The English?' This from Jean-Michel.

'I joined a regular French vessel at first, but we were captured within weeks by an English privateer and indentured. I found myself serving with the British Navy in the Mediterranean — until we were outnumbered by the Spanish.' He looked at Jean-Michel grimly. 'Are you familiar with the expression 'Fall into the hands of God, not the hands of Spain', sir?'

Jean-Michel's voice held an edge when he replied, 'You were captured by the Spaniards.'

'And imprisoned, thanks to a gallant but stupid British captain, who thought he could outwit the enemy. Instead of blowing the magazine and sending us all to painless eternity, he made a run for it.'

'They were faster.' Jean-Michel's voice held a note of heartfelt commiseration.

'Indeed they were. And crueller than any I have witnessed, or care to again,' Morgan added bitterly. 'Suffice it to say, I was one of the few to survive. I escaped thanks to the wiles of an Englishman from another captured vessel, and we found our way to

England. By this time, my English was as good as my French, and I decided there was more to be made on that side of the Channel, so I joined a privateer by the name of Brankscombe, operating first out of Liverpool and then Halifax. I made enough in a year to buy two ships of my own.' He shrugged. 'I licensed one as a privateer and used the other for the Caribbean trade. Eventually, I had more than twenty ships.'

Sophie felt cold deep in her bones, despite Jean-Michel's warm grip on her shoulders. 'But despite all this wealth, you never returned to rescue your family, even though you must have known your wife was destitute.'

'I knew no such thing!' His eyes were dark with pain. 'I returned to Georgia at the very first opportunity, but you were gone. No one knew where, no one seemed even to remember you. Damn it, Sophie, I could not find my wife and child! For all I knew, you were dead, too.'

She sighed, feeling decades of hatred crumble into despair. 'You are right. We had so few friends. Mother said we should just make a clean start, put the past behind us. She told me you were drowned at sea. I suppose it was the only reason she could ascribe to your disappearance.'

There was a short silence. Morgan stared at the floor.

'I even went to the churchyard,' he said at last, avoiding their eyes. 'Pascal's grave was covered in weeds. When I saw that, I knew you had gone. The woman I married would never have let her little boy's graveside go neglected.'

'No,' Sophie agreed, staring into her hands. Her eyes filled and she sniffed. ' 'Twas her greatest sadness that we had to leave him behind when we went to Guadeloupe.'

She stood, pausing for a moment, and then crossing the floor to the man who was all but a stranger to her.

'I came to Acadia hoping to find my uncle and some last remnant of my family,' she said softly as she stood before him. 'But instead I have found my father, which is more than I ever dreamed.'

He gazed down at her, his eyes deep and soft and full of sadness. Then he opened his arms and she stepped into them, enclosed by their warmth as she had been so many many years before.

They left the inn soon after, leaving the body of Daniel Blackthorn to be collected by the undertaker. Morgan wanted them to go straight to his house on the hill above the town, but Jean-Michel insisted they must free his crew first, and Sophie wished to find Zamore and the injured sailor.

The first was easily accomplished by messenger, and the men were housed in various hostelries near the harbour while repairs could be effected to the *Némésis*. Zamore proved somewhat more elusive, but he was finally located in the care of the constable, who had interrupted him in the process of spiking the guns aboard the *Kestrel II*, the brigantine that had been responsible for their capture.

Morgan growled, threatening to have Zamore personally rebore the cannons, but Jean-Michel made amends by offering him the guns from the *Némésis* instead.

'Why did you do that?' Sophie whispered, as they waited for Morgan to join them in his coach for the ride to the house.

Jean-Michel shrugged. 'I have lost my taste for piracy. I nearly ruined your father, when it should have been Blackthorn I was after. A careless error I should not have made and one I shall not risk repeating.'

She sat back. 'I'm glad.'

'I am not.'

Sophie frowned, but something in his expression told her he did not want to be pressed on the matter. His eyes looked bleak.

'What will you do?' she asked gently.

He gave a self-deprecatory laugh. 'Do? As my brother Robert would say, gentlemen should not 'do' anything. Being rich should be an occupation unto itself.'

'You don't give a fig for Robert's opinions.'

'This time he may be right.'

At that moment, Morgan joined them and the conversation turned to other matters, but Sophie was left with a deep feeling of unease.

As the horses pulled the small coach up the hill, her father surprised her with some other news.

'So, you were on your way to find Bernard Dalibar, eh?' he said. 'You know he lives in Québec?'

Sophie's pulse quickened. 'Indeed, Jean-Michel had heard of a man by that name living there. Do you know him?'

'I've kept an eye on him, no more. Like you did, he thinks I am dead, and I deemed it safest to keep my own counsel. So I do not know him personally, but I do know he is a successful lawyer and a member of the *Assemblé*. Also that his wife is called Margot and he has nine children and, at last count, two grandchildren.' He grinned. 'Does that satisfy your curiosity?'

Sophie was astonished. 'But how can you

know all this if you have not made yourself known to him?'

Morgan spread his hands. 'Several of my ships make regular runs up and down the St Lawrence in the summer. I have no remaining family myself, so I made a point of keeping abreast of my wife's. I have a friend who moves in Dalibar's circle, and he passes me news of them from time to time.'

Sophie was delighted to discover such a bevy of relations, and yet their existence, while comforting, paled beside the discovery that her own father was alive.

The carriage drew up and they dismounted before an elegant two-storey house with chimney stacks at each end puffing white smoke into the increasingly blue sky. Two dormer windows broke the steep roof line, and the impressive portico was finished with grey stone columns which drew Sophie's eyes to the broad stone steps leading into the mansion.

They were ushered inside, and since rooms needed to be readied for the unexpected guests, were taken straight to the dining-room. A hastily prepared meal reminded both Sophie and Jean-Michel how long it had been since they had last eaten and they ate ravenously while Jack Morgan regaled them with talk of his shipping business, leaving Sophie with the impression that her father was certainly quite a power in this city.

'Why do you not call yourself by your real name?' she asked, as she enjoyed a dish of scrambled eggs and hot fresh rolls.

He gave a short laugh. 'This is an English colony, and we are at war with France's revolutionary government. A man with a name such as Edouard Lafleur would barely be tolerated. Anyway,' he said, brightening, 'I have become quite fond of the persona of Jack Morgan. But we shall have to think what to call *you*, shall we not, my dear?'

Sophie flushed. She glanced quickly at Jean-Michel, but he was studiously attending to his boiled mutton.

Her father's eyes, on the other hand, were intent upon her. She poked aimlessly at her food with her fork. 'You need have no concern on that score, sir,' she said, not sure quite how she should address him. 'I came to Canada to follow a vocation, not impose myself upon the goodwill of my family. I shall travel to Québec, I think, for there is an order of Ursulines there who may be glad of my services.'

Morgan, to Jean-Michel's satisfaction, choked on his coffee.

When he was sufficiently recovered, he

blotted his mouth with his napkin. 'You're going to be a nun? Where in God's name would you get a fool idea like that?'

Sophie's cheeks turned bright pink and Jean-Michel almost felt sorry for her, although he shared Morgan's feelings on the matter.

'Sophie feels she must make amends for her sin in this life, so she may enjoy an eternity of bliss in the next,' he explained. 'Don't glare at me, Sophie. I am merely repeating your own assertions.'

'You are making fun of me.'

He was instantly contrite. 'Then I beg forgiveness.'

'What the devil are you two babbling on about?' Morgan interjected, looking from one to the other.

Sophie set down her fork. Given the long time since they had last sat at table, Jean-Michel was surprised her appetite was so quickly sated. He, on the contrary, found his increasing with every outburst from her father. An unexpected ally, to be sure.

'When I told you at the Grey Goose that I had killed a man,' she explained to her father, 'I spoke only the truth.' She went on to describe the event and its antecedents, then how she had fled capture by stowing away on the *Deliverance*. This last caused the man no little astonishment.

His face became grim as she described how Jean-Michel and his gunner had sunk the vessel, and Jean-Michel had to be quick to point out that he had mistaken the actions of Blackthorn for those of his partner.

'Damned expensive mistake,' Morgan growled.

'Damned expensive choice in business partners,' Jean-Michel replied mildly.

Morgan chuckled. Jean-Michel thought he was coming to quite like the man.

'So,' he said, turning his attention back to his daughter, 'you are planning to knit yourself a hair shirt, eh?'

Jean-Michel laughed aloud. 'Were those not Father Cassel's very words, Sophie?'

She glowered at him. 'There are some people on this earth, *Monsieur le Vicomte*, who believe in helping others. I thought you of all people would comprehend that notion.'

He remained undaunted. 'It no longer signifies, anyway,' he continued. 'You have no need of it. If I am not mistaken, you saved my life today. Surely my life is worth no less than that of Louis de Guillaume?'

Sophie stared at him, licking her lips. The tiny movement made Jean-Michel squirm a little on his seat. He dipped his head and applied himself to eating.

'I do not believe I did anything of the sort,' she retorted. 'It was Mr Morgan' — she glanced awkwardly at her father — 'who saved you.'

'You do yourself an injustice, my dear,' Morgan stated. 'Had you not come in with that ridiculous pistol, I would have dealt quite harshly with Monsieur Chambois. But the instant you looked at me, I knew who you were, even if you did not know me. I could scarcely expect that, I suppose, after eighteen years.'

'How could you possibly know it was me?'

'You have to ask?' He seemed surprised. 'Why, you are the image of your mother, my dear, as she was when I first met and fell in love with her. Times were hard, of course, and she aged too quickly, especially when the boys died.' He turned to Jean-Michel, explaining for his benefit that his wife had borne three sons. The eldest, Jules-Edouard, had died at two, before Sophie's birth, and one was stillborn. But the real blow had been when Pascal died of fever at the age of six. 'My wife never recovered her spirits after that. Nor I. I felt a wretch for not being able to provide a proper life for them, the kind she had been used to in Acadia. But we were no better than refugees when we lived in Georgia. We had no lands, no belongings, no heritage.' He sighed. 'At first I blamed the English for deporting us so they could control this part of the Atlantic; later I blamed myself. But there comes a time when a person must simply stop looking back and go forward. It's do that or die, if you ask me.'

Jean-Michel stared at the man, his thoughts far away at a graveside in Boston. How extraordinary it was, that this man, so apparently different from himself, should have had so similar a tragedy to contend with. He, too, had lost a wife he loved. The difference was, Jean-Michel had never lost his daughter. Suddenly, his arms ached to hold little Rose-Marie.

'Anyway, my dear,' Morgan said to Sophie, 'perhaps if you would call yourself Sophie Morgan, 'twould make things a little easier. We'll say you've been living in the French Caribbean since you were a babe and so you have yet to learn English.'

'And how shall I say I became separated from you?' she asked, faintly astonished by the ease with which he was reconstructing her life.

'Demmed if I know. Let's go whole hog, shall we? Say you and your mother were stolen by pirates right off one of my ships.'

Jean-Michel choked on his wine. Sophie gasped. 'I will do no such thing! To cover one's sins with more lies is too much to ask.'

'What would you have me do then, Sophie? Tell them the truth?' His eyes grew serious, sad almost. 'You can if you will. But it will be the end of me, you know.' He shrugged when she made no move to respond. 'Bah, after what I did to you and your mother, 'twould be no more than a man deserved.' He jumped up from the table, tossing his napkin upon the cloth. 'But for now, I have business that cannot be delayed, and you two must be tired. Rest, and I will see you this evening. We'll decide what's to be done then.'

He bellowed to Mrs Bellamy, his housekeeper, concerning the readiness of rooms for his guests, and was soon stomping out the door to the stables.

Jean-Michel looked at Sophie, concerned by the deep silence that had overtaken her since her father's parting words.

'You have hardly eaten, Sophie. Are you ill?'

She shook her head, not meeting his eyes. 'No.'

'But?' he asked, when she did not continue.

She shrugged, getting up to wander to the window and stare out at the lush garden where tulips and narcissus nodded in the spring sunshine. The day was turning more promising by the minute. Yet she looked so lost, so alone. He followed her, yearning to enfold her in his arms, but sensing that in this strange mood she would not welcome his gesture.

He leaned his back against the side of the window alcove. She did not acknowledge his presence, merely stared out, her eyes unfocused. He wondered what she was seeing in the troubled recesses of her mind. The sun lit upon her face, enhancing the blueness of her eyes and turning her softly curling hair into strands of living silk. He reached out a finger and tucked a stray lock behind her ear.

She jumped. 'Wh-what are you doing?'

'Forgive me. You seem so sad. I had thought now that you were here and had met your father, you could finally be content.'

'I am happy to have found my father.'

'Then what ails you?'

Again her slight shoulders lifted in a shrug, and her eyes were touched with a despair that tore at his heart.

'Naught but that I am confused,' she answered with a sigh, turning from the view.

She spread her hands as she walked across the fine Chinese rug. 'Now that I have found my closest family, I feel no pressing need to seek my uncle in Québec, yet I cannot live here with my father, not while he is an Englishman and I an Acadian.' Her voice broke suddenly. 'And what of my vow?'

Jean-Michel crossed to her in a single stride and dragged her into his arms. She went willingly, burying her face in his shirt. He let her cry, for she was exhausted and in shock from the ordeal she had endured these past two days. They stood there, with Jean-Michel rocking her in his arms, until she relaxed. Finally, she pulled away.

'I believe I should like to visit the church,' she said, wiping her eyes on the handkerchief he proffered. 'Do you know if there is a Catholic establishment here?'

He nodded. 'St Peter's, if I recall, on Spring Garden Road. But it will still be there on the morrow. You are exhausted, Sophie. You need rest more than prayer just at the moment.'

And brooking no argument, he summoned the housekeeper and shooed her away in the woman's motherly care.

★ ★ ★

Sophie slept the day away, and to her astonishment, the whole of the night that followed, and rose to a bright May morning with a great deal of her energy restored, though a *mélange* of emotions still warred in her heart. She lay in the soft bed, gazing about at the elegant bedchamber with its rose curtains and matching bed drapes, the cheerful rug upon the floor, and the flowered porcelain jug and bowl on the washstand. Though the furnishings were by no means as grand as those of François and Léonie in Boston, they bespoke a very comfortable lifestyle. Her father had become a man of means.

Had circumstances been different, she mused as she sat up and began unweaving the long braid in her hair, she might have left Madame Guillaume's service and returned here freely, making a life for herself, learning English even — She stopped, falling back upon the soft goose-down pillows. Ridiculous. Had it not been for her crime and subsequent escape, she would never have encountered Jean-Michel de Chambois, and without him and his hell-bent dedication to ridding the world of evil, she would never have discovered that Jack Morgan was really Edouard Lafleur, the father she had lost so many years ago.

Chance. Her life had ever been a series

of chance events. Where was the notion of free will, the simplicity of choice and consequence, when one's life was governed by accidents and fickle Lady Fate?

One thing was clear, though. If she was to find her own path in life, she must do it at once. She reached for the robe thoughtfully provided by her father's housekeeper and tugged it on. She would seek out the priest at the Church of St Peter this very morning. Surely within its walls she would find the answers she so desperately needed.

She attended to her ablutions and dressed herself in one of three simple but fetching cotton gowns she found laid out upon the chest in her room. She wondered idly to whom they had belonged, thanking the unknown donor as she chose a pretty concoction in blue and white dimity, with a matching white shawl.

There was no one below, only a note from her father saying he would return at luncheon, and that Jean-Michel was seeing to the repairs of his vessel.

Mrs Bellamy brought her a simple breakfast of fresh-baked bread and fruit preserves with a pot of the most delicious coffee Sophie had tasted, with the possible exception of the excellent beans Léonie's husband imported. She wondered how many of her father's ships were engaged in fully legitimate trade. At the memory of the slave ship they had been tricked into attacking, and the subsequent death of Daniel Blackthorn, she shuddered, pushing aside her cup. That the man had deserved his fate she did not doubt for a moment. She would, however, have much preferred not to be a witness to it.

She leaned back in her chair, toying with the crumbs on her empty plate, and thinking how very calmly her father had despatched his partner to the next life. He claimed it had been a kindness, which perhaps it was, given the retribution the natives might have extracted, but to kill a man with such ease, such nonchalance . . . She shuddered. Men were entirely different creatures, that much was certain. Her father had not appeared in the least repelled by the notion that his only daughter had killed a man. Quite the opposite; he seemed almost amused.

She pushed herself away from the table and set down her napkin. This would never do. She was beginning to think like a man, to make excuses for her appalling actions.

Without further ado, she accepted Mrs Bellamy's offer of the small *calèche* and a driver and set off for St Peter's Church, ignoring the puzzled expression upon the housekeeper's face.

18

Jean-Michel de Chambois was pleased with the relatively minor damage to his ship. The *Némésis* had lost some planking on her upper deck, and there was damage to the railings and a little to his cabin, but otherwise, she was unharmed. She did not even need new spars cut, for his quick surrender meant the masts had escaped Blackthorn's cannon.

The carpenters were busy at work and assured him the vessel would be ready to sail by Monday. Meanwhile the crew were busy clearing the debris caused by the cannonball, and a group of local painters had been employed to restore the vessel to her former glory.

'When would you like to sail, sir?' Zamore asked, coming silently upon Jean-Michel as he stood with his back to the main-mast watching the work.

Jean-Michel jumped, his thoughts having been fully occupied by the way this little ship reminded him of Sophie these days. Of her laugh and her hair blowing like spun gold in the breeze.

'You walk like a cat, Zamore,' he

complained gruffly. Then he waved one hand at the work underway on the deck. 'I gather she'll be ready in two days.'

'Perhaps less. The Halifax shipbuilders are very experienced.'

Jean-Michel grunted. 'And so they should be after all the privateers and naval vessels they've outfitted in their shipyards.'

Zamore coughed, pulling on his sleeve. Jean-Michel allowed himself to be led further out of earshot. 'At present, they believe they are working for Jack Morgan, sir. They would not offer their services for a vessel that was French.'

Jean-Michel raised his eyebrows. 'The *Némésis* is not French, Captain. She is American. Time you recognized that fact.'

Zamore tilted his head in acquiescence. 'I trust they would see it that way, sir. However, with France and England once again at war, I thought it best to — '

'Yes, very well. Your point is well made. However, your English is as good as mine, so as long as the crew don't blab about, you should be safe enough.' He looked at the blackamoor, a man who had become far more than an employee over the time they had spent together. Zamore was a friend, and a man of considerable talent. The time had come, he thought.

'Follow me to my cabin, Captain — if we can get in. There's something in my desk I wish to give you.'

Ignoring Zamore's puzzlement, he led the way below. The carpenters were happy to break for a moment and leave them alone. Jean-Michel opened the desk, extracted a drawer and then unlocked the small safe built into the back of the space behind. He withdrew a scroll of parchment sealed with wax, relocked the box and replaced the drawer. Nodding to the carpenters who were waiting outside, he led Zamore to the *grande chambre* where they could talk privately.

'I had this drawn up a while ago. It is time you had it.'

Zamore took the paper without a word and broke the seal. For a moment he read in silence, then he looked up, amazed. 'Are you quite sure about this, sir?'

'I am.' He patted his shoulder. 'I should have done it months ago, but I didn't know then what I would do without my ship.' He sighed, turning away. 'Now all it does is remind me of Sophie, and of the many mistakes I have made and the lives I have endangered. Enough is enough, Zamore. You will put the *Némésis* to far better use than I.'

The Negro's face lit up, his teeth gleaming

403

in the morning light. 'Then sir, with your permission, I would like to rename the ship, sir. I should very much like to call her the *Danielle*.'

Jean-Michel's brows shot up. 'Indeed? So that is the lie of the land, is it?' He laughed. 'Well, I wish you well of both the ship and the lady, Zamore. You are a lucky man.'

'I believe I am sir, thanks to you.'

Jean-Michel set out to return to Jack Morgan's house with mixed feelings. He stopped at the end of the wharf and gazed back at the little Baltimore Clipper, its perky masts topped with the American flag fluttering in the balmy breeze. He was glad he'd deeded the vessel to Zamore; equally glad he'd never again be tempted to wreak revenge on a stranger and in so doing punish the innocent. But that only left him with a greater concern: just what was a wealthy but aimless man of thirty-seven going to do with the rest of his life?

Suddenly a voice hailed him. He turned, startled to hear his name on anyone's lips in a strange town.

'Monsieur de Chambois! Is that really you? Can it be?'

A thin black man dressed in patched breeches and vest over a plain white cotton shirt approached. He wore a battered hat which he tore from his head as he bowed deeply.

Jean-Michel frowned, feeling a faint stir of recognition.

'You do not know me, sir? No, nor should I expect it after so many years. John Samuel Henry is my name, sir, and I have been here in Halifax, a free man, ever since you helped me escape in '88.'

'Ah!' Jean-Michel suddenly recalled a badly beaten young slave about six years ago he had rescued from a particularly unpleasant owner.

'You won me at cards, sir, then you sent me to that farm of yours to learn and to get well. I came up here after that and now I have a wife and three children, another on the way, sir, and all of us free as the birds, sir.' He beamed at Jean-Michel, displaying a row of white teeth. 'I always said to myself — John Henry, if you ever get a chance to shake that man's hand, don't you ever pass it up.' And that was exactly what he did — he took Jean-Michel by the hand and pumped it up and down till his shoulder felt like it might fly entirely free of its socket.

Jean-Michel gazed in dismay at the man's threadbare attire. 'What . . . what work do you do in Halifax, John Henry?'

'Me, sir? Why I'm a clerk sir. Thanks

to that farm school you sent me to, I can read and write and do my sums, and I do all those things, sir, at one of the shipping offices down by the wharf. Not too many black men can do what I do, no indeed.'

'And do you make enough at your clerking to house and feed a family?' Jean-Michel asked him as they walked side by side along the busy street.

'We manage well enough, sir,' came the more subdued reply. 'Though not all have as many skills as me. Lots of the Negroes have left again, say there's nothing here in Halifax but jobs for white folks. Some of them even took a ship back to Africa, sir, in '91, imagine that. But not me, no, I'm settled here. We make do, me and my Evangeline.'

They parted company soon after and Jean-Michel, finding his mind completely occupied with the disturbing picture of life that John Henry had painted, ducked into an inn. He sat in a dark corner nursing a jug of ale and contemplated all that he had learned about himself in the past two days.

It was not a pretty picture.

★ ★ ★

Sophie's morning was scarcely more productive. She had not managed to find a priest, but had visited the little wooden church on Spring Garden Road, been admitted by an elderly lady sweeping between the pews, and had knelt before the simple altar praying for guidance. All she needed was some indication, some feeling that might enter her heart and provide direction, anything which would lead her towards a future while providing some certainty that she had chosen the correct path.

She came to the conclusion, after a fruitless hour upon her knees, that God must have been either uninterested or occupied elsewhere that morning.

By the time she returned to her father's mansion, she had reached the dismal view that she had made her vow in undue haste. She sighed as the *calèche* drew up in front of the stone steps. A life of piety dedicated to good works had seemed like the perfect penance for the sin of taking the life of another human being. But Father Cassel had been right all along: Sophie did not find it easy to contemplate a life in cloisters.

She entered the parlour to find her father in conversation with Jean-Michel. The latter seemed in a very sombre mood, and she felt a sudden presentiment of gloom.

'My dear Sophie,' Jack Morgan said, his eyes lighting up when he saw her. He crossed the room and bent over her hand. 'I trust you had a successful morning.'

Sophie glanced quickly at Jean-Michel before answering. 'I regret I was not able to speak to the priest at St Peter's, but I enjoyed a time of quiet in the church.'

Morgan smiled. 'Wonderful. Then you must be ready for luncheon. While we eat, I have a matter I must discuss with you.' He led her away towards the dining room, leaving Jean-Michel to follow behind, and settled her into a chair before seating himself at the head of the table. A maid brought soup, another bread hot from the oven, and a footman poured white wine into crystal glasses. Sophie almost felt as though she were back at La Tour House in Boston.

'I have received an invitation to attend a ball at Government House,' her father said, as they bent to their meal. 'To honour His Royal Highness, Prince Edward.'

Sophie's eyebrows shot up. 'I was not aware Halifax had such a noble visitor.'

'Ah, yes indeed, my dear. The prince is quite the soldier of his family, and has been appointed Commander in Chief for Nova Scotia. He is preparing our defences in case of invasion by the French.' At this, Sophie's eyes met Jean-Michel's. Clearly, he, too, was disturbed by the turn of events.

408

'For that reason, I fear it might be unwise for me to accept on either of your behalfs, for although the prince's consort is herself of French extraction, one cannot be too careful in times of war.'

Sophie set her spoon down, her appetite having left her suddenly. 'I see. You are saying that it is not wise that people know you have a French daughter, is that it?'

Jack Morgan's expression clouded. 'I don't give a damn for myself. But until I have a chance to see how things stand — '

'It is perfectly all right, sir,' she interrupted. 'I have no desire to become a part of Halifax society, at any rate. I shall not be here long.'

There was a sudden silence. 'But I thought — ' Morgan began.

'Where will you go?' Jean-Michel said suddenly entering the conversation.

She looked at him, then at her father. 'I have not decided. But as I speak so little English, it would seem futile for me to seek work here.'

'You have no need to work!' Jack Morgan expostulated, throwing his soup spoon upon the table with unnecessary force. 'I thought you understood that. I shall settle a dowry upon you and — '

'I shall not marry,' she replied quietly,

gazing at the bowl of primroses on the table. 'I have come to Canada to do God's work and there is only one thing I would ask before I begin.'

'And what is that?' her father demanded, clearly dumbfounded by her quiet assertion.

'I should very much like to visit my mother's old home.'

There was a moment's silence. Then Jack Morgan patted his lips with his napkin. 'Ah. Well, that could be difficult.'

Sophie looked at him, wondering why he should be suddenly so evasive.

'I've not been there myself, Sophie,' he said quietly, 'but I've heard there's precious little to see. The English burned everything as a way of forcing everybody out. My parents' property in Cape Breton — not that it was much to start with, mind — was quite gone when I went back. Nothing to be seen but grass on a hillside.' He reached out and squeezed her hand. 'I'm sorry, but I don't think there's anything to be found.'

Sophie fought the ache that burned behind her eyes. 'Nevertheless, I should like to stand on that land, to see the ocean and feel the same wind on my face that Mama did.'

He stared at her for a moment, then nodded. 'And so you shall. I cannot get away myself at present, for there is a Court

410

of Admiralty auction soon and I cannot be absent.' He turned to Jean-Michel. 'Your vessel is under repair, I gather, but perhaps if I were to lend you my own schooner you might oblige me in this. My crew is first-rate and they know the waters of the Bay of Fundy — '

'Baie Françoise,' Sophie interjected quickly. 'Mama always referred to it by its French name.'

He sighed. 'I have become more English than I know. You are right, my dear. Baie Françoise.'

'I would be honoured to take her,' Jean-Michel said softly. Sophie looked into his eyes then, feeling a deep message that she was at a loss to interpret. But her breathing quickened and she felt a heightened sense of anticipation as they finished the meal and discussed preparations for the voyage.

'The *Sophie II* is always in readiness,' Morgan explained, 'you could leave tomorrow if the tides are favourable.'

'The *Sophie II*?' Sophie asked, her eyes widening. 'You named your ship after me? But what became of the *Sophie I*?'

His eyes twinkled. 'Why, you are here in the flesh, of course. And quite a sailor yourself after all your adventures.'

She blushed, touched that he should have

411

named a vessel in her honour. 'Thank you . . . Papa,' she said, feeling a surge of love for the man she had given up for dead almost two decades ago. God was smiling upon her, she thought, surprised to be found deserving of such bounty.

Jack Morgan laid his big hand over hers. 'Thank you, my dear, for your courage and bravery. Chance, it seems, has brought us together again, and I hope you will reconsider leaving Nova Scotia, for it will pain me greatly to lose you again.'

Her eyes filled with tears, but she blinked them back, quickly changing the subject to where she might procure some clothes and other necessities without delay. She did not want to think about leaving her father. Not yet.

★ ★ ★

They waited until nearly noon for the giant tides of Baie Françoise to rise sufficiently on the inland waterway at the mouth of the River Dauphin. The waters of the tidal estuary closed rapidly over the red mudflats, forcing the flocks of busy sandpipers and plover higher up the beaches. Then, Jean-Michel, upon the advice of the able captain of the *Sophie II*, ordered a dinghy to be

412

lowered. They would have three hours.

Two sailors rowed them towards a rickety jetty that struck out bravely from the overgrown shore like an accusing finger, crying its thirty years of neglect to Sophie's soul.

'Is it safe?' she asked dubiously, as the sailors pulled up to the rotting wooden structure. Jean-Michel translated her question into English.

'Good enough, if you watch where you put your feet, miss,' came the reply.

The men waited while Jean-Michel helped Sophie from the dinghy and then pulled away once more, leaving them alone on the edge of a grassy meadow.

Sophie turned her back on the wide river and stared up at what was once her mother's family's landholdings. The land showed evidence of diking, rising up sharply from the saltmarshy beach and then flattening out into a wide field. The meadow was wide and verdant, alive with red-winged blackbirds in a frenzy of spring courtship and nest-building, and edged beyond with a heavy band of pine and spruce trees which sloped gently up towards a grassy hill.

She stared about her, clutching her wool cape closer against the fresh sea breeze that blew at her back, though the sun was warm on her face. 'Look,' she said, pointing, 'there is some kind of a path.'

She glanced quickly at Jean-Michel, to find him gazing quietly at her. Something in his eyes disturbed her, but she shook the feeling off. This visit was for her benefit, not his. It was a pity he could not revisit his old family haunts in France; perhaps then he would understand how important this was to her.

She pointed to a narrow rut that disappeared into the overgrowth up the hill. The grass grew patchily over the old track, the weeds still different from what had once been a fertile meadow, despite more than thirty years of disuse.

'If we follow it, perhaps we will find the house,' she said, indicating the rise beyond the trees, 'up there, somewhere?'

He nodded, his lips pressed together.

Sophie turned to the path, disappointed that he was not entering into the spirit of this adventure. Why did he have to be so prickly this morning, when he had seemed more than happy to bring her all this way in her father's schooner?

She heard him hurry to catch up and turned her head to wait. At that very moment, her feet, clad only in modest shoes, sank abruptly in the thick red mud of the meadow.

'Oh!'

The next instant, he picked her up, his strong arms swooping her off her feet and holding her against his chest as though she were a child.

A low rumble of laughter alerted her to the fact that her shoes had remained stuck in their oozy prison. How dare he improve his mood at her expense, she thought crossly, but much as she would have liked to assert her independence and struggle free of his arms, the sight of her bare stockinged toes let common sense prevail. But she did not have to like it.

Jean-Michel bent down and pulled her shoes free. The mud gave way with a strange sucking sound, which caused him to laugh once more.

'You should have worn boots like me,' he said as he proceeded to stride across the field, still holding her muddy shoes in one hand and carrying her easily with the other.

'I do not possess any boots,' she retorted with as much hauteur as she could muster, disgruntled to find that she was obliged to wrap her arms about his neck tightly. She had accepted his company on this trip only because her father was unable to take her, and she was determined to keep relations between them as formal as possible. In a few days his ship would be repaired and he would be gone. She doubted she would ever see the man again. And yet here she was, alone with him in the middle of an Acadian field with only the birds and the bees as chaperons. Her face flooded with colour.

'Am I going too fast?' he asked, frowning down at her.

'N-no! But I can manage now.'

He shook his head. 'It's still very wet underfoot. These fields were reclaimed from the sea by the Acadians and they are still soft. Hold on, Sophie, or you shall get more than merely your feet muddy!'

She clutched his neck more tightly, feeling him hoist her weight more snugly against his chest so that her head was tucked firmly beneath his chin. She tried to be still, tried to ignore the enticing smell of his skin mixed with the salt tang of the breeze, tried not to think about how her face was pressed against his neck, or her head against his chin. Heaven knew, despite her best intentions she was tempted to tilt her head up and kiss that firm jaw, but if she did, he would probably be so surprised he would drop her on her rear in the mud!

So she focused on the sunny spring meadow instead and tried to ignore the steady beat of his heart against her ear, and the mysterious ache of longing that pooled deep within her, no matter how much she tried to deny it.

She sighed with relief when they reached the edge of the meadow and the ground began to rise. He set her down on an outcrop of rocks, then turned to wipe the worst of the mud off her shoes. He wasn't even breathing hard.

'I-I can do it, thank you,' she said, reaching for the shoes as he bent to put them upon her feet.

' 'Tis no trouble,' he replied mildly, though the shock that jolted through her as he took her chilled feet in his warm hands was anything but mild. She jerked away.

'Did I hurt you?'

'No!'

'Then hold still.'

Sophie sighed, steeled herself against the rush of emotions and allowed him to slide the shoes onto her feet. The instant he was done, she jumped up and headed off into the trees, where, as in the meadow, there was the remnant of a track to follow. But the forest she had expected was no more than a small copse which gave way to a delightful orchard planted with all manner of apple trees. The blossoms were finishing now, the last pink and white petals giving way to spring-green leaves, but the smell was still heavenly.

'My mother described this precisely,' she cried in delight, running between the trees. 'All the different kinds of apples they harvested and how her grandfather had planted them in the seventeenth century. They made cider, you know.'

Jean-Michel watched her running up the hill among the trees with a faint smile on his lips, but he did not join her. A few weeks ago, she was certain he would have grabbed her hand and been as silly as she, maybe he would even have kissed her . . . She stopped that thought, for it reminded her of a certain rainy day in Boston.

So much had happened since then, she thought as she plucked a flowering twig from a tree and brought the fragrant blossoms to her nose. Now she had found her father, and . . . and this. She turned, surveying the orchard. I wonder if Mama knows I am here, she thought. She would be glad, if she could see.

'Shall we go on?'

Jean-Michel's voice so close to her ear made Sophie jump.

'Yes, of course. The house should be beyond the orchard, on the hill. I am sure Mama said you could look both ways across the peninsula from there, to both the sea and the river.'

When they reached the hilltop, Sophie's eyes widened with dismay.

'Jean-Michel, it is not here!' She turned all about, seeing nothing but a few trees, a piece of broken fence, an odd wilderness of vegetation . . .

'You must not expect so much, Sophie,' he said softly. 'It is thirty years since your family was forced out. Much can change.'

'No,' she said stubbornly. 'A beautiful house like that, the finest in the area, would not just disappear.'

He shrugged. 'Perhaps we should look further.'

She stomped off across the long grass, determined that she must simply have remembered her mother's description badly, or perhaps her mother had recalled some of the details awry. Anne had been a mere child of thirteen when they were evicted from their homes and packed onto boats, and things often seemed larger, or different —

'Oh!'

Jean-Michel was at her side in an instant, his mouth grim. Sophie drew a deep breath and pressed her lips together, for they quivered suddenly.

In front of her, half hidden in a tangle

419

of wild honeysuckle, stood the remains of a once-grand fireplace.

'I-I think perhaps we have found it after all,' she whispered, going forward to pull at the twisting vines that clung to the giant stones. The mortar crumbled a little as she pulled back the branches, but the beauty of the original fireplace was clear to see. The chimney itself was gone, leaving only a small broken spire of stones like a dead tree trunk sticking up, and the mantel, once of elegant hardwood, was mostly burned away by the fire that had doubtless consumed the house.

'They burned it,' she said sadly. 'Just as Mama feared. Why did they do this, Jean-Michel? Why did they hate our people so much?'

He enfolded her in his arms and this time she allowed herself the comfort of his hard, warm chest.

' 'Twas not that they hated the Acadians, Sophie, but that they wanted control, and the French settlers would not sign an oath of allegiance to the British crown.'

'Why should they do any such thing?'

'Because the British had conquered Nova Scotia, my sweet. It was a simple choice between living in peace under British rule, or leaving.'

'Being forced out like criminals,' she amended bitterly.

'Perhaps. But some chose to sign. Others, like your uncle, hid. The rest . . . ' He waved a hand around the clearing on the hilltop where her grandparents' house had stood. No further words were necessary.

'It is so unfair,' she said in a subdued tone.

'It was harsh,' he said, stroking her hair absently, 'but they thought it necessary. If you stay here, you will be required to sign that same declaration. You will have to face that same choice.'

She pushed away from him, looking up into his serious grey eyes. 'Are you saying I could not live in Nova Scotia unless I agree to this?'

He nodded.

Sophie walked away, fingering the old bricks of the fireplace and looking down at the hearth in which some small creature had undoubtedly made a cosy nest for her babies in early years, the hideaway now exposed by her work. She knelt on the ground. If there had been a fireplace this large, then surely beneath this thin covering of grass and moss might lie a flagstone hearth. She began pulling at the weeds, which came away in her hands with surprising ease, revealing a patch of uneven stones some three feet wide. Jean-Michel helped her and soon the whole construction was clear of overgrowth and stood, mute testimony to a glorious past.

'It must have been quite a house,' Jean-Michel said.

'Look!' In her hands, Sophie held a shard of porcelain, caked with mud. She wiped it with her fingers, revealing that underneath the grime it was white and almost translucent. Part of a crest could be seen engraved in gold on the fragment.

She held it out to Jean-Michel, who took it, examining the pattern closely. 'This looks like a D,' he said, pointing to an elaborate flourish, 'for Dalibar, *sans doute*. This is your maternal grandfather's pattern, Sophie. Where did you find it?'

She showed him, and together they began searching in the weeds around the base of the chimney, but could find nothing further except a small pewter plate, lacking any marks save a simple decoration around the rim. Yet to Sophie it was a treasure. She held the item in her hands, thinking of the people who had used it, handled it every day of their long-past lives. It was a tangible link to her grandparents and it moved her more than she would have believed.

The wind whistled in the pines that grew

close by, and Sophie shivered. She glanced over to where Jean-Michel stood gazing across the narrow neck of land to Baie Françoise. His boots were muddy, his tan breeches stained from kneeling in the dirt, and he had cast off his coat during their work so that he stood with his white linen shirt open at the neck. It stirred her heart to watch him, and with a pang she realized that this might be one of the last days they would ever spend together.

Sensing her scrutiny, he turned and looked at her. Sophie smiled, her heart beating the traitorous tattoo that she had almost come to find comforting whenever he was around. There was something in his eyes, a look that she could not interpret. It had been there many times since he had proposed to her, and she wished she knew what it meant, what he could possibly be thinking. But she knew better than to ask.

Her eye was caught by a sudden movement within the pines and maples that grew wild along the crest of the hillside, beyond what had once been the garden of the Dalibar house. Sophie turned sharply, but at first could see nothing, then a pair of dark eyes peered out at her once again.

'*Qui est là?*' she called, hurrying towards the trees. But the face melted into the gloom.

She stopped. Perhaps she had imagined it.

Jean-Michel saw Sophie turn towards the trees, thought he had heard her call out, but before he could open his mouth, she was gone, plunging into the wood like a dog after a fox.

'*Parbleu*,' he grumbled to himself as he strode across the long grass. He snatched his coat from the old mantel and hurried after the woman, wondering why he seemed to be spending so much of his life doing that these days. He was always trailing about after Sophie Lafleur, wasting his time when he should have been going back to Boston and creating some kind of a new life for himself. Trouble was, he really couldn't develop any enthusiasm for the idea. He didn't know what he wanted to do, except be with Sophie, and heaven knew, *she* didn't want him. She'd made that abundantly clear.

He cursed as a broken spruce branch scraped across his hand, drawing a thin line of blood. He stopped, rubbing the scratch absently as he peered about him. Now where had she gone?

The forest was cool and green, the light filtering through the high canopy glowing with that special bright colour of new spring leaves. A chipmunk darted through the undergrowth at his feet, making him jump, and far above in the unseen sky came the call of a meadowlark.

He saw a sudden flash of colour in the distance, lower down the hillside, and resumed his pursuit, glad when the trees began to thin out and the thick firs and pines give way to wider-spaced maples.

★ ★ ★

Sophie was breathing hard, but she would not give up. Twice she had seen the child — a girl of perhaps ten — darting away through the trees like a frightened hare, but she never got close enough to call out again.

The trees were thinning now, the vegetation changing as the forest reached its end, but the light undergrowth had given way to a tangle of wild mulberry vines and shrubby cedars that made the going more difficult. Her gown was torn in a dozen places, and her shoes, so gallantly rescued by Jean-Michel, were now soaked and stained, but she didn't care.

Just as she was about to concede defeat, she found herself in the open again, close to a small cottage made of rough-hewn boards with a wooden shingle roof. In front of the dwelling grew a substantial vegetable garden enclosed within a rail fence, and a yellow dog sat on the dirt in front of the open door, sleeping in the sun.

Of the child, there was no sign. Sophie felt foolish, now, and looked back up at the hill she had just descended by way of the forest, wondering where Jean-Michel was. Just as she was trying to decide whether she could safely return by the same route, the child's face appeared in the doorway of the cottage. At the same moment, a boy of perhaps fourteen came around the side of the house carrying firewood. He stopped when he saw Sophie, but did no more than stare curiously. Sophie stepped forward, knowing she could not possibly sneak away now. She crossed the meadow, sighing with relief when she heard Jean-Michel come crashing out of the forest a few feet behind her.

'Damn it, Sophie,' he complained as he came up beside her, 'what on earth made you run off like that?' His expression was one of relief rather than rage, and Sophie felt instantly contrite.

'Forgive me,' she said with a quick glance at the house. 'But there was a child watching me from the woods. I wanted to speak to her, but she ran off.' She turned and indicated the cottage. 'Perhaps these people know something of what happened to my grandparents' house and lands.'

At that moment, several more figures appeared in the doorway, one a woman carrying a baby in her arms, then several more youngsters and finally an older woman in a black gown with a striped apron and cap. She carried a pitcher in her hand and wore heavy sabots on her feet, as did the older of the children, though the little ones appeared to be just as happy in bare feet.

For a moment there was silence, then the older woman shrieked, dropped the pitcher to the ground where it smashed into a thousand pieces and ran at Sophie, arms outstretched.

'*Mamselle*! *Mamselle*,' she called as she ran, 'you have come home! Thanks be to God!'

She threw herself upon Sophie, who was too surprised to move, clutching her shoulders and kissing her hands and sobbing, all the while babbling incoherently.

Finally, Jean-Michel peeled the woman forcibly away, just as one of the older boys came up and restrained his mother.

'*Maman*,' he said in a low urgent voice. 'It cannot be she. This lady is too young.'

The woman stopped, staring at Sophie in horror, then snatching at her apron, wiped her eyes vigorously and blessed herself.

Sophie remembered her father's words,

and his reaction to seeing her for the first time, and knew what had transpired.

'*Madame*,' she said gently, 'I believe you have mistaken me for my mother . . . Anne Dalibar?'

The woman's eyes widened and then she blushed a furious red, dropping a curtsy. 'Forgive me, *mamselle*!' she blustered, her work-worn hands waving about in distress. 'I never gave it a second's thought. For a moment, 'twas like 1762 all over again, when we were girls together. Anne and I, we were *copines*, dearest friends and confidantes, never apart when we could be together, and when she left . . . ' Her voice trailed off and she wiped her eyes again, but still stared at Sophie as though she'd seen a ghost. 'You are so — '

Sophie laughed. 'Like my mother,' she interjected. 'So I have discovered. Forgive me for upsetting you, but I saw one of your children in the woods and wanted to question her, but she ran away before — '

'Ah, Mamselle Dalibar, you have come home,' the woman said. 'I always knew you would come if you could.' Her eyes, now that she had got over the shock of her error, were searching the trees at their back. 'Is she with you — Anne? I would so dearly love to see her again. Is my Anne come home, too?'

Sophie shook her head sadly, taking the woman's hand in hers. '*Non, madame.* My mother died some months ago. In Guadeloupe where we lived for many years.'

The woman's lips formed a silent 'Oh' and her eyes were filled with a desolation so absolute that Sophie felt as though she had wounded her physically.

'Perhaps you should go inside and rest,' she said, glancing at Jean-Michel, who quickly stepped forward and took the lady's arm. The woman seemed suddenly ten years older, and Sophie felt wretched that she had been forced to break the news so baldly, without any chance to prepare her for the shock.

'You are most kind,' the woman murmured as they steered her along. 'But I shall be quite all right in a minute.' As they neared the house, she called out to the younger woman holding the baby. 'Jeanne, fetch some refreshment for our visitors!' She allowed Jean-Michel to escort her into the house where they were seated at a long wooden table. The house appeared to comprise a single room, heavily beamed, with a simple wooden ladder that led upstairs, presumably to the sleeping quarters. Sophie looked about her at the large number of children and wondered how so many could manage in so small a place.

'Forgive my manners, *mamselle*,' the woman said as she smoothed her crumpled apron over her broad bosom, 'I am Albertine Sauvé, a widow since my dear Joseph passed away last spring, and this is my eldest daughter, Henriette Babour. She lives in a cottage nearby, but her husband is away with some of my boys fishing in the bay, so we are two women here with a lot of little ones today.' She began to name the children, some hers, the others her grandchildren, and Sophie quickly gave up trying to remember who was whom, especially when she realized several of the children, sharing the same godmother or a godfather, bore identical names! How she could be expected to tell Pierre, aged ten, from Pierre aged four, Sophie was not clear, and when she discovered that Madame Sauvé had not two, but *three* daughters who were all baptized Jeanne, she gave up completely.

But the child who had led her to this house, a shy, dark-haired girl, painfully thin beneath her ragged dress, was Anne.

'For your dear mother,' sighed Madame Sauvé.

Sophie smiled at the child, holding out her

hand to her, but she scampered up the stairs and would not be persuaded down.

They drank apple cider and ate small tarts made with dried apples and raspberries left over from the precious winter store, while Sophie plied Madame Sauvé with questions about her grandparents' property and how she herself came to be still here.

'My father was determined we should not be deported,' Madame Sauvé explained, 'so he took us away by birchbark canoe. We were nearly sunk by the tide coming up the bay, but we made it to New England, where for a while we lived in secret. My father fished, and we were fine until the winter came. But then we knew 'twas hopeless. He signed the oath and we were allowed to return.' Her eyes filled as she recalled their arrival in an early snowstorm to find their house — much grander than this poor dwelling, she hastened to add — burned to the ground, their stock gone and even their fields destroyed. ' 'Twas a cruel winter that first year, but my parents were determined, and what few Acadians were still here had true charity and shared whatever they could. Come spring, we replanted and, *Grâce à Dieu*, we prospered well enough.'

Sophie, glancing about her at the simple rustic house, wondered how prosperity could be measured in the face of such straitened circumstances. But she said nothing, for then their hostess began asking questions of herself and Jean-Michel: was that his ship they had seen in the estuary that morning? Was she sad that her family's property had been sold?

'Sold!' Sophie exclaimed. 'What do you mean? Who could possibly — ?'

'Not long since, I hear tell,' said Madame Sauvé. 'Of course, the government had taken it over — owned it, so they said. But now we are afraid the new people will call us squatters and we'll be thrown off.' She glanced about her at the quiet huddle of children, her face troubled as she sipped at her cider and lapsed into silence.

'But who has bought the land?' Sophie persisted. Her mother had told her that Grandfather Dalibar's *seigneurie* had encompassed a hundred families ranged along the river. Such a piece of land, were it to have been purchased in its entirety, would cost a pretty penny at today's rates.

Madame Sauvé's eldest daughter Jeanne answered from near the fire where she was jiggling her babe in her arms to get it to sleep. '*Un américain*,' she said, all but spitting out the word.

Sophie's heart sank. 'Is there nothing you

can do? Can you not obtain title to this portion of the land for yourselves?'

Jeanne shook her head. 'Not us. We can't read or write — what chance do we have against lawyers and notaries!'

Sophie turned to Jean-Michel, who had sat silently throughout most of the visit. 'Can they do this, Jean-Mich? Is there nothing can be done?'

He shrugged, looking uneasily at the Acadian women. 'One could enquire, perhaps . . . I know little of Nova Scotian law. Perhaps your father — '

'*Absolument*!' Sophie cried. She turned to Madame Sauvé and grasped her hands. 'I shall speak to my father the instant we return to Halifax. I am sure he will know a way to help you.'

Jean-Michel did his best to tone down her enthusiasm, for fear she might set the Sauvés' hopes too high, but Sophie was too excited to listen. She said her farewells to the family, promising to visit again, and after a fierce hug from her mother's erstwhile best friend, they found their way back through the forest to the top of the hill. The tide had reached its peak and was now ebbing and the *Sophie II* could be seen riding at anchor in the bay, awaiting their return.

'Time to go, Sophie,' Jean-Michel said

433

quietly, but she made no move. She did not want to leave. She stood on the hilltop, looking north across Baie Françoise, watching the rolling waves of the Atlantic Ocean, now in full swell, and feeling the wind cutting into her face.

She had found her answer. It came to her with the force of a vision and filled her with peace and certainty. So powerful was it that she knew she finally understood what Father Cassel and Jean-Mich, even Léonie and her father had been trying to say all these weeks — a vocation was more than a simple decision to travel down this path or that. She had found her true vocation today, and it was not within the cloisters of the church. It was right here on this wind-blown hillside. It was down there in that swampy reclaimed dikeland among the poor half-starved and illiterate Acadians.

'These are my people,' she said, turning to Jean-Michel. '*These* are the people I was sent to help, and now that I have found them I can never leave.' She spread her arms, letting the wind catch her cloak and tug at her hair, tasting the salty breeze on her tongue. She leaned her head back and watched as an eagle soared majestically into the vast blue sky. And suddenly she, too, knew how it felt to be free.

'This is *my* land, Jean-Michel, and I will find a way to come back to it if I am forced to build my own wooden cottage and squat alongside the descendants of my grandfather's *habitants*.'

19

They reboarded the *Sophie II* just as the tide began falling in earnest, causing some consternation on the part of the crew as they prepared to navigate the narrow neck of the estuary. The waters here fell almost thirty feet between high and low tides, and the captain of the schooner had no desire to run his ship aground on a sandbank.

As the schooner cleared the rivermouth and headed for the open waters of the bay, Jean-Michel and Sophie stood on the deck watching the land slip away. A gaggle of squalling gulls escorted them out to sea, wheeling hopefully in search of a few morsels from the slop bucket. Eventually they floated away on the air currents, their efforts unrewarded. Perhaps the cook had not yet begun preparing the evening meal.

The breeze on the open sea was cool, and Sophie was glad of the heavy cloak she had brought. Jean-Michel, too, donned his woollen topcoat with its high-standing collar, and they stood enjoying the feel of the vessel ploughing through the waves.

'Look!'

Sophie turned to where he pointed and saw a sudden splash in the waters, then a huge body rose partly into view and sank quietly, followed by two more. Suddenly, a giant creature flung itself from the waves, turning a somersault onto its back so that the sunlight glinted off its white underbelly. It crashed into the sea, sending an almighty splash skyward.

'Whales!' Sophie cried in delight. 'Do you know what kind they are?'

'Minke,' Jean-Michel replied, resting his booted foot on the lower bar of the railings as they watched others in the pod executing the same joyous flips. The whales were running alongside half a league to starboard, heading out of Baie Françoise with the tide, but they posed no threat to the schooner.

Sophie's delight in observing such a display was catching, and he found himself enjoying the spectacle, though he had seen many similar sights over the years. He watched her almost as much as he observed the enormous beasts of the sea, enjoying the way her cheeks grew pink with the breeze and the excitement brightened her eyes. Her silken hair caught in the wind no matter how she tried to tuck it securely into her cloak, blowing about her face like gossamer.

He wanted to kiss her. So badly it was

almost a physical pain of longing. But he would not, for to do so would only be to submit himself to even more torture, and he doubted he could endure any more.

She turned suddenly, feeling his scrutiny. Their eyes met and held, asking and answering unspoken questions, and he saw the slight movement as she swayed towards him. Her eyes roved over his face, coming to rest on his lips and he almost groaned aloud. Then her tongue darted out and moistened her lips and he stepped back sharply.

'Don't,' he said without thinking, and immediately saw the hurt in her eyes.

'Don't what, pray?' she replied, her cheeks reddened by more than the wind as her eyes flashed at him. 'You flatter yourself, sir, if you think I hoped to seduce you into staying here with me, now that I have found my real home — '

'*I* seduce *you!*' That was rich, he thought, after she had almost kissed him. 'I made you an offer of marriage, Sophie. You turned me down. Do not imagine that I flatter myself in any way where you are concerned.' He glared out at the whales, now growing more distant. 'Doubtless, you will find yourself some strapping Acadian boy to keep your bed warm at nights, once you are ready.'

Her eyes blazed. 'I shall do no such thing.

I have not the least intention of marrying, thank you. I shall find a way to buy my grandparents' land back and I shall devote myself to helping the last of the Acadians there, just as I vowed to do. I have no need of a man to tell me what I may do and when I may do it.'

'Indeed? And how, pray, do you intend to pay for this vast estate you have set your heart on? By asking your father — a man, after all — for the money?' He grinned suddenly, seeing the point he had scored reflected in the woeful look in her eye. 'I suppose you could always swallow your pride and offer to marry the mysterious American if he is in need of a wife. That would be by far the straightest route.'

'But not the shortest, this time,' she replied stiffly. 'They say that every man has his price, but I am a woman, and my freedom is priceless.'

'You mean you would not resort to such a marriage of convenience, even were there no other possible avenue to achieving your objective?'

She glared at him. For a moment, he thought she might strike him, but then she turned away, tugging the hood of her cloak up over her head. 'I shall not marry any man, for land or money.'

She could not tell him why, though her heart ached to say the words. Let him think what he would, but Sophie Lafleur would never marry unless it were for love — love that was felt by both partners. She knew she loved Jean-Michel de Chambois, and always would. Yet he clearly held none of the same deep regard for her, for his shameless 'proposal' had been the merest trick, a ploy to get her to stay with him in Boston and live the life he chose. And now, barely a few days later, he was suggesting she behave like some shameless adventuress and throw herself at a total stranger, offering her body to him in exchange for the privilege of living at his beck and call on her own family's land. *Her* land, for that was already how she viewed it.

No, Jean-Michel de Chambois was leaving for Boston as soon as they returned to Halifax, and it could not be soon enough for her! If she had to, she would borrow the money from her father in the form of a mortgage, and she would find more settlers to populate the farms and create income, just as it had been in her grandparents' day. She would see to it that their lives were made easier and that their children could attend school. They would learn their letters and they would learn their own language, in safety, and secure from the threat of eviction.

Somehow she would find a way.

★ ★ ★

The voyage back to Halifax, and the two days following were spent in an uneasy truce. Sophie, for her part, set the wheels in motion to discover the identity of the new owner of the Dalibar *seigneurie* in the Bay of Fundy, through her father's agent. Meanwhile, having advised her father of her desire to regain the land if she could, and if not, to reside close by, she set about obtaining the supplies she deemed necessary: basic furniture, serviceable kitchen items, wooden sabots for her feet, sturdy clothing and the like. Jack Morgan, for his part, seemed both disappointed and relieved. He expressed concern that she might soon become bored with the privations and isolation of the life, reminding her that she was always welcome to return to Halifax society. And if not? Well, he was glad she at least seemed to have abandoned her plan to journey on towards Québec and the cloisters.

Of Jean-Michel she saw little. Her outburst

441

on the *Sophie II* had clearly driven a rift between them that he was in no mood to bridge. And since Sophie knew that there was not the least likelihood she would ever see the man again once he departed for Boston, she felt it best ignored.

But if she had hoped to be able to part company with the viscount as she would from any other acquaintance, with a simple farewell in the presence of her father, she was to be sadly disappointed.

He sought her out in the parlour one morning while she was busy making lists of the garden implements and seeds she expected to need. She had got as far as the easier vegetables, such as potatoes, peas, corn and turnips, allowing for several times the quantity she could possibly need, since she intended to cry ignorance and beg Madame Sauvé to share her surplus. The more difficult decisions, concerning quantities of livestock, were occupying her thoughts when Jean-Michel strode into the room.

He was dressed in an russet coat that emphasized the Titian colour of his hair, and his long legs were encased in skin-tight tan breeches tucked into black boots.

He nodded briefly to her as he entered, then strode about the small room glancing distractedly at this and that as though preparing himself for something. Sophie, observing the taut lines of his face, set her pen in its stand and folded her hands in her lap. She wondered if she could persuade Mrs Bellamy to bring tea or otherwise insinuate herself into the room at this point.

'Would you care for some refreshment?' she asked hopefully.

'*Quoi?*' He seemed not to have heard, then he waved a hand. 'Er, no, thank you.'

She sighed inwardly and straightened her back. 'You are leaving Halifax today, my father tells me.'

He looked at her fully then, his eyes dark as he ran a hand through his hair. 'I am. The tide turns at three.'

There was another silence, then Sophie spoke. 'I wish you a good journey, with no . . . side trips to distract you,' she added, referring minxishly to their entrapment by Daniel Blackthorn on the way to Canada. She suppressed a smile when she saw him frown.

'You need have no fear of that. I have taken passage with Captain Wilmington, who is in no way given to such escapades.'

'But the *Némésis* . . . I thought — ' She frowned. 'Was she not repaired several days hence?'

He clasped his hands behind his back

and turned to stare out the window. 'I no longer own the *Némésis*. I deeded her to Zamore.'

Sophie clapped her hands together, jumping up from her chair and crossing halfway towards him until his expression stopped her. 'I — I am delighted to hear it,' she said, tangling her fingers in her gown to stop them reaching out to him. 'He is a man of considerable ability.'

He nodded curtly, and in the ensuing impasse, Sophie took herself back to the table and her lists. He watched her in silence as she added two more items to her notations, and she wished he would just say what he had come to say and be done, for she was having the greatest difficulty in maintaining her patience.

She stiffened her spine as he came to peer over her shoulder. 'So, your plans are well advanced then.'

'They are progressing,' she replied, more calmly than she felt.

He moved to the empty hearth and propped an elbow on the mantel, staring at her long and hard until she was forced to look up and meet his gaze.

'Did you come to say goodbye?' she asked quietly.

'If that is what you want.'

444

'What *I* want? I thought 'twas what *you* wanted. Your life, your family is in Boston; what possible reason could there be to keep away?'

'And you?' he asked, his eyes glittering with an emotion that Sophie could almost taste. 'Where is your life to be? With the widow Sauvé in a wooden hut?'

She tilted her chin. 'I shall live in La Baie Françoise, whether I am able to do so on my grandfather's land or not. It is my heritage — in my blood. I belong there.'

'I see.'

She stared at him, wondering what had become of the fun-loving pirate she had known and loved. Since Madame Guillaume's unexpected arrival in Boston, that man had progressively disappeared until he was now deeply buried beneath this veneer of black ice.

He crossed to the door, grasping the brass handle but not turning it. 'Then there is really nothing more to be said unless you have reconsidered my offer of marriage,' he said, staring at the wooden panels before him.

Her eyes widened. 'Indeed, I have not.'

He bowed his head. 'Then I shall not ask again.'

Her heart was pounding so hard she

thought she might faint, but she took a deep breath and willed the nauseous sensation away. 'I am sensible of the honour, Jean-Michel, but I have decided to stay and serve my people.'

He half-turned and her heart cried silent tears as she saw the remoteness in his eyes. How much she wanted to say yes, to ask him to stay with her, help her make a life they could both share, but she knew it was futile. He had not the least interest in Acadia.

'Very well,' he replied, bowing but not taking her hand. 'Then I must bid you *adieu*.'

He wrenched open the door and Sophie gasped. 'Wait!'

He stopped, turning to hear what she had to say with all the coolness of a complete stranger.

She twisted her fingers in front of her, wanting to say so much, yet tongue-tied by the rigid set of his jaw.

'Give my love to Rose-Marie,' she said with a catch in her voice. 'Tell her . . . tell her I shall write to her. Soon.'

He nodded. 'I will do as you ask, though I don't know if I shall be able to explain this,' he added.

And then he was gone.

20

Sophie blew a loose tendril of fair hair off her sticky forehead and stretched her back with a sigh. It was damnably hot, reminding her of what now seemed like another lifetime in Guadeloupe. Perhaps she'd become accustomed to the cooler northern climes and hadn't expected such sticky weather even in July.

Or perhaps it was the effort that went into baking bread, she thought ruefully. She punched the dough on the heavy wooden table and began the final kneading, her well-worn copy of *La Cuisine Bourgeoise* open beside her. It was seldom closed. Its inestimable advice had opened her eyes to an amazing world of bains and brioches, brochettes and bouillabaisses. And after a month of experiments and disasters, she was becoming quite proud of her new skills as cook and housekeeper.

The door of the cottage was open to admit as much of the sea breeze as could be persuaded to blow through the little wooden dwelling, and Sophie turned as she heard a voice outside. She went to the door and stood with hands on hips looking across the estuary. Little plovers, their feathers the colour of wet sand, wandered back and forth across the mudflats, issuing their *too-li, too-li* calls with that odd questioning inflection that had become so familiar. Overhead, gulls wheeled and turned in their never-ending ballet.

'*Mamselle!*' called a young voice. She turned from contemplating the estuary to the little creek nearby that emptied into the River Dauphin. It was partially blocked by a weir of sticks, to allow small fish to be trapped when the tide receded. And it was from there that Pierre — one of Madame Sauvé's children, who, with his 11-year-old sister Jeanne, now lived with Sophie — was calling.

She beckoned to him and the boy came running across the sandy grass, his strong brown legs pumping and his dark face serious. She had employed the children partly because it would have been foolhardy to attempt living alone in a colony altogether too short of eligible women, and also because there was so much to be done before winter set in. She could not possibly cope without the extra pairs of hands. That she paid good wages was a bonus she knew her mother's old *copine* was grateful for as well.

'*Qu'est-ce que c'est*, Pierre?' she asked as he reached her, not the least out of breath.

'On the hill, *mamselle*. A whole group of them today, and they've brought lumber and stone on a wagon this time.'

'Stone? Up the hill?' Sophie seemed sceptical.

'*Oui, mamselle*.'

Sophie considered this information, patting her pocket unconsciously where the latest missive from her father lay. 'Very well, Pierre,' she replied absently, reaching inside the door to take a plate of cooled oatmeal cookies from the worn sideboard. She gave him two and watched as he returned to his duties, cleaning the fish from the day's catch and setting them out to dry for their winter stores.

She sat down upon the sun-warmed step and unfolded the letter from her pocket, smoothing it with floury fingers.

Halifax, 7 July, 1794

My dear Sophie

What can I report? Your grandfather's seigneurie *has been sold to a company in New York City by the name of Compton and Giles. As far as my man can ascertain, their interest in the matter is entirely*

449

pecuniary, and when casually approached as to their interest in parting with the said tract of land, they appeared entirely uninterested.

My dear, I fear it is as I warned: the land has been purchased by way of a long-term investment and no more. To sell so precipitously would not seem to their advantage, and unless one were willing to pay vastly beyond the value of the land, it would seem impossible to recover the title.

Do not despair. Their uninterest probably means that you and the others squatting on the property should be safe from danger of eviction, for it seems unlikely they will visit the site themselves.

I shall enquire concerning other parcels of land that might serve your purposes equally well in the vicinity. In the meantime, I shall visit shortly and bring whatever supplies you so instruct. Perhaps I can persuade you to return to Halifax before the winter snows! I should rest a great deal easier with you here beside me.

As ever

Your devoted father,

Edouard Lafleur.

Sophie blinked back a tear. The fact that her father, if only in correspondence with herself, had reverted to the use of his real name, touched her deeply. But as to the contents of the letter . . . She gazed across the creek and up to the hill from whence, now that she listened for it, she could indeed hear the faint sounds of hammers and chisels biting into wood and stone. She frowned, glancing down at the letter that still lay spread upon her lap: ' . . . *a long-term investment and no more . . .* ' If that were so, then what possible purpose could be served by constructing a building, if that indeed was the activity being undertaken so mysteriously beyond sight of the trees?

She tucked the letter away and returned to her dough, slicing it deftly into loaves and placing them in their tins. She covered them with a muslin cloth, not bothering to move them near the fire to rise on a day as warm as this, and untied her apron.

A walk would do her good, she thought, snatching up a round basket as she left the cottage. She could walk in the cool of the forest and mayhap find some early wild berries at the same time.

And if her steps took her up towards the brow of the hill, well . . .

But first she walked around the back of

451

the old abandoned fisherman's cottage she had renovated for her own use, to where the sizeable kitchen garden was now flourishing. Jeanne *la moyenne*, as she thought of her — since there was both a younger and an older sister of the same name in the Sauvé family — was bent over the potatoes with a hoe, her black hair peeking from beneath her straw bonnet. She straightened when she saw Sophie, her sweet face breaking into a smile.

'Don't tire yourself in this heat, Jeanne. There's cool water in the pitcher inside, and some cookies on the sideboard.' She glanced at the row of neatly mounded potatoes and smiled. 'You have worked a miracle with this garden, my dear. I shall have to increase your wages.'

'Oh, no, *mamselle*!' the girl replied with a shy smile. 'Maman says you already pay too much — and you give us lessons.'

Sophie patted her arm and headed for the gate that kept the pigs from wandering into the garden and wreaking havoc. 'We shall do some more this evening after supper, Jeanne. You can read to me from the new book my father sent.' She explained that she was going for a walk in the woods in search of berries, and hurried away before the girl could offer to follow. She did not want an audience if she did find someone up on the hill that she could talk to. Her greatest concern was that she would encounter only English-speaking workers. Her efforts to master the tongue were moving slowly, especially as she had no one to correct her except when her father made one of his brief visits from Halifax.

She crossed the meadow, where the tall grasses had been cut and dried to make winter bedding for the animals, leaving the lush shorter grass open to the sun. Two fat cows grazed now on the new pasture land, watching lazily as she climbed the stile in the rail fence at the far side and entered the forest.

It was cool and quiet among the trees. The maples were in full leaf, the pines fresh and green and pungent, and everywhere birds flitted about their daily business high in the trees, while squirrels and chipmunks scampered about on the ground.

Halfway up the hill, she stopped to rest, sitting on a rock in a small clearing populated by tall ferns and redolent with the pungent aroma of rich brown earth. She closed her eyes and breathed in the sweet humusy scent, searching for that inner calm, that feeling of belonging and fulfilment.

But it was not there. There was no doubt she had come to love this land, from its hot, sultry, summer days like this one, to the times where the Atlantic rose up in a fury and reminded her never to take anything for granted. The first time that had happened she had lost her brand-new birchbark canoe, her only means of transportation between the cottage and the settlement of Annapolis Royal up the river; the second time, it had torn the unlatched shutters right off the walls of the cottage and flattened her very first row of runner beans. And all that in summertime. Winter, she mused, would certainly be interesting.

She heaved herself to her feet, turning once again in the direction of the crest of the hill where her grandfather's house had once stood. Her footsteps dragged the closer she got, for she knew that to find others despoiling the spot would lend an air of finality to her hopes. Sophie was not ready for that. She had only just found her family, and she was not ready to have a stranger obliterate all trace of them from her life. Not yet.

There was another reason, of course, why her feet became heavier as she grew closer to the sounds of desecration. She had not set foot on the meadow at the top of the hill since she and Jean-Michel were last here. Not since she had made herself a promise that she would make her life here among her own people, no matter what. Not since she had sent him away, telling him there was no earthly reason for him to stay in Nova Scotia.

She paused when she spotted a small patch of half-ripe raspberries that would make perfect conserves. She began to pick, popping the occasional fully ripe fruit into her mouth and delighting in the sharp tang of the juice on her tongue.

I wonder what he's doing now? she thought as she picked. No doubt he has gone into business in some way or another, perhaps with François. Without a doubt, he would be enjoying his life once more, free of his constant need for revenge, but no doubt still enjoying a successful night at the tables, to say nothing of the sampling the delights of the most eligible ladies of Boston . . .

She pricked her finger and gave a most unladylike epithet. It scarcely mattered to her. Sophie had always known there could be nothing between them, despite Léonie's assertions that he was fond of her.

Not fond enough, it seemed, for he had sailed away without the least compunction after their last scene in the parlour, and from that day on she had heard not a thing from him, had received not even one line to say whether he was alive or dead, happy or not . . .

She shook her head, scolding herself for such sensitivity. It was she who had rejected Jean-Michel, not vice versa. She had not the slightest right to complain of his actions when it had been her refusal to accept his proposal of marriage that had sent him on his way. Though she wished with all her heart that they had not parted on such acid terms.

She abandoned the raspberries suddenly, having no more patience for berry picking, and hooking her basket over her arm, set off once more up the hill.

Madame Sauvé asked after Jean-Michel every time they met, and when Sophie replied that she had not the least idea, the old lady would tut-tut and ask her if she was happy! Sophie insisted that she was, although in her heart she knew she had yet to learn the meaning of the word. Perhaps she expected too much. No doubt that was the problem. She had anticipated that her little rented cottage, however basic its amenities, would feel like her own little corner of paradise, and yet while it gave her satisfaction to see the garden taking shape and the cows' milk yield rising, there *was* something missing in her life. Something that seemed to occupy an awfully large part of her thoughts.

That something was over six feet tall, with dark red hair and eyes as grey as a thunderhead, and she knew, to her chagrin, that if she lived to be a good deal older than Madame Guillaume, she would never forget that face, nor the way his lips curved and the deep chuckle that issued from his throat when he laughed. She could never forget the heat and passion that ignited those eyes when he looked at her. The memory still caused her cheeks to flame.

She had never dreamed a man could excite her the way Jean-Michel de Chambois did. That she would live with this empty feeling of loss — foolish, self-imposed loss — was perhaps the greatest irony of all. She could have said yes. With just that one little word, they could have been together for always as man and wife. The very notion sent her heartbeat flying and strange yearnings stirring deep within her. To think she could have been a mother to that dear little girl with the innocent brown eyes and the sweet baby smell — all for the sake of one little word.

But he had not given her the word she had so needed to hear. Not once had he said he loved her, she thought sadly as she ducked beneath a broken branch. She could scarcely blame him. She was, after all, a murderess. Oh, he had called her by various endearments — my sweet, my love — but such expressions were commonplace enough. Even Léonie sometimes used them.

Sophie had discovered there was quite another form of love. The type that made her mouth dry, that caused her face to burn and her tongue to tie itself in knots at all the wrong moments. Every time Madame Sauvé mentioned Jean-Michel by name, Sophie nearly had a conniption!

She had fallen in love with the Vicomte de Chambois, although she had never wanted to, and now she had lost him. It was hard to tell which was worse.

She stopped as the sounds of a chisel cutting into stone invaded her thoughts. She tried to compose herself, to cut off the painful memories and the futile self-recriminations.

She had what she wanted: her own people to live amongst and care for, her own family rediscovered. It was more than she deserved.

She took a deep breath and tilted her chin. Somehow she would find, if not happiness, then satisfaction in her new life, and with that she must be content.

She reached the summit of the hill where the forest gave way to a sunny meadow that had once been the lawn of the Dalibar *seigneurie*. She paused, one hand on the rough trunk of a tree. There were three men in view. One was cutting lumber while another atop a trestle was rebuilding the chimney with uneven blocks of stone. A third stood below, passing him pails of mortar with the help of a crude pulley, talking and joking in English. She wondered who was in charge, spying another two men cutting shingles with a flat-edged axe a little further away. If none of the men spoke any French, she would never get the answers she wanted.

And then she heard something that caused the breath to catch in her throat.

A small, high-pitched voice, giggling with babyish laughter, carried to Sophie on the breeze.

'*Viens ici, Toutou! Viens ici!*'

No, surely it could not be! She froze, staring in wonder as a small dark-haired girl, straw bonnet bouncing on her shoulders by its ribbons, came over the rim of the hill straight towards her. A small black-and-brown dog, his puppy tongue dangling from the side of his mouth, loped a few feet in front of the child, easily keeping out of reach.

The dog reached the trees, looked straight at Sophie in that unerring way of dogs, and

459

ran up, tail wagging.

'Toutou? Toutou?' came the little cry, but then the child spotted her pet and ran full tilt to where Sophie hid, stopping with a squeak when she realized someone was there. Then her little brown eyes widened and a smile that could have melted an ice cap spread across her face.

'Mamselle Sophie! You are here just as *Papa* said!'

She threw herself into Sophie's arms, treading on the puppy's tail in the process and causing a loud squeal to emanate from the dog.

'Oh, *mamselle*, I have missed you sooooo much. And *Papa* has been soooo cranky, and he said I could have a puppy if I wouldn't talk about you all the time, 'cause it makes him cross.'

Sophie could imagine that it might. 'Is . . . is he here?' she asked tentatively, looking around the clearing but meeting only the curious stares of the English workmen. Surely Rose-Marie would not have come here with anyone else, and yet . . .

She felt a sudden prickling sensation run up her spine and turned her head sharply, her heart stopping dead and then beginning to pound so fast she thought she might faint.

Standing with the sun behind him on the

edge of the clearing not ten feet away was Jean-Michel.

He was leaning on a rock, his long legs crossed at the ankles, his hair burnished by the sun and his face in shadow. For what felt like a lifetime, neither spoke, but Sophie was unable to break the eye contact that bound her to him. He had come back. Here, to her grandfather's land. Not to Halifax, but right here, to —

Then suddenly everything made sense. An American had bought this land! And was it not Jean-Michel de Chambois who always insisted he was not French, but American? Anger flamed in her breast. She disentangled herself from Rose-Marie, looking down at the child. 'Why don't you take Toutou over there and play fetch with him,' she suggested, pointing towards the sloping meadow on the other side of the clearing. She bent down and picked up a long stick, broke it in two over her knee and handed a piece to the child. Rose-Marie ran off eagerly, the puppy at her heels.

Sophie watched her go for a moment, uncomfortably aware of the man now strolling towards her. She forced herself to be calm, though what she really wanted was to pick up the other half of that stick and aim it at his head. How could he? How dare he?

She turned, her fury returning with blinding power, but as she opened her mouth to speak, he crushed her into his arms, his mouth claiming hers with an intensity that stole all conscious thought.

Sophie whimpered beneath the onslaught at the same moment as her arms came up and encircled his neck. As his tongue plundered her mouth, questing and tasting, her fingers twined themselves in the thick strands of his hair and her body pressed up against him, feeling the hard contours and recognizing the hunger that he ignited. He shouldn't be doing this, she thought as his mouth left hers and moved to her chin, her neck, the sensitive spot behind her ear. She shouldn't be letting him . . . He shouldn't even *be* here!

She pushed back suddenly, rubbing her tingling mouth with the back of her hand. 'You . . . ' she spluttered, 'you . . . ' Then, as he said nothing but just stood looking down at her with those storm-grey eyes, she found her wits and stepped back, distancing herself lest he should care to repeat that performance. Undoubtedly the workmen were enjoying the spectacle.

'It's you, isn't it?' she said with ice-cold certainty. 'You are the American who bought my grandparents' land.'

His shoulders lifted in an almost imperceptible shrug, shattering the last of Sophie's illusions. She turned away, folding her arms tightly across her chest and staring out at La Baie Françoise in the distance. A schooner was coming down the bay, its sails full in the generous breeze.

'How could you do such a thing?' she asked, without turning to face him, for her heart was in such pain, she wasn't sure she could bear to set eyes on him again. 'How could you steal this land from beneath my nose when you knew how much it meant to me?'

She bit her lip when she felt his fingers grip her arm and swing her roughly around to face him. His grey eyes were remote, cold as the north wind, and Sophie shivered.

'I did not steal this land; I paid handsomely for it. If anyone were robbed, 'twas most likely me.'

'Then if you were, it was no more than you deserve — sneaking about under my nose to take the one thing that was most precious in all the world to me! Why did you do it, Jean-Michel? You can have no possible interest in the land.'

'That's where you are wrong, Sophie. I have extraordinary reasons for doing what I did, but first answer me this — are you still happy here? Now that you have been living in Acadia for two months, are you still convinced that this is where you want to spend your life? Is this piece of windswept land what you care about more than anything in the world?'

She stared at him in dismay, wishing she could shout 'No. You are more important!' but her heart could not bear the rejection that would inevitably follow. 'If you did this just to deny me the chance to rebuild my grandparents' house and force me to live like a peasant, then you have failed. I have learned a great deal these past months, and not once have I wished to return to my father's comfortable house in Halifax. I have learned to cook and to milk cows, to fish and to look after myself. I am teaching some of the children their letters, and when winter comes I shall open a school so that they may use the inclement months in the pursuit of learning.'

She tilted her jaw at him, daring him to contradict her. He had broken her heart, but he would not break her spirit.

'I see.'

She frowned. 'I doubt that.'

He looked down at her, his eyes unreadable. 'You do not have a very high opinion of me,' he stated. 'No doubt you are right about that, too. But whatever else you may believe about me Sophie, I did not buy this land in order to thwart you.'

'Then to what possible purpose would you part with such a sum?'

He was silent for a moment, turning to watch Rose-Marie in her game with the little dog. Her childish laughter was in stark contrast to the bleakness in his heart at that moment and he found himself wishing he was anywhere but here. He had not known what to expect when he returned. He knew he would meet Sophie, had thought himself prepared for it, but now he found himself feeling awkward and angry.

He turned to her, to find her staring at him, her own expression one of righteous indignation. He could scarcely blame her. Perhaps the time had come simply to lay his cards upon the table and let her see what he held in his hand.

He dragged his fingers through his hair.

'You need have no fear of me as your neighbour,' he mumbled finally. 'I shall not get in your way.'

She looked puzzled, glancing from him to the busy workmen and back. 'But — '

'The house will be completed before the first snows. You can move in before winter.'

'I . . . ?' Sophie stared at him, not quite

believing her ears. 'What did you say?'

'The house is yours, Sophie, as is the land. The deeds are in your name and your father's agent has the papers.'

Sophie thought about the last letter she had received from her father and pressed one hand against her pocket to reassure herself that it was not a figment of her confused imagination. 'My father bought the land from you?'

Jean-Michel shook his head, making her realize how weary and dispirited he looked. 'No. 'Twas always in your name. I bought the land for you.' He gave a self-deprecatory laugh and turned away, heading for the slope where his daughter waited. 'Actually, I bought it for all three of us, but you would not have me, so 'tis yours alone now.'

Sophie ran to catch up, her heart in a turmoil of mixed hope and dread. Surely she had misheard! She grabbed his sleeve, forcing him to stop. They were only a few feet from the half-rebuilt chimney now, and she was vaguely aware that the stonemasons had paused in their task and were openly listening.

'Why did you do that?' she asked, tears flowing freely, so that she had to blink to see him at all.

He remained stone-faced, looking in front

466

of him, rather than at her, a muscle jerking involuntarily in his jaw. 'Because I thought we could do something here, together. Make a new life, improve the lot of the Acadians with a school, perhaps a hospital. Help create some work for the young men that would give them some choice other than subsistence farming or fishing. But you are doing all that anyway, so there's no point — '

'There's every point!' she objected, pulling him around to face her.

His eyes connected with hers suddenly, and the anger in them was so bitter she could almost taste it on her tongue. 'Is there? You don't want a family, remember? You're too afraid to commit yourself to a real relationship with a man. You only want to love this — ' He bent down and grabbed a handful of red dirt between his fingers, flinging it into the wind. 'Not real people, with real hearts and minds and needs and fears.' He grabbed her hands and held them tightly so she would look him full in the face. 'I bought this land long before you even came to Nova Scotia, but I didn't tell you about it, because I didn't want to bribe you with it. You wouldn't marry me just to get control of the place, you told me so yourself. You had too much pride.' He gentled his hold, rubbing the balls of his thumbs across the backs of her hands. His voice grew softer, regretful. 'Sophie, I wanted you to say yes just because you loved me. For myself — the bitter widower, the pirate and blackguard, the ordinary man with ordinary devils at his back. I couldn't live with myself if I thought for a second that you had married me for any reason other than love.'

'But I do love you!' she cried, her tears falling freely now so that his face shimmered in the sunlight. 'I have always loved you, Jean-Michel de Chambois, and you are no blackguard. You are the finest, noblest man I have ever known.'

She dashed away her tears, anxious to see his beloved face clearly, but he was not smiling.

'It is too late, Sophie. I said I would not ask you again, and I meant it, for to do so now would be to leave me forever wondering — '

'Very well,' Sophie said, grabbing him by the hand. 'Then if you will not, I am not afraid.'

Still holding his hand, she knelt upon the sun-baked earth and looked up at him, her eyes shining with love.

'Jean-Michel de Chambois, will you be my husband, to love and honour me all the days of your life, as I shall love and honour you? Will you stand by my side in darkness and in light, in fear and in pain, in joy and in bliss, and will you promise to kiss me under the apple blossoms each spring and shelter me with your coat in the rain?'

She gazed up at him, their eyes meeting and melding for the longest time, until, when she could stand it no more, he finally replied.

'I would be honoured, my love.'

There was a resounding whoop from the trestle above them, followed by the smack of the trowel into the pail of wet mortar, but Sophie was oblivious to it all. She was conscious only of Jean-Michel's strong arms about her, lifting her from the ground, clutching her to him as though his life depended upon it. Her arms gripped his neck fiercely and her tears of pure joy caught the sunlight as he spun her around, turning her world into a kaleidoscope of brilliance and hope.

When at last he set her back upon her feet, it was only to claim her mouth in a shattering kiss, tasting and plundering as though he were a man starved, and she responded in kind, wantonly and without regard for their audience. She pressed herself against him, feeling the hard muscle of his chest, the power of his arms. She breathed in the exotic mix of sea and man that was so uniquely his, and when she became aware that their kiss was having an altogether unmistakable effect upon his person, she did not shy away. Jean-Michel de Chambois was going to be her husband, and she would give herself to him as completely as any wife who had ever lived and loved.

She drew back a little, laughing breathlessly. 'I believe we are creating something of a scene!'

But he had eyes only for her. As he leaned forward to close the small gap between their mouths, he murmured, 'Let them watch. I have waited too long for this moment.'

The second kiss was no less soul-shattering than the first, but it was suddenly interrupted by an indignant, high-pitched voice.

'*Papa*! You're eating Mamselle Sophie!'

Sophie pulled back, horrified that she had been so thoughtless, but Jean-Michel merely laughed, picking up his daughter easily in one arm while keeping the other tucked firmly around Sophie's waist.

'Rose-Marie, you once told me I should marry Sophie and make her your *maman*. Would you still like that?'

Her little eyes widened and she clapped her chubby hands together. 'Oh, yes, *Papa*,

I should like that more than anything. But please may we stay here, because Toutou has run away in the woods and I cannot get him back! If we go back to Boston, how will he get home?' Tears threatened, and Jean-Michel gave her a quick hug.

'We shall most certainly stay here, *ma petite*. And I think there are some small children who live close by who might help you look for Toutou. Would that be a good idea?'

She nodded eagerly and without further ado, the small party tramped off through the woods, calling to the dog and following the path to Madame Sauvé's house where they could be relied upon to find help.

What they found, however, was 4-year-old Jeanne sitting on her mother's step in the sunshine, feeding a large dish of creamy milk to the puppy. And within minutes, Rose-Marie had made her absolutely newest, bestest friend in all the world.

21

They were married six weeks later in the parlour of the rebuilt house. Rose-Marie and little Jeanne-la-jeune carried baskets of flowers, while Father Cassel, brought up by François and Léonie aboard the *Lady L*, performed the ceremony.

All the de la Tour children were in attendance as well, although Sophie was disappointed that the Duke and Duchess de Chambois had already returned to England and were unable to be present. Robert she was not sorry to miss, for he, too, had departed, declaring American society to be deplorably ill-bred. She wondered whether he would finally find the courage to set a date for his marriage to unlovely Lady Alice Rutledge and so fulfil his destiny as a man for whom spending a fortune was a true vocation.

Jack Morgan, who had not only rediscovered the daughter he'd believed to be dead, but had gained a son-in-law and a noble family of in-laws, beamed from morning to night. By the time the festivities were over he had shaken hands with François on some mutually lucrative business dealings, and was even challenged to a swordfight by the irrepressible duchess, Léonie. He declined, of course, for he could not decide which was worse: to vanquish a lady at sports or to have her make a fool of him. He decided discretion was definitely the better part of valour.

Rose-Marie had fallen asleep with her new friend, little Jeanne, long before the festivities ended and the two girls had been carried off to spend the night in the care of Madame Sauvé, whose cottage had now been deeded outright to her, and even extended with the help of Jean-Michel's carpenters.

The guests sailed away in the *Lady L* at the apex of the tide that evening, and Jean-Michel and Sophie watched the beautiful little vessel sail out into the estuary. By the time they had walked back up the path to the house they were able to spy the white sails as the ship sailed south out of Baie Françoise and on to Halifax.

Sophie leaned her head on her husband's shoulder, thinking of the night to come, the night during which they would at last show the depth of their love, and knew that her heart was so full it could hold no more happiness.

The sun began to set in the west as they

gazed out to sea, trailing wisps of golden silk across the fading blue of the sky. The river at their back, the ocean before them, and the enduring land in between, all seemed somehow part of her, now. Sophie knew she could never live anywhere else. Despite everything that had happened during her short life, this was what was meant to be. It was as though the land, the sea, the tides and the wind had bound themselves to her and she to them.

Acceptance of her destiny, once she had truly found it, had been altogether too much temptation to resist.

THE END

We do hope that you have enjoyed reading this large print book.

Did you know that all of our titles are available for purchase?

We publish a wide range of high quality large print books including:
Romances, Mysteries, Classics
General Fiction
Non Fiction and Westerns

Special interest titles available in large print are:
The Little Oxford Dictionary
Music Book
Song Book
Hymn Book
Service Book

Also available from us courtesy of Oxford University Press:
Young Readers' Dictionary
(large print edition)
Young Readers' Thesaurus
(large print edition)

For further information or a free brochure, please contact us at:
Ulverscroft Large Print Books Ltd.,
The Green, Bradgate Road, Anstey,
Leicester, LE7 7FU, England.
Tel: (00 44) 0116 236 4325
Fax: (00 44) 0116 234 0205

Other books in the
Ulverscroft Large Print Series:

WHERE SHADOWS WALK

Angela O'Neill

Patrick Hegarty, elder son of farmer Joseph and Mary Ann, has no intention of carrying on the farming tradition. He sets off for Scotland to work with the navvies, but an encounter with a stone wall leaves him with a broken ankle. Nursed back to health by beautiful young Kate Kinard, the pair fall in love and are married without delay. But husband Patrick is a very different proposition from the romantic youth who courted her. The divide between them widens and Kate discovers that the saying 'Marry in haste, repent at leisure' may be more than just an old wives' tale . . .

THIS MORTAL COIL

Ann Quinton

'PETS. Exits arranged. Professionally. Effectively. Terminally. Apply: The Coil Shuffler.' Thus reads the business card of a professional assassin. When physiotherapist and lay reader Rachel Morland stumbles across one of these cards on the body of a frail parishioner, her suspicions are at once aroused, not least because she has seen it before — when her beloved husband apparently committed suicide. Policeman Mike Croft, a friend of Rachel's, also realises the significance of the calling-card and, together with his former boss, Nick Holroyd, sets out to track down the killer . . .

GRIANAN

Alexandra Raife

Abandoning her life in England after a broken engagement, Sally flees to Grianan, the beloved Scottish home of her childhood. Running Aunt Janey's remote country house hotel will be a complete break. Sally's brief encounter with Mike — gentle, loving but unavailable — cures the pain of her broken engagement, but leaves a deeper ache in its place. Caught up in the concerns of Grianan, Sally begins to heal. And when fate brings Mike into her life again, tragically altered, she has the strength and faith to hope that Grianan may help him too.

AN INCONSIDERATE DEATH

Betty Rowlands

In the sleepy Gloucestershire village of Marsdean, Lorraine Chant, wife of a wealthy businessman, is found strangled. But why, when both the Chants' safes had been discovered, was nothing stolen? What was Lorraine's relationship with Hugo Bayliss — a man with a dubious background and a penchant for attractive married women? How did Bayliss come to meet Sukey, police photographer and scene of crime officer, before the investigation became public? Then, in a cruel twist of fate, Sukey unwittingly plays into the hands of Lorraine's murderer . . .

THE SIMPLE LIFE

Lauren Wells

Lawrence Langland has had enough of corporate politics and fifteen-hour days. He wants out, to a simpler life. Isobel, his wife, whose gold-plated keyring says 'Born to Shop', has her own reasons for wanting to escape. Fortunately for Jacob, their eight-year-old son, it means leaving his horrible boarding school, although his elder sister Dory needs more persuading. And so the Langlands become 'downshifters', exchanging a comfortable house in suburbia for a small cottage in the countryside. Making the decision was the easy part — but can they cope with the reality?